Ouida

Puck his vicissitudes, adventures, observations, conclusions, friendships, and philosophies related

Ouida

Puck his vicissitudes, adventures, observations, conclusions, friendships, and philosophies related

ISBN/EAN: 9783742818102

Manufactured in Europe, USA, Canada, Australia, Japa

Cover: Foto ©Raphael Reischuk / pixelio.de

Manufactured and distributed by brebook publishing software (www.brebook.com)

Ouida

Puck his vicissitudes, adventures, observations, conclusions, friendships, and philosophies related

COLLECTION

OF

BRITISH AUTHORS

TAUCHNITZ EDITION.

VOL. 1120.

PUCK BY OUIDA.

IN TWO VOLUMES.

VOL. II.

PUCK:

HIS VICISSITUDES, ADVENTURES,
OBSERVATIONS, CONCLUSIONS, FRIENDSHIPS,
AND PHILOSOPHIES.

RELATED BY HIMSELF,

AND EDITED BY

OUIDA,

AUTHOR OF "IDALIA," "TRICOTRIN," ETC.

COPYRIGHT EDITION.

IN TWO VOLUMES. — VOL. II.

LEIPZIG

BERNHARD TAUCHNITZ

1870.

The Right of Translation is reserved.

CONTENTS

OF VOLUME II.

P U C K..

CHAPTER I.

La Pipetta.

ABOUT ten o'clock in the morning the valet was commonly used to knock at his master's door, and being bidden to enter, would carry in some coffee or some soda and brandy, and such letters as had come by the early post. At that hour I was always accustomed to run in likewise; and, perching myself on Beltran's bed, to eat the coffee-sugar, and watch him whilst he glanced through his correspondence. It was generally a great amusement to me, for being of quick intelligence, I had soon learned to guess from what fair hand each epistle came by its very air and aspect, to say nothing of its monogram, and it was a little comedy to me to see the weariness, the impatience, the contemptuous amusement, or the curt dismissal, which were what he generally bestowed on these delicate, tempting, and glossy letters, which the writers doubtless had conceived would be so welcome or so terrible to him, according as they wooed him or reproached him. This morning, for once, the servant's rap was not answered by a permission to enter; but Beltran, with the only savage oath I ever heard him use, bade the man begone and the letters also. Even to my whine and moan no heed was paid by him; and I sat outside the inaccessible chamber, tired in patience and wounded in heart.

Neglected by my master, bewildered, saddened, and perplexed by the strange events of the past night, I did a foolish thing. I incautiously wandered down the stairs, and finding the house-door standing open, I went forth into the street.

It was a sunny frosty morning, and people were astir; it was bright and busy and tempting. There are, in our race, natural and nomadic instincts that no education or captivity can eradicate—an inborn passion for freedom and enjoyment. This, in man, is damned with texts by your priests, and, in dogs, is chastised with stripes by your keepers. But, as a rule, being of itself innocent, and desirable, and even noble, it is too strong always for either priests or keepers; and under the damnation or the dog-whip will turn the man criminal and the dog mad. This instinct awaking in me, and I, being a little foolish guileless thing, deprived by my mode of life of many of my proper qualities of self-preservation and of foresight, and rendered helpless and dependent against my very will, was vaguely moved by it, and, knowing no better, moved to my own destruction.

I wandered down the street, playing with the rusty leaves that blew along the pavement, feeling pleasure in the fresh wind that wantoned among my curls, and thinking of no evil, because meaning none. The leaves were always escaping me, and always running gaily on; and I ran after them, wondering, indeed, how such poor, shrivelled, brown, and aged things had heart in them for play, when they knew, as they could not fail to know, that their day was done for ever, that they never more could toss in western winds and summer suns, but had no other thing to do than to drift dully on, and die.

For I was young, and did not guess that the leaves, though so worn and sere and useless, are all unconscious of their fate, and murmur amongst each other of their spring-time and their forest as though they were tossing still aloft, and had not known decay, even as the old amongst you "babble of green fields," and do not see their grave. I chased the leaves, and the leaves outstripped me. I ran unwittingly through many tortuous turns of streets. Just as, triumphant at the last, I caught my playfellows and found them rotten, useless,

frail as timber, a black shadow fell between me and the light;
a black cloth was flung over my head and body; I was seized,
crushed into silence, and borne away.

When I saw the light again, I was in the horrible den of
Bill Jacobs.

"He's got to be a cussed pretty beast," said the brute as
he surveyed me. "I sha'n't chance a reward: rewards is plants
now with them swells. He's worth two ponies, and I'll get
two ponies for him."

     *   *   *   *

I have a dim recollection of blows, bruises, foreign
tongues, bewilderment, dark dens, sharp whipcord, sickness
from a curious motion, and imprisonment in some floating
dungeon. But what I distinctly recall, as the first picture
on my mind after the renewal of the hideous scenes of
bloodshed and suffering at Bill Jacobs', are, a sky of the
deepest and most radiant blue, and a vivid quivering sunlight, that seemed alive in its intensity; a crumbled wall,
all clothed with a green that I knew later as that of the
acanthus; a herd of goats, a huge barrel upon wheels, and a
small cream-hued, fox-like face, that was peering close
against mine.

"*Ruzzola*—Pepe—I do not understand?"

"Well, I can tell you no more. Pepe is a servant to a
marchesa, whose villa is close by; and he had been sent to
fetch you from the English ship; some English friend had
bought you as a gift to the *marchesa*; and lo! as Pepe was
between the town and the villa, we overtook him at a little
village. The *contadini* were playing *ruzzola*; and Matteo was
giving them wine; and he challenged Pepe, and Pepe set
you down and went to play in right fierce earnest. They
are all alike, these Italians: give them a spade or a mattock,
and they die perspiring in ten minutes; but show them a
ball, or a disk, or something to gamble with, and they will
fag themselves at it from siesta to sunset! So they got to
play, these two, and they presently waxed furious at it.
That wine is fresh from the vats, and Matteo does not water

it for his own drinking! Old Pepe had staked every coin he had on him before they had played half an hour. The luck was at see-saw, and lured him on; then it set dead against him, and still he played. He staked his pipe, he staked his buttons, he staked his shoes, and before he had done he had stripped himself nearly bare. Then he went mad, and he staked you."

"Hush!" said the owner of that face, in the tongue of my own kind. "Hush! I will not hurt you—I am Spirka."

"Spirka," I echoed—the name conveyed no meaning to me, and I did not know where I was.

"Yes; I am Spirka, the Pomeranian. I live in the little hooded house there up on the wine-cart. That is Matteo, my master, yonder, giving a drink to the goat-herd. O, it is no matter; he will fill up the cask from the well! No one will be the wiser; and the wine is not his, you know. Are you in pain now?"

I groaned that I was.

"That is bad," said the sympathetic Spirka. "You have been in my house three weeks, and have seemed to know nothing."

"I know nothing now. What has happened? Where am I?"

"You are on the road between Civita Vecchia and Rome. And you are in my wine-cart. You were knocked over by one of the wooden rounds at *ruzzola*. That is one of our games, you know. Matteo got playing at it with your Pepe, and Pepe knocked you over; they thought you were killed. So did I—"

The Pomeranian paused, and I shivered; though you make your own selves so often into helpless counters on the green-table of fortune, you have no idea how horrible it is to a dog to feel that he has been a mere stake, thrown for as a thing of no feeling—of no volition—of no vitality. A man very often will game himself away till he has no more shame or sentient power than his dice; but a dog never does this, and never loses either his self-respect or his sensitiveness.

"Staked—and lost you," continued the communicative Spirka. "You were the property of his mistress—a present from a foreign land—a thing of price intrusted to his care. He shrieked, he raved, he cursed himself and you; then up he lifted his wooden disk, and let it fly with furious force. It struck you as he meant it should; and as it stretched you senseless on the grass, he took to his heels and fled, howling like a beast—fled before Matteo's knife could reach him. Every one thought you were dead; but Matteo thought not. Anyhow, he put you up here beside me, and gave you a chance of your life. And you are alive."

In my present state, the declaration appeared to me premature and unconclusive; however, as I certainly breathed, heard, and saw, I did not dissent openly from it. I ventured to ask why Matteo had not taken me to this *marchesa*, who was to be my fate.

"Pooh!" said Spirka contemptuously. "He won you, fairly, at *ruzzola*. It was not for him to turn out of his road for a strange woman and a foreign dog. What would she have given him for a little beast with two ribs broken, as yours were? He would have had the stick for getting at games with Pepe, and you would have been thrown neck and crop down a well. Do not get asking rude questions, or I will give you a shake with my teeth."

"Would it be rude to ask what is Rome?" I panted timidly.

"Rome? I heard a man say once that it was an eternal archaism, uttered in marble—whatever that may have meant. It is the place we take our wines to, that is all I know. We shall soon be there."

"Is it in England?"

"England! England is a little bit of mud floating in the middle of a duck-pond—I have heard Americans say so."

"It is not! It is a noble place—a great place!" I panted, patriotism coming on me, though I knew not one country from another.

"Pshaw! Nothing is either noble or great except Raulthelhautszeim!" responded Spirka, swelling with scorn and pride.

"And what is Raulthelhautszeim?" I asked, appalled at the mere rolling grandeur of the quadrupedal word.

"My village!" responded the Pomeranian with dignified emphasis; and thereon fell a-barking at a goat who had strayed nearer the cart-wheels than Spirka deemed fitting.

I, with my scarcely-healed ribs, lay still and silent among the straw in the little pent-house over the shafts. The extreme strangeness of the scene, and the marvellous effulgence of the sunlight, stupefied me.

"What time in the year is it?" I asked faintly at length.

"December," the Pomeranian answered in a brief pause of his breathless tirade at the obnoxious goat.

It had been in November that I had been seized by Jacobs. Ignorant as I was of time, or of occurrence, I arrived at the conclusion that I must have been sold by the thieves to some purchaser who had consigned me hither. And this conclusion very naturally explained all the imprisonment, suffering, and bewildering torments that I had endured, and which were all blurred in my memory into one indistinct maze of half-obliterated wretchedness.

Matteo came to his place on the cart; the horse, with its bedizened leathern harness, jogged on; the wheels creaked, the bells jingled; the huge wine-cask was drawn slowly along; and I lay motionless, exhausted and frightened, amongst the straw.

And thus we moved on through the great, golden, silent waste, all alive indeed with glorious-coloured insects, and waving various-hued grasses, and shrill grasshoppers trilling under the leaves, and wise-faced bearded goats straying under broken arches and gazing down from vine-wreathed ruins; but yet withal so still, so strange, so death-like.

The road was uneven; the day was hot; Matteo did not urge his horse—in point of fact, he was asleep almost all the way, trusting doubtless to the vigilance of Spirka.

Slumber, and your dog will guard you; it is only your

human friend who will seize that hour of your eyelids'
closing to steal your purse, or press adulterous kisses on
your darling's lips, or bid your children mock you for a
sluggard.

So we moved slowly on, through that wondrous blinding
sunlight, which seemed as though no clouds could ever
darken, and no rainfall ever soften it; moved on through two
days, resting innumerable times, and covering but a very few
roods in an hour.

The horse paused at a little town, whose name is needless
here; a little cluster of dwellings lying, as your Campagna
village often does, among deep cork-woods and old chestnut-
trees; with quaint gray houses, and ancient walls made lovely
by the lichens, and great wells everywhere, into which for
ever waterspouts were emptying themselves with sweet cool
soothing measure.

Spirka barked loudly; Matteo awoke; looked lovingly for
a moment at the open door of a tavern, then descended before it. The wine, to whomsoever it belonged, seemed likely
to be long upon its journey Romewards.

A handsome, good-tempered, dark-eyed woman bade him
welcome joyfully; and after setting him down to a meal at a
little round table in the ivy-hung balcony, brought to me and
to Spirka a plateful of rice, and of what they call macaroni.

Before I had a chance to touch a portion of it, Spirka
swept the whole up with his tongue.

"What right had you to do that?" I murmured woefully;
"some was mine."

"Right!" snapped Spirka; "I like your impudence. Why,
I am a Prussian!"

Who does not believe in nationalities?

I wonder if Europe will ever do as the good-natured
Roman woman did? She boxed Spirka's ears (who took it
quietly, as she was so much bigger than he), and then she
served me afresh with some food by myself.

There was a black-browed, handsome, thievish-looking

man sitting in the balcony with a box of musical puppets
beside him. He looked at it, and spoke to Matteo.

Soon afterwards he came down from the balcony, and
took me out of the wine-cart, and shook and pinched and
tormented me in that peculiar manner whereby you men
imagine that you test an animal's value, and health, and
temper. He was clad in greasy sheepskins, he had a sly cruel
gleam in his great black eyes, and he looked sluggish,
brutal, and a rogue to boot. I trembled beneath his slightest
touch.

"What didst give for him, Matteo?" I heard him ask.

"I won him at *ruzzola*," the wine-carrier replied.

"Art in the mood to sell him?" asked the puppet-player.

"Ay, ay," assented Matteo. "I have no wish for him.
I'll stake him again at a game of *morra*, if thou wilt, against
five *baiocchi*."

"Done!" cried the other Roman, with all his nation's passion for hazard and for lottery set on fire.

So they commenced playing.

I, trembling in the hooded house of Spirka, was powerless
whilst my fate swung in the balance. It was one of the
greatest moments of mental agony that I have ever known.

They played that wild, strange, ancient game of *morra*,
which with its antics, its vociferation, its twinkling, dazzling,
ceaseless movement of the fingers, so utterly bewilders the
stranger who watches it. They looked to me like maniacs.
But to be sure if dogs ruled in the world they would very
often raise the cries of "Rabies!" against very many human
actions and grimaces.

A man wheeling round in the maze of a waltz; a man
frantically tearing over the turf in a running match; a man
laboriously beating the water with two flat wooden blades;
a man solemnly blowing forth fire-smoke from his mouth and
nostrils; a man furiously battling with twenty others for the
right to kick a big ball into space—do not all and any of
these look infinitely more like insanity than a poor dog just

speeding in a straight line to the river-side on a hot summer's day?

This frantic and foolish battle came to an end in favour of the puppet-player.

My heart sank within me. The wine-carrier had a frank, good-humoured, sunny face that inspired me with some trust, but the mere touch and glance of this *fantoccini* owner froze my blood.

He saluted me with a blow by way of greeting, on entering into possession of my little captive body.

"Ho! In a week's time thou wilt jump about like an eel in a frying-pan!" he cried to me; and nodding and laughing a good-bye to Matteo, he threw me roughly on the top of his music-box, and hoisting it on his shoulders, departed from the hostelry.

"What an ass thou hast been, Matteo," the woman of the house said, as we moved away. "To have lost at a game of *morra* a little beast like that, who looks worth his weight in silver!"

Matteo hung his head, looking wild with himself for his greed and his loss. Spirka barked a loud farewell, but I think he was glad to reign once more alone on his throne of the wine-cart, where he had so long been supreme.

As for me, I went with a bitter heart, and a trembling brain, forth on fresh travels, seated on the slanting roof of the box in which the puppets of my new master reposed. Ah! how I wished—the first of a thousand such futile wishes— that since we were made to be delivered over to be the slaves of man, we had been created deaf and dumb, as those wooden *burattini*, and not cursed with nerves, and fibres, and affec- tions, and instincts, that are never of any other use to us save only to make us suffer!

I had indeed cause so to wish; for the time of my most intense torture was now at hand. I had never suffered like it ere then—in truth, I doubt if any human being ever knows such suffering, even in the worst agonies of your prisons, your mines, and your mad-houses.

My taskmaster, whose name was Giacone, known amongst the populace as Giu, proved the tyrant his look had betokened. He was indeed merciless beyond all description; and the brutalities and privations he inflicted on me came, of course, with tenfold more torture to me because of the peace and comfort—and latterly the extravagant luxury—of the life I had chiefly led. With the exception of the time passed in Jacobs' power, I had never had anything to prepare me for the misery I endured with this Roman slave-driver.

In the first place, he scarcely fed me, save just enough to keep my life in me; in the second, he fettered my limbs into a little coat and cap that were to me what the fetters of iron are to your prisoners; in the third, he exercised every ingenuity of torment in the process of what he called my education—*i. e.* the endeavour to make me dance, jump, posture, and go through card tricks to the sound of his organ-music.

And this reminds me to tell you what idiots you are when you beat your dogs as you do; a puppy is thrashed within an inch of his life to teach him "intelligence!" Intelligence, forsooth! when you have dazed the poor bewildered brain, and confused all the struggling senses, with physical pain! In educating a dog for sport, for instance, remember that you are educating him *against* all his natural instincts, though to your own uses—*i. e.* you want him to stand still and point, when nature would tell him to dash forward; you insist on his not ruffling an inch of either fur or feather in retrieving, when instinct would lead him to eat up the whole bird or beast; you swear at him for not sneaking step by step at your heel, when every fibre of his body, and every pulse of his limbs, are quivering with longing to be "at them;" you require, in a word, every law of his being to be either violated, or altered, to serve your purpose and pleasure.

This being the case, you proceed to instruct him in these offences against his own habits by the brutal stripes of that foul instrument of torture, a dog-whip; and when you have made every muscle throb with pain, and bewildered all his mind with internal suffering and piteous terror, you wonder

at his "stupidity," and curse him or shoot him because he
does not obey your word on the instant. O, how wise you
are and how just!—if there be a spectacle on earth to rejoice
the angels it is your treatment of the animals that you say
God has given unto you!

It is not for me, a little dog, to touch on such awful mysteries; but—sometimes—I wonder, if ever He ask you how
you have dealt with His gift, what will you answer then?

If all your slaughtered millions should instead answer for
you—if all the countless and unpitied dead, all the goaded
maddened beasts from forest and desert who were torn
asunder in the holidays of Rome; and all the innocent, playful, gentle lives of little homebred creatures that have been
racked by the knives, and torn by the poisons, and convulsed
by the torments, of your modern Science, should, instead,
answer, with one mighty voice, of a woe no longer inarticulate,
of an accusation no more disregarded, what then? Well!
Then, if it be done unto you as you have done, you will seek
for mercy and find none in all the width of the universe; you
will writhe, and none shall release you; you will pray, and
none shall hear.

Where was I?

Ah, let me pass quickly over the pain of that cruel time!
I do not wish to dwell on this portion of my life.

Già was at his best but a rough taskmaster, and at times
a very brutal one. He taught me many accomplishments, as
I have said, such as begging for food, as erect as a sentinel;
marching on my hind legs; shouldering a piece of stick as a
musket; taking wondrous leaps over a stretched cord; and
finally putting a little cap on my head, and sitting gravely in
a chair with a pipe in my mouth. As I was excessively small,
the pipe was a very small one also; and as this was a very
favourite attitude with my audiences, I gained the name in
Italy of Pipetta.

Like most other brilliant amusers of the public I was weary
enough at heart; and though I looked so gay and gilded to
the *contadini* in my little scarlet coat, and my little cap with

the gold band, as I went through my tricks, I wished over and over again that I were dead, and ached in every bone of my little body from blows and from hunger. I went through my dances and my postures trembling with terror, till in the burning days I was as cold as ice; and I only costumed and capered from dread of the lash and starvation, as your men of wit coin their brain from the dread of poverty and a prison.

It was a miserable, toilsome, sordid life I led; one mechanical routine of stereotyped antics; one ceaseless round of mimicry of that joy of which my heart gave not one echo.

I was the envy of all the children for that little red coat of mine, that little gilded cap, that little pipe I smoked, that little tambourine I played.

Dogs were too wise to envy me, for they knew I was not free; and I—I envied every dog I saw that roved at large, though with a soiled coat and a hungry body; every dog that barked from his heap of straw outside his master's *loggia;* every dog that drove his herd of goats to and from their milking; every dog that followed some homely, honest, simple duty, and owned a kindly hand that would caress him now and then, and a wooden house that he could call his own.

To be a goat-herd's dog; to sleep on a fragrant bed of dried wild thyme; to bask in the soft warm dawns, and slumbrous evening shadows; to wake to the memory of a pleasant duty to be done to the chime of tinkling bells; to drink and splash at will in the hillside brooks, and to watch the old wise-looking bearded goats nibbling at the green wild vine shoots,—what happiness it seemed to me! How passionately I envied, as I passed, them; all shabby and shaggy though their coats might be!

Some of these dogs, doubtless, were sometimes roughly treated; sometimes hungered, and smarted, and were footsore, and sun-heated. But they were free; and they had not to go through that dreary desolate pantomime of mimicked gaiety, while their hearts were breaking!

Ah! you pity your hewers of wood and drawers of water,

you weep for those who do your rude hand-toil that needs no thought, and live in the open air of moor and meadow blown on by all fresh winds of, heaven. Guard your compassion rather for those who must still pipe for you, though you no longer dance; who must wear the festal robes of frivolity though famine gnaw at their entrails, and despair devour their hearts.

You laugh! You can see no parallel betwixt a little woe-begone anticking dog, and the men and the women of genius? Well, it may seem foolish; yet believe me they have nearer kindred than you think: that one close terrible kindred of woe, and solitude, and bondage, and the iron cruelty of mimicked mirth.

My life endured thus for a year. I saw and heard much in the many wanderings which we made through all the Papal States; much which remains on the copper-plate of recollection, in sharp and defined outline; since there is no aquafortis that bites in so sharply as misery.

There are many beautiful pictures which arise in my memory, of earth and sky, of colour and form, of night and day; of the majestic old-world beauty of the women, and of the quaint, poetic, rich-hued life in the vineyards and cornfields, in the hill-side *osteria*, or the harvest-season's out-door camp. But other and worthier than I have painted these again, and again, and again, ever since the world was young. All the universe knows the smell of the Parma violets, and the taste of the waters of Trevi; the wail of the *pifferari*, and the chant of the barefooted monks; the frank sweet light of the Roman smile, and the deep strong stench of the Roman cabbage. Why should I dwell on these?

Though the sun was so cloudless, and the smile so fair, and the sod so thick with flowers, the time was dark and drear to me. A time of desolation.

Now and again some girl, drawing the metal pail up from her fountain, would pity my little, dust-stained, wayworn face, and give me a drink from the clear Virgine water, and a kiss from her arched, ruddy lips.

2*

Now and again some old woman, seated at sunset under the vine-hung gallery of her house, telling her beads in the cool calm decline of day and of age, would lift her voice, and bid my master cease to beat me, as he passed.

Now and again some gentle-eyed priest, with a wistful pain and peace together on his face, would take me up, and murmur a kind word to me, and pause at a stall in the street to buy me a little fried fish, all golden and shining from the stove.

But these were few.

For the most part people are cruel, cruel if only from lack of thought. And they were cruel to me. The children in especial; children are cruel everywhere. Few indeed of the virtues are inborn; and the virtue of mercy rarely—very rarely—ever runs in the quick, gay, self-moved blood of youth.

The children were cruel always. When they wished me to dance, I had to dance, though I died. When I made, through fright, an error in my tricks, they stoned me, and bawled at me. When I had walked round and round on two feet, till I was sick and giddy with the strain, and fell, they screamed to my owner to beat me for the fault—that fault of my weakness which injured their pastime.

The children were cruel always—those brown, handsome, graceful creatures, with the limbs of gods and the eyes of angels. So cruel they were, that at length when I saw children drawing nigh I would shiver, and moan, and seek to hide myself under a stone. In vain! Unerringly they would hunt me out, and riot, and scream, and tear me from one and another, till Già, for the sake of my value, would rescue me from their clamour and their grip, half dead.

Therefore, that time is very hideous, very hateful, to me. And it seemed to me always, that in this Latin land the very earth, by reason of its drought, and pain, and the innumerable dead it hid, was cruel likewise; and that even the sun, burning through so many weeks and months without one drop of rain, grew hard, and horrible, and rather shed death than begat life, with its unquenched rays.

There used to come upon me an infinite longing for the cool gray mists, the cool brown shadows, the dewy grasses damp at noon, the wild west wind sea-fed in summer, that I had known in that old north-country of my birth.

It is a *thirst*, I think—such as birds caged in cities feel—which devours us with so terrible a desire when we, who drew our first breath in the shady stillness of green northern woods, burn, and stifle, and grow blind in the merciless glare of southern suns. I suffered far more, also, because of the indulgence and luxury of my late brief enjoyment of a life of fashion. I had known what it was to be an idol of society, to be sunned in the smiles of coquettes, and to be caressed by the hands of great ladies; my palate had been attuned to dainty living, and my taste to all the gay frivolities and charming follies of the world of pleasure, only—as it seemed —that I might suffer more acutely from the degradation of my fate and the misery of my captivity.

I thought how wicked I had been to scorn all those poor dancing girls, who slaved for the popular amusement on a miserable pittance. I, too, knew now what it was to be the slave of the public, to be in the dress of the mime, to have to dance with aching limbs, and play with an aching heart.

How often I had joined with Fanfreluche in her merciless ridicule of these poor jaded, tired, rouged, and spangled coryphées of the burlesque; how often I had scoffed with her at their poverty and 'their sorrows; at the faded prints and the ragged shawls of their own day-attire, contrasted with the gorgeous dresses in which they flashed and glittered in the gaslight; at the hard bread and strong cheese they nibbled by stealth, while they waited for rehearsal; at the tears that gushed into their eyes, under the coarse oaths and brutal vituperations of their stage tyrant; at the piteous fashion in which they would trudge forth on foot into the rainy or snowy midnight, they, who went skipping and bounding, and whirling and laughing before the footlights, as though they had not a care in the world, or a need in the universe.

I knew now what it was to go through this mimicry of gaiety, this ostentation of radiant mirth, with grief in the heart and famine in the body. I knew what it was to long to lie down and die, yet be forced to rise and caper, and seem merry, because a ruthless Public cried,—"Dance, dance, dance! Shall ye dare to be weary or sorrowful when *we* have bid ye be joyous, and have bought your joy with our money?"

Alas! If I had been cruel from the levity and the thought-lessness of young years, my sin was visited very heavily upon me.

And another sin too,—my momentary oblivion of my first beloved home, seemed to me now but justly avenged by the wretchedness of my doom. Puffed up with the sudden fashion and luxury of the eminence to which I had been raised; inflated by the compliments and caresses that I received from noble lips and gentle hands; esteeming myself amongst the great ones of the earth, because I fed off silver, and ate of costly wonders out of their season, and drove in coroneted carriages, and looked from the windows of noblemen and gentlemen; conceiving myself, in my foolishness, to be far lifted above the good and gentle companions of my infancy; I had, wickedly and shamefully, thought scorn of their simple and hardy life, and had dreaded lest people should ever know that my first year had been spent beneath the roof of that rose-thorn cottage.

Wicked ingratitude, foolish shame!—that now had bitter punishment.

And it was not for the gay rich life in London, but for the innocent forest life in the green pinewood of the Peak, that I yearned with such an agony of longing as I was dragged through the towns and villages of Italy, footsore, bruised, bleeding, worn-out with fatigue, sore all over from blows, devoured by hunger, driven half-mad by thirst, and never hearing any other voices than those that rained their curses on me, or shrieked to me to dance though I were dying.

A year passed with me thus.

It was a hard life enough for Già himself: all such lives are, however romance may colour them, or their vicissitudes make them seem adventurous to the eyes of imaginative youth.

To tramp all weathers on foot, with a heavy box of *fantoc-cini* strapped to your back; to sleep where you can, in a hay-loft or a corn-barn; to walk fifteen miles to a town where, maybe, you do not get as many pence; to play in the scorch-ing heat, under the balconies where the happy people lounge in their pleasant idleness, which seems to insult you with its insolent prosperity and peace;—all this was hard enough, even for him.

But then he had many easy hours withal: welcome at some wayside *trattoria* where trade was dull, and a fritter was tossed, and a stoup of wine poured with eagerness for him; mirth at some rustic bridal, where the fun was at its height, and he, though a stranger and a wanderer, was frankly bidden to join; a turn at *morra;* a stroke at *pallone;* a cast of the *boccette;* a game at dominoes when the day was done, and the men and the maidens were jesting and dancing in some little village under the cork-trees. He had all these things; for he was a man of ready tongue, and comely enough in person. But I had none of these—I starved whilst he ate his stew; I ached with bruises whilst he laughed in the inn-porch; I was the sport and the prisoner of the brutal children whilst he was flinging his heels in the measures of the dances. I was infinitely miserable; and it seemed to me that my misery would have no end.

In the Eternal City, as in the Campagna, I was but a little, lonely, friendless, miserable, suffering thing. To me, therefore, it was horrible.

A victory looks but a sorry thing to the boy conscript lying cramped, and bleeding, and crushed, and woe-begone in the ambulance wagon on the red evening-tide after the battle. Rome looked but a motley, blinding, cruel, uncanny, eldritch place, full of noise and colour to me, as I lay, aching and terrified and heart-broken, on the top of the wooden *fantoccini* box.

I have heard you speak often since then of its sorcery, of its sadness, of its wonderful hues, and its unutterable beauty, and all its mystical, awful charm that none who have once been under its spell can resist; well—I never felt any of these. To me it was only a place where I suffered.

Believe me, it is the light or the darkness of our own fate that either gives "greenness to the grass and glory to the flower," or leaves both sickly, wan, and colourless. A little breadth of sunny lawn, the spreading shadow of a single beech, the gentle click of a little garden-gate, the scent of some simple summer roses—how fair these are in your memory because of a voice which then was on your ear, because of eyes that then gazed in your own. And the grandeur of Nile, and the lustre of the after-glow, and the solemn desolation of Carnac, and the wondrous beauty of the flushed sea of tossing reeds, are all cold, and dead, and valueless, because in those eyes no love now lies for you; because that voice, for you, is now for ever silent.

The narrow, crowded streets; the bray of mules and asses; the eternal wail of the beggars; the stench of stews and fries from the cooking-stalls in the alleys; the overpowering odour from the great mounds of fruit and flowers; the squalor and the glitter, the filth and the beauty; the glimpse through the butchers' doors of a dying kid, or lamb, as it struggled beneath the knife; the shriek of a goose or a fowl, as it was seized from the living flock to have its neck wrung at the market stall,— these were what I saw of Rome; what I always see now when I think of it.

Moreover, I was harder tasked in the City even than in the Campagna. In the latter there had been but a scant audience at best; two or three performances had always sufficed to gain what coins were to be had in the district. But in Rome there was an audience the whole day long, save at the brief noon-hours; and all through the starlit evenings, till late into the night.

When one crowd had dispersed another gathered. No sooner was the round of tricks finished than it had to be commenced afresh. There was scarce a moment that I was not either dancing, or telling fortunes on the cards, or walking round with my toy tambourine to collect *baiocchi*. Già had no mercy, and the people had no mercy either. It was one perpetual toil, one everlasting misery. At last it so wore me out that I went through the whole programme mechanically, with a noise like the rushing of winds in my ears, and the darkness of a sickly swoon before my eyes. More than once I dropped from sheer exhaustion; and then was roused with a kick and curse.

I think if you knew what you did, even the most thoughtless amongst you would not sanction with your praise, and encourage with your coin, the brutality that trains dancing-dogs.

Have human mimes if you will; it is natural to humanity to caper and grimace and act a part: but for pity's sake do not countenance the torture with which Avarice mercilessly trains us "dumb beasts" for the trade of tricks.

. All through those long, sickly, burning days, with their scorching sun streaming on the parched ground, the lash of my taskmaster kept me at my tread-mill of mimicry. It was as bitter, unbearable, agonising toil to me as any that your galley-slaves suffer is to them. The strain on the muscles and limbs was an intense physical torment; and the incessant nervous apprehension, the terror of ill-usage and blows, were yet more excruciating still.

"The Clown-dog draws throngs to laugh and applaud," says some advertisement: yes, and I knew a very clever clown-dog once. His feet were blistered with the hot irons on which he had been taught to dance; his teeth had been drawn lest he should use his natural weapons against his cowardly tyrants; his skin beneath his short white hair was black with bruises; though originally of magnificent courage, his spirit had been so broken by torture that he trembled if a leaf blew against him; and his eyes—well, if the crowds that applauded him had once looked at those patient, wistful, quiet eyes, with their unutterable despair, those crowds would have laughed no more, unless they had indeed been devils.

Who has delivered us unto you to be thus tortured and martyred? Who?—O that awful eternal mystery that ye yourselves cannot explain!

CHAPTER II.
The Dog and the Devil.

AFTER a space Giù quitted the city. What he did I know not; but it is certain that he displeased the priestly authorities in some manner, and had to go stealthily and swiftly out of Rome. For I heard many dark ominous words pass between him and his mates, the *pifferari*, and the *pifferari* counselled flight; and he departed thence, all hurriedly, by night, taking me and the box of *fantoccini* with him. From the muttered fragments of talk that I heard, I have a fearful fancy that he had killed some hapless woman in a drunken brawl, and that the woman being a priest's light-of-love, existence no the Seven Hills was on longer safe or even possible for him.

You will always find that these sluggards who are too lazy to labour for themselves, and seek their support by means of some poor performing animal, are great brutes as well as great cowards. Were you wise, you would forbid all such performances; for, if the man who works neither brain nor body be deemed by you useless and of evil example to the community, what then must he be who, in order that he may live in a sot's idleness and indulgence, does daily beat, fatigue, and torture a creature delivered into his power?

Hiding and skulking, and by means, I think, of false papers and names, Giù got across to Ostia; and thence went by sea to Marseilles. The horrors of this passage I cannot dwell upon. I was starved, sick, beaten for moaning, and drenched in a deluge of rain that swept the whole Mediterranean with almost the force of a water-spout. Had it not been for the goodness of an old weather-beaten sailor, who wrapped me in a morsel of tarpaulin, and tied me with a rope to the seat, I must have been driven overboard, or have perished of wet and cold, whilst Gih below drank brandy and played dominoes with the half-drunk skipper of the rotten, groaning, olive-laden felucca.

There is this that is consolatory in life: its darkest hours rarely have *no* ray of light; its woes, its tyrannies, its agonies, commonly give birth to some act of kindliness, or of courage, or of compassion, that arises in their midst as a palm in the desert; it is little enough oftentimes, but it is something; something that just saves the earth from being hell.

Marseilles lay white and blinding, and scorched with a hard burning sand-laden wind from the African shores, when we at length reached it after a hideous voyage of storm and heat, of hurricane and drouth united; a voyage through which the skill of the old sailor I have named alone brought the vessel, whilst its captain lay drunk in the cabin, and the crew shrieked and roared to the saints.

In Marseilles we tarried some time, and thence passed across France to Paris.

It was the same old miserable life; the same tramping, and playing, and performing.

"O, what a happy little thing art thou!" said one day to me an honest, but rather stupid dog (the only dog ever unwise enough to envy me), who lived in a hut amidst the fields of the great south-west, with a goat-herd. "Look at me—I fare so hardly, I am out in all weathers, I never taste anything except a bit of black bread or rancid meat, I am all the year round with those silly goats, I never see anything all day long but a plover or a henbarrier flitting by over the marshes. How lucky thou!—to ride on the top of that box, and to be tossed sweet cakes and biscuits, and to have nothing at all to do but only to dance for thy living!"

Alas, he little knew the perpetual travail of my existence,

and how gladly I would have changed places with him, and taken his black bread and his liberty together!

There is no labour so utterly weary and cruel under the sun as the labour which takes the semblance of pastime. For the dullard is free to go to his solitude, and weep his heart out, if he will, for the dead whom he laments: but Verdi must write his new opera though the mistress of his youth lies scarce cold in her coffin.

Our passage across France occupied long; going so slowly as we did, pausing at every little hamlet or wayside wine-shop on the road. The people on the whole were more cruel than those of the Campagna; the women were toil-hardened and sun-dried, and had not that frank sweet smile of Rome. There were often fairs, or fêtes, on Saint-days, in the townships through which we went.

These were very quaint and picturesque, I admit; all the colour and the movement; all the gorgeous charlatans and conjurers; all the saints and images and banners; all the white-robed choristers with their censers; all the flower-crowned girls with their crosses; all the chanting priests and singing women; all the green branches, and floating ribbons, and ringing music, chimed in so well with the old gray walls, and the high-peaked roofs, and the straight poplar trees, and the quiet narrow streets.

But on such popular days as those I was so maddened with the noise and tumult, I was so worn out with over exertion and pitiless demands on my frail strength, that at length, whenever we drew near the gates of a town, and I saw the gleam of the golden host uplifted, or heard the clamorous *charivari* of the fifes and drums, I trembled and sickened, and strove vainly to escape in any ditch or any hole, and was only dragged within the gates by sheer force, by curses and cuffs, and kicks and blows.

Of course I had no power against my tyrant. I was a little weakly timid thing, and all the natural agility and spirit I possessed were cramped by the garb in which he had imprisoned me, and cowed by the hunger to which he subjected me.

So my life passed: and I had been one year and a half with Già, when at last we drew near to Paris. I dreaded the city beyond all words to tell. I thought that there I should always see the host uplifted, and always hear the shrill din of the *charivari*.

In the country sometimes I had a respite, a breathing space; some woman milking her cattle gave me a drink from the foaming pail; some lad lying deep amongst the hay made me a nest beside him; some gentle cow would let me rest amongst the fodder of her stall; some big rough-coated dog about a farm would bring me food and call me to his kennel; some young girl, leaning out of her lattice in some hostelry we stopped at, would call to Già not to beat me, and would come down and caress me, and beg me of him for the night, and take me to her little bed under the eaves, and lull me to slumber like an infant against the warmth of her soft bare breast.

But in the cities there were no pause, no pity, no peace, from morn till midnight. The very animals themselves in agony grew selfish, and had but little mercy for their kind, because, for their own dumb helpless lives, men had none.

As we drew near Paris we came to a long steep stony street, uncleanly, unsavoury, full of noise; I heard them say that it was Sèvres. I have ever since shuddered at the name when I have heard it spoken before those pretty porcelain things it christens.

Here there was a crowd; the porcelain makers and painters had finished their work for the day; they were lounging and gossiping and singing, and sipping their coffee inside their house-doors.

Già, as usual, wherever he could command an audience, set his box upright on its pole, opened its case, and began to play, bidding me dance to the music. The puppets never tired, of course; and I suppose he thought that I was like them.

Now as it chanced I had performed all day long in the town of Versailles, hard by. I had scarcely had any rest;

and I did not know how to commence afresh. Dancing and performing are as severe a trial to us as the hardest rowing or wrestling is to you; more so, indeed, because you, after all, are only doing that which you choose to do, and which is in a manner natural to you, whilst all these actions which you teach us are to us painful, unnatural, and full of an arduous strain and contortion, for which our nerves and muscles are utterly unfitted.

The puppets danced gaily, as the organ handle turned; I moved to and fro, as I had been taught, on my hind legs; I smoked my little pipe; I struck my tiny tambourine that was hung round my neck; I did all to the best that I could, and the youths, and the young girls, and the children, and the sturdy tanners of Billancourt and the wan pottery painters of Sèvres applauded gleefully and shrieked, "Encore, la Pipetta! —encore, encore!" so that I had to go again and again through all my antics, and yet they were not satisfied.

Now, I had been performing all day long since sunrise; I had eaten nothing but the handful of boiled rice he had tossed to me. I was very sick, and tired, and worn out; and it so came to pass that, when in obedience to the "encore, encore" of the impatient and delighted little crowd, Già shouted to me the word of command to commence afresh, I tried to dance again, but—my strength failing—tottered, and moaned, and fell, breaking in twain my little painted tambourine.

I lay, stupefied and sick, in the white dust. Già furious, threw himself on me, and seized me by the neck, and beat me;—ah! I can feel the rain of the blows now.

"I will teach thee to tire! I will teach thee to fall!" he screamed aloud, and with every word the biting lash curled round my little quivering body.

"Beast! would you kill the dog?" cried one of the porcelain makers, though he did not stir to succour me.

"It is mine!" cried Già, a coward though a brute. "It is mine, I will kill it surely;—the little sluggish devil!"

Scarcely were the words uttered, when suddenly a

ponderous body flung itself on my tormentor; a row of white and glistening teeth seized and shook him with tremendous force; he dropped me with a shriek of terror; and my deliverer, in whom I recognised one of the princes of my own kind, caught me up in those massive fangs which had wrought my freedom, and bounded off with me in a stretching gallop.

.The pressure of his jaws; the speed of his going; the heat; the bruises; the terror; all combined, made me insensible; this manner of deliverance was well-nigh as fearful as the torture itself had been: and I knew not where I was carried nor how long I remained unconscious.

When I recovered my senses, I was lying on long grass beneath the trees of a garden: and over me stood my friend —a gigantic tawny-coloured Muscovite dog. Huge though he was, and with the grip and the claws of a lion, his eyes were soft and even tender, and gleamed very gently and benevolently on me from under the leonine waves of his shaggy mane.

He addressed me in that universal tongue of ours which is one of the many superiorities which we enjoy over men:— you, poor humanities, born on different banks of a river, or opposite sides of a plain, jabber jargons mutually unintelligible to each other, and on a public mart, or at a *tir national*, stand bewildered amidst a score of unknown tongues spoken by your next-door neighbour. But place a Labrador dog with a Pyrenean dog, let one of Poland meet one of Peru, and lo! you behold them intelligible to one another at once, able to exchange converse by a freemasonry to which the widest-spread of your brotherhood is as naught. For our race being too wise ever to build either a Babel or a Babylon, no curse of confusion rests on us; and though scattered all over the world, we are yet even as one great nation.

"I am Russ," said my deliverer. We always give our names frankly to each other; that base human device, an alias, is wholly unknown amongst us. "I am Russ. I will not hurt you; you know that. We are far away from that brute, your taskmaster. No man can emulate my speed. I have raced even with rein-deer; and have beaten them. You poor little frightened thing!—he would have killed you if I had not interfered. Are you a dancing-dog?"

I groaned an assent: I was ashamed of my profession, and of my little red jacket, and of the broken tambourine about my neck.

"Ah, that is so like a man!" said the giant Russ grimly. "'To case your little supple body in a tight bit of cloth, and to force you to strut awkwardly about on two legs, and to then call that sort of disfigurement 'training' you. Well—I am glad that I saw you. I fly at all such creatures as Gih. Wretched, lazy, lubberly ruffians, who are too idle to labour for their living, and torture a bear, or an ape, or a goat, or a puppy like you, to get the coins that they want for their food and their drink! I have had a tussle ere now with this Gih. Too idle a sot to work for himself, he is for ever pressing some innocent thing into his service, that he beats, and starves, and drives mad for his profit."

I shuddered with the remembrance of my sufferings as he spoke; and with the pain of the bruises that covered every inch of my body.

"You are very good," I faltered. "But how can you keep me from him?"

"Why, see here. I will get you permission to stay in this place. You need not go out of the garden walls; and Gih will never dare to track *me*. Ask every one in Paris who Russ is and what he can do. If you feel well enough now, come within."

He stalked like a lion towards a low white stone building; and I feebly followed him, still wondering, dazed, and affrighted. My limbs ached, and my coat impeded my movements; but I managed to crawl after him meekly and feebly, through some winding grassy paths, all yellow with golden dandelions and shadowed with hanging boughs. At last we approached the low stone house; with a thatched roof on which pigeons sat pluming themselves; an old carved oak porch half smothered in that white creeper you call traveller's joy; and some deep stone-embayed windows hidden likewise in ivy and creeping roses. Amongst all this verdure and blossom, there hung, half seen, a wooden board on which glistened a couchant silver stag.

Russ crossed the threshold and mounted some broad wooden stairs, so black with age and slippery with polish that I had much ado to climb them after him. On the head of the staircase he pushed open an unlatched door, thrust himself through it, and advanced into the chamber.

It was broad and low, with casements looking out on sunny meadows; it was filled with what to me seemed lumber, quaint shapes and devices, shabby draperies, and strange wooden skeletons that filled me with terror. At what I afterwards knew was an easel, stood a young man painting; at a little distance sat a girl in a blue-serge gown, and with a white peaked cap.

It was to the woman that Russ advanced; taking me in his mouth, and laying me at her feet; then retreating a little, he gazed at her with eyes of wistful entreaty, thumping his bushy tail weightily on the floor.

The young painter laughed.

"Another protégée, Russ? Verily thou art the most benevolent of all four-footed Christians!"

It was a misnomer. We have ever been pantheists; pagans, if you will. Had the dogs of Jerusalem been Christians, be sure that Pilate would have been torn limb from limb, and Peter with the lie upon his lips been bayed from out the hall of judgment. Where one dog lives and loves, there at least is one friend faithful.

However, the speaker meant well, I doubt not; and Russ, understanding him, leapt on him in gratitude, knowing that he had obtained asylum for my helplessness.

"Poor little thing! How thin it is, and how frightened!" said the young woman, who stooped over me and touched me gently. "This is the fifth dancing-dog that Russ has brought to me!"

Russ thumped his tail in confirmation.

"The fifth! Where are they, then?" the artist asked.

"O, I have placed them out; people around took them; they are happy," the girl answered him, smiling and freeing me from my coat. "Ah, forgive me, Monsieur Carlos, I forgot that I was sitting; I have disarranged the pose!"

The painter looked down on her tenderly.

"No matter! The sun is low. We will put the canvas aside till to-morrow. Then I will paint you with the sick dog in your lap; that soft pity becomes you so well!"

She smiled again, and a bright warmth came over the cool clear olive of her check; then she rose and bore me from the chamber, followed by Russ. In a few moments I was lying on some hay in a corner of a fragrant-smelling loft, and being fed with fresh milk and bread, whilst Russ surveyed the operation with a good-natured and self-approving air.

"That woman is an angel," he said to me as she passed out, leaving me cleansed, comforted, and refreshed.

"Who is she?" I asked feebly.

"Our Madelon," he returned, as though all were uttered therein. "I have lived with her ever since she was fifteen. She is twenty-two now. Philip Ferrand left me here when I was young. He never paid them, either, for his six months' board and lodging. I have heard painters say since then that he has risen to great eminence in England. Well, if he have, he has never thought of either his dog or his debts. The old Mère Bris, too, here nursed him through a dangerous illness; and not so much as a kerchief for her throat has Philip ever sent her in payment."

"But they have been good to you?"

"Good! Indeed they have. I was never happy with him. He would swear at me, and, what was worse, sneer at me. You know a dog would sooner be kicked than be laughed at. Here I have been happy all my days. It is such a still, quiet, pleasant place; and one does as one likes. Sometimes I go out for a long ramble; when I do, I am sure to meet some animal in distress, and I rescue him, if I can, and bring him to Madelon."

"That is very noble of you."

"O dear, no! It is just commonly right. Life would get too smooth and too sleepy here if I did not go out sometimes, and have a fight and a tussle over some bit of evil-doing. For what else was I made so big and so strong? Do you know what they say in my country?"

"No. In Russia?"

"In Russia. They don't let dogs enter churches, because they say that a dog once betrayed Noah to the devil for the sake of getting that thick warm coat which we northern dogs now all wear. Now, that is a lie. It just shows the way men distort things. Amongst our traditions, which of course men can know nothing about, is one on that very point; and it runs thus, having nothing to do with Noah:

"In the very early age of the world there was a dog, very wise and brave, and who hated a lie most of all the sins under the sun.

"Now, this dog one day came to a church, where a preacher was being listened to as though he were an angel from heaven. The dog knew better, and sprang on him, and tore off his robes, and showed a cloven hoof and a tail beneath them. 'Foolish people!' cried the dog, 'your priest is the devil of Falsehood;' and he drove the devil out of the sanctuary.

"He went to a second church, and found the priest the devil of Greed, and drove him out the same.

"He went to a third, and there exposed the devil of Lust; and to a fourth, and there unmasked the devil of Self-love; and to a fifth, and there sprang upon the devil of Empty-words; and the people all stood aloof and wondering, and cried, 'Eh, then! are our priests all devils?'

"But the devils themselves were sorely frightened, and said, 'If the dog tear off all lies, then the trade of devils and priests will be gone!' So they banded themselves together, and persuaded the foolish people that the dog was a wizard, and must be killed for the weal of the world. And in the end, the wicked people stoned the dog to death; and he died be-

cause he had dared to witness the truth, and had not left
those fools alone to their worship of falsehoods.

"And from that day, devils still having great influence,
and, above all, being strong in all pulpits, whence they throw
dust in the eyes of the multitude, they have always hated all
dogs, and have forbad them out of their churches.* This is
the true tradition. The other fable is a devil's device."

I thanked him for his instruction, but being still faint and
weary, longed in my soul to be quiet and sleep. Besides,
when you have just been in the grip of a cruel man, it seems
to you that the devils themselves can hardly be very much
worse to deal with, and you hardly feel that proper ab-
horrence of them which you would do at any other time.

Returning to present matters, I asked him who was that
youth whom I had seen in the painting-chamber.

"O, an artist!" answered Russ, with a little good-natured
contempt. "All the men who come to this place are artists.
That one has been here since the first days of March. By
name he is Carlos Merle. He is of very great genius certainly; but I am not sure of him for all that. He is fitful.
He works with great spurts, and then does nothing for days,
except lie on the grass and dream, or murmur to Madelon.
Genius is a great thing, of course; but it is not everything.
Genius is like a spirit flame; but genius must have its armour
of application, as the flame must have its lamp-shade, or both
will go out under a blast of rough wind."

"What was he doing when I saw them?"

"Painting her portrait. All of them like to do that. It
occupied Jean Stenlinck six weeks last year to get the portraits of a brown pipkin and a market-cabbage; and Jean
still is mad with himself because the pipkin won't look old
enough, and the cabbage will look too green on his canvas,
do what he will to alter them. Ah, the ecstasies I have heard
him go into over a well-painted wooden pail, or a pinch of
snuff in a paper! They see naught to adore in real pails and

* Except in Scotland; where I suppose that the people's gratitude to
their Colley-dogs is too strong for Satan to vanquish it.—ED.

papers of snuff, then how can the mere imitation of the thing have any worth?"

I was too tired and ill to take any interest in his disquisition. Since that time I have heard plenty of art-jargon talked by half the connoisseurs of Europe; but I am not sure that I ever heard anything more direct to the point, or more truly sensible, than this objection from Russ. But Russ is not the world; and meantime Meissonniers fetch the same prices as Raphaels.

"I like artists," continued my instructor, laying his massive form down to rest. "They are stupid, you know. They will stare for hours at a ripple of water, or a few twisted twigs, and they always talk as if heaven and earth depended on their hog's bristles and their oil-tubes. But they are a kindly, simple, genial race as a rule. They are so ignorant, and know nothing about a bird except the hue of its feathers, and nothing about a dog except the tint of his coat, and nothing about a woman except the red in her lips and the white in her limbs, going altogether by the surface of things, and fancying they have got 'atmosphere' in dabs of gray and yellow, and 'distance' in streaks of flake-white, and 'sunset' in scumbled lakes and ochres. Yet they are very happy in that innocent blissful stupidity of theirs, and, like all happy people, are good-natured. Of course no dog was ever so ridiculous as to draw an imitation dog, and take pleasure in the canvas creature that could not bark, or move, or smell, or feel. But then so many of men's pursuits do look so trivial to us that I scarcely think Art, as they call it, is much worse than anything else. And it hurts nothing, which is more than can be said of the generality of their pastimes."

"You do not think well of men?"

"O yes, well enough," said Russ carelessly, as a giant will speak of pigmies. "There are only two animals in all creation that I hate, and they are a cat and a woman."

"You think these two alike, then?"

"Alike! My dear little soul, they are one and the same! When cats die, they become women. Did you never know

that? Look at their pretty little teeth, their velvet skins,
their agile grace, their idolatry of warmth, and ease, and good
living; their chilly sensualism; their frolics, that always end
in a scratch to their playmate; their passion for chasing a
mouse or a lover, that, once caught and slain, is valueless
vermin for evermore in their sight. The cats keep all their
characteristics when they turn into women. We become men,
it is said, though I doubt it myself; for it would be hard to
descend in the scale of creation. But dogs who believe this
affirm that our singular antagonism to cats is instinctive, as
against our future betrayers in our future state of existence.
The dog that kills a cat will, it is said by our poodle-pundits,
meet that cat as a woman when he is a man, and will marry
her. There seems no justice in so terrible a punishment;
but, if true, it serves to explain the 'cat and dog life' of most
marriages."

And with that Russ, fatigued by his long gallop through
the heat of the noon, composed himself to sleep; and slept
with fits and starts, and mutterings and growls, caused, he
afterwards told me, by a dream which he had of a tortoiseshell
cat, whom he had once slain in the days of his youth, incited
thereto by his master, and who appeared to him in his slumber, with prophecies of her vengeance.

I, overpowered with pain, joy, fear, and fatigue, all commingled, slept also, and forgot in slumber all my bruises, my
woes, and my exile.

Ah, when I awoke, how delightful it was! No coat im-
prisoning my limbs, no stick shaken in my eyes, no kick
thrust into my ribs, no curse hurled at my defenceless weakness! It was all calm, and still, and sweet. The bright
summer sunlight came streaming in; the apple-boughs, fruit-
laden, swayed against the windows, the cocks crew near at
hand, the sheep bleated afar, the pleasant scents of fruits
and of blossoms and of herbs blew in upon the south-west
wind; and I rejoiced in all this freedom, peace, and loveliness,
with that gratitude which is a dog's religion.

Why have you not more of it in yours?

The Romans, I have heard tell, veiled their faces in prayer: that was fear. The Greeks stood, with eyes fastened on the earth: that was meditation. The Christians kneel: that is entreaty. There were but the poor Peruvians, who bowed low, lifting their eyes to heaven, and showering kisses in the air: that was rejoicing, thankfulness, and adoration, all in one.

And you think you are holier than they were?

Well, think so if you like.

CHAPTER III.

The Silver Stag.

IT was a tranquil fragrant place, this little hostelry of the Silver Stag. It was quite old, and very rustic, though yet so near to Paris.

Its gardens were famous for their peaches, and its hives for their honey. It was a drowsy, shady, odorous place, full of the murmurs of birds, and of bees, and of ever-tremulous leaves. Untrained roses bloomed in every nook and corner, and pigeons and doves by the hundred flew all day in and out of a great square stone dove-cot, that had been built in the years of the Dame de Beauté. For human life about it there were only the cheery old woman, Manon Bris, her daughter Madelon, and the painter Carlos Merle.

Their house was much frequented by artists, who came thither for sake of economy, fresh air, solitude, and the beauty of the woods; men could live there for a few francs a week, enjoy all the stillness of the country, watch all the charm of woodland life, and yet withal be in Paris in less than an hour. The place was indeed consecrated to artists, and few others ever intruded there, unless it were some gay group of students and grisettes on a Sunday, after a childish frolic in the wood, and some wild rounds of games and dances under the orchard-trees. All the week it was very still, still as death, except for the fluttering of the doves, and the sing-

ing of the birds, and the turning of the water-wheel, and now
and then the bay of Russ.

For old Manon Bris, being well off, and her daughter well
dowered, and being, moreover, an honest, fearless, pure-living
old woman, cared not if she displeased her patrons; and set
her face straight against all those Greek-limbed models and
Egyptian-eyed companions whom the painters would fain
have brought thither; and she would have none of them—no,
not if it were ever so—and made her will felt on her guests,
who laughed indeed, but yet obeyed, and came there only
with male comrades.

It is needless to say what a paradise this place was to me
—a poor little terrified, agonised, hunted creature, who for a
year and a half had only known blows, and kicks, and hunger,
and thirst, and suffering. They let me dream or doze all my
hours away; play at will in the sweet unshaven grasses; roll
the fallen apples about as balls, and roam from dawn to
twilight in the deep old leafy ways of the fragrant-scented
garden.

It seemed to me happiness exquisite enough only to
stretch my limbs in peace on the cool moss; only to pass the
whole blithe day without one voice raised in anger at me;
only just to be fed, and to be clean, and to be left quite free.
The passion for freedom is intense in dogs. Men do not
much mind the gall of fetters, if so be that those fetters are
well gilded. But the gilt on a chain makes it none the better
to us; and we pine, and fret, and thirst for liberty, with a
force you can never know—you, who so continually sell yourselves into bondage for the sake of the purchase-price.

Moreover, there was one person very good to me—ever
gentle, ever thoughtful, ever kind. This was Madelon
Bris.

She had not very much beauty, this Madelon; not at least
after the vivid colouring and the exuberant outline of Avice
Dare, who had the scarlet bloom on her cheeks and the
northern gold in her hair. She was very slender, and very
pale, with great dark changing eyes, and swift small feet, ·

and a mouth which, though somewhat large, yet had a smilo so sweet that it had loveliness.

In every iota she was so unlike to what Avice had been in the old Peak days, that the contrast was almost startling to me. She was so skilled at every sort of work; so rapid and lithe in every kind of movement; she seemed so perpetually content; she sung so constantly over her labour, indoor or out.

She know every fowl by name; she would twist the humblest grasses and flowers into such pretty forms; she did all household things with so neat yet so elegant a touch; she dressed so simply, yet with so much grace and suitability for the work she did; with never any ornament save only one plain and massive cross of gold hung on a string of ivory beads. Everything about her was in harmony, and her life "seemed set to music," though it was a life of continual industry, and of even prosaic cares.

Her mother was very old, and did little save sit in the sun and read her well-worn book of Hours. All the toil and the thought of the place fell upon Madelon; and there were no boards so white, no brazen pans so shining, no pottery so clean, no honey so clear, no poultry so plump, no plants so healthful, no omelettes so lightly tossed, no beds so sweetly lavender-scented, as those of the Silver Stag.

This life of hers was prose, even as had been Avice's; but there was a poetry in it.

It was not heavy-weighted with tawdry follies; it was not fevered with discontent; it was not disfigured by an everlasting straining after something unpossessed; it was not hideous with that dead incurable poverty of spirit, and abject slavery to the dominion of ignorance, that are so appallingly hopeless in the lives of your English poor.

Avice had wreathed huge glass beads on her throat, red and yellow and blue; Madelon never wore but the ivory necklace that had been her great-great-grandmother's. Avice had worn a gown of many colours and of as many rags; Madelon wore one of dark-blue serge, but whole and doftly shaped. Avice, gathering radishes for the dinner-table, had thrown them all together, wet and soiled with the clods of their native earth; Madelon washed them heedfully, set them in little dainty pyramids of red and white, and garnished the whole with blossoming thyme. Avice at her work had kept her mouth sullenly tight set; Madelon at her work sung like some blithe bird. In Avice poverty had been dire ugliness and sulky wrath; in Madelon poverty was smiling patience and thoughtful content.

But there is no need to amplify examples; the one was Gallic and the other British.

Life went very softly and happily at the Silver Stag: old Manon Bris was a cheery old soul, with a stock of quaint legendary lore from her native province and a mirthful temper combined with a sturdy will. There was no one at the house that summer save Carlos Merle, and he lived almost like their son and brother. He was a man of seven or eight-and-twenty, Bohemian, enthusiast, and artist; he had few friends and little gold, but in compensation he had a most singular personal beauty and as singular a genius for art.

I have never in my life seen a man more beautiful than Carlos; he was like some perfect classic statue, and was radiantly fair with golden locks, though the country of his birth was far away south, touching the Pyrenees. They did not know very much about him; but from what he had said it had transpired that his mother had been a woman of noble family, who had contracted a low marriage with an opera-singer. Both were dead now, leaving him their beauty, their artistic dreams, and their poverty.

It was easy to see that there was more than friendship betwixt Madelon and her guest. She was reserved with him; and as shy as the natural dignity about her, and her clear and candid nature, permitted; but he never addressed her without the blood tinging her pale cheek, and he never entered her presence without her deep dark eyes kindling with a richer glow. As for the young man, he seemed irresistibly drawn to the peace and purity of this character so opposite to his own; he watched her swift yet soft movements as she went about her household labour, *ohne Hast, ohne Rast*, with the same pleasure that he watched the graceful flight of a dove; he appealed to her continually for her opinion of his art, and listened to her with loving reverence. For Madelon, though by no means what you term an educated woman, was of that natural intelligence which to a great extent supplies education by observation, and had heard and seen so much of art from her childhood, that her power of criticism was considerable when her modesty allowed her to give judgment.

She had a strong influence over Carlos Merle: when he, with his native southern indolence, would lie all through the long sunny hours under the acacia shadows, dreaming of many pictures but executing none, she would approach him gently and murmur: "Dreams are the artist's heaven; but they are not the highway to fame, my friend." And he, roused by that hint, would then rise, and shake himself, and go within, to work at his great picture for the Salon, or bring his tools into the open air, and sketch all manner of living things and floral life around him.

"They love one another," I said to Russ, when I had been there a week or two.

"I suppose they do," he answered reluctantly. "But I hardly approve of it. There have been many better men here than Carlos; and she has never cared for them."

"What is amiss with Carlos?" I asked; for indeed I liked the young man myself; he was gentle of nature, and often played with me.

"There is this amiss," said shrewd Russ. "He is the weaker of the two. Not in talent; he has superb talent; but in character. And there is always woe in such cases."

"May she not strengthen him? inspire him?"

"Where did you catch up that human cant? Do not believe that women ever do that. When a man is strong, but has fallen, a great-minded woman may raise him to her height, to above her height; if she only move him with passion enough. But where a man is radically weak it is not in any woman to do it. A mistress may, perhaps, because the tenure of a mistress is always uncertain, which piques and spurs him to retain her; but a wife never will. Her attraction falls away into habit; and her spell dissolves in familiarity."

"But look what influence Madelon has over this painter already."

"Ah—yes. Because he is a little in love with her; and is under the first charm of her sweet modest worth, her lofty pure wisdom. But if he were to marry her these would soon grow only wearisome to him, if only by reason of their superiority to himself; and he would be sure to forsake them for sake of some warmer, fuller, and more merely sensual charm. Madelon is an angel to those who have studied her nature; but she is only a quiet good girl of the people to others, and she cannot, you know, be called beautiful."

"Are only beautiful women beloved then?"

"O yes! I have seen men mad for a woman who had scarcely a good feature in her face; but then she had a *diable au corps* that supplied the place of beauty and seduced them."

"A *diable au corps!*"

"*Au corps, et à l'esprit, et à l'âme!* A woman who was once a cat, my dear: which Madelon never can have been."

I said nothing; though I wondered greatly why a woman was likely to be less beloved because she was an angel, than if she had been a cat; and I wondered also why a *diable au corps* should be such a great attraction.

I do not wonder now: nor will you either, if you have studied the sex, and know all that Russ meant by the three little words.

However, despite the chill that he threw on it, I continued to weave my little romance in those pleasant summer days, under the great blossoming lilacs and lindens of the place of my refuge; and I think that Madelon and Carlos Merle wove theirs too.

She was seldom alone with him, for the white tower of Mère Manon's head-gear was ever in sight, in the same chamber or through some open door. But continually when she was out among the flowers, or the poultry, or the beehives, tying up the sweet-scented stocks, or gathering the rose-leaves to dry for *pot-pourri*, or calling the pigeons around for food, Carlos would come down from his painting-attic, and saunter forth likewise, and stand beside her in his picturesque linen blouse, with the sun on his handsome golden head, smoking, and smiling, and sometimes tendering a nominal help.

And at such times he would talk tenderly to her, wistfully and sadly too, for he was alone in the world, and poor, and very ambitious; and Madelon would let the rose-leaves roll down on the turf again, or the grain all tumble in a heap at her feet, whilst she listened with tears that did not fall just gleaming in her great soft eyes;—the tears of a yearning sympathy which was, though she scarcely knew it, love.

At such times, also Russ, would growl where he was stretched full length under the trees.

"There have been many better men here than he," he would grumble in my ear; "and she never hearkened to one of them like that. O, he is well enough; I do not say anything against him; but he is of the stuff, look you, to make a great name by his genius one hour, and kill himself for a courtesan the next."

I, with the obstinacy of youth, disbelieved his verdict, and thought much better things of this sunny-haired southerner.

I lived a good deal in Carlos' *atelier;* in rainy days I was there entirely; and I think that I got to understand him better than stout old Russ, with his preconceived conclusions, ever did. Experience is an excellent spy-glass; but it has this drawback, that prejudice very often clouds the lens.

Carlos, with all his beauty and talent, and mingled force and indolence, had had but a rough life; and had been sorely ·

tossed and evilly entreated, and had suffered much from poverty and other ills.

This place in its peace and poetry was much such a haven to him as to me; its calm idyllic days were sweet to him as to myself; life here, under these blossoming limes, these clouds of foliage and flowers, seemed so still and fair a thing, so fit for dreams, so free of pain.

There are pauses in all your lives in which a balmy rest comes unto you, and you say, "It is well with me; I will look neither at the years that lie behind me nor before." It was such a pause in this young painter's. In such a season a young man's "fancies lightly turn to thoughts of love"—love for any woman near to him; any woman youthful enough to have in her the likeness of an ideal, and fair enough to seem to him the source whence his peace comes. Madelon was both these; and she was more. She was a woman who won his reverence by her pure straight thoughts, free of all guile; who charmed his eye with the grave grace and the lithe ease of her movements; and who made that poverty, which so long had been the King of Terrors to him, wear an aspect of sweet serene simplicity, which appeared of higher worth than riches.

He loved her therefore; loved her truthfully; if in such a season of summer and of rest he would have thus loved equally any mindless, laughing, red-lipped girl, or any dark-browed, lustrous-eyed faithless wanton, who should have been beside him in that soft maturity of the full year.

The influence Madelon had on him was very genuine, if not destined to be very enduring. She seldom advised; she never preached; she was disposed rather to undervalue her own powers of judgment, than to exalt them. But the very sight of her, in the untiring industry of her simple life, was of itself a tonic to the indolence of genius; and beneath her honest humility there was a force of enthusiasm for all high purpose and achievement, that acted as a fulcrum to the too facile talents of her guest.

What he felt towards her it was plain to see; her own

feelings were deeper hid, and less easy to guess. But that his presence was welcome to her, and his success dear, there could be little doubt; and her sincere belief in the greatness of his future was in itself enough to stimulate a man of spirit and of sensitiveness towards the realisation of its inspiring prophecies.

So the summer sped sweetly away with us all; the passing of time scarcely noticed except by the change of apple-buds to fruit, and the appearance and disappearance of the ruddy gold-starred strawberries underneath their leaves.

Two other artists passed part of the season there, but they were two aged men, severally painters of landscape and of animals; and their presence in no way jarred upon the harmony. Indeed, in a manner they contributed to it, for they had both fame and influence in the world of art, and they also saw great things in the works of Carlos Merle, and bade him be sure of that ultimate victory over the world, of which he often despaired: the ten years in which he had studied art having been a decade of failure, neglect, and privation.

With fresh heart put into him, the young man laboured hard during those long, clear, midsummer days; taking his recompense in the cool of the dewy evenings, with the great stars shining out, and the nightingales singing in the orchard, whilst Madelon, sitting in the porch, let her work fall upon her knee, and listened to him as he murmured passages of the *Nuits d'Octobre*, or of the *Chants du Crépuscule*, their melancholy and fervid poetry seeming, indeed, to be the very voices of the night.

I did not share Russ's contempt for Art. To me it always appeared a marvellous sorcery this, through which, by means of pigments and of oils, all things of nature were made to have their being on a dull, dead piece of pine-wood or of paper. I have moaned at the misery of Landseer's "St. Giles;" I have barked furiously at the hunting scenes of Snyders; I have howled with grief before the "Dead Trumpeter's" dog at Avignon; I have longed for old Trust to see

the sheep of Bonheur and of Verbœckhoven; I have thirsted
to pull the meat out of the basket of that bloated "Jack in
Office;"—therefore there cannot be a doubt but that I have
the true feeling for art in me. For this lies, I humbly submit,
not half so much in the sharpness of criticism, as it does in
the credence of sympathy.

Hence I watched with interest the progress of the great
picture with which Carlos was about to challenge the verdict
of Paris in the winter exhibition of the Salon.

It was a very peculiar picture; in a style that is not
popular in these days, when you are fond of little cabinet
sketches of every-day life, and of a realism that faithfully
reproduces every rent in a worn carpet, every knot in a
carpenter's piece of deal.

This picture of Carlos' was gorgeous in hue, shadowy in
meaning, had but little detail, and was of a terrible force and
a passionate poetry. And yet the subject was very simple.
It was only a man lying dead in a hot glow of sunset, with a
wondrous fair face, and a fearful woe set upon it; self-slain
it was easy to tell; and away from him, looking back over her
shoulder, was stealing, through the hush and the heat, with
the light of the west all about her like a fire, a woman, with
a wicked laugh upon her mouth, and her bosom all bare, and
her hand gathering up rich disordered gold-broidered robes.
This strange work, which had no story, was called simply
"Faustine," and it spoke for itself.

It was of this subject and its treatment that the painters
who came and went that summer at the Silver Stag predicted
such great things.

There was a little one, a highly-finished study also, which
he intended to send with it, for sake of the contrast, as I suppose. This was quite a small picture of a woman sitting in
cool, gray, silver-toned light, that came in through an ivy-
hung lattice; her work, a common shirt of serge, had fallen
on her lap, and her eyes were lifted to the soft night sky
without, where the first stars were gleaming. The subject
was of the slightest and simplest; but the colour, the patience,

the tender poetry in this moonlit face, made it beautiful. It
was on this that he had been engaged when Russ told me
that he was painting the portrait of Madelon Bris.

"Send them both," said one of the aged artists to him.
"They show that you can feel and fathom the two extreme
opposites of woman's nature. Without being able to do this,
neither painter nor poet can be great."

Doubtless, the old man was right.

But how many of you men write, think, paint, and speak
as though there were but one of these two sides to womanhood—according as the brazen, or the silvern, round of the
shield has been turned to you.

It was into autumn when those two paintings were altogether completed. Madelon looked at the one which so much
resembled her, of which she had indeed been alike the theme
and the inspiration, with a shy sweet pleasure, that blushed a
little in her pale cheek, and spoke eloquently in her dark
eyes. But before the Faustine she stood far longer, lost in
thought; gazing at it with an intensity, a wistful wonder, a
fascinated horror—even as a woman may gaze at a rival who,
though steeped in sin, is yet through sin victorious.

It was in the hush of an October evening that she stood
looking at it thus for the hundredth time, his latest touch
having been put to it; making more wicked the laugh of the
courtesan, more lurid the sunset glow, more glittering her
robes of cloth of gold, more white and rigid the face of the
dead man.

The evening was very warm. The leaves of the creepers
around the wide lattice were tinged with amber and crimson;
the sun was burning in the west; the great golden pears hung
motionless amongst their still green leaves; the fragance of
ripened fruit, and of damp earth, and of late roses, came in
on the western wind.

The large wooden chamber was half in shadow, half in
light; the only sound upon the silence was the lowing of the
cattle in the distant fields, and the coo of the doves ere they
settled to rest. All was cool, and still, and balmy.

Carlos approached her when she stood in front of the Faustine.

"Why will you look so much at that picture?" he said gently. "Why not look rather at the other, which is like yourself?"

Madelon did not answer for some moments, and I thought a faint shudder came over her.

"It has the fascination of the unknown for me," she answered simply.

"The unknown, indeed! But that is not all?"

"Not quite all. I am trying to see wherein lies that woman's power—that terrible power which has ended in stretching him there—dead."

"You cannot. No woman can see it—unless she be like that woman herself."

"Are you sure of that? I am not."

"Why? You say it is the sorcery of the unknown. In saying that you have said you cannot comprehend it."

"I ought to have said rather the unfamiliar. It cannot be unknown to me, since I feel it. It hurts me; it oppresses me; it is an awful thing—that witchery of sin, that has such irresistible seduction for all men!"

And whilst she spoke she still gazed with the same peculiar intensity of regard into the wicked eyes of the Faustine, till it seemed as though she read a living mind, a living vice, a living lie, in that pictured semblance of a gold-decked crime.

Carlos, in answer, moved the other picture before her.

"Nay," he said softly, "if Faustine triumph over some, others are saved—saved by such pure eyes as those that win them to their higher dreams,—to duty, peace, and honour. For a season Faustine may allure; but the gold on her garments is bought by blood, and the cruel hot sun of passion kills. Men seek to rest for their lifetime in the holy light of those calm stars."

Madelon smiled: the smile of a woman who believes, and for whom belief is beatitude. Yet the smile died soon upon her face, and she looked not at the woman who sat dreaming in the starlight, but still on the wicked eyes of the Faustine.

"It may be so," she said, under her breath; "but your pencil was closer to truth than your words. Look!—he—lies dead; and she—she sits there by the lattice *alone*."

Then she passed swiftly from the painting chamber, as though fearful that her answer bore some interpretation that she could ill endure to hear him give: some self-betrayal which for one brief moment had escaped her.

Alone! Carlos echoed the word as he stood before the little portrait, which caught the fading light of the west upon it. The word seemed to strike heavily on his ear; dully upon his heart, as with the melancholy of a foreboding.

This little slender, simple study had more sadness in it than he had ever noted whilst occupied in creating it. The weary folding of the hands, the meditation of the uplifted eyes, the thoughtful shadowy smile upon the mouth, the faint gray light that seemed to float around the form;—all were sad with the infinite sadness of resignation, the sadness of a woman alone with her perished youth;—alone for evermore.

The face was the face of Madelon; but on it was a grief, around it was a solitude, that were as yet far from her; that as yet had never even touched her cheerful tranquil life.

"It is Faustine, who dies alone!" he muttered, as though he repelled the thought her words had conjured up. "Not such women as Madelon. They die in the ripeness of time, after a life of peace, with their children and their grandchildren about them."

He went to the open window and leaned his arms on it, and looked down on the garden below. He was very thoughtful and touched, I thought with a reflex of Madelon's sadness.

I wondered if he had ever been beneath the sorcery of such as that Faustine whom he had painted there; or, whether it were only by some foreboding of a fate to come that he had dreamed that dark and awful story, and wrought it out with colour till it seemed the record of a fact.

I could not but fancy it the last.

The fair face of this young painter was very frank, and tender, and eager; it had sorrow, and unrest, and desire upon it, but these were all untainted by evil; it had rather the longing for a fuller life in it than the fatigue of one by whom the uttermost possibilities of life have been exhausted.

Perhaps I hardly reasoned thus, then; but I felt it: and now, looking back to that time through the light of my experience, I am certain that I translated aright the look upon his features.

As he leaned on the wooden window-sill, in the still green garden beneath, where the moonlight already was stealing, he saw Madelon. She was walking amidst her flowers, that grew half wild amidst the grass and bushes. Now and then she stooped and raised some fallen carnation, or lifted some rose, which, overladen with dew, drooped downward and trembled, as a human heart that is too happy sinks and trembles with apprehension.

Now and then, too, she moved aside, that her foot should not crush some tiny crawling thing, that had its one short hour of harmless joy amongst the leaves and grasses: now and then she lifted some little brown glow-worm, with its brightly burning lamp, up to some place of safety, on a leafy bough, or in the cup of a late lily: nay, even a beetle creeping with its load homeward, or even a sand-worm crawling in the gravelled way, she stepped aside from, leaving them their life.

Would that more amongst you had that tender pity; had that reverence for the wonder of existence which is as great in the tiniest fly that wings its way as in the great leviathan of the sea. All things must suffer, and must think, since all things dread and trust: can there be fear without mental torture? Can there be trust without emotional power? Ay —and thrusting a pin through the beetle's body and cutting the brain from the living pigeon, in your hideous dissecting rooms, will not teach you this; it will only teach you to be blind to it.

The young man, leaning from the casement, hidden himself amongst the thick screen of the ivy, watched her as she moved. Perhaps that gentle compassion for the "lowliest thing that lived" had greater sweetness in his sight because, to him, the world of men had been cruel and hard; and the world of women had had for him some scorn, since he had not owned the gold that buys their kisses.

When the stones of poverty and of disdain are rained from many hands upon one single head, he on whom they fall—being defenceless—grows one of two things beneath the storm: either he becomes case-hardened and ruthless in revenge, or he grows weak as water, and is ready to sell his soul for the sweet balm of pity. To Carlos Merle—with the heart of a woman in his godlike young form—pity and comprehension bore so fair a likeness to love that, paying them with gratitude, he dreamed gratitude was also love. This error is common with you all; commonest with the tenderest of your natures: but it is an error which often costs you more heavily than sin itself. For, amongst you men and women, though there be absolute passion without love, there is no absolute love without passion.

He watched her thus awhile, where she went amongst the trees, with the dark graceful folds of her dress sweeping aside the dews.

On a sudden impulse, as it seemed, he left his studio, and ran lightly down the old broad oaken stairs, and went out into the garden. He was at her side ere she had heard his steps that fell so lightly on the grass. She started a little, and turned from him, as I noticed, having followed him myself out into the balmy evening air.

"Madelon," he said to her, with a tremor in his voice, "Madelon,—if you will let it be so, you shall never sit at the lattice alone."

She gave him one quick glance under her dark deep

lashes; then she was silent, her hand gathering the feathery crowns of tall seeding grasses that grew round her.

"May it be so?" he murmured. "Have you faith enough in me to let me enter your life? You can make me what you will: will you give me place beside you always?"

She did not answer, but her drooped face flushed till all its colourlessness changed to a hot scarlet radiance, like the flush on the latest autumn roses.

"Tell me," he murmured eagerly. "Can it be—that you have less pity for me than for that glow-worm that you lifted out of harm a moment ago? I love you, Madelon; you must have known it all this summer through, and I think—I think —you have some love to give in recompense?"

The glow died from her face; great tears stood unshed in her eyes; she trembled greatly whilst she left her hand in his.

"It is not a question of my love," she said, scarce audibly. "It is of your peace,— your greatness,—your future. These lie far apart from me."

"They lie with you: with you alone!" he answered her, with passionate belief in his own truth as he drew her nearer and nearer, and stooped his golden head, and kissed her where they stood beneath the great shadows of the dying limes.

For a moment Madelon surrendered herself to that sweet intoxication. But the breathless trance endured but a little space; she drew herself from him, and looked straight up into his eyes with that deep glance of hers that had in it such exhaustless tenderness and power of sacrifice.

"You speak in haste," she said tremulously. "I am the only woman near you; you have found some comprehension and some sympathy in me; you have a noble nature;—and you offer me love. But, though I love you, Carlos, I am not fit to be your wife!"

"Not fit! My God!" he cried, "what grace, what excellence, what purity of womanhood have there ever been found lacking in you?"

She smiled faintly; but her eyes never lost their steady, meditative wistfulness of regard.

"Nay, I speak the truth," she said gently. "I am but one of the people; I have ever laboured with my hands; I am ignorant, even if sympathy teach me some few things. You will be great, my friend; you will have fame, and fame brings fortune; I shall be no meet companion for you in that new life which so surely waits for you. I love you—"

She paused, and stretched her hands out to him in a gesture of infinite tenderness, though her face the while grew yet more deadly pale.

"See! I do not seek to deny it or to hide it. I love you, Carlos, but *because* I love you, I know—I know—that there will be no place for me in your future!"

He seized her outstretched hands, and poured forth poetic burning words of eloquence, that thrilled out upon the stillness of the autumn twilight, and seemed to scorch and stagger her as they pierced her heart. But for her he swore he had been worthless; crushed beneath the load of poverty and of the world's neglect. Her influence alone had breathed into him the strength to give form and substance to the fair dream of an idle brain. He had no name nor place in the world as yet: should he win either ever, it would be through her inspiration; through that brave acceptance of the yoke of toil, which, beholding in her, he at length had followed.

So he urged and pleaded till the ardent eloquence of words was as a whirl of fire in which her thought and her will were caught, and blinded, and consumed. Yet not wholly; for this woman's love was—unlike the love of her sex —without one taint of selfishness, or of vain desire, or of untrue appraisement.

"You speak generously," she murmured, whilst her heart heaved and her lips quivered. "But you speak in blindness. You love me now—O yes!—but for how long? Nay, it is not that I distrust you. I distrust myself. I may be well in your sight here—here in solitude and in summer—but with the moment that brings you fame, and that the world usurps

you, I shall be no more than a kindly memory in your
heart—"

"A memory! If ever I love you less, if ever I leave your
side, may God—"

"Hush! The future is not in your hands; not in mine.
Call no curse upon it. It will not be possible that you should
love me always. I have not beauty; I have not knowledge;
I am only, after all, a peasant trained to household labours.
If I were to become your wife, what would you say in the
years to come?—you would say this woman has no likeness
with my life as it stands now; no kinship with my fame; no
fitness for my career. You would say it—assuredly—in your
own heart—"

"Are you mad?" he cried with impetuous interruption.
"Am I a noble or a prince, that you should look on me with
this proud humility—treat me thus, as though I were some
creature of a higher sphere descended to you? You know
my history, my poverty, my dependence on my own labours;
the neglect the world has had of me, the chances that I shall
never be able, do what I may, to give my name to fame. As
I stand now, I am barely your equal. You have certain
possessions; I have none. To me this sweet and tranquil
place is the happiest home that I have ever known. Is it a
little thing to ask you to let me share it always?—to ask you
to let me, in the fever and disappointments of a painter's
career, always have its rest and innocence to return to for
shelter and for hope? No! it is because it is so great a
thing—a thing so utterly beyond my rights to claim and my
power to requite—that you draw yourself aloof from me, and
plead your own unworthiness, in the noble falsehood of a
woman's pity!"

The words poured from his lips with all the vivacious fire
of his southerner's temperament, and with all the fiery reproach of that upbraiding selfishness which always sounds
upon a woman's ear as love itself incarnate. It moved her
strangely. The colour came and went upon her face; her
limbs trembled; her lips parted with swift uneven breaths.

She looked up swiftly in his face with the great tears heavy on her lashes.

"Ah, if I could be of use or service to you," she murmured; "if I could be sure that you never could repent."

She needed to say no more: he stooped again his beautiful fair head, and his lips rested on hers unchidden.

They wandered long together that evening, through the lonely moonlit orchards, and the deep cool gardens; on which the last glow, and the last breeze, and the last sigh of the dying summer were lingering, as though loth to pass away and leave the earth to silence, snow, and shadow.

CHAPTER IV.

Faustina Victrix.

LIFE at the Silver Stag, which had been full of peace before, now deepened into happiness. The beatitude of confessed and mutual love was there; nor was there any hindrance to it, nor any shade to mar it.

The old Mère Iris had grown to regard with unusual favour this golden-haired young stranger, who treated her with all a son's reverent kindliness; and she offered no opposition to his marriage with Madelon, desiring only that he should achieve some public success that should be a guarantee of his ability to add somewhat to her own slender store. And to this Carlos Merle offered but little opposition: he was too proud and honest to seek to live in idleness upon these women; and, indeed, though he knew it not, so much of the desire of rest, and so little of the desire of passion, was in his love, that it was almost enough to him to be certain of this simple asylum and this innocent affection that he had already gained. So all things went smoothly and joyously in this primitive and pleasant spot. His pictures were completed; his time was his own; he could spend it at will with Madelon; aiding her in her out-door tasks; watching her in her in-door occupations; listening kindly to the old dame's legendary lore; and

even spending his strength in such useful fashion as the hew-
ing of wood for the winter firing, and the fetching of buckets
of water from the distant well in the orchard. As for Madelon
—there was in her fathomless eyes such a look of tranquil
intensity, of unutterable joy, as I have never seen on any
human face; she spoke but seldom; but her voice as she sang
at her work had the sweetness in it of one continual hymn of
praise; and to her the russet autumn was as the golden dawn-
ing of years of perpetual summer.

Russ alone was ill-satisfied.

"It is not well," he muttered to me. "It is not well. He
is sincere?—O yes, he is sincere; men mostly are whilst they
talk of love. But it is only affection with him; there is no
passion in it; and no man, with his beauty and his nature,
ever passes by passion all his life long. He will know that
one day—and she too. But we can do no good. Don't let
us talk of it."

"Is passion such a good thing, then?"

Russ growled a whole satire.

"Good? It is a devil, my dear: and one that the dog I
told you about never succeeded in driving out, whether from
church, or castle, or cottage. It is a devil that will tempt
Carlos Merle, sooner or later; and it will drag him away from
her in the end, let him seek or strive as he may."

The winter soon came. It was very cold, but very bright.
Carlos sold a little landscape to a stranger who, resting at the
Silver Stag, chanced to see, and paid five gold pieces for it;
and he spent all the five in purchasing a set of furs for
Madelon. She chid him gently for the extravagance, but
smiled on him for the love shown therein. She wrapped them
about her mother, and moved blithely in the snow to feed her
poultry and her doves, quite warm in her dress of serge,
from the rapture and the peace that dwelt together in her
heart.

The broad low kitchen of the place was always ruddily
bright from the big fire of wood that burned on an old-
fashioned hearth, built long, they said, ere stoves were

known. It had a pleasant odour always in it, from the many
herbs that hung from the ceiling beams; knots of dried
thyme, and marjoram, and sage, and rue. The reddened
light of the stormy winter days played cheerily upon the
brass and pewter that, shining like gold and silver, filled the
black oak shelves.

All day long the little birds would crowd under the casements for food that Madelon threw them; and the droll-
visaged ducks, and the neat coquettish hens, when wet or
cold, would come through the door she opened for them—the
former with solemn march, and shrewd all-seeing eyes, the
latter with coy dainty steps, and shy sidelong glances—and
go straightway to the hearth, and there sit and dry their
plumage and dress themselves, and turn their heads over their
shoulders to survey themselves, precisely as I have seen great
ladies do before their mirrors. When dusk closed in, and
the fowls were all at roost, and the oil lamp lighted, Russ
and I would lie alone within the warmth of the logs, watching,
with dreamy pleasure, the big copper kettle of soup swinging
in the chimney; while old Mère Bris dozed in the corner, and
Madelon, with her great eyes all dilated and eloquent, listened
to some *chant du siècle* read aloud to her by her lover's inclo-
dious vibrating voice.

It was a happy winter time; and in it I almost forgot my
two past years of misery. Not quite: for a dog never wholly
forgets; and, having his spirit once broken, is never altogether the same dog again. Naturally the eyes of creatures
of our race are fuller of glee, mirth, readiness, and gladness
than the eyes of any other living things; but most of them
are clouded by sadness, by terror, and by the constant apprehension which your brutal training leaves on them, long before they have even reached their prime.

It was a hard winter, so far as cold went. The great black
woods were ice-bound, and the water of the duck-pond had to
be broken every morning for the old carp to breathe. Madelon
put over the doorway a little oat-sheaf for the birds, in a
fashion she had learned of some German artist; and the case-

ments were thick with dense, white, glittering frost with every dawn that rose. But though so chill without, life went within gladly and brightly. The first real chill of the year seemed to fall when it was no longer possible for Carlos to longer defer his visit to the Salon.

His pictures had been accepted; he went to the assembling of the critics. He was to rest there the night, and was to return on the morrow, bringing his tidings with him. As he quitted the little porch Madelon thrust a covered basked into his hand.

"It is the carrier-dove Fleurette," she whispered to him, while her voice was full of love not spoken in phrases. "She has often come between this and Paris. If all be well with you, loose her. She will be back here in two hours."

So Fleurette went with him on his pilgrimage; for the electric wires were a costliness not dreamed of by these poor and simple people. Russ, and I, and Madelon tarried behind in the old, oaken, dusky chamber. It was a drear, dark day, with fitful gusts of storm-wind, and sudden driving clouds of rain—a day full of melancholy and of foreboding; a day that makes dogs howl, and men pen satires, and women sit all day long wearily watching the sweeping on and off of the black mists. Madelon did her household work of the day none the less quickly or well; but every now and then she started, as a blast shook the house; and when her labour was done, sat with fevered cheeks by the casement, looking out with wistful eyes for the clearance of the skies that should allow the dove's soft, slender wings to beat their safe way home. Her whole soul was in her lover's fame, even though she knew fame was her cruellest rival.

The day passed very wearily to us all.

There came back no Fleurette.

Madelon kept the shutters down an hour later than was her custom, and stood gazing out into the shadowy bleak night for the white small form of her messenger of hope.

"Close the window, *ma fille*," called her old mother from

the chimney-corner. "It is quite dark, and there may come beggars around, or worse—drawn by the light in the lattice."

Madelon obeyed with that curiously implicit obedience which characterises French filial duty, and came and sat down by her lamp, and began to sew—mending a worn summer blouse of Carlos Merle's. Her mother did not see that her eyes were wet with tears—but I saw. *Je reste: tu t'en vas!* Such is eternally the requiem over all women's loves; when the woman has loved well.

The long evening went slowly, very slowly. The bubbling of the copper pot, and the crackling of the fire logs, were the only sounds upon its stillness. Russ once moved towards her, and laid his great head on her knee, and gazed into her face with great loving eyes of sympathy and reverent pity. Madelon stooped and kissed him, and tears fell on his forehead.

"It is thus that it must be, Russ," she murmured over him.

The evening and the night passed; the morning broke fairer, though still cold. About noon a little flash of white glimmered in the steely sky; there was a murmuring noise; and, beating against the casement, there fell down the dove. Madelon caught her with a low cry.

She was not cold nor wet, and could not have been loosed until that morning. He had forgotten to send her home.

Beneath her left wing was a note. As Madelon read it she grew pale—paler than she ever had been through all this winter-time.

"What does he say?" cried the old mother from her chimney-corner, eager to learn the best or worst.

Madelon waited a moment ere she replied. When she did so her voice was calm.

"Only three words, *ma mère.* 'Success! Return to-morrow.'"

"'To-morrow!" cried Mère Bris. "He said this day—this day, beyond a doubt."

"Yes. But how likely it is that he has met with friends,

and—see, *mère*—he has success at last.   No wonder he stays
from us!"

Then she left the chamber; closing the door upon her,
and carrying with her the tired, thirsty, ruffled dove.

Carlos did not come that day, nor the next, nor the
next.

Madelon said nothing, not a word, save at such times as
she answered, to her mother's petulant quibbles, that it was
natural and fitting he should stay; that he was his own
master; and that he owed them nothing.

But the time dragged drearily; and she never sent
Fleurette back to the city.

With the fourth day indeed he came, sweeping through
the snow, with his yellow locks on the wind, and his fair face
hot with proud passionate glow. He rushed straight to where
Madelon stood, having risen in startled amaze; he clasped
her hands, he kissed her dress, he showered letters, and
papers, and gold upon her lap; at last he flung himself at
her feet, and letting his head drop down upon her knees,
sobbed like a woman.

"I have the desire of my life!" he cried to her. "I have
the desire of my life—I am famous!"

It seemed, as I gathered a while afterwards, that he had
in truth achieved the most singular success of the winter ex-
hibitions, and redeemed, almost in a day, the painful and
long decade of disappointment and of failure. The general
crowds of Paris flocked to stand before the Faustine; but
some half-score of perfect judges offered him well-nigh its
weight in gold for that little study of the woman at the
lattice.

Faustine was one of those wonderful and instantaneous
successes which sometimes seize on the world with a force
quite outside criticism, and quite beyond attack.

People flocked in herds to see it; and on the class of which
it was the representative it seemed, they said, to exercise the
strongest and most irresistible fascination.

The day of the first exhibition had been a day of unshadowed triumph for Carlos. His name had leapt to all the lips of Paris; and great artists, long neglectful and contemptuous of him, had turned and surveyed him with a curious puzzled look, as though they said, "Eh, then, who is this that has been amongst us, and that we have denied?"

They denied him no longer. The popular voice is very seldom indeed the voice divine; but occasionally it does speak with the prescience, the spontaneity, the irresistible verdict of a god-like fiat. It spoke thus in his election; and against such a choice his rivals had no power.

The Faustine had been sold ere it had hung two hours— sold for an enormous sum, as many said. For the Woman at the Lattice he had, with an artist's and a lover's improvident, unwise spirit of fanciful attachment, refused all the offers made to him.

"Are you mad?" painters had whispered him. "Faustine in a year will be worth to you millions of francs, and that little panel will never again fetch so much as they tender you for it now." But Carlos had shaken his head, and been firm. "Shall a man sell his soul?" he had said in his heart. So the Faustine hung there, sold at her birth, as befitted the likeness of a courtesan; but for the woman in the moonlight there was no gold chaffered.

And he came back to us, wild and drunk with the wine of his fame; he wept, he laughed, he threw himself like a child before the crucifix; he scattered grain in huge golden showers to the birds upon the snow; he waltzed, he sang, he was like one possessed; and all this was beautiful in him, because his own youth had so much beauty, and all his ecstasies had so much truth. Then he grew very quiet, and came and stretched himself upon the hearth, and lay there with his head leaning upon Madelon's knee.

"I shall be great," he murmured passionately to her. "Already—in a day—my name is famous, and men say of my work that it has in it the germ of the eternal. And what should I have been without you—you, to whom riches, and fame, and honours, and life, all are due?"

Her face was in shadow, and he was not looking up to it, but into the burning embers of the wood; or he would have seen a smile upon it that only the martyrs wear.

"Be great; be greatest," she whispered to him. "So shall I be content."

And yet I think she knew so well that, saying this, she also said, "Go from me, and never more return."

Division already had commenced: passion and ambition will scarce ever live together. They are as two fierce parasites which will not share with that which they cling to and corrode, but must have all or nothing. Here and there, indeed, they may grow side by side together; when they do, the world has no strength to stand against that furious fusion of strange forces.

The first note of fame to him brought the first note of pain to her. He needed now to be perpetually passing to Paris. It seems that fame is such an *ignis fatuus* that a man, if he once lose his personal watch over it, fears to see it sink into the marshes of oblivion.

It was natural that he rejoiced in his fresh-won success; that the new voices of praise were very sweet upon his long-thirsting ear; that the new life which had opened for him allured him with an enchantment he scarcely sought to resist.

It was natural, moreover, for his name's sake, or he thought it was, that he should have a studio in the heart of the artist-world, now that this world was busied with his works. All Madelon said was simply, "What is best for thee, is for me happiest."

The old mother grumbled at the thought of his considering some other abode so needful for him, just because he had won his way a little on to the tongues of men.

But he pleaded his excuse with his graceful kindly filial fashion.

"Nay, *mère*, it is not a home that I seek; my home is here," he answered her. "I do but go to Paris as to an armoury-shop, where I may be nigh at hand for the battle; to circumvent my foes, and to secure my victories."

And Madelon urged his cause also. "It is best, indeed, *mère*. All painters must have a working-place in Paris. The world is never so fond of genius that it will ever run far into strange corners and village-hearths to seek it. It is best out in the mart, with the rest of men's merchandise."

"You do not want to be happy, Madelon!" retorted the old woman sharply.

Madelon smiled—that same sweet dreamy smile that had such an unfathomable meaning in it.

"Nay, *mère*," she answered, "let him be so first."

So it came to pass that, when the turn of the year came, and the first signs of life were stirring under the bark of the trees, and the ice of the pools, and the dark sodden mould of the gardens, Carlos Merle had a studio of his own in the heart of the Art-world of Paris, and stayed there all the week, and only came to the Silver Stag at the close of each sixth day.

It was inevitable, I suppose; they said so. Paris had a place for him now, and he went to fill it; the voices were glad about him, they were pleasant on his ear. The world spoke his name; he liked to hear it sounding. Men pointed him out when he passed; he was proud of that finger-homage. Crowds stood all day long about his pictures; he was pleased to stand near also, and see that worship of the multitude which worships the artist as it worships the god—blindly and yet unerringly. It was natural, I suppose, that Paris should draw him thus, daily and daily, more and more towards it. It was natural, doubtless; but at the Silver Stag the spring was dreary.

The sweet scent of the russet fallow turned upwards under the plough; the bees began to boom about in the pale sunshine; the ducks found shoots of cress under the chill water; the swallows came from Africa, and as they twittered underneath the eaves, told to the home-staying doves a thousand stories of the old Libyan world. It was earliest spring with all things; but it seemed to us rather like the setting than the resurrection of the year.

Yet Carlos came with every seventh day—came with burning eyes, and eager words, and proud glad laughter, and spoke incessantly of the great life that had opened to him with his victory. The world was transfigured to him. He was no longer poor, or neglected, or alone. He had present ease and future wealth secured. Men sought him; houses opened to him; friends came around him; he was known; and in that one word there lies for genius all the width that yawns between heaven and hell. The very suddenness of it made it the sweeter; and he went to the phantasmagoria of the world with all the eagerness, and almost all the ignorance, of a child.

Vice had had scant temptation for him earlier, because clothed in rags rather than in robes. But now pleasure, for the first time, smiled on him from the sweet gay eyes of dainty, velvet-footed, silvery-voiced women. Their allurements were not easily forgotten when he returned to the quiet homely innocence of his little woodland shelter. Not that he loved it less, or less loved Madelon; but he seemed like the carrier-birds, which, though they are never easy until they have reached their home, yet, resting but a moment there, desire to fly forth again.

He poured out on her the same passionate gratitude. He still beheld in her the force whereby he had been lifted up to greatness. He came to her for all his highest inspirations. He brought to her, as of yore, all his thoughts, and his hopes, and his dreams. He beheld in her the most perfect of created women, whose shoe-latchet he was not worthy to unloose. But still, with the sunrise of every first day of the week he went, as an arrow from the bow; and though his eyes oftentimes looked back, his swift feet never tarried once.

On some of these seasons of departure he would take me with him, having grown to like me in a fashion, though not deeply. Take me into the great white gleaming city, that seemed all colour, and tinsel, and marble, and foliage; and into his little *atelier*, where already the world was flocking, because he had painted a courtesan in such sort that all of her kind recognised their own likeness.

The *atelier* was somewhat high in air, in a famous part of the artist-town. He had taken it from a rich young amateur, and it was full of eastern stuffs, curious woods, cabinets, cushions, and all manner of quaint glittering rubbish brought from Asian bazaars. Its window looked on a pile of zinc roof, and its spiral staircase was dark and narrow, and its north light was obscured. If I had been an artist, I think I should never have painted so well in this small, luxurious, gaudy chamber, with its stuffs, and metals, and skins, as in that broad, low, wooden room, all open to the light, and swept by the free winds of heaven, and scented by the odours of the woods and fields without. Indeed, I know not why it was, but I felt a curious fancy that in this Parisian studio Carlos would never paint again as he had painted when the Faustine rose to life.

This little, dusky, bedizened, crowded, gilded chamber, with its pieces of art and its fabrics of India, might be a paradise to him, because to him it represented resurrection from a death in life, and was as the temple of victory. But to me it was only a den, pastille-scented, charcoal-heated, stifling with artificial aroma, and bounded by four narrow close walls, all hung with fantastic gold Japanese shapes, on a ground of black, that made me shudder whenever I looked at them.

It was not dull, for there were throngs all day long coming in and going out; men and women also, who came because the Faustine was the fashion. Beside, that singular beauty which he possessed was fair in the sight of the sated dames of the capital, as in the thoughtful wistful eyes of Madelon. It was beauty untamed and yet soft, virile and yet appealing, that had a sorcery for women; and ere long the great ladies of Paris vied to seat this superb young painter at their board and welcome him within their presence-chamber. "*Je suis pauvre,*" he would object to their flattering overtures, with his gracious half-proud diffidence. "*Qu'est-ce que c'est ça?*" they would answer.

So, though he waited within all the day, I was always left alone at twilight, and the key was turned in the studio-door, and rarely ever again unturned until the first streak of dawn. He painted scarcely at all. How could he? He had done so much in the summer and early autumn, because he had gone to bed almost with the kine, and risen always with the lark. But now that his days and evenings were all spent either in the gay wild laughing company of wits, and rhymesters, and playwrights, and artists, or in the dazzling brilliancies of the great world of society, work was impossible.

Do not think that Carlos spent all his gains upon himself. O no! He spent them royally; and every manner of good thing and gracious gift found the way to Mère Bris or to Madelon. He had received as many orders as he would have been able to execute, working at the hardest, in the coming two years; and no thought that an hour's illness, a street accident, a horse's kick, might turn his Eldorado afresh into a desert, ever weighed on the sunny sanguine glow of his fervid temperament. He intended to labour assiduously, he said—when—when all this novelty should have worn off—when he should have, in a measure, received his recompense for his ten years of weariness and pain.

So that when with every sixth day he went to the Silver Stag, and the old mother would ask petulantly of him what the week's work had beheld done, he would murmur hurriedly a thousand picturesque words, sketching a thousand picturesque scenes. It was the spring; it was just April; it was the height of the world's follies. All things seemed so fair and new; people were kind; and the days fled so fast; and friendships such as those he made were fame and fortune likewise. And Madelon, who never asked him questions such as these, would call softly across to her mother from whence she sat at work by the casement, "Carlos is right, *mère*. It is such people as these that are fitting for him; their voices are fame."

But I think she only said it to disarm the sharpness of the old woman's irritable tongue; for I think that Madelon knew that the greatness of the artist cannot come from without; that genius is a curlew best rocked on the tossing crest of a roughened sea; and that for him by whom a thirsty ear is lent to the world's homage, the tocsin of feebleness, if not of failure, has already sounded.

The gladness of the man is come when the crowds lisp his name, and the gold fills his hand, and the women's honeyed adulations buzz like golden beesabout his path; but how often is the greatness of the artist gone, and gone for ever!

Because when the world denies you it is easy to deny the world; because when the bread is bitter it is easy not to linger at the meal; because when the oil is low it is easy to rise with dawn; because when the body is without surfeit or temptation it is easy to rise above earth on the wings of the spirit. Poverty is very terrible to you, and kills your soul in you sometimes; but it is like the northern blast that lashes men into Vikings; it is not the soft, luscious, south wind that lulls them into lotos-eaters.

In the north wind Carlos Merle had staggered to his feet, and been proud, and been strong, and had conquered; in the south he was ready to say, "It is sweet; leave me alone; I have lived!"

CHAPTER V.

"Cléopâtre."

"It is as you said," I lamented to Russ.

"Of course," he made answer, "where two people love it is always the deep heart that breaks itself for the shallow one. O—I do not say his is shallow really, but it is for this passion. Do you not know that a man's passions are just like the channels of water-courses? some seasons they are narrow as runlets, others they are as broad as rivers; sometimes a child can straddle athwart them, and plumb them with his little forefinger, and at others a man shall not cross them with safety to his own life. It just depends on how the storm has come down."

Which was no doubt true; and the storm-drum never yet has beaten that has warned men of a fatal passion.

So the spring time came, and went, sadly at the Silver Stag; though there was no lack of guests and of passers-by all through that lovely cowslip time. There were always artists, of some standing or another, staying there, from the gray-headed masters to the laughter-loving students, and one and all these talked of Carlos Merle.

By Madelon's desire no one knew aught of the relationship between them, and so they spoke of him fully and frankly as of a familiar mutual theme of interest. It was only when they touched, as she thought, too closely on the personal matters of his life that she would check their converse; as though, in the pure undivided loyalty of her soul, she feared to seem to do him the dishonour to glean by hearsay what he withheld from confidence. But old Manon Bris, less scrupulous and more inquisitive, asked all she could of his life in the city from the men who came beneath her roof, and caught many glimpses in it of extravagance, and heedlessness, and pleasure, that wore the look of evil to her sturdy peasant's mind.

"Carlos lives as a prince in Paris," she muttered to her daughter.

"O no, *mère*," Madelon answered her in deprecation. "He lives as every artist that is at all known must do. Do not believe that boy Looloo's chatter; he is a little scaramouch, who thinks it a feast to get a full meal of roast chestnuts, his people have always been so poor, and he is such a child; he can be no judge of how a man should live."

"Carlos was as poor two months ago!"

"Not quite, *mère*; and beside, if he were, he has earned a large wage, and a just, since then; he may surely have some pleasure from the price of his own labours."

"He will never marry you, Madelon," muttered the old woman, in discontent and doubt.

"He would marry me now, *mère*, if I would have it so," Madelon answered her gently.

And this was true, for every time that Carlos came back thither he renewed with almost feverish entreaty his offers of an immediate union.   But perhaps Madelon detected the accent of honour only, and not of passion in his words; or perhaps she felt, that he sought to bind his will by law, because he felt it unstable in inclination; at any rate she answered to him always, "Not yet."

It was not from any fear for herself I am sure.   Madelon was not the kind of woman that fears; I think it was rather that she feared for him, and that she desired to leave this beautiful future, which was now unclosing to him, altogether free and entirely without claim or lien on it.

"Servitude is well for women," she would say to him; "they are hardly happy free; but with men it is otherwise: —liberty is the very marrow of their bones."

And she would not wed with him earlier than that late autumn time which her mother had originally fixed.   Yet though she was so resolute, her cheeks grew thinner, and her eyes larger and brighter every day; and I think that, if she had once heard the pleading of actual lover quiver in his voice, she would have put her hand in his and never have withdrawn it till the priest's benediction had made it his own.

Maybe those women are happiest who easily deceive themselves.   Madelon was not of them.   The essential truthfulness in her made her, no doubt, specially keen to feel any grain of truth that was lacking in others.   "He does not really love me," she had told herself the very night on which she first heard of his love; and the lowliness of her self-esteem made it appear to her impossible that he ever should do so.

The full deep spring came; the great plumes of the lilacs nodding everywhere, and the grasses all yellow with cowslip bells.   The days began to grow long, and be sultry at noon. The mavises and linnets sang all the light hours through, scarce still even at the noontide.   But over the place a certain

sadness fell—in the deserted painting-room the shadows lay
unbroken by any passing foot; to the well in the orchard
Madelon went alone; nor ever now would she wait to bind a
coil of ivy round the handle of the pail, or gather the big
white marguerites that grew there, to make of their petals a
sundial for love. In the few times that brought thither a
laughing group of students and of girls, she served them
silently with wine and milk, honey and meat, coffee and cake,
and then withdrew herself, so far as might be possible, from
out the hearing of the mirthful cadences of laughter; and in
the evenings, when the day was done and the little latch lay
quiet in the gate, she would take her work and sit beside the
open lattice, looking ever and again at the calm gray sky
beyond, as in the picture he had drawn.

But the look that was in her eyes no longer seemed the
same. The hush of maidenhood was gone, the rapture of
marriage and maternity had not come; there was only the
vague, passionate, dumb anguish of the womanhood, which,
in the same hour that it learns passion, learns likewise aban-
donment.

Now, amongst those youths who came and went in the
golden April days, amongst the lilacs of the Silver Stag,
young painters of careless tongue and mirthful mischief, there
were many who spoke of the doings of Carlos in Paris, and
tangled many names with his, as young men will. But chiefly
they quoted one, a name of melody and meaning,—Cléopâtre.

Madelon grew paler whenever the name was mentioned;
but she never asked whom it might mean. Perhaps she knew.

"You are painting the portrait of Cléopâtre?" she said
straightly to him when he next came. He started and looked
at her.

"Who told you so?"—it was the first thing that he had
not of his own accord related to her.

"The students say so," she answered. "Is it true?"

"Yes; it is true, for that matter."

Her voice sank very low.

"She is a bad woman, Carlos?"

"A vile woman—"

"Why have you aught to do with her, then?"

"To do!—she is a perfectly beautiful woman; she sought a portrait of me. She is an empress in her way. Was it worth while to refuse?"

He spoke hurriedly, bending to and fro a bough of blossoming lilac.

"I thought you would never paint portraits?"

"No, nor do I,—but this woman is like no one else. She is a woman that comes once in five centuries!"

"She is so beautiful?—I understand."

"No, you cannot understand," he muttered. "Madelon, Madelon, I swear to you that I never hated the Faustine of my fancy more than I hate this hell-born Cléopâtre!"

She looked at him earnestly; and a shudder ran through her.

"You defied Faustine!" she murmured with a shiver. "O, my love, my love, my love,—beware!"

It was one of the few moments in which the great affection in her broke up into yearning and passionate speech.

Carlos stooped and kissed her; but his face was flushed, and his caressing answer was incoherent in its breathless and vague promise.

And with the dawn of the morning he went back to Paris.

During the week, which was now May, there came many parties of students to the gardens of the Silver Stag; and they often spoke this one name—Cléopâtre. So they had christened a strange woman, come two summer seasons earlier to Paris. They spoke of her great torch-light fête, of her carriage with silver wheels, of her great sapphire hollowed for a sweetmeat box, of her domino powdered with fire-flies in gold, of her enormous stakes won at games of dice, of her tiny house, that though so small was as perfect as a palace, and filled with all fabulous worth. And they said, also, with gay laughter, that her last caprice was Carlos Merle.

"Your old friend will fare ill, Madelon," they laughed to her, not meaning cruelly, because they knew not where they wounded. "He goes every day to paint the portrait of Cléo-pâtre—O, hé—and no man can look long upon her and live! They say that seeing how he had painted the Faustine, she was minded to have her vengeance."

Madelon never made answer; except once, when she said, gravely, that to speak at all of such as Cléopâtre to honest women was not well. Which silenced the reckless youths; and made them mute on the subject, for they held her in reverence and love.

As for me, where he left me in the quiet country place, I wondered ceaselessly what she could be, this strange and marvellous creature, whom they had christened thus; they had depicted her in their words till I seemed to behold her, with her full-lidded lustrous eyes, that had such magnetism in them; with her curling lips; that so seldom spoke, yet breathed a sorcery over men; and with her chain of tawny topaz, that seemed like a yellow snake about her throat.

Any way,—I felt that she was evil.

As the season grew, and the summer came, the men who spent their leisure at the *auberge* ceased to speak of Carlos Merle when Madelon or her mother were by. When they were alone, I heard them talk of him, of how his head was turned by the delirium of success, of how he was like one drunk with his triumphs; of how he flung his gold broadcast, so that he must soon be more utterly than ever a beggar; of how he was devoured body and soul by one passion, and of how his genius was consuming as a reed in a flame.

"It is Cléopâtre," they said. "She kills them all so. You remember the Prince de Ferras?—ruined in one winter, and run through the heart for her by a Russian, when she had pillaged him to her will. Recall too how it was with Ber-naldés, when he had wakened up all Europe with that Venus of his—how she set herself to steal the nerve from his arm, and the cunning from his hand, and the fire from his brain, till he never rounded a line of marble more, but died raving mad in Bicêtre! It will be the same here."

"It is Cléopâtre," another echoed one day; an old wise

man, grown gray in the service of Art. "There are women who abhor genius; women to whom it is horrible that a man should live who can be sufficient for himself; women who set themselves to tempt, and corrupt, and destroy it, as the devils of the legends set themselves to kill innocence. It offends them, insults them, escapes them, outrages them, because it defies them—and they set themselves to have their vengeance on it; and to drag it down into the dust, where they can spit on it. There are women whose whole life is a war against all that lifts men out of hell; they are scorpions who spit death upon every holy thing."

Did Madelon hear as well as I heard?

Sometimes I feared that she did, for her face grew utterly weary, and she never once now lilted a song as she worked. What could she do?

Ah, nothing!—only wait, and wait, and wait with that sublime patience which is the heroism of such women.

The throbbing summer came; all heat, and colour, and storm, and wondrous light. There seemed fire in all the scarlet roses and all the electric skies, and all the hot hard days, in which the very bees seemed drunk, and the very cattle drugged. Everything was silent, and gasping, and white with furnace heat, all things languished, stupefied yet burning, as a man may lie in the height of a mortal fever.

In the sultry height of the summer the visits of Carlos altogether ceased.

There came no word of explanation from him, there was only silence.

The long evening stole away on every Saturday, and sank down into night, and the little click of the latch sounded no more through the stillness. The Sunday noons brought with them the gay glad parties of youths and maidens who romped together through the tall seeding grasses and the yellowing corn, who loaded themselves with fruits and garlands of green leaves, who danced in the dewy starlight, and sang, and shouted, and chased each other through the shady espaliers and the blossoming lime-tree walks. But he came no more with either noon or night; we heard no more the gladsome challenge of his voice, we saw no more the proud, bright, golden head like the head of a young god.

To the incessant questions of old Manon Bris, the painters who strayed thither only muttered now in answer that he was well, that he was much sought in the world, that he was busied incessantly upon the portrait of Cléopâtre; and they would add no more, or had no more to add.

"You are sure it is well with him?" Madelon once asked of a white-headed artist, laying her hands upon his arm, with a look from which his eyes turned away.

"It is well with his body, with his fame, with his riches," the old man muttered. "Not well with his soul."

On the morrow Madelon told her mother that she was about to go to Paris. The old woman did not seek to oppose her, and she was merciful enough to ask nothing of her errand.

Once she grumbled that, in her own youth, she would have thought it shame to go seek one who neglected her for a wanton; in her own girlhood women had deemed that a lover who was not kept by his fancy was ill kept by his troth-ring. But her daughter only smiled as she heard—the faint fleeting smile of one whose thoughts lie too deep for tears, and whose love lies too high to be gauged by mortal eyes; of one who is indifferent to appearance or to misconstruction. And at noon she went, wrapping about her a large dark cloak, and letting the fierce sun beat upon her unshaded head.

To Russ she signed to stay and guard the house; for me she stooped, as though seeming to pity my wistful look of unspoken petition, and bore me with her beneath her arm.

I believe that in a manner the presence near her of a little living thing which he had cherished had its consolation, and that I brought her sympathy because I loved him.

It was a very burning after-day as we entered the city. The dust was thick and gray upon the streets, and the glare was great from the whiteness of the houses; there was not a

breath of wind stirring, and the air smelt hot and sickly, and
as though it were loaded with wine fumes, and the reek of
opium smoke.

Here and there a mosquito hooted, and a hornet buzzed,
above the thronging crowds.

Here and there the scarlet glitter of a troop of soldiers
flashed through the shadowless sunlight, like a blood-red
shape of death.

She walked on long, not seeming to heed the oppression
of the weather, or the scorching of the stones. She was not
very certain of her way, and mistook it, and traced her steps
only again to retrace them very often. Presently we came to
a place that was thickly thronged; and the people were coming in and out of a house, and talking very eagerly amongst
themselves, and she could hear the word that constantly re-
curred,—"Cléopâtre, Cléopâtre."

"Is it there?" Madelon asked, and I saw her lips were dry
and white as she did so. They told her that it was. She felt
for a small coin, and paid it in, where she saw others paying
theirs, at a hole in a wall, where a money-taker sat; then
she passed through with the rest into a chamber hung with
crimson cloth, into which the people were pressing eagerly.
I was hidden beneath her cloak, and passed in with her.

The room was lighted by a flood of light pouring downward from the top, and this light was so managed that it fell
wholly on a solitary picture at the further end, set in a carved
frame of ebony.

It was not a large picture; but the multitude were breathless before it, as they had stood before Faustine.

"It is her living self!" they murmured.

They meant the Cléopâtre.

She lay on a couch of purples and of lion skins, with her
head leaning back on her arm, and her limbs lightly crossed
on each other; she was unclothed save where some heavy
folds of a Tyrian robe were flung across her, and save for
heavy rings of massive gold that clasped her ankles and her
wrists; she seemed just waking from slumber, and her eyes

looked out from under their languid lids with a peculiar glittering, furtive, voluptuous, merciless regard, whilst with one hand she drew against her scarlet lips one gorgeous blossom of the pomegranate.

In the distance, beyond a marble archway, were the reeds reddening in the after-glow, the ruby skies of sunset, and one slender palm shaft cutting sharp against the gold of an Egyptian night.

It was a wondrous picture: marvellous, because in its revival of the dead beauty of old Nile it also gave the living presentment of that beauty which Paris saw amidst it every day.

It was Cléopâtre—but Cléopâtre living, no less than Cléopâtre dead.

"It is she!" they murmured in ecstasy; for Cléopâtre was in a measure dear to them, by reason of that supremacy in infamy, that mercilessness in destruction, which made her heroic and deified in their sight. And it was she indeed they said, as they stood about the picture; all the dreamy sensualism, all the dormant power, all the oriental languor, all the leonine force that were in the living woman were in the portrait also.

"Before he could have painted *that*," muttered an aged artist as he gazed, "he must have sold his soul to her."

Madelon gazed on it as on some dread thing that compelled her regard, even whilst it blinded her, as the lightning fascinates, yet withers up the eyesight. I felt her tremble as she looked; and she seized for support the brass rod that ran before the painting, severing the niche where it hung from the crowd of the sight-seers.

The cruelty and the splendour of this beauty seemed to fascinate, and to paralyse her, almost, as they did all men that gazed on them. She gazed, and gazed, and gazed, until every drop of blood faded from her lips and cheeks; as though it were drawn out and absorbed by that imperial, scornful, deep-hued face, that made her own pale as a corpse, and poor as a faded violet.

"How shall you be remembered one hour beside such as I?" the mocking, changeless, lustrous eyes seemed to demand of her in their scorn; and Madelon seemed to shiver, and droop, and die out as it were, beneath that gaze.

Those smooth, opal-hued, glistening limbs; that soft velvet skin, with the golden bloom of a fresh peach upon it; that dreaming repose of a half-banished sleep; that curling mouth that half-caressed the flower; that deep full bosom that heaved above its ceinture of dead gold: how could the man who studied these, from their warm life abandoned to his sight and touch, have had a thought, or wish, or memory left for any other thing?

She blamed him no more; she marvelled no more; but her head dropped like one who has been stricken a physical blow, and she turned, and went feebly out of the little crimson chamber, with the unsteady flickering step of bodily sickness.

To resist, to hope, to believe in herself were no more possible to her: with her own eyes she had beheld this power against which she long in blindness had contended; with her own eyes she had seen what manner of thing it was, this sorcery of the senses, this lust of the flesh, this temptation by the breath of a woman, wherein the strength of her enemy lay; and she contended no more, she no more resisted, but went feebly out into the sunshine, knowing that never again could she have either place or memory within his life.

Ah! I have seen the same warfare many times; the same contest betwixt the soul and the senses, betwixt the love that is sanctity and the love that is devilry, betwixt the woman who seeks a man for the god-head there is in him, and the woman who seeks a man for the beastiality there is in him; and I have never seen it end in any other fashion than this; never seen it come to any other close, than for the lily to die away, crushed beneath his foot; and for the passion-flower to grow high, and wild, and free in triumph, above the ruin of his house.

Madelon was a woman pure of soul, high of thought, loving nobly and with innocence, desiring the greatness of that which she loved, and seeking its honour before her own joy; Cléopâtre bared her limbs to the painter's gaze, and looked into his with her burning cold eyes; and gliding forth from her bath to her mirror, with the water glistening on her polished skin, said in her soul that he should love her in such wise, that this love should kill all manhood, all conscience, all godliness, all genius within him, and deliver him over to her prostrate, worthless, a mockery of men.

Yet it was Cléopâtre, and not Madelon, that he loved.

Wherefore? Well, not because he was base: because there is a marvellous sorcery in the mere bodily beauty of women; and because there is a madness and a drunkenness in love, that go best, as it seems, with the liberty and fever of vice.

And this is why in love there is so much of woe, and so little of contentment; because pure women are too cold, and passionate women are too vile; and when men stoop for kisses, their lips are either chilled to ice, or scorched with flame. Then, being content with neither, they break the bonds of love, and are pointed at as faithless,—not with much justice in the charge.

Madelon went out into the street with the same feeble wandering gait; and her face had a wan, scared, paralysed look upon it, as though she had seen some sight that had frozen her blood and stopped the pulses of her heart.

She moved mechanically out of the throngs, and into some cool quiet gardens of the public, whose trees threw their shadows opposite the house where the portrait of Cléopâtre was hung for exhibition. The gardens were almost deserted, and she sank down into a wooden chair under the shelter of a great sweet-chestnut. One of the guardians of the place approached her, and brought her a drink of water, thinking she was faint. She put it aside gently, and asked him only to leave her in peace. She sat there quite motionless, it must have been nigh an hour; and the gray, rigid, startled look upon her face never faded away.

On the clear air the voices of the crowds, from the other side of the rails, came plainly to where we sat. They kept going in and out of the picture-chamber by hundreds all the afternoon long. Cléopâtre was known to all Paris, and this painting of her had a fascination as wide as the city.

Ever and anon there floated on the wind little fragments of their talk; words of wonder, praise, and homage; the artist of Faustine had been great, but the artist of Cléopâtre was greater. It was well with his genius as yet.

Madelon writhed as she heard.

The desire of her prayers had been given to her, he had fame, and the world gave him honour;—and she sat alone here, forgotten by him as the picture of the woman at the lattice was forgotten by Paris before the portrait of a courtesan! She had voluntarily delivered him up to his art, she had willingly surrendered him to the claims of ambition; —and all that art and ambition had done had been to bring him to the murderous embraces, and reward him with the poisonous kisses, of the deadliest temptress of Paris.

"O, could he but have been content without fame," she cried; but she knew that he never could have been this, and that, if in selfishness she had striven to bind him down to the obscurity of her own humble and innocent life of labour, tho stifled desires and the feverish unrest within him would have killed his peace in a slow torture as surely as hers was now slain at one deathblow.

She had done that which was right, though the issue thereof was evil.

After a while she rose and left the gardens, and asked her way to the place where his painting-rooms were. I do not think she knew clearly what she meant to do. I believe she only felt some vague impulse, such as a woman, whose great love yet made her humble, might well feel to look once more—and for the last time—upon his face, and leave him for ever to the infamy of the temptress who had robbed him of her.

People guided her willingly towards the artists' quarter.

She knew little of the city, and in her misery seemed to have
forgotten all she did know.

It was now quite late in the day, though the sun had not
set; it was still intensely hot, and the crowds were growing
larger, as all those whose work was done came out to seek a
breath of air under the sultry yellow skies.

She made her way with some difficulty to the street where
his *atelier* was: there was no one in the building except an
old negress who had the charge of it, and who did such little
housework as the four or five painters living on its several
floors required. This negress knew me again, and roughly
bade Madelon enter her little porter's lodge, and rest. But
Madelon scarcely heard, she only asked if Carlos Merle were
now within the house.

The old black woman looked at her curiously, standing in
her grimy den, a little old uncouth figure, black as soot, with
all rude vivid colours in her ragged dress.

"Carlos Merle!" she echoed. "No, Carlos Merle rarely
comes here now."

"He lives elsewhere?"

"Elsewhere!" the negress laughed grimly, "elsewhere!
Who are you that do not know of the caprice of Cléopâtre?"

A shudder passed over Madelon's form, but she was a resolute woman, and brave, and she asked still:

"What caprice is it that you mean?"

"Why! her caprice, for sure, for this golden-curled youth
whom you speak of, this Carlos whom Paris for a little season
has taken to calling a genius. Cléopâtre is very famous, very
rich, very powerful, she can afford such fancies! and she
laughs to see all her princes and nobles so mad because she
will for a while look at none but this painter."

"But she—she—" the words died on Madelon's mouth;
she leaned against the wooden shaft of the lodge door, and
her breath came in painful gasps.

"Well!—she what?" chuckled the negress. "She can
afford such a caprice once in a while, I tell you. Her world
will only be the madder for her when she shall have tired of

her young yellow-haired god, and that will be before the last
summer roses are dead. He was hard to conquer, look you;
he had a horror of her at the first, he shunned her, and fled
from her, and that set her harder on this fancy to beat him.
She will have no man look on her face and keep sane. So
she set him to paint her portrait—you can see the thing now
in Paris; it has taken him three months to do; and she would
have it painted in the noon hours, at her own dwelling, that
is all marble, they say, and gold, with purple couches, and
strange plants, and all the floors of silver. Well—well—he
went, and before the painting was one-half done the world
only held for him that one woman. It is always so with them
all. And now it is her caprice, I tell you, to have none but
him near her; whenever she goes abroad he is by her; and
he seldom or never leaves her roof except with her. It is a
base life?—O, well, that is as it may be. I think he has
shame of it,—bitter shame sometimes, but he is drunk with
it, as it were; he has no will but hers. He would fling himself in the river at a sign from her."

Madelon leaned heavily against the timber of the door,
her eyes closed, her mouth panted for breath, under her clear
pale skin the veins looked black.

The old negress looked at her, and seemed to take a cruel
pleasure in the misery she saw she dealt.

"He is your brother, maybe? Well,—you will scarce get
him out of the hold of Cléopâtre. 'Till her fancy slackens,
at least!—and then he will be little worth getting. Last
autumn she had a like caprice for Hugo Cabarrus, the composer. They all said he was the man of the future,—just as
they say of this Carlos,—how did he end when she had played
with him a season and spent her will on him? Why—shot
himself through the head one night, after burning the score
of his great opera, that they said would have ranked him with
Rossini. She has done something the same with a score."

"And such a woman lives!"

The words broke with a shriek from Madelon—the only
utterance she ever gave to all the agony within her.

6*

The negress grinned.

"Lives! She will live every hour of her life, however long it be. There is not a second that she does not enjoy. Look at her great, brown, sleepy, scornful eyes. No one ever sees them change, and how they smile at you poor fools that fret yourselves with sorrow!"

Madelon put out her hands with a piteous gesture as though praying peace; then, tottering like a woman quite worn out with age, she turned across the threshold, and passed again into the streets.

She had forgotten me: I followed her closely in and out a winding maze of roads. I think she had no sense nor knowledge where she went.

The day was wholly dying now. It was scarcely any cooler, and the great furnace glow in the west had the same red of Egypt in it that burned in that accursed picture, and made the very marble of the houses flush to colour, and gave the faces of the women all a weird and fevered look.

She wandered aimlessly, stunned with this one grief that left her no other memory than itself. None noted her; a pale, dust-stained, weary-footed woman, without beauty and with poor raiment, there was nothing to mark her from the crowds that parted to let her pass through them, without so much as noticing the agony upon her face.

Once or twice a moan broke from her; but it was too low to reach any ear in those busied and heedless throngs.

The great doors of an old church stood open; within all was cool, and dark, and silent. She sought its shadow, in-stinctively; turning aside from the red hot glow, and the whitened glare, and the sea of shifting and unpitying faces.

She dragged her tired limbs into a distant corner of the place where one little silver star of light burned before a picture of the Mater Dolorosa.

There she fell on her knees,—and at last wept.

It was quite night when the peal of the choir aroused her, and she crept forth from her shelter once more into the streets.

"*Ma mère!*" she muttered, as she raised me in her arms; her face was calm again, and the long habits of self-sacrifice and self-control had made her remember that her old mother would be ere that time waiting, and watching, in doubt and anxiety for her long-delayed return.

The church was in a rich and famous quarter of the city; though so still, and gray, and old, the tide of gayest and of wildest life surged round it; the broad highway in which it stood was brilliantly illumined, and the buildings that flanked and fronted it were all ablaze with light likewise, and bright with floating banners and with gilded balconies.

As Madelon went out, from under the dark porch, all this radiance seemed to blind and to confuse her: she covered her eyes with her hand and gazed upward with the helpless look of those that are stricken sightless.

Straightway, in front and above her, was a square balconied window, open to the night. The balcony was of stone, and jutted out, canopied with amber silk, and filled with leaf and blossom; there was a strong light within that poured out through the yellow draperies into the street beneath, and in that light there leaned two forms; one that of a woman, who was carelessly thrown against the cushions, and carelessly watched the movement of the shadowy crowd below; the other that of a man who in his turn watched her, with all that passionate ecstasy, that rapt worship in his gaze, which none ever see in a man's eyes but once. And where he bent above her, half shadowed in the curtain's shelter, he stooped his head, till his lips touched the fragrant hair that loosely lay upon her shoulders.

The woman, not changing her position, smiled, and let her broad, calm, dreamy eyes rest unmoved upon the crowd beneath.

Then she stretched out her arm, that had one great eastern bangle of dead gold upon it, and pointed to the portico of the church:

"See! There is your poor fool," she said, with the same

calm scorn upon her smiling mouth. "Will you go to her?
—now?"

Why did this woman, who had every earthly gift and
grace, and every joy in absolute possession, thus set herself
to the destruction of a creature, innocent, obscure, neglected,
who had never harmed or crossed her? I cannot tell—there
are women who love to murder, and women against whom all
innocence is crime.

The brutal mockery of the words galvanised Madelon into
sudden consciousness. She raised herself erect, and looked
straight up at the broad golden casement, with its blaze of
colour.

She was a proud, pure, brave-hearted creature, and she
found strength in that moment to give back scorn for scorn.

He, leaning there over the white shoulder of his wicked
witch, and gazing whither she pointed, met that full, upward
look of unutterable rebuke, and of unchangeable forgiveness.

Their eyes rested on one another.

Carlos, seeming to lose all courage and comeliness, as
under some stroke of sorcery, shivered, and covered his face
with his hands, and shrank back into the abyss of blazing
light behind him.

Madelon passed onward with a steady step, and with her
hands clenched upon the ivory cross above her heart.

The shadow of the church had screened her from the view
of her destroyer before the time that she staggered and fell
down upon the stones of the great city, as Ben Dare had fallen
in the market-place of the little northern burgh.

A sweet gay burst of riotous music broke over the crowds
and through the summer night. It came from the open
windows of the house where Carlos had made his choice to
dwell.

CHAPTER VI.

In tho Quartor of the Poor.

Tue first thing that I remember subsequently was the loosening of some violent pressure about my throat, and a rush of blood through my head and throat that made me blind and dizzy.

When I fully recovered consciousness, I found myself in a small low place crowded with innumerable flowers, dead and living, which filled it with an intense odour that recalled to me, till I shuddered, the beautiful flower-filled road of the *infiorata* all covered with a sea of gorse, and roses, and wild thyme, and snowy cistus-buds, and all fair summer things that grew; that road on which in Italy I had been hunted and stoned, and singed with torches, and beaten with sticks, and kicked from side to side, in the common fashion at that poetic religious rite.

A boy with a pale sympathetic face leaned over me; a woman of noble stature stood beside me. She was silent; he was speaking eagerly to a withered old man in a blue blouse.

"So the little dog bit, and tore, and foamed, and raged, grandpère," he was saying, "because they would move him from this poor sick woman who had fallen there, and whom they wanted to carry to the hospital; and the gendarmes bore her off upon a litter, saying she was not dead, only senseless, and they kicked the dog amongst the crowd because it strove to follow them. Then the people shrieked that it was dangerous and mad, and they called out to one another that it should be killed; and a soldier caught it and twisted a bit of cord about its throat. He was for stringing it up straightway to the lamp-iron; and would have done it too, but that madame stayed his hand, and bade him not be so brutal to fidelity, and forced him to give up the little beast, and put it in my hands for me to bring here; and the cord was tied so tightly, I could not loose it till I came home to get a knife,

I do not think the dog has any harm in it; it was not mad, it was only faithful."

"Fidelity is madness," muttered the woman wearily, as she turned to the old man. "The dog is innocent enough. Let it stay here; it will be a pleasure to your grandson."

"As madame pleases," murmured the man, not best pleased himself, but respectfully submissive as to one he honoured and obeyed.

The woman passed up some narrow, dark, crooked stairs, in which a little dusky oil-lamp was burning; and the boy followed her until they reached a chamber in the roof. It was a small bare attic, clean as any brown stone that lies in bright brook-water, but without any sort of ornament, or indeed any sort of comfort.

The boy talked to me, stroked me, and made me a little bed of straw in one corner of the garret; the woman seemed to have forgotten both his presence and mine as she laid aside her outdoor garments, and went to a table under the lattice, where she seated herself at some kind of work—what, I could not see.

"May I leave him with you, madame?" the boy asked after a time, when his efforts to make me eat of some bread and milk were all unavailing. "He moans and whines—I suppose for that poor woman—and grandpère might not like him down below with Tambour."

"Yes, leave him, Rémy," she answered him absently; and the boy went out, closing the door softly.

I supposed from what they had said that my efforts to serve Madelon had been futile, and that I was severed from her in all likelihood for ever. For several days and nights I mourned unceasingly with restless, feverish grief, refusing to be comforted; the woman bore with me, and was good to me in her silent, passionless, weary manner; and the gentle-hearted boy did his utmost to console me.

He was the grandson of the old herbalist in the little shop below—a kindly tender-natured child. They were quite poor people; and the various chambers of the old, dull, antique dwelling were let by them to persons no richer than themselves—penniless students and labouring women who lived on black bread and bitter coffee, and studied or toiled early and late, and seemed only to exist to carry on that endless warfare with starvation and ruin which is all that the very poor know the world of life to mean.

I saw but little of the boy, for a few weeks later he went away to some religious place, where he was in training to be made a priest—poor gentle child, who gave his birthright of the future up in such pathetic ignorance of his immeasurable loss. The old man I rarely encountered; he was learned in simples and other herbal lore, and passed all his time in studying when he was not vending his shrubs, and herbs, and flowers. Thus I was left entirely to the woman who had saved me from the hangman's cord. This woman was called Madame Reine.

Whether this were in truth her name, or whether it was but one she had adopted for the purposes of her life in Paris, I could not tell; the people of the place she dwelt in knew, I think, nothing of her. She lived quite alone, and seemed never to seek to hold any sort of social intercourse with any one of those around her.

Only to those who were aged, or such as were in trouble, she was always merciful; with that noble, silent, unceasing charity of action, which so often, amongst the poor, supplies the place of that charity of alms which poverty denies them the power to show to one another.

Herself, she gained a barren living by continual hard toil. She modelled in leather (or, rather, carved the leather as a delicate wood-carver does his wood) for a Palais-Royal house that dealt largely in such things, but paid for them grudgingly.

She did the work marvellously well; she could imitate in it the most perfect wood-carving, a fern-leaf, a dead woodcock, a branch of pine, a water-lily on its green raft of leaves, —she would execute these, or any other similar thing, in leather, until the keenest eye could scarce have told the work

from a most delicate and exquisite oak-carving. But it was
a slow and toilsome labour; the single feather of a bird would
take two hours in its execution—even more; and the wage
for them was exceedingly small, beautiful though they were.

She was all day long at this species of sculpture, sitting
at the little deal-table, with her tools, under the single small
square lattice in the roof: and the life was very dull for me.

There was no sort of change from dawn to sunset. My
heart was heavy for all those whom I had lost. It seemed to
me that life was but a sequence of tender ties, formed only to
be ruptured, and leave the torn heart aching. I missed,
moreover, the glad, sweet, summer season in the open air;
the freedom of the old fruit-gardens and flower-covered ways;
the homely, happy sounds of all the stirring bees and chirm-
ing birds, of the ducks in the dark cool pond, and the lowing
cattle in the poplar-belted meadows.

This little garret was very clean indeed; but it was bare,
and dull, and lonesome, exceedingly. The scents of a city
made hot and sulphurous the winds that blew in through the
lattice; and all the hours through there came up from the
streets below the one unceasing muttering of wheels, and
cries, and drums, and engines, and all the ceaseless noise of
men. It was a quiet ancient quarter, it is true; but the
quietest quarter of a city, after the lull of country silence,
makes you know all that your poet meant when he wrote of
"the ear *aches* with sound."

Of Madelon I never heard.

But once, whilst the boy Rémy was still in the house, and
when he took me with him across the bridges to the old green
Luxembourg Gardens, as he was wont to do in the pleasant
evening time when all Paris was out in the sunset hour, I
saw a carriage with scarlet liveries and fretting horses and
gay harness all hung with noisy silver bells, and I heard the
people round us say to one another, "There is Cléopâtre."

And as it went through the white gilded streets and the
green lines of leafy trees, and the air that was bright, half
with the gleam of the lamps and half with the glare of the

sunset, her face came fully in my sight, lit with that evening
light, and I knew her then—knew her entirely—as that memory stood out clear and fixed before me, which had haunted
me, though vague and troubled, when I had gazed at the
picture of Egypt.

Carlos Merle was not with her; beside her sat a dark,
slender, gipsy-eyed man, whom the crowds about named,
whilst he passed, to one another, as a prince of some Danubian
province, fabulously rich, who had lavished on her black
sable skins, and diamonds, and opals, and strange Byzantine
things of untold worth.

And my heart was sick for Carlos; for it seemed to me
that already somewhere in that hot, brilliant, amber-coloured,
magnolia-scented summer night, the last rays of the setting
sun were seeking out his colourless face and weary body in
some haunt of death; while she, the Faustine, the Assassina-
tress, the Hell-born, was gathering up her skirts, heavy with
the golden wage of infamy, and fleeing, with the wicked
laugh upon her face, to passion, and to pleasure, and to
riotous mirth, and to the witches' sabbath of the senses.

I longed to seek for him. Alas, what could I do? a little
powerless, insignificant dog; dragged along with a cord over
the asphalte; kicked aside by the hurrying happy throngs
that went trooping to theatre and dance-garden; deafened by
the music that swelled from the open-air concerts where the
soldiers were playing; terrified by the savage glance and
word of the gilded and belted gendarmes; and glad to hide,
trembling, beneath the chairs of the gay indifferent people
who sat before the café doors, and ate their ices, and laughed,
and cried, "Holà, there is Cléopâtre!"

Ah, I wonder if you ever think of the woe that it is to us,
that utter inability to serve or to aid those we love!

The life was dreary. To watch the stiff brown sheepskin
gradually moulded under the worker's hands into the sem-
blage of some drooping, lifeless, moorland bird, or some
lovely curl of clematis-flowers, was all the distraction that I
had. I was thankful—since ingratitude is a human monopoly

—for my bodily safety, for my corporeal welfare; thankful that I was not beaten, nor starved, nor chained. But I was very sad. I had lost all my friends into the night of an unknown fate; and I could not forget, for I was a dog.

The sole interest that this existence awakened in me was an interest in this woman, who had delivered me from death. I wondered about her ceaselessly.

Her garments were of black, and very worn, but they clung about a form fit for a sculptor's dream of a Greek goddess; her hands were for ever working at the manual toil by which her scanty bread was gained, but they were long and white and slender; her face was very worn and attenuated, as though with infinite want and sorrow, and there were silver threads amongst the luxuriance of her hair; but the shape of her head and throat were haughty and full of stag-like grace, and the eyes were still wondrously beautiful, though the lids were so swollen above, and the shadows were so dark beneath them.

She had a look that was very far above the place in which she dwelt, and the poor people of the tenement. Although she lived more poorly still than many of them, and never appeared to hold herself greater in any way, they yet treated her with a curious reverence, and called her Madame with more of courteous meaning than always lies in the common term. I was ashamed to fret at the monotony and obscurity of my own existence, when I saw how utterly joyless and cheerless her days were.

To a woman like this, who must once have been of rare beauty, and who evidently had a proud nature and a delicate taste, the manner of her life must have been almost intolerable. She rose at dawn to go to the little work-table under the lattice; she rarely ate anything save some thin soup, some coffee, and some poor rye bread; she saw no one unless it were some creature, yet poorer than herself, who came to her door for an aid that she never refused; she rarely went forth save very early, to sell what she had modelled, or to

obtain the bough, the fruit, or the dead bird that she needed
to copy in her dried-skin carving.

I was sometimes with Tambour, the dog in the place below—that little flower-shop of herbs and plants and roses and
immortelles, that smelt fragrantly always, and gave a lovely
flush of colour in the dark and crowded passage-way; and he
told me some few things of her.

He was an old brindled mastiff, very old; so old that he
remembered the Days of July, and had seen his first master
shot down in his youth upon the barricades; but he was very
kind and very pitiful. All our race are. Was it not the dogs
that succoured Lazarus, when the rich of his own kind scorned
him?

Tambour told me that this woman Reine had dwelt with
him three years, coming, he believed, from across the Alps.
She had never in all that time lived differently to what she
now did; nay, she had indeed lived worse, for at first finding
none who would recognise her talent in the leathern carving,
nor even purchase sufficient of it to gain her money enough
to buy sheepskins and birds for models, she had been forced
for some six or seven months to earn her daily bread by the
hard coarse toil of sewing the hempen shirts that the populace
wore. Saving a few coins from this ill-paid labour, she had
been able at length to obtain the materials which she needed
for her art, and had succeeded in obtaining also a market for
that art at a shop in the Galérie d'Orléans.

"Why that woman works so, I cannot think," said the old
dog to me, where we rested together under the little low
ceiling of the flower-shop, among the quantities of broom,
and lilies, and roses, and sweet herbs, that lay dying sadly
here in the heat and dust and turmoil of the city; flowers
sick with longing for the cool touch of the dew, as your hearts
get faint with longing for the freshness of truth in the fever
and the falsehood of the world. "I cannot think. Why does
she not set a pan of charcoal in her chamber one quiet night,
and make an end of all this toil for ever? Julio did that, here
in this very house; and he was only twenty. He was a

Bordelais; he was a musician; he wrote very beautiful things in music; at least they sounded so upon his violin, which he would play from dawn to midnight up in that very little garret where you live now with madame. I have seen the people in the street all gathered mute as the dead under our casements, listening—listening, ay, and sobbing like children too. It must have been good music that could move them so? I do not know why it was, but none would listen to it in Paris, save these poor work-people, out of these courts and alleys, who were, I suppose, no good to him. Any way, I know Paris would not listen; no one would take his opera—not even try it. And they said—my people did—that when he went to one of the great masters, this great man derided him. It might be so: men, you see, will not recognise that all human genius is like all sun-rays, coming from the same source, and therefore the same light, whether shining on Europe or Cathay, whether beaming on a king's diamond or on a cotter's tuft of daisies. No; they are so feebly and so foolishly jealous. The setting sun denies the sun that rises! Well, Julio could get no hearing; and he was exceeding poor, and the hunger of him killed his soul; and rather than sink down into this soulless, sightless, bitter life, he chose to die. They found him dead one morning—his breath stifled by the fire-fumes, that were kinder than men's neglect. Why does not this woman do the same?"

"Perhaps she thinks it a sin?" I suggested, for I knew that Madelon, or Ben Dare would have held it to be so.

"Perhaps," assented Tambour. "It may be one. We always endure, you know; we never slay ourselves. Yet it seems strange—how she can go on with that dreary life. All these three years, no friend has ever visited her. No letter has ever come to her. It must be worse than death to be utterly forgotten, to be utterly alone, like that. However, I fancy it will not last much longer. That woman is marked to die."

"To die?"

"Yes; hark at her cough! Look at the flush in those

hollow cheeks! See how weak she is when she rises in the morning! She is marked to die, and that soon."

I shuddered; it seemed terrible.

"You are unwise," said the old French dog; "very unwise, if you wish the woman well. What is life to her? A burden borne for duty's sake alone. She will be as glad to lay it down as a hunted bird is to sink into its nest. There has come a certain peace upon her face of late; I think it has come because she knows death near."

"But she is young still?"

"Ah, what does that matter? I have seen a girl of seventeen years thankful to die. Her beloved one had been slaughtered in the African raids, and for her the whole world was laid desolate because that one poor soldier was dead, in a nameless grave. You do not understand men and women much; they are very curious in that. They are at once the most selfish and unselfish—the most sublime and the most sordid of all created things. See! one of their women will kill her lost lover's fresh mistress rather than let him be happy through another, and then kill herself because she cannot endure to exist without him! There is not the slightest sense in any of their actions; but there are continually the most wonderful egotism, and the most marvellous martyrdom, side by side together."

"You think the life of Madame Reine a martyrdom?"

"Well, I do. There is the look of a woman who has *renounced* upon her face. It is she who has forsaken the world; not the world that has forsaken her."

"There is a difference, then?"

"A difference! The poles are not wider asunder. Look you—I was once a convent dog. It was the happiest time of my life. I never went beyond the garden walls it is true; but then the garden was so large, it was a little kingdom. I was there six years; years of perfect peace. My only office was to guard the convent fruit from marauding children who would, undaunted by the sanctity of the place, climb the high walls at twilight for sake of the bursting plums and luscious peaches. The nuns made a favourite of me; and I came to know them all perfectly well. The greater number by far were women whom the world had abjured; whom nature, denying beauty, or love, or sweetness, or some other gracious charm of living, had driven to this solitude; or who, disappointed of marriage or ambition, or of whatever desire their souls were set on, had come thither because naught else was possible to them. But, again, there were a few whom the world would fain have kept; women gifted, beautiful, victorious, who had been beloved and tempted; who came of their own will to a self-chosen sacrifice; laying down out of their hands the glory, or the passion, or the homage they enjoyed. Now, of these first women the look was always regret, discontent, sadness, helplessness; but of these latter women it was always half conquest, and half captivity—an agony indeed. And that is the look this woman Reine has on her face; and death with it, as theirs mostly had."

And then he would compose himself to sleep under the yellow plumes of the broom, and the sheaves of great white lilies, and dream, I doubt not, that he was once more amongst the deep unshaven grasses and the drowsy shadowy ways of his old convent-garden.

This talk of his moved me to quicker and more curious interest than I might otherwise have felt in this lonely, proud, weary woman, who had stood between me and the hangman's cord. There was a strange fascination, too, about her; a fascination that seemed the stronger now that he had shown me that death was hourly stealing the cunning from her hand, and the brilliance from her eyes.

There seemed in that mute, haughty, passionate, colour- less face, so eloquent a story of a soul so hard to crush, of hopes so hard to die, of a spirit so hard to break; a story of strong love, of strong powers, of strong woes, of strong will, that had fought so bitter a battle with fate, and at the end been worsted.

It seemed an idle fancy, of a woman who modelled, in a garret, woodcocks, and ferns, and wild vine-clusters for the

Galérie d'Orléans; yet I could not help believing that she had once been famous in the blaze of the world's light.

Once, one twilight, Tambour and I were lying underneath the lilies; the beautiful pure lilies that the flower-girls bore forth every evening to perish in the gas glare of the streets and cafés, as women take their innocence and honour to wither in the corruption of base sins and venal vices.

There was more stir than usual in the little place that night; there were eager voices, and sobs and laughter, and flushed wondering faces, all pressed together in the light of the little single oil-lamp, whose feeble rays struggled through the dusk of evening. In the centre of the breathless groups was a girl of one of the adjacent houses. Her name was Mariquita. She was of Cordovan-Jewish blood, though Paris born, the daughter of a poor fruit-vender, who dwelt under the tawny leathern awning of the melon and grape stall opposite.

The girl was handsome, and of a vivacious, electric, untamable temper; she had a voice too, mellow, sweet, far reaching, and a form as lithe as a serpent's.

She stood, the centre of the excited crowd, with her brown arms outstretched, and her whole body quivering beneath her picturesque rags, and her black eyes full of fire, and her white teeth glittering with an hysterical laugh of joy. Evidently some great joy or wonder had just come to her, in which the sympathetic crowd was sharing; for Mariquita, despite her gusts of passion and her lioness-like rage, was a favourite with the people of her quarter, by reason of her beauty and her keen and witty tongue.

As Tambour and I, roused from slumber by their cries and exclamations, lifted our heads and watched them, wondering what had chanced, Madame Reine entered the shop; which was the only passage from the little street without to the staircase of the dwelling which led to the garret which she occupied. She had been out on one of the two only missions which ever took her forth; either the sale of her carvings, to

the Galérie d'Orléans, or a visit of charity to some dying or
ailing creature.

She paused beside Mariquità, who was, in a manner, fa-
voured even by her; Mariquità, tameless to all others, had
ever been docile to her, and had always shown a curious attachment and veneration for her.

"What hast thou, Mariquità?" she asked, arrested by the
girl's aspect, and by the excitement of the little throng that
filled all the dark den, whose only light came from the colours
of dying flowers, as the only poetry of your world comes from
the sadness of ruined lives.

The girl flashed her glowing eyes upon the weary face of
the woman who questioned her.

"Madame, Madame!" she cried breathlessly, the words
coursing each other off her lips. "Madame! my fortune is
made—my fame is made! I shall be great—great, only think!
The director of the Ambigu has seen me and has talked with
me, and says that I have the genius of Rachel in me, and that
if I will serve him, and him only, for five years, he will bring
me out before Paris, and make me the talk of all the world,
because I have the three sole things that women want for
greatness—beauty, and passion, and voice! O, look! it has
come at last,—the chance for Paris to hear me, to see me, to
know me. And I have it in me to conquer them; I feel it!
I fear nothing, I heed nothing, I hark to nothing—only to
this surety in me that tells me I shall be great—great—
great!"

She was a ragged Jewish girl; she spoke in the tongue of
the populace; she had lived all her short life under the yellow
leathern awning, selling the slices of water-melon, and the
handful of roast chestnuts, in which her father dealt. But
for all that there was the fire of truth in her, and none who
heard doubted that her self-prophecy came, not of vanity, but
of vision.

Over the face and form of the woman who heard her—
of the woman to whom the world was dead—there passed a
curious and terrible change. She trembled and recoiled, and

seemed to sicken, as one might do who saw the grave of some lost and beloved thing suddenly forced, and flung open, by an alien hand.

"Great, great!" she muttered in her throat, while her eyes gazed, without sight or sense in them, at the dilated triumphant form of the young girl. "Great! Ah, God! I dreamed just such a dream—once!"

Then, without seeming to have any memory or knowledge of those about her, she moved mechanically forward, and up the familiar stairway into the darkness of the steep and gloomy shaft; away from the rays of the little lamp, away from the fragrance of the fading flowers.

The group around Mariquita looked after her, suddenly checked in their riotous wonder and joyous felicitations; they dimly saw, that in some vague way they had touched and struck the broken chord of this silent life, whose melody was gone for ever.

The young Israelite stood, hushed, and afraid.

"Will it be so with me, ever?" she murmured, and her head sunk on her bosom, and the light died out from her face.

I stole up the stairs into the desolate chamber in the roof, where the woman who had succoured me had passed alone.

In the faint reflection from the sunset in the evening skies that still lingered here, above, though darkness brooded in the street below, I saw her kneeling as I had seen Madelon kneel in those weary summer nights which had closed the days that had failed to bring her Carlos.

But Madelon's hands had clasped her crucifix: this woman's hands were empty.

From that day her health declined more rapidly and visibly. Her weakness increased, so that she could scarcely move from her chamber. She would drag herself wearily from her bed to the table where her work stood, and strive to model some feather, or leaf, or blossom; and then would let fall the tool she held, and sink down from absolute exhaustion.

She could eat little; and the hard tasteless food she had was ill fitted to tempt appetite. She coughed continually, and her hands were wasted and diaphanous.

It was touching to see the poor people of her quarter bringing some little fruit, a golden peach, or a leaf full of mulberries, and begging her to taste it for their sakes. They had grown to hold her in great reverence and affection, sad, and silent, and proud though her aspect was; and they knew that only for a very little longer could this stranger tarry with them there. To her the young Jewess devoted herself with a passionate attachment: Mariquita seldom spoke, but she would watch for her every want with her great radiant wistful eyes; and would crouch on the floor sleepless and motionless through all the night; and would never tire, or be tempted from her side. Once or twice she brought some clear crystals of ice, some golden luscious wine, some clusters of violet grapes; the dying woman looked at them and murmured some wonder as to whence these costly things could come. Mariquita grew red under her soft brown skin, and muttered hurriedly of gifts made to her father.

But Tambour whispered to me:

"Look you. She has not that golden sequin that she always wore on the silk cord round her throat, the only ornament she had. She has bartered it I doubt not to get the ice and the wine in exchange."

And neither do I doubt that the girl had done so, though the golden coin had been the pride of her eyes and the delight of her soul; an amulet of potent charm, no less than a jewel of price in her sight.

Mariquita again and again urged her to see some physician. She always refused.

"What use?" she would reply; "no skill can cure consumption. And if such skill even there were, I would not employ it."

This was all she ever said in reference to herself, or to the death which she knew to be so near. Usually silent previously, she had sunk now into almost perfect apathy, although the same desolate calm, the same proud serenity, that had always characterised her, were with her still. There was this difference only, that whereas before she had seemed a woman to whom no hope of any sort was possible, she had now this one certainty of death which was release. Where the look in her eyes had been agony it was now resignation.

Several months had passed with me here. Autumn was deepening into winter. The only plants in the flower-shop beneath were the immortelles and the wreaths of ivy leaves for tombs. All the rest were pods and seeds, withered foliage, and sheaves of dried herbs, that gave forth a curious faint odour like the scent of herbs that are laid beside the dead in coffins.

Paris around, doubtless, was awakening to its utmost gaiety, its wildest whirl of pleasure; but here we knew nothing of it—we only knew that bread would be dearer, and that the very aged, and the very young, would soon perish of cold, and that wood would be scarce for the stove, and that in the little chamber under the roof there lay a woman dying.

Ah! that is all the poor ever do know of what there is on earth. That there is pain, and there is cold, and there is death.

With other things they have no part nor portion.

And all the while I shivered in the dreary attic that was scarce warmed at all by the little fuel that alone was burnt in it; and pondered ceaselessly and longingly of all those whom I had known and lost; and wondered if in truth I could have ever really been the little gay white creature, happy and playful and prettily proud, that had been caressed by the hands of fair women, and praised by the voices of nobles.

One day, one very chill dark day, in that drear winter-time I sat huddled beside the bed. The embers had quite died in the stove; the gray December light struggled feebly

through the scant inlets of the lattice; the strong scents of
the herbs came up the stairs like the odours of sepulchres.
Mariquita was perforce absent, gone to her taskmaster, who
was to give her fame as wages. Madame Reine, half raised
upon the hard narrow pallet that served her as her couch,
had drawn some letters from beneath her pillow, and was
reading them—very slowly—one by one.

She had been weaker that day than any heretofore. All
the night through convulsions had shaken her wasted form;
and the hæmorrhage of the lungs been only stayed by the ice
that the Jewish girl had held to her parched lips. Although
I had never beheld death, it seemed to me that there could
not be many more hours to her life; it seemed that very soon
this mute, desolate, proud existence, without a history, without a friend, without a lament, or a sigh of self-pity, must
end, and take its secrets and its sorrows to the silence of the
grave.

The letters were many, and were hours in her hand; tears
had long been scorched dry in her dark weary eyes, but as
she read them, one by one, the anguish was upon her face
that I had seen on Madelon's when she had heard that her
lover dwelt in the house of Cléopâtre.

They were letters in a man's hand; letters doubtless in
which a man's heart had been spent in all a man's frank and
honest passion.

When the last had been read by her the day was done;
the light was well-nigh spent, the evening shadows were long
and dark within the chamber. She dragged herself, with
slow laborious effort, from her bed to where the scant wood
burned in the poor cold stove, and crouched down before it,
and slowly thrust one of the letters amongst the fuel.

Her own secret she could take with her to her grave, but
his she could not: she would not leave it for another's eyes to
learn.

One by one the letters were drawn within the heat and the
smoke, and curled, and crumbled, and fell away, a little heap
of ashes. And to her it was even as though, with each, her

own life consumed and passed away in fire; even as her
years had perished in the furnace of the past, so perished
these records of a passion that was dead.

They were all her hold on life; all the bonds that still
bound her to some old sweet unforgotten time; all the ties
that still held her to some divinest season when she had
known of joy; all the witness that still told her she also once
had lived.

When the last letter alone remained she paused—so long
that the cold white moon of winter rose and shone in through
the lattice in the roof. She waited, as the suicide may wait
ere he drives home the thrust that shall kill memory in him
for ever, and make him dumb, and still, and senseless, as the
earth that will yawn open to receive his corpse.

It was quite night, the moon was high and full, and the
chamber was dark as a grave, when at last she stretched out
her hand and let the cruel fire take those living, breathing,
throbbing words of a love that wrote itself as deathless; and
burn them, as time burns passion till it dies; and leave them
there, a little coil of wind-blown, silent, hueless ashes.

Then, as though her own life indeed went out with theirs,
her hands moved feebly as though seeking some other hand
to hold them; her great dark eyes gazed upward as though
searching for some other look in answer; a convulsive shudder
moved her once—only once—then stretching her arms out
wearily, in the darkness and the solitude and the silence of
the night, she bowed her head and died.

CHAPTER VII.

A Torn Letter.

THEY buried her in the quarter of the poor. They had
loved her, these people, and they would not leave her in her
death to chance, or charity. They did what they could to
honour her in her grave; and the Jewish girl, weeping passionately, and refusing to be comforted, laid on that nameless

grave the earliest white-ladies that bloomed, pure and spotless out of the winter-snows.

Amongst the trifles of her daily work, of the art that she had prosecuted, they found a written fragment in her handwriting, a sheet of paper torn obliquely, seeming to be a letter that she had penned upon her dying bed, and then had half-destroyed, in doubt whether or no to leave it to speak for her to some other when her voice should be for ever silent.

The fragment was this—many words probably had preceded it.

"It is selfish to send you this; when I am dead it can but rend your heart, if your heart still holds a place for me. And yet I feel that I must write to you this one last word,--must bid you know why, why only, I fled from you. O God, you cannot doubt why it was, surely!

"I left all, I lost all, when I gave up the world for you. I had vanquished them; I had vindicated my own powers. I had reached success, if not fame; I had talents, if not genius; I had touched celebrity and brilliancy, and wealth and pleasure; I had learnt how sweet the praise of the world can be; I had tasted how precious is the homage of watching eyes and listening ears: and I gave it up all—all—for you. Only for you. It was not my duty as a wife, he had forfeited all claim to it. It was not my honour as a woman, you were dearer to me than that. It was neither of those that made me leave you to think me dead so long. No:—it was for your sake alone.

"It seems such a little thing for a woman to give her life up to love; and it is little, truly, so little that do you think I should have paused one moment out of selfish fear? But it is a great thing for a man—a terrible thing;—a thing not less than ruin.

"You and I have known the world—have we seen any fate less deadly to a man than that surrender of himself to the wife of another, in a union that has all the bondage, and none of the honour, of marriage?   And the sweeter, the truer, the more loyal the man's nature, the worse is the bondage for him.

"It was not because I doubted you that I dared not become your mistress: it was because I trusted you so utterly. You loved me with such noble and perfect love; you would have surrendered your life to mine as indemnity for what you would have thought my sacrifice; you would have held that the world's scorn gave me upon you a claim fast as iron, imperishable, eternal.   You would never more have been free; and I—I, O my love! should have been your gaoler, your injurer, your curse.

"I had strength to save you from myself—from yourself; to set my will for your sake between your passion and my own...... Will you understand this? you must at least believe.   Since for it I have lost all.

"Do not seek to learn how have I lived: it has been by simple hand-labour alone.

"The mock passions, the counterfeit woes, the mimicked embraces, of the stage seemed profanation to me when once you had looked into my eyes.   Moreover, had I remained before the world, I could not have been withdrawn from your sight, your voice, your presence; and women are so weak, I could not have been sure an hour of my strength.

"It was for you—for you alone.   I knew so well the loyal knightly sweetness of your nature; I knew so well that you would have deemed yourself mine till death; I knew so well how it would have ended—the old, old history!—when some higher, happier, purer love should have arisen to you, and I—your mistress—should have stood between you and all fair things of innocence and honour.

"Will you believe?—My God! you *must!* For you I have borne worse than death;—for you I have killed myself in my youth, my beauty, my power, my victory;—for you I have died, and yet have kept the agony of life awake in me; yet in my grave have I heard the laughter of the happy world, and all the glad and busy sounds of earth.   Will ever woman love you as I have loved! No—never, never, never!...."

There the words ceased, and the paper was torn asunder, as though, when she had written these, she had feared to send them to him lest in them she should leave a legacy of pain, lest by them she should deal the stroke that she so long had spared, lest through them any sort of selfish pity, any breath of unconscious rebuke, should seem to him to linger in her dying memory of him.

Mariquita took the torn sheet, and caused it to be read aloud to her by some Jew of the quarter who understood the English character in which it had been penned. She heard it with wondering eyes, all ablaze with fire, and yet all dimmed with tears; then she folded the paper reverently, and laid it within a little curious leathern locket that she owned; and thrust it within her bosom.

"Some day I may meet him," she muttered to herself; and she went on her way with the first snowdrops of the year to that nameless grave in the quarter of the poor.

CHAPTER VIII.

"The Child Gladys."

For a brief space afterwards I remained in the little flowershop. Mariquita vehemently implored for permission to possess herself of me, entreating, and commanding, and execrating, and conjuring all in one breath, in her own impetuous volcanic fashion, but all her prayers were useless. The time had not come for her to have entered on the career that looked to her the high road of glory and of affluence; she was exceedingly poor; and she had nothing to offer for me save a few old battered centime pieces. The florist shrugged his shoulders and answered that I was of value; that he had a right to me, as his dead lodger had cost him more than she had paid (this I am certain was untrue), and that he should keep me until he could make an advantageous sale. All the low cunning and the hungry avarice of the low French nature had awakened in him, without any other counteracting influence to combat it, now that the one woman was gone towards whom he had felt forced to yield a certain reverent submission. So I remained; dull, weary, spiritless, ill fed, ill cared for; knowing no moments of pleasure except when the Jewish girl would beg me for an hour, and warm me beside the little stove at which her father roasted his sweet chestnuts, and sit with me under the broad old red weather-stained umbrella that in winter replaced the tawny awning of spring and summer. But these times were few and far between, for Mariquita went daily now to the theatre, at which she was to acquire the rudimentary grace and science of that Art which, as seen in her marvellous visions, was to make her meet with the empresses of the earth.

I did not seek to run away, though I was miserable. I had acquired that sad knowledge which the young are so rebellious against—that there are things worse even than a dreary and desolate monotony. I had known the lash, the goad, the life of the public toy, the endless labour of an ever-renewing task; and I knew that there were worse fates than to see the days and the nights drift dully by, sitting amongst the stores of evergreens and the pale winter roses, even as men and women, when their life is done, sit amidst deathless memories and faint sickly hopes.

Awhile earlier I should have rebelled passionately against this colourless and weary existence; but now I knew that not actively to suffer is almost, in this life we lead, the nearest approach we get to joy. So I took the broken crusts and the begrudged shelter, and the chilly hearth where the stove was cold; and tried hard to be thankful because the snow-flakes could not cover me, and the hail could not pelt me, and the shivering mountebanks, who came into the quarter of the poor to dance on the icy ground and to shake their spangles in the blue hard frost, could not seize me as a brother and claim me as a slave.

"Ah, little one! shall we ever *live*, thou and I?" cried Mariquita to me one day, rebelling in her wayward youth

against the poor barren life of hardship and of solitude that
she led at her father's fruit stall. She might, I knew—for
she was a woman, and beautiful, and to such the apple of
life will ever be tossed if they do not mind the black speck at
its core of dishonour. But to me it seemed that never more
could mirth or joy return.

Yet, as often chances, I think, in this life, both were nearest to me when I deemed them farthest. The time came when
the old man sold me—sold me just as the new year began. I
was now so sick at heart, so tired, and so homeless, that indeed I cared little whither I went, nor what my fate might
be. Only I dreaded, with a terror untold, the stick of Gih
and the little red coat of La Pipetta.

There were the usual chaffering of strange voices; some
broken weeks of unrest and captivity; some misery in strange
lands and binding chains; some piteous, dumb, wondering
woe, that none seemed to note or care for; then there came
a day of travel by land and sea, and when my cage was
opened and I was loosed from it with eyes blinded by the
rush of light, and senses half numbed and half maddened, I
thought that I was dreaming a dream of my old dead life.

The chamber was strangely familiar. The place seemed
to me like "a tale that is twice told."

Its cabinets, its bookcases, its mirrors on their ground of
ruby velvet, its grand piano in a half-lit recess, its single
small marble statuette of the "Gott und die Bayadere," its
exquisite copy of the "Départ pour Cythère," hung between
photographs of Rachel and Ristori: did I dream of these in
one of the many dreams of them which had haunted me
among the long dry Campagna grasses, under the orchard-
trees of the Silver Stag, and amongst the white lilies and yellow broom of the flower-shop in Paris? Or was I, in truth,
once more in the supper-room of the Coronet? The door had
closed behind me; I was alone. I gazed around in eagerness
and amaze.

There behind the bookcase-glass were the cream-hued
faces of Scribe and all his brethren; there on the couch were

the sealskins, and the black laces, and the painted fan of a woman; there on the table were the Majolica fruit-stands that I knew so well, and the little silver wagon that held the cigarettes, and the claret-jugs with their swan-like necks, and the quaint old flasks of Rhineland wine. Yes, surely, it was no dream. I was once more, after my wanderings, in the pleasant festal-chamber of the unforgotten theatre; I was once more in the old charming life of ease and fashion, where the wheels of time were oiled with gold, and if Care still clung behind, Pleasure at the least ran on before.

And I felt half blind with joy.

For, write as you will of the glory of poverty, and of the ennui of pleasure, there is no life like this life, wherein to the sight and the sense all things minister; wherefrom harsh discord and all unloveliness are banished; where the rare beauty of high-born women is common; where the passions at their wildest still sheathe themselves in courtesy's silver scabbard; where the daily habits of existence are made graceful and artistic; where grief and woe, and feud, and futile longing for lost loves, can easiest be forgot in delicate laughter and in endless change. Artificial? Ah, well, it may be so! But since nevermore will you return to the life of the savage, to the wigwam of the squaw, it is best, methinks, that the Art of Living—the great *Savoir Vivre*—should be brought, as you seek to bring all other arts, up to uttermost perfection.

I sat down and gazed around me in a tumult of memory and of expectation. It was very still, except for the roll of the carriages in the street below. In this room you never, at any time, would hear one sound to tell you that an audience of three thousand people was shouting with applause, or shrieking with mirth, only a few feet beyond.

In this strange silence—strange because such intensity of life was so near—I thought, I knew not why, of the boy-statesman who had killed himself upon the hearth of this very chamber, to have his jewels rifled, even whilst she kissed his dead lips, by the woman for whom he perished.

Was it always thus, I wondered? Always the love, and

the loyalty, and the faithfulness that suffered; and all that
lived in peace and plenteousness the Faustine—the Cléopâtre?

As I mused the door opened, and a woman entered.

Have you never seen, in life or on some old master's canvas, a beautiful child's face, fair, tender, serious even to sadness, with the golden hair, cut low and square over the brow,
and the dreaming eyes gazing straightly out—beyond you,
very far beyond you? If you have, you have seen this woman's face as she came into the lighted chamber, with black
folds of velvet sweeping after her as she moved, with that
grave grace of motion which always seems to belong to other
centuries—to the terraces of Marly, to the halls of Rambouil-
let, to the studios of Vandyke, to the palaces of Charles the
First. And which you have lost—yes, lost strangely, in this
day of yours, when, all lovely and thorough-bred though
many of your women be, they smoke their papered cigarettes,
and talk their stolen slang, bet on their gunners in a drove of
grouse, and land their gasping grilse to their own line; take
a double and drop like a workwoman, and "get on" for a
"good thing" at the Craven or the July, with a reckless auda-
city that never flies at anything less than four figures.

She looked at me with a smile which seemed, I thought,
surety that I should have to endure from her neither harsh-
ness nor caprice.

"What a pretty creature!" she said as she stooped to
touch me; but I stayed not for her caress—I forgot her very
presence, for beyond her I saw Beltran.

Time had not dimmed my memory of him, nor had it
quenched my affection. With a bark of delight, I escaped
through her hands and sprang on him, recalling myself to his
remembrance with all the innocent arts of which I was master.
He was in nowise altered; but had he been so ever so greatly,
my instinct would have been true to him.

We, who can only love dumbly, cling to the creature of our
affections, no matter how time have blanched his locks, bowed
his frame, shattered his whole being. You, who talk so

grandly of elective affinities and the unions of souls, pass your
early love in the street without knowing her, if she have but
wrinkled a little; and break off your marriage troth with your
lover if a shower of shot chance to change his handsome face
to deformity.

He looked at me in my ecstasies with amused surprise;
he had no sort of knowledge of me; but as he turned to her
to speak of my value, the little collar that I wore caught his
sight, and he raised me to read the inscription upon it.

The bit of metal that had been fashioned for me at the
forge in the woods of the Peak was still about my throat; it
was not worth a brass coin, so none had cared to rob me of it.

If you wish to keep a thing, let it have naught to attract
the eyes of others—a rule which sometimes seems to influence
you too often in the selection of your wives.

His face changed as he read.

"Puck!" he muttered; "as I live, it is the same dog that
belonged—"

The phrase was left unfinished; the woman beside him
turned with a flush of surprise, in which one saw how very
youthful was that lovely face.

"Puck! Puck!" she echoed, as though my name brought
also to her some memories. "Can it be the same? That is
strange, indeed!"

"It is the same dog, oddly enough," said Beltran, as he
gave me to her; but there was an annoyance, almost a dis-
pleasure, on his face as he spoke. Whatever might be her
remembrance of me—for of her I had none—to him evidently
I bore but one association, and that the unwelcome one of
Avice Dare. For me personally, I suppose, he cared nothing.
Alas for us! it is almost ever so in the intercourse between
our race and yours. Between human beings, when two measures of love are weighed out by the hand of fate, to be mingled together in union, one scale is always light and the other
always heavy. How much more so between men and dogs!

Although we spend all that we possess of loyalty and
strength and courage in human service, and break our hearts

oftentimes for human friends, we are seldom much loved in return. A careless touch of the hand, a rough kindly word or two now and then, a broken crust, a tossed bone: these are payments enough for a dog—"only a dog."

Here and there a Rab will find a chronicler; a St. John will beg with his last breath that his bones be laid beside Lion's; a Byron will value his "one friend;" a Walter Scott will think, amidst woe, and debt, and the exhaustion of a mortal disease, of "the dogs;" and tombs will be raised to lost and lamented dog-comrades, as in the little shadowy yew-circled cemetery of Wrest. But these exceptions are very rare. For the most part, we are but little loved, little heeded, and not at all remembered.

The woman, bending over me, caressed me with a dreamy tenderness, as though thinking of other things that my presence brought from some past time. Her eyes seemed dim as she looked at me, with a sweet vague sadness, as for some remembered season of great woe. Beltran drew me away from her.

"If he bring you those memories, he shall not stay. I would never have bought him if I had known—"

"Why?" she answered him, still dreamily. "I shall care more for him. As for those memories—when do I ever forget them? And do you think I would forget if I could?"

"I wish that you would at least. There is only one thing you can want to remember—"

"And what is that?"

"That you are famous now—and happy. You *are* happy?"

There seemed, I thought, some little doubt and vague apprehension in his question.

If there were, they must have been contented by the look in her eyes as they turned on him: a look so eloquent that it needed not in its confirmation the half-sigh of joy with which her lips breathed the answer.

"Happy? Ah, yes! Happier than it can ever seem right to me to be—"

He did not ask her why this should be so,—perhaps he knew.

Almost at that moment the door of the supper-room, which they had left open to the passages beyond, was filled by the forms of five other men: three were strangers to me; in the two others I recognised the fair features of Lord Guilliadene, and the lofty form and dark guerrilla-like head of Derry Denzil. To me it seemed so marvellously strange, so breathlessly bewildering, thus to be tossed back once more by the battledore of chance into the heart of these old associations and unforgotten memories that I cowered, dumb and dizzy, in a corner, wondering still if I were not dreaming all these things under the dying lilies of the florist's little den, or the golden-fruited pear-trees of Madelon's orchard.

But, with them, there appeared a presence which did assure me beyond all doubt or question that I was in the region of fact and not of fancy; for into the chamber there entered a little black slender figure, hung about with golden bells, with piercing eyes, diamond bright, and a pert, proud, consequential carriage. Need I say it was Fanfreluche?

She darted at me, angered, curious, brimful of irritation, and readiness for insolence; then dropped her nose to mine, and cocked her ears, and screamed, "Mercy! If it's not that little fool!"

The salutation was not courtly nor complimentary; yet it fell sweetly upon my ears. Is not the roughness, or the sarcasm, of a friend more welcome than the suave insincerity of conventionality-clothed foes? It is so to us: not perhaps to you; for humanity has learnt to love a daintily-dressed falsehood. What matter to you if garden snails, pulled off the cabbages, have made your soup, so long as you don't know it and are cheated by a clever cook into murmuring, "What a good *consommé!*"

Fanfreluche knew me, instantly; and was glad to see me, with that warmth of heart which had always underlain her cynical assumptions. Quickly, as though we had never parted, we were talking fast in that tongue of ours, which you under-

stand as little as you—deaf in your own conceit—understand
what the rooks talk to one another in the sweet still evening-
time; or know the meaning of the night-birds' signals, as they
move in the world of shadows; or catch the word of warning
with which the blackcock, on his tussock of heather, tells his
brethren of the rifle-gleam; or comprehend the coquetries of
the prairie-fowl's quaint ceremonious country-dances; or know
by what rule of command and subjection the great armies of
porpoises move with such precision and wisdom; or tell what
amorous poetry the stock-dove murmurs to her mates through
the sweet green summer silence; or translate any other of the
innumerable tongues that daily and nightly fill the woods and
waters, the meadows and seas, with their meaning. A meaning to the full as intelligible and as useful as that of your
own speech; only you are too vain to believe it, and too li-
mited indeed in your intelligences to be able to do so much
as perceive it.*

"Where on earth have you been all these years?" began
Fanfreluche, showing the passage of the years herself no
more than does your "frisky matron." "And you look as
much of a baby as ever you did, you poor little atom of
swansdown!"

This was insolent, for I was treble her size, but I was too
content to meet her once more, to pause to vindicate my dignity; and indeed she gave me no time to do so, nor any peace
until I had related to her all my vicissitudes from the period
of my disappearance. For them she evinced some compassion, and more contempt: as I believe your friends are in the
habit of doing when you tell them how your wife has gone
wrong, your bank broken, your horse proved a non-stayer,
your pigeon fallen outside the enclosure, or any other mis-
fortune of your existence.

* I hope a certain contemptuous tone of self-glorification, that runs
throughout, will be forgiven to my friend Puck. It is perhaps pardonable
when we reflect that his race always smell out a rogue, however he may be
clothed; and that we seldom or never detect one provided only he be, as
the French say of their *abricots, très bien doré.*—ED.

"I am sorry you have ever been professional," she said disdainfully,. when she had heard of the days of La Pipetta. "You haven't lost caste. We don't: a thoroughbred's always a thoroughbred, if he come down to drawing a cart. But the stage never suits us. It suits *them*. Human beings are always acting off the boards; they may just as well do it on; a lie or two more or less, when they are about it, doesn't matter much. But we—"

"Tell me all about yourself. What have you done?" I interrupted her, remembering of old her disposition to chatter epigram, or what she thought was such, with about as much reason as your ignorant diner will take a bit of mutton, smothered in sauce, to be an *epigramme d'agneau*.

"Done!" she echoed. "*I?* My dear, I should talk all night if I attempted to tell you. You've lived in a puppet-box, an *auberge*, and an attic. I've lived with one duchess, one marchioness, three Anonymas, a rector's wife, a horse-couper, an ambassadress, a tinker, and a manufacturer of truffles—india-rubber, and so true to life that nobody but a dog could have told the difference; people went into ecstasies over their flavour! Done? Why, it's an eternity since I saw you! A bride whom I was bought for when you went off the scene—such a pretty creature, and quite a love match!—has had time to get into the 'Court of Probate, &c.,' and out again, and is just going to marry her lover. By the way, I saw her throw her arms round her husband, and kiss him with her pretty innocent lips, the very night she ran off with the other one from old Lady Tynemouth's 'small and early.' O! those dear women!"

"And what became of the husband?"

"How out of fashion you are, thinking of *him*—that comes of living in puppet-boxes and garrets. O, he went mad, I believe: is mad now. A fine gallant-looking fellow, too; but I knew from the first he was a great fool: he always preferred sweet champagnes, and never could eat a raw oyster."

"But tell me all that has happened here?" I urged, breathless and curious, as I gazed at the familiar faces, and the familiar things, and heard Beltran's slow melodious contemptuous tones, and Denzil's deep frank laughter. "Has he restored the theatre? And who is that lovely woman?"

"That lovely woman you will know more about than I,— for you are going to live with her, I believe. He restored the theatre, at a ruinous cost, directly after it was wrecked, partly because, out of kindliness, he wouldn't turn his employés adrift in mid-winter; and partly out of pride, because he wouldn't have the town say that the success of his stage depended on Laura Pearl, or Avice Dare as you used to call her—"

"And she is in Paris? She is Cléopâtre?" I demanded, scarce able still to disentangle past from present, dream from fact.

"She is Cléopâtre—just now—yes," assented Fanfreluche; "what she'll be before she dies nobody on earth can say—a peeress, or a princess, I shouldn't wonder. That woman understands the great rule of success—'*frappez vite, et frappez fort*'—and don't care a hang where you strike. I was in Paris all last winter, and I thought she was having a very good time, as the Americans say: she spent her thousand francs aday; she had peaches before anybody else, she changed her dress four times in every twelve hours, she had the best horses in the Bois, the Court wore a robe Watteau she had revived, a new liqueur was christened after her, and tortoiseshell fans became the rage because she carried one. I don't know what a woman wants besides all this to be in paradise!"

I shuddered. I thought of Carlos.

That history seemed too terrible to speak of to this gay satirist.

"What are you thinking about? You are not the livelier for your exile," cried Fanfreluche. "Ah, my dear, you should have lived as I've done; with men who make up delicious truffles out of a little india-rubber, and women who make up lovely faces with dead hair and their paint-boxes! They are the comedy of life. You've been with people dreadfully in earnest, who ate dry bread, and wore their own hair, and looked sallow with sorrow, and did no end of fools' things, and

went through life as through a tragedy—I know! There can't
be a greater mistake. Everything is amusing, if you'll only
look at it in that light."

"Life has gone so well with you," I retorted.

"O, well enough, my dear! And why?—I bite everybody's
legs if I'm unhappy; you should see how quick they get to
make me comfortable! The secret of being happy yourself lies in the capacity to be intensely disagreeable to other
people."

"That sounds very unamiable."

"Unamiable! what does that matter?   An amiable dog is
a fool—every little cur in the streets snarls in his path, and
every scamp of a boy throws stones at him!"

"But his own people love him?"

"O yes, love him so dearly that they give him a sound kick
in the ribs—knowing he won't return it!"

I thought she had grown soured by growing older, female
creatures will; or at least on our ear, a *mot*, that only sounds
prettily piquant when the speakers are young, has a spiteful
ring in its tone, we fancy, when they are young no longer.
Indeed, these sharp trivialities annoyed me at this moment,
when I was all agitation and excitement at my sudden return,
and full of eagerness as to all that had happened in this
little world during the dreary seasons that I had been absent
from it.

"We are just the same as we always were, my dear," she
said pettishly. "Bless you! in our world we never alter anything; our hearts may be broken, our honour be blasted, our
peace gone for ever, the one friend we trusted dead, the one
woman we cared for lost, we never change anything; we dine
and drive, and smoke and saunter, and laugh and drink, and
make love just the same. Why not? Our one canon is, not
to show that we're beat. *Beau joueur ne faut se plaindre.*"

"It must be hard to do that sometimes."

"It is hard to the canaille; it is second nature to the gentleman," retorted this determined aristocrat. "If you want
news, of course we have always plenty of that. No end of

marriages, and divorces, and scandals, and turf-ruin, and co-
cotte-ruin, and all the rest of it; there are fresh stories every
day, just as there's fresh butter for breakfast. But nothing
makes much difference—nothing—unless perhaps it's the
grouse disease."

"'The grouse disease!"

"Well, yes; there's nothing exactly to put in those birds'
places; but men and women get supplied quite as fast as they
get bowled over. 'Durham's gone,' they were 'saying last
autumn everywhere; and he was 'gone' for some four hundred
thousand; nothing in the world left him except his bare title;
for Royeldene wasn't entailed. Now, Sir D'Arcy Durham—
you remember him?—was, take him all in all, the best-loved
man in the country; witty, sweet-tempered, generous to madness, brilliant exceedingly, he was yet of happy enough nature
to have scarcely an enemy, and to be adored nearly as much
by man as by woman. Well—who thinks of him now? He's
ruined and has gone to Norway, or—no one knows where.
'Durham would have handled these line hunters better than
that d—d fool;' or 'Durham wouldn't have squandered a fine
lot of foxes like this duffer,' they have said now and then when
wrathful with some M. F. H. And that's all; except that
two or three women have looked white, for a month or two, in
spite of their rouge."

"Do hold your tongue," I entreated; "or else tell me why
I am here, and what has happened to them all, and who is
that beautiful fair woman."

"As to why you are here I don't know. Simply, I believe,
because Beltran wanted a dog of your sort, and bade some
fanciers look out for one; in consequence of which you were
sent him. No design, my dear; nothing but coincidence—the
one odd-tempered deity that rules the world. When those
poor devils of novelists jumble a lot of impossible coincidences
all pell-mell together without building-plan or sequence, or
any sort of sense, they are all wrong as to Art, clearly, but
they are awfully true to Life. As to them—as I tell you, nothing makes much difference to them. They've dined, and

dressed, and shot, and hunted, and played whist, and made
love, much the same as ever they did. They're always saying
they're tired of the life, but I don't think they can be, for they
never seem to try any other. Beltran's been to Africa and
killed a lot of things; and a mare of Guilliadene's won the
Oaks, spread-eagleing in splendid style all her field, though
the very merest outsider; and Derry Denzil's published another book that the men swore by in the smoking-rooms, and
the women cried over, and the critics called immoral, so that
I suppose it was a great success with three such vouchers for
it. *Du reste*—I don't think there's much to tell. There's
been plenty of news, of course; but now-a-days, when nobody
ever takes up a paper without seeing some friend or another
divorced, bankrupt, breaking a bank, or writing a novel, no
news seems to have much taste in it—your *bombe* is all water-
ice."

"But the theatre?" I persisted, out of patience.

"O, the theatre is doing wonders, they say, since this new
miracle came into it. All the cellar flip-flaps done away with,
you know, my dear, we go in for nothing but high art, or at
least as nearly high as is possible in an age that prefers high
feeding."

"But who is *she?*"

"I can't say. Our stars are seldom lost Pleiades that can
be named and placed: they are generally '*étoiles qui filent—
qui filent—qui filent et disparaissent!*' You are going to live
with her. You can't want to ask me."

"And where do you live?"

"With Beltran."

I could not repress a sigh of envy and of sorrow; my
pleasant place in those pleasant chambers! Nothing looks
so sweet to us as a lost home in which a stranger is installed.
The flaming sword, betwixt the infuriate cherubim of the
brazen gates, was more merciful by far to the Eden-banished
sinners than would have been the sight of other human
creatures sunned in the lost light of that fair forbidden kingdom.

"You are fortunate," I said with a sharp pang.

"I don't know about that, my dear," she made answer. "I suppose I am. I have always made it a practice to pilfer anything that looks tempting, and bite everything weaker than myself that I meet with; I believe that is the sort of practice that makes men's fortunes, so it ought to make ours. I wished to live with Beltran, so last season I just walked into his rooms and stopped there. They couldn't get me to go out, do all they would; so they ended by making themselves agreeable to my staying. If you want to get a place, try that way. I've seen so many public men keep in offices, that everybody wanted to turn them out of, only by that power of theirs of sticking tight, as a sea anemone sticks to its rock! 'A masterly inactivity' is never so masterly as when it glues you fast to a good berth, no matter whether you're fit or unfit for it. They understand that so well in all cabinets!"

"You must know everything about him, then?"

She turned her nose in the air.

"My dear! There are four orders of creatures that always know everything—they are journalists, ladies'-maids, priests, and toy terriers."

And therewith she left me in the half-lit recess where the grand piano stood, and trotted out into the full light, where she put herself into a pretty pose in order to get bonbons thrown to her.

Whilst she was gleefully catching the burnt almonds and crystallised cherries, and cracking them with a monkey-like unction, I sat in my corner, not knowing rightly yet whether I were awake or dreaming.

The very familiarity of the aspect of all around me only increased the confusion of my ideas. There was nothing but what I had dreamily remembered, a score of times, in the visions which had visited me lying under a *contadina's* tent in the harvest-fields of the Campagna, or watching the pale moon glide above the metal roofs of Paris; nothing except the picturesque head of this beautiful fair woman, the like

of which I had never seen either in life or dreams. I sat
still and gazed at them; gazed beyond all at Beltran. Having so long beheld nothing but the passionate, black-browed,
sun-bronzed faces of the Roman peasantry, and the lean,
swart, keen, eager visage of the Parisian workmen—save
when I had seen the golden beauty and fervid youth of the
painter Carlos—these men, once so familiar to me, with their
handsome colourless faces, their low serene voices, their
tired laughter, their look of fatigue, their consummate tran-
quillity and indifference, seemed like the creatures of another
world.

Could passion stir them? pain move them? want con-
sume them? life be known to them through any other thing
save its pleasures and satieties? Idly I wondered this, judg-
ing foolishly from the surface. I might have known that no
passions burn fiercer, no romances wax stronger, no courage
ever flames higher, and no hearts perchance ache more
wearily, than in these lives that look so passionless, so
tranquil, so cynical, so selfish, and, as your world will have
it, so culpable.

If you doubt what these men are whilst you see them
live, go and see them die, as they have died again and
again, at Steinkerk, at Edgehill, at Vittoria, at Hougoumont,
at Inkermann. Jacques Bonhomme shrieked and struggled,
and writhed and screamed, as they led him to the scaffold;
but, think you that Rohan cared nothing for the sweetness
of life because the proud blood never paled before the axe,
and the mute lips never once lost that smile of serenest
disdain?

I cannot tell why these disjointed thoughts drifted
vaguely through my mind as I looked at Beltran, even in
that moment of bewilderment and of restoration. Except,
indeed, that in the faces of men like himself, as they lie at
length on the heather, or pace their yacht-deck, or smoke
their cigar on a battle-field, or murmur love-nonsense in an
opera box, you can trace the old *race* so curiously. The old
race with all its reckless daring, and its feudal insolence,

and its courtly gentleness, and its imperious temper, and its
loyal honour, and its simple religion of *noblesse oblige*, still
alive under all the changes of manner and habit; the old
race, which is still, whatever be its faults or follies, what a
mob will cower before, and a soldier will follow to the death,
and a people will look to in its hours of action or of need,
and a woman will choose before any other type of manhood
to be beside her in any time of menace or of peril.

From my dusky corner I watched, and wondered, and
listened, and puzzled my brain: the room was the same, the
men were the same, Fanfreluche was the same, the very
silver box that held the cigarettes was the same, and yet—
there was a great difference. The voices seemed much
gentler; the laughter seemed much quieter; the wines were
but little touched; the conversation, as I caught snatches of
it, seemed artistic, pleasant, sometimes playful, sometimes
earnest, but at all times the conversation of men, talking at
their ease indeed, but still troubling themselves to talk ably,
and conscious of the presence of a woman who could discern
such ability. Above all, their speech was fit for a delicate
ear even in their sharpest witticisms, and there was not a
flavour of that cynical indecency which had been so general
to the same speakers here in the days of Avice Dare.

What had wrought the difference I wondered? Certainly
she who now sat there with that fair, childlike, and yet
queenlike head, and those dreaming, luminous, grave eyes,
and that voice which made the simplest words of common
speech sound music, and that rich old-world velvet dress
without a single jewel or ornament of any sort, was very
different to the form that I had used to see there; blazing in
sapphires or in rubies, and full of the supreme vanity of its
own wanton, deep-hued, gorgeous, physical perfections dis-
played to the eyes of others, as the peacock spreads its
plumage to the sun.

Men are very much in society as women will them to be.
Let a woman's society be composed of men gently-born and
bred, and if she find them either coarse or stupid, make

answer to her;—"You must have been coarse or stupid yourself."

And if she demur to the *tu quoque* as to a base and illogical form of argument, which we will grant that it usually is, remind her that the cream of a pasturage may be pure and rich, but if it pass into the hands of a clumsy farm serving-maid, then shall the cheese made thereof be neither Roquefort nor Stilton, but rough and flavourless and uneatable, "like a Banbury cheese, nothing but paring."* Now, the influence of a woman's intelligence on the male intellects about her is as the churn to the cream: it can either enrich and utilise it, or impoverish and waste it. It is not too much to say that it almost invariably, in the present decadence of the salon and parrot-jabbering of the suffrage, has the latter effect alone.

"Pray tell me who this exquisite creature is?" I begged of Fanfreluche, who returned to me when she had eaten at her own sweet will of bonbons till she was tired of them.

"You'll hear enough of her, my dear," she retorted, "the town talks of her, and crowds this place to see her. She does act well, that I grant; but if she only knew it, she don't want her genius a bit; she might act like a stick; they'd come just the same,—once set going."

"But to set them going requires the genius?"

"Gracious, no!" returned my ancient monitress, with unutterable contempt. "If you can just get it well bruited about that a woman's very pretty, or very immoral, or has tried to poison some people, or has got fabulously little feet, or is going to play a shockingly scandalous character, any of these things will draw a great deal better than any amount of talent. What made this one's fame? Not her capabilities, though they are great; but just this one line in the *Midas*— 'She is the loveliest woman we have ever seen upon this or upon any other stage, and her attire is simply—perfection.' The men went to see the face, the women to see the dress: her fortune was made. *Voilà!*"

* Jack Drum's Entertainment, 1601.—Ed.

"She is a great actress, then?"

"She is a charming actress. I don't think we can have a
great one. We are not barbaric enough; and we are too incredulous. You want a good deal of barbarism and a good
deal of faith in an age, to get a really great stage out of it.
To us, after our late dinners and with our pleasant indolent
spleen, Lady Macbeth looks ridiculous, and Othello seems
very bad form. We are as wicked as ever other ages were,
as passionate and as vile and as guilty as ever they were; but
it is all in a very different fashion: and the fashion is one
which it is much easier for the satirist to deal with pungently
than it is for the dramatist to render artistically. Chignons,
and co-respondents, plunging and panniers, Americanism
and cocotteism, are so much better suited to a Sheridan or
Beaumarchais, than to a Shakespeare or a Sophocles. The
odd thing is that, in the dearth of the poetic drama, not one
satirical comedy has as yet held up the mirror to all that
tempts such a mirror so strongly. The odd thing is that,
with such a field for them, we have no Sheridan, and no
Beaumarchais."

"I did not ask for a dissertation on the drama," I
interrupted her impatiently. "I want to know about this
woman."

"I'll tell you all I know, my dear," said Fanfreluche,
seating herself comfortably. "You remember the wreck of
the theatre, of course?—Well, he restored it, as fresh and
pretty and dainty as any enamelled *bonbonnière*. It is nicer
than ever it was, with statuettes in its corridors, and little
boudoirs behind its choicest boxes, and leaves and flowers
everywhere. It cost enormously; but he did it chiefly out of
pride, no doubt, that none might say the house had depended
on Laura Pearl. Many persons wanted it: when a thing or
a woman is known to be certain ruin it is always bid for so
eagerly! But Beltran would not part with it. 'I shall
chance it till the lease is ended,' he always answered; and
the time came when I thought I knew why he had so
answered.

"The performance was much the same for a time: Maude
Delamere and melodramas first; burlesque and ballet afterwards. Money was lost every night. I don't know why; I
suppose old Wynch did. The losses were so profitable to
him that he retired, bought a small place in Surrey, and lives
at ease. Last autumn twelvemonth I belonged to Mrs.
Riversleigh—pretty; notorious; husband vaguely 'in the
city;' good for water-parties, fish-dinners, drag seats; and
doesn't resent being cut if you meet her in the Park when
you're driving with your wife or your mother: you know the
style I mean? Royston Wressyl was her chief friend at that
time: a Major of Lancers in the old Sixteenth. She was in
town because the Sixteenth were at Hounslow. One night
Wressyl and she went to the Coronet with a few others; they
were to sup at the Leviathan afterwards; and to take me with
them for a wager, which they did. Wressyl carried me hidden in a big lorgnon case; but he needn't have troubled himself, they knew me there.

"'What do they play to-night, Royston?' she asked as
we drove.

"'I'm not sure,' he answered her, 'but I'm awfully afraid
it's some old duffer's dry-as-dust play. They were saying
something to-day, though, in the Rag, about a new actress
being announced.'

"She didn't ask any more. She only went to a theatre to
show her diamonds, and have a pleasant supper somewhere,
with lots of champagne-cup. They neither of them knew
Beltran personally, and had heard nothing.

"At the entrance we met Guilliadene, who was intimate
with them.

"'What's up, Ned?' Wressyl asked him.

"'*Much Ado about Nothing*,' said the Earl. 'And a new
actress as Beatrice. Never played publicly in her life, they
say. What a part to start with!'

"'Awfully plucky,' said my Lancer. 'Safe to make a
mull of it, I suppose? Who is she?'

"'I don't know much about her,' replied Guilliadene,

'Merest novice, I think. Beltran's always picking up stars that turn out to be sticks, like the rockets at Cremorne.'

"And he went to his stall, and we to our box.

"The play had begun. This woman was on; you see what her beauty is, and she was costumed superbly; her hair was cut square on the forehead and waved loose behind, an anachronism, doubtless, but the very poetry of Coiffure. Her audience, which seemed an ordinary one, was apathetic and even hostile. It was the most piteous thing I ever saw. Her tones were almost inaudible; her colour kept coming and going; her agitation was very great; and she looked so young, such a child with it all, you would have thought that the public must have been touched. But it was not. It hissed a little; it yawned a great deal; and Mrs. Riverleigh and one or two women laughed loudly behind their fans. I think she heard the laughter, for I saw her shiver. Ah! it must be a terrible thing, that first sound of your own voice in the vastness and stillness; that first sight of the unknown crowd of satirical, indifferent, unpitying faces!

"The impersonation all through the first act was utterly tame and meaningless. If it had not been for her beauty, I think the house would have howled. As the curtain fell and Wressyl left the box for a moment, I managed to slip out and through the passages, till I got 'behind,' where there were only Beltran, Denzil, Dudley Moore, and Steinforth, the great author, you know. As the girl had come off the stage she had rushed away to her room before they could stay her. Beltran looked grave, and more anxious than I had seen him do one race-day when a beaten horse had cost him half an estate.

"'One can't say much for your new wonder!' they were muttering to him.

"'No,' he answered, very quietly. 'But I believe she will do well in time. You have not seen her act in private—I have.'

"'I don't doubt her charms for any private performance,' said Dudley Moore drily; 'but we have really tried to float

as great geniuses so many pretty women, with only their
prettiness to recommend them, that I am getting rather
doubtful of the utility of the process—it can't claim novelty,
and I fear it can't claim propriety.'

"Beltran did not show either annoyance or impatience.
'Don't judge her just yet,' was all he said, very quietly
still.

"When the actress was called again, and left her room,
her face was quite white and her eyes all black and humid
with a bewildered sort of terror.

"'I have acted so ill! I feel so frightened!' she murmured breathlessly to Beltran, not seeming to see that any
others beside himself were present. He stooped to her very
kindly and gently.

"'You have not done great things at present, certainly.
But you can—and you will. Try and forget that any
one is listening; and only remember how I want you to
succeed.'

"The last words were murmured so low that only she and
I heard them. She drew a deep breath, the colour flushed
her face, a sort of inspiration seemed to seize her, and she
went. From that moment her acting was entirely changed.
Her voice rang clear, and full of exquisite cadences; her
beauty grew radiant with pride and strength. She seemed
to feel her own force, and to be filled with the powers of art.
All the beautiful insolences, all the changeful colours, all the
splendid audacities, of genius shone out in her; and tri-
umphed. Her audience, indifferent and even alienated before, were first startled and then captivated. They realised
that this creature to whom they had been at best contemptuously indulgent, as to a lovely child whose failure they
pitied, but whose weakness wearied them, was in truth their
mistress, through the dominion of great gifts; and could force
them to rejoice with her, to weep with her, to laugh, and to
suffer, and to love with her, at her will and at her fancy.
They woke from their apathy into a sort of fury of admiration; and the house rang with raptures of applause.

" 'And there's not an ounce of that *bought*,' murmured Beltran.· 'It's genuine, whatever it's worth.'

" 'We were right to suspend judgment,' said Dudley Moore, taking snuff. 'I have never seen anything more poetic and more sincere, more delicate, and more vivid'—and what he said the town was certain to say after him on the morrow.

"Her triumph was very great; only the greater it seemed because heralded by failure. The house was convulsed with excitement; they called for her again and again; the women laughed no longer, and the roof rang with a tumult of applause.

"When she came off the stage, for the last time after the recall, her face was deeply flushed; her eyes gleamed like two stars; her whole frame trembled; she had the look of a creature in delirium. She stretched out her hands to Beltran with a little, breathless, hysterical sob, 'Have I done well—at last?' He took them in his own and bent tenderly to her. 'Better than the best: I cannot say how I thank you.'

"At that moment one of the officials of the theatre, whom Wressyl had sent to seek me, bore me away, and back to Mrs. Riversleigh's box, where that lady was in wrath and dudgeon because the Lancer, in an excitement of admiration at the new Beatrice, had, unauthorised, flung her bouquet of red and white camellias upon the stage. We did not stay for the burlesque that evening, as the delicate little suppers at the Leviathan are too perfect to be kept waiting, and I saw no more of the actress. But from that night her fame was made, and her name heard upon the lips of London."

"And what is she to Beltran?" I asked, as she closed her narration.

Fanfreluche grinned: her worst grin.

"Ah, my dear! That's what the town's been asking ever since, and never has got an answer yet. But look, they are going. Good-bye till to-morrow; I'm very glad to see you here again."

When the little gathering broke up, the actress drew about her those black laces and scalskins lined with rose, which I had noticed on the couch, and stooping for me, raised me so that I could lie curled upon the soft sea-furs.

An elderly woman, who was in waiting in the ante-room, offered to take me, but she refused the offer, as she had declined those of the men about her, and carried me herself through the various passages to the entrance of the theatre, where a carriage stood. They accompanied her, talking the while with her, as men and women do who have the custom of daily association and familiar friendship; and bade her goodnight at the door of her brougham, which rolled rapidly away. She and her maid drove on in silence, whither, of course, I could not tell. When the carriage paused, we passed through a fragrant garden, whose leafless boughs were very dark and still in the dim moonlight, and thence through a very small square hall, and up a staircase in which the lights were burning low; it was too dark to see much, but all seemed pretty and luxurious about me; and as she carried me into a room on the right, I perceived that it was the chamber of one to whom both art and gold had ministered.

It was of small size, and of much simplicity; but it had an exceeding elegance and harmony in all its arrangements. She laid me down upon her sealskins, then sank into a chair before the hearth on which a fire was brightly burning. Her attendant asked her, with a solicitude that seemed quite genuine, if she were not very tired?

"I am often tired; that is no matter," she answered, with a smile, which though fatigued was very sweet and glad. "Take these things off me, please, and bring me some tea."

The maid obeyed, wrapping round her some cashmeres, and letting loose all the fair masses of her hair; then brought her the tea in a miniature old-fashioned service of egg-shell china, and left her alone by her desire. She called me from my resting-place and raised me on her lap; stroking me, and even laying her lips on my forehead.

"I shall love you for his sake. Had it not been for you I

might never have known him," she murmured. "But still you can never be to me what my dear old friend was!"

And, looking at her thus, with the fire-glow upon her, I knew her, despite all the magic changes wrought by time, and gold, and fame. I knew her to be—Gladys Gerant.

CHAPTER IX.

A Story of the Sea.

I THINK Fanfreluche spoke with reason. Coincidence is a god that greatly influences mortal affairs. He is not a cross-tempered deity, either, always; and when you beat your poor fetish for what seems to you an untoward accident, you may do wrong; he may have benefited you far more than you wot.

Not very long ago, a man and a woman loving each other well, were parted by misunderstanding—one of those sad, dreary, proud fantasies, that so often arise between you human creatures and your happiness. Neither would stoop to explain, they were divided during two long years; for it is strange how people living in the same society may yet grow utter strangers to each other; how passing one another daily in the park, how brushing against one another in the opera corridors, how hearing one another's names uttered by many lips, how beholding one another's faces in the crowded rooms of great assemblies, or of private views, they may yet remain as utterly divided from one another, as though oceans rolled between them.

Well, the time came when the woman, haughty, lovely, and brilliant, was, through a series of family calamities, doomed to an exile that galled her bitterly, in a far-away lonely German forest-land.

Awhile later, the man, by what he deemed the bitterest injustice and injury to him in his service, which was diplomacy, was consigned as envoy to a miserable petty state, in which his talents rusted, and his name was unheard, and his weeks and months passed by in an unutterable weariness and inaction.

One summer day, in a deep old Teutonic wood, where no footfall but a forester's or charcoal-burner's ever fell, and the millions of pines were wrapped in twilight even at noon, these two, each unwitting of the other's presence in the hated land of banishment, met face to face suddenly, in that stillness and that solitude. And in that moment their hearts went out to one another, and the veil fell from their eyes, and the old love reigned alone!

Pride had been strong in the press of the world; but here, chance touched and startled them, and surprised from both their secret; and thus from the thorns of harsh accident, there blossomed for them sweet flowers of passion and of peace.

("And, my dear, there was something beside chance, for there was ennui," said that matter-of-fact iconoclast, Fanfreluche, when she heard of them. "He must have been awfully bored, you know, and so was much readier to make it up with her, than he had been when decently well amused in London. It's an immense pull for a woman, you know, to get at a man when he is thoroughly bored. He's so much more glad of her then." But this was only the comment of a shallow cynic; and the story truly ran as I have told it.)

Coincidence now had tossed me back amongst life, and luxury, and friends; and I was glad and grateful: not querulous as you too often are when what you have long coveted comes to you.

When the morning broke I found myself in a small elegant house, as warm as an eider-bird's nest, and as pretty as an enamelled snuff-box; such a house as may be seen by the score along the Thames or the Seine; shut in amidst miniature gardens, that doubtless were one mass of foliage and flowers in summer, to judge by the maze of greenery that was now snow-powdered and silver-frosted.

It was so small and so pretty that it was like a toy; but in common with those little jewelled teapots, and stags, and other trifles that hang to your watch-chain, it was only such a toy as gold could purchase.

Once more there were the softness, and the smoothness, and all the nameless pleasantnesses of life when money rounds its angles about me. Once more I slumbered on silken cushions; and was fed on dainty forms of nourishment; and was prankt up* with bright ribbons upon my throat. And it was sweet to me to be thus soothed, and fed, and caressed, and decked, and dighted, as in my early days of fashion and of favouritism, for such outward symbols show that the world goes well with us, and that we are of value and of ornament in it. For it is all very well to call these things fribbles and frivolities, they may be so; but they are a great portion of the pleasure and the ease of existence at any rate. I know a man who was always inveighing against them (he was rich and possessed them, mind you), he was deeply bitten with many stern philosophies of equality, and was wont to sigh for a time when bread and broth in even portions to all should vouch for the perfect isonomy of the State.

But whilst he thus theorised, I never knew any one more particular than he as to the age and delicacy of his wines; and in the autumn when he was belated, and perforce detained by a broken ankle, in a rough and remote Highland inn, his rage at the peat, and the fleas, and the oaten cake, and the rusty bacon, and the wretched rooms, was so dire that none durst scarce approach him.

"Equality would be very charming, dear—but still—I don't think you'd *do* for it," said his pretty provoking wife, as he swore right and left at the Gaels.

This house in which I found myself was, as I say, exquisite; on that first morning breakfast was served in the daintiest

* Puck seems fond now and then of retaining some of the archaisms of the language which he learned no doubt in the north country, where many of the strong picturesque words of Shakespeare and Piers Plowman are still in daily use. Why should such words be lost? Talkers may perhaps shrink from the charge of eccentricity incurred by using them; but writers surely need not care for it.—Ed.

fashion, in a bewitching little warm violet-hued room, in which you caught here and there the glint of dead gold; and the mistress of it all (in whom beyond a question I saw the child whom I had once seen so sad and desolate in the streets striving to sell her dying harebells) was fully in keeping with such a chamber, as she sat in a low chair, beside the fire, reading her letters and papers of the early day, whilst her maid served her with chocolate and delicate bread, and purple hothouse grapes.

It was all perfectly charming: the fire, the chamber, the colour everywhere, the silence only broken by the singing of a bullfinch in the window; this beautiful woman, the very cream and biscuits that they brought me for my food, all were charming beyond measure on that winter morning, so cold without, so bright within, so vivid in contrast with those cheerless dawns which had broken so gray and biting in the attic of the house in Paris. And yet—my blood for a moment ran as cold as though I were hungry and homeless in the falling snow.

How could a friendless, penniless, helpless young creature, such as had been Gladys Gerant, have come to attain such comfort and such elegance as were present here, except through the ways of evil? For I knew that such transmutations can only be wrought by casting into the crucible of fate the pearl of honour that, perishing, leaves in its stead the coveted philosopher's stone, which is gold.

And yet I felt ashamed of my own thought, as I looked at her delicate proud face, that from its childish innocence and sadness had changed into this exceeding beauty; altering so greatly, and yet retaining the same grave lustrous meditation in the eyes, the same dreaming sweetness on the mouth.

Whatever her life might be now, it was certain that she was a creature of most unusual loveliness, and grace and genius; and no less certain that she was happy—happy with more than the mere feverish joys of fame. And to me, remembering her in her great misery and her desolate youth, it seemed that she could not be so entirely content as this, unless she had in some way killed her conscience.

For in my brief life I had seen that all which was noble and loyal, and of purity and honour, was most usually doomed to a long and weary thole; capable indeed of joy in its highest, but seldom if ever knowing it.

She sat beside the hearth reading; her room seemed filled with papers and new books; and I sat gazing at her wondering, wondering where was Bronze, who had made the wandering child into this exquisite empress, was the poor dead poet forgotten—above all, what was she herself to Beltran?

I shuddered as I thought: that pure child whom I had seen kneeling in the moonlight, with the prayer for her lost brother on her lips, could never have learned the wicked ways, and taken the wicked wage, of Avice Dare?

And yet, otherwise, how came she hither in this affluence and ease?

The morning passed very quietly; I was tired and slept a good deal, overcome with fatigue and excitement. I was awakened by the striking of the clock, and the appearance of a light luncheon. She scarcely touched it, and went afterwards into her drawing-room, carrying me with her; the room was as perfect as all the rest of the house, and was quite full of the bloom and odour of flowers, although the time of year was still winter.

She moved about a little, touching her flowers, pausing beside a picture, rearranging some china in the pretty way women have, then seated herself once more amidst the books.

Between two and three o'clock there were the grating of wheels in the carriage drive without, the sound of a man's step, the tinkle of little bells, and there entered Beltran, followed whether he would or no by Fanfreluche.

He cast down a loose coat of sables, came to the hearth, and seated himself in a low lounging chair with the manner of one accustomed to frequent the place daily.

By the quick turn of her head, by the brilliance in her eyes, by her smile as she saw him, it was easy to tell how welcome his advent was. No formal greeting passed between them; they began to converse as though they had been together the last hour: people only do this betwixt whom there is an entire accord.

"Well, my dear, how do you find yourself?" asked Fanfreluche with a grin.

I said that I found myself very well.

"I daresay you do: it's a pretty place," she said drily. "On the whole Platonics don't seem such economical things as one thought they were—"

"What do you mean?"

"Never ask a person that. If his epigram or his argument be pointless or involved, you shouldn't show him that you think so, by asking him what he means. I told you I'd see you to-day: we come here most days when we're not hunting or shooting."

"You don't hunt?"

"No. A terrier isn't such a fool. *We* nip our prey in the necks in a second; we don't run it across half a county, and lose it in a drain after all. And to see what the hunting is now too! Knocking the horses all to pieces over cramped ground for sake of a fast twenty minutes! This is a pretty little house, isn't it? The rent's three hundred a year, furnished just as it stands; only the china, and pictures, and bronzes, and things are all hers,—or his."

"But how rich—"

"Well, he pays her at the rate of fifty guineas a week, or rather has it paid to her, for she don't know exactly that it's his. O, she's worth it, no doubt. She'd get it at any theatre, now. Gladys Gerant? O yes, she is Gladys Gerant; acts in the name too. People think it a fancy name because it's pretty. You see we have so many Polly Smiths and Betty Browns who are Amandevilles and Fitzosbornes upon the stage, that we think no woman can have a good graceful name really hers, unless she be in the *Libro d'Oro*, and has 5000*l*. a year of her own. I told you he'd keep his promise, didn't I, when we were at Ascot?"

"But how has he kept it?" I murmured; it was well indeed with her, so far as success, affluence, ease, beauty, talent went, but otherwise?—

"I don't think that's any business of yours, my dear," snapped Fanfreluche. "I can't tell you anything. I knew nothing about her till that night she came out as Beatrice, and then, of course, I recognised the name, and remembered the story you'd told me."

"But Bronze?"

"I know nothing about Bronze either. I was abroad, in different places, almost all last year, with my ambassadress, and my *prima donna*, and my truffle-maker. But there's a little low beast here, who can tell you, I daresay. He's called Patch, and lives in the kitchen by choice."

"A cur?"

"Well—yes. A cur. Not that I like that word. They have snobs and cads, but we have no curs,—not in the sense of disparagement that they use the word to imply. Even the Lurcher, the lowest type amongst us, is immeasurably superior to their Rough. With a poached hare in his mouth, he has a brisk, innocent, pleased air, and a conscience well at ease. He has no idea of dishonesty, and has only done his duty as his master taught it him. He is loyal, as far as his light goes; he has served the power he reveres; he has obeyed the law-giver of his humble life, in ignorance, indeed, but in fealty and faith. When can they say as much? No—we have no curs in the sense that they have cads; for we have none in our race who strain to seem what they are not; who are made hideous by vulgarity, made grotesque by assumption, or made infamous by lying. The lowest, ugliest, most hungry, most honest mongrel is always natural and always faithful. It is impossible, therefore, for a dog to be a snob."

"Does she suffer still for her brother, or still remember him?" I asked, not attending to her didactic digression.

"I can't tell you, I am sure," she said, with a sniff of scorn. "I never think much of their feelings at any time.

They are all words. Creatures that take out their grief in crape and mortuary tablets can't feel very much."

"There are many lamentations, from Lycidas to Lesbia, which prove that whether for a hero or a sparrow—" I began timidly to suggest.

"That's only a commonplace," snapped my lady. "They chatter and scribble; they don't feel. They write stanzas of 'gush' on Maternity; and tear the little bleating calf from its mother to bleed to death in a long slow agony. They maunder twaddle about Infancy over some ugly red lump of human flesh, in whose creation their vanity happens to be involved; and then go out and send the springtide lamb to the slaughter, and shoot the parent birds as they fly to the nest where their fledglings are screaming in hunger! Pooh! Did you never find out the value of their words? Some one of them has said that speech was given them to conceal their thoughts. It is true that they use it for that end; but it was given them for this reason. At the time of the creation, when all except man had been made, the Angel of Life, who had been bidden to summon the world out of chaos, moving over the fresh and yet innocent earth, thought to himself, 'I have created so much that is doomed to suffer for ever, and for ever be mute; I will now create an animal that shall be compensated for all suffering by listening to the sound of its own voluble chatter.' Whereon the Angel called Man into being, and cut the *frænum* of his tongue; which has clacked incessantly ever since, all through the silence of the centuries."

"Where is that legend?"

"In our traditions, which differ as much from the human ones as the human ones do from each other: *on ne pourrait plus!*"

"It is a great pity we were denied the power of the art of writing."

"Do you think so? We should never have kept our honesty if we had learnt it. Don't you know what that poor ruined Sir Robert said when he was dying? 'If I had never known how to write my name upon paper, I should have been a good man, and a rich one now.' My dear, if we had known how to write, we should have taken to 'bills at 60 days, &c.,' and a hound's kennel would soon have been no better than a club-room, with a sweepstakes card up on the mantelpiece!"

I yawned irritably. I was impatient of her talk. Your *pique-assiette*, as Lever has aptly yclept the professional dinner-table jester, is very agreeable over the turtle soup and the trout à la Chambord; but as a continual companion he may be almost as tiresome as the bore of whom he relieves your dinner.

I prayed her to be quiet a little, and turned my attention to Beltran.

He was reading through several letters that Gladys had given him.

He looked at home there, stretched on the low long chair beside the fire, with that exquisite woman's face opposite him. He was not in the least altered; only I thought that his mouth had not quite so sarcastic a curl as of yore, and that his eyes had a very gentle and almost sad look in them that was new to their languor and coldness.

"You need not answer those at all," he said, laying three of the letters aside. "To these two dinner invitations send a brief refusal. To this manager, answer him that you have no intention to enter into any other engagements. For these fellows who want to send you ms. plays, silence will show them that we don't want their wares."

"I would rather let them send their plays, and look at them," she said pleadingly, as though she were not much used to place her wish in opposition to his.

"Why? They are certain to be trash."

"Most likely. Only—you know, some one among these authors may be a poor boy, breaking his heart over his writings as *he* did. They are all unknown names, and it will not be much trouble to look through them; and there may be some touch of talent, some glow of genius, in one or other of them, that will die out altogether if treated always with silence."

He smiled.

"Well, let them come if you like, though I fear they will hardly be worth the paper they are written on; and their verse will be emphatically 'blank' as regards wit, grammar, meaning, or measure. As for these other two letters—have you read them?"

"No. They seemed—flattery and folly. You told me once it was best not to read letters that commenced in that strain, and so I never go further than the beginning—now."

He looked content, but not surprised.

"I think you are right," he said simply. "Just read the signatures, however, and send them back whence they came —without any comment. They *will* write these things to you —there is no help for it."

"I suppose they admire me?" said Gladys thoughtfully, "or they think it is the fashion to say so."

He laughed; his old, curt, contemptuous laugh.

"Of course they admire you. There is no doubt about that. What a child you are still! Is there anything else?"

"Only this note from Lord Dammerell. He sent it up quite early with a wonderful little coffer, that, you see, he says belonged to the great Catherine. It was a beautiful thing; malachite crusted with opals, and the lock and hinges of gold. I wrote him my thanks, and begged to return it. His messenger took it away."

She spoke quite indifferently, as of an every-day uncon- sidered trifle; but his face darkened as he took the note.

"Cis Dammerell!" he muttered; "I introduced him to you myself."

He said no more; but he tore the note into many little pieces, very slowly, and as if the action expressed anger that he did not put into words.

"I remember that coffer—at Christie's," he said, after a pause. "Dammerell will be slow to forgive you; he never had a rebuff before."

"You said last night you were quite happy?" he asked her a few moments later abruptly. "Are you very sure that is true?"

She looked up with surprise; her wondering smiling eyes answering before her words.

"True! Indeed it is true! I am so happy that I feel sometimes that I must be dreaming of this marvellous life. You see, it is still wonderful to me. All my childhood was so uneventful; we had so much sorrow in our pleasantest days; we had always the woe and care of such anxious needs; it was always so still there, and so simple, and so plain, just like one of those peaceful households that we read of in the old Puritan days; that you, who have had the world with you always, cannot understand how the colour and movement and change and beauty of this existence you have given me, seem to me half miraculous still. In the old time, when Harold and I used to walk at evening under the orchard trees, and talk to one another of all our fancies and our dreams, we used to picture just such a future as you have made my present. I have only one sorrow, only one—that I should have it all, and he never have enjoyed one hour of it! It seems so like avarice, selfishness, sin! And to think he cannot even know—"

She paused, with a quiver in the rich eloquent sweetness of her voice, which told me that her brother was unforgotten.

"You ask me that question often now," she said, after a little while. "Why do you doubt, how can you doubt that I am happy? Think how much I have, how much I enjoy; and what a desolate, friendless, hopeless child I was when I knew you first."

Beltran flung the torn fragments of the note into the fire.

"I hardly know why I asked you. Only—I cannot do exactly as I would for you. You should not have such letters as these if I could prevent it; but it is difficult, without doing you more harm than good."

"They do not hurt me; and they go—there," she answered him with a pretty half-haughty gesture of her hand toward the flames. "I remember your warning me before you let me come to the stage, that in an actress's career, annoyances, humiliations, even insults were inevitable; because, her art being a public one, the world always deemed her life a public plaything too: and I told you what I thought then; that though she might be annoyed, she need neither be humiliated nor insulted, unless she chose to merit such abasement. I am an actress now, and yet I think so still."

"You are but a child now, and therefore you think so still."

"But is it not so? Humiliation is a guest that only comes to those who have made ready his resting-place and will give him a fair welcome. My father used to say to me, 'Child, when you grow to womanhood, whether you be rich or poor, gentle or simple, as the balance of your life may turn for or against you, remember always this one thing—that no one can disgrace you save yourself. Dishonour is like the Aaron's Beard in the hedge-rows, it can only poison if it be plucked.' They call the belladonna Aaron's Beard in the country, you know; and it is true that the cattle, simple as they are, are never harmed by it; just because, though it is always in their path, they never stop and taste it. I think it may just be so with us; with any sort of evil."

She spoke with all the mingled poetry and simplicity, all the tender thoughtful seriousness that I had heard in her when she had told her story to the dancer Nellie. She was a lovely woman now; sitting there on her own hearth, clad in velvet and in lace, and conscious of celebrity and of victory in her career; but there was the same nature in her as in the days when she had gone, a famished, desolate, houseless child, to the little garret in Westminster; and the same accent was in her voice, the same accent of mingled pride and innocence, of strength and trustfulness.

Beltran listened, with a certain trouble in his gray, calm, weary eyes. Something in the words touched him, I think; for he got up and began to tease the bullfinch on its perch, and to criticise the hanging of some cabinet pictures.

"You have put the Frère and the Tadema together," he said, going up to them. "For heaven's sake, don't do that! Can't you see how they harm one another? The stately elegance and ceremonial of the Roman patrician life beside the little Bréton interior, with two cottage-children at play with some faggots of gorse! Look how they hurt each other, and make each other look, respectively, coldly artificial and insignificantly homely! Pictures, like beauties, kill each other; I am afraid no sort of skill in the hanging of galleries will alter the fact, that the exhibition of many paintings amounts virtually to their extinction. We are getting too many, even into this little room."

And they altered the place of the Frère and the Tadema, and talked of art, to which I did not care to listen. The thoughts of art made my heart ache; it brought to my memory the low, sunny, wooden chamber at the Silver Stag, with the white fruit-blossoms swaying at the casements, and the long shadows asleep upon the floor, where the Faustine had taken her birth from that prophetic passion which is at once the inspiration and the destruction of human genius—a flame which consumes even while it illumines and conceives.

"Can you tell what she is to him, my dear?" grinned Fanfreluche.

I admitted that I could not.

"Well, ask Patch; see if he can tell," she responded. "One isn't fond of intercourse with common dogs; but still when one can get anything out of them—How civil my Lord A. and the Hon. B. and Sir C. C. can be to a low brute on the race-course, when they want to get at any straight tip, or be on for a dark thing! I don't see why we need be more particular; and we have no class so low as their bookmakers, touters, and nobblers. A dog may be unpolished; he may gnaw a bone on the hearth-rug; he may go wild after a herring-trail; he may carry his flag badly; he may demean himself to eat tripe; he may whine instead of bite when he's hurt; he may do many things which show him an under-bred one; but he is never a

Snob, or a Cad, or a Rough, as I said just now; and, thank heaven, he's never a Blackleg!"

"Is it under-bred to whine when one is hurt?" I asked, conscious that, despite my aristocracy of descent, I sinned in this particular.

"Very, my dear," averred Fanfreluche; "when you are hit, *bite*—bite deep, and bite often. All success lies in the teeth; I told you that long ago."

"But if we bite, we are chained, or, still worse, we are killed."

Fanfreluche grinned.

"There was once a dog, my dear, that was hit by three men, one after another, as they went by him where he lay in the sun; and in return he bit them—deep—and they let him alone then, and ever after sought to propitiate him. Well, the first he bit in the arm, where there was a brand for deserting; and the second he bit in the throat, where there was a hideous mole; and the third he bit in the shoulder, where there was the mark of a secret camorra. Now, not one of these three durst speak of the wounds in places they all wished to hide; and when ever afterwards they passed the dog, they gave him fair words, and sweet bones, and a wide berth. It is the dogs, and the satirists, and the libellers, and the statesmen who know how to bite like that—in the weak part—that get let alone, and respected, and fed on the fat of the land."

At that moment, there entered the drawing-room Derry Denzil and Florance Fane of the Guards; two or three other men followed in a little time—men of similar rank, who had come to town, I suppose, for the sake of their clubs, in the frost which made the "grass countries" untenable at that moment. By the way, the other day, this autumn, I heard a woman whose dinners enjoy an excellent reputation ask an ex-Coldstreamer, famous with Tailby and Pytchley, when he would come to dine with her in the winter, which she was about to pass at her town quarters. "I'll come *the first frost*," said he, and she felt no offence; she understood thoroughly that herself and her *menu* played second to the "little red rover," and would be relegated if no frost came till the April days of budding chestnuts, and spring chickens, and new operas.

These men were all pleasant companions, as your thorough-bred man of the world almost always is, with his lazy sarcasms and his good-natured ironies, and his acquaintance with all the fresh mischief afloat, and his facile touches of art-knowledge and political knowledge, and his racy history now and then of some field-sport which he loves; in the telling of which all his pococurantism fades away, and all his restless recklessness gleams for a moment on the surface of his half-amused, half-weary discontent.

Such were these now; the fire burned brightly behind the broad banner-screens; the light played prettily about the delicate colours of the room; the dainty five-o'clock tea came, with sodas and seltzers; there were pleasant talk, airy nonsense, good-humoured disputes, melodious laughter.

It was with difficulty that I could bring myself to believe that I was not in one of those regal country-houses where, in the frosty weather, the men had gathered at the tea-hour in library or morning-room round some fair titled châtelaine.

"She is very much in society, it would seem?" I murmured to Fanfreluche.

"She is not in society at all, my dear," averred that dic-tatress. "Ask the Countess of Ben Nevis, who has had *liai-sons* with every handsome *lion* out; or Lady Charles Whyte, who has her cottage in the Forest, to carry on her intrigues with the Guards; or Mrs. Vereker, who goes to Paris with Hailes Haynes the tenor, and is none the worse for the escapade, because her own people never have dropped her; ask them if they'd know Gladys Gerant the actress—their outraged virtue would be aghast!"

"Does she know no women, then?"

"None, my dear. He wouldn't let her know the bad ones; and the good ones—or the pseudo-good—wouldn't know her."

"How shameful! how sad!"

"Not a bit. As for the sadness, I don't think myself that the British matron, whether heavy or frisky, is any such very great loss; and the British maiden, in her day of slang and salmon-fishing, of 'big coups' and 'awful yawners,' certainly isn't. As for the shamefulness, that's nonsense. Every pleasure has its penalty. If a woman be celebrated, the world always thinks she must be wicked. If she's wise, she laughs. It is the bitter that you must take with the sweet, as you get the sorrel flavour with the softness of the cream, in your soup à la Bonne Femme. But the cream would clog without it, and the combination is piquant."

"Only to jaded palates," I retorted, for I have often tasted the Bonne Femme, and detest it.

By the way, what exquisite irony lies in some of your kitchen nomenclature!

"Perhaps not," assented Fanfreluche, forgetting for once to disagree. "But in this case a very choice hand prepares her portion, and the cream of it is made so sweet, that I don't think she's even found out yet that the sorrel-leaves lie at the bottom."

And she left me to digest this dark saying as best I might, while she followed her master and the other men out of the drawing-room, and out of the house, as the little timepiece chimed the sixth hour.

At eight the young actress went to her art and her public. I strove to accompany her, but was not permitted.

Left to myself, I wandered through the various rooms to dissipate my ennui, and also to search for Patch.

There was a little chamber, down a few steps, into which I peeped; it was cosy and warm, but simply furnished; there on the hearth I saw a small, broken-haired, mongrel dog, with a white spot over one eye, which had doubtless gained him his name.

He was a little, shabby, wiry, good-natured-looking creature, and I made acquaintance with him—a little arrogantly, I fear; for, with the first glimpse of the blue-ribbon of revived aristocracy round my neck, I had consigned to oblivion the remembrance that I had ever danced for gain in the streets, and walked on my hind legs to beg for a copper coin.

"Yes, I am Patch," he said. A little, straightforward, simple dog, evidently in nowise ashamed of his humble aspect and station.

Indeed, you never see any kind of base or petty pride amongst us: we will guard a knife-grinder's barrow, or sit beside a tinker's wayside work, with perfect loyalty and content, if grinder or tinker be our friend. Not so you. I have noticed in the best of you a certain failure in these respects.

In the old Oxford days, Bertram Byng, your young rough north-country comrade at Balliol, ground fine, with the wheel of his high intellect, the somewhat blunt edge of your own intelligence, in many an hour by Isis. And in that sad dreary winter at Nice, when you had just lost the woman you loved, and could not find in écarté the whole end and aim of existence, as the apostles thereof said you should, that poor, witty, dubious, dark-historied Ina Raby amused you immeasurably, and bore with you patiently, and served you in many ways, and gave you many wrinkles for the *quatre à* and *la belle*.

But when Bertram comes up now, rough and shabby, from his Devonian curacy, poor exceedingly, and with those old tendencies to roll Greek out so fearfully loud, and to heed not how many days' dust lie on his boots and his coat, only more intensely developed, you don't take him to the Athenæum or the Guards' Club for dinner; you dine him alone in your rooms, and tell your man "Not at home." So, too, when Ina Raby comes to you, and men drop their eyes and say, "What, *that* fellow! thought he was dead years ago, you know, &c."—you make excuses for not riding at noon, and back out of taking him to Hurlingham, though you offer warmly to take him to Sydenham; and you continue to pass most of your time with your schooner where she lies in the Thames, and where Demi-monde and Bohemia can cruise with you—a hint which poor Ina, having been a gentleman

in his day, quickly takes, and so pleads business in Paris,
and goes back to the old weary life of whist and winter cities,
of écarté and exile, of piquet and poverty, with a pang the
more, maybe, in his heart.

It is thus with you. Whereas we—well, I will tell you a
story.

Once at a great house in the west I saw a gathering on
the young lord's coming of age. There were half the highest
people in England there; and a little while before the tenantry
went to their banquet in the marquees, the boy-peer and his
guests were all out on the terraces and the lawns. With him
was a very noble deer-hound, whom he had owned for four
years.

Suddenly the hound, Red Comyn, left his titled master,
and plunged head-foremost through the patrician crowd, and
threw himself in wild raptures on to a poor, miserable, tattered, travelling cobbler, who had dared to creep in through
the open gates and the happy crowds, hoping for a broken
crust. Red Comyn pounced on him, and caressed him, and
laid massive paws upon his shoulders, and gave him maddest
welcome—this poor hungry man, in the midst of that aristocratic festival.

The cobbler could scarcely speak awhile; but when he
got his breath, his arms were round the hound, and his eyes
were wet with tears.

"Please pardon him, my lord," he said, all in a quiver
and a tremble. "He was mine once, from the time he was
pupped for a whole two year; and he loved me, poor soul,
and he ha'n't forgot. He don't know no better, my lord—
he's only a dog."

No; he didn't know any better than to remember, and be
faithful, and to recognise a friend, no matter in what woe or
want. Ah, indeed, we are far behind you!

For the credit of "the order," it may be added, that Red
Comyn and the cobbler have parted no more, but dwell together still upon that young lord's lands.

10*

"I am Patch," said this little cross-bred fellow, "and I belong to Margett Llansaint."

"And who is Margett Llansaint?"

Patch with a glance showed me an old woman asleep by the fire.

"She is my mistress. She is Welsh."

"And what does she do here?"

"She is here by Lord Beltran's wish. She was house-keeper to two generations of his family. They gave her an annuity and a little cottage on the Island."

"It was where he took Gladys?"

"I don't know exactly what you mean. One summer Gladys Gerant came to us with a blue-eyed girl called Nellie, who did not remain very long. It was by Lord Beltran's desire; and he visited her twice or thrice himself, not often. She was in infinite woe because of the death of her brother. She did not gain health or strength at all till the spring came round."

"And he kept her there at his cost?"

"I cannot say. Margett was well paid for her; but I think it came from some moneys that some book of her brother's had brought. So, at least, I know that our lord told her. She was with us all the summer. Our cottage is so quiet and so fragrant, with the sea just seen through the great sweetbrier hedges, and the trees of dog-roses and myrtles. She used to dream all her days away by the sea. It seemed to bewitch her; she would gaze at it for hours."

"Did he come often?"

"No, very seldom. But I think she measured time by his coming only. With the winter we moved near London, to a little quiet place in Esher. I believe still by his direction. Here she had teachers and masters of divers kinds. And she studied hard, and long into the nights. Her eyes grew brilliant; her loveliness increased; her whole soul seemed filled with some great ambition. Then Lord Beltran came oftener, and at the close of the time brought two or three others with

him, and I heard them talk of some eminence to which she
would rise. One night in the late autumn she went away for
several hours, and I suppose it was to this theatre, for ever
since I have heard that she had become a great actress; I am
not sure what that is, I do not understand much that they
say. With the turn of the year we came to this pretty house;
we have been here twelve months. I believe Lord Beltran
desires Margett to be with her; but for me—I shall be very
glad to go back to the Cottage."

"And what is he to Gladys?"

Patch looked at me in honest surprise.

"What do you mean? I don't know indeed.   Her friend
of course, for he is very good to her."

I felt abashed at my own thoughts.   But this is the worst
of seeing the world, that you see so much evil that you suspect
it everywhere.

"You cannot tell me any more, then?" I asked.

"Anything more? I don't know what you mean. I do
not like exactly what I do see. This Gladys was a woe-begone, white-faced child when she came down to the Island;
and she used to sit staring at the sea, as I say, with her great
melancholy eyes; and she was only a poor yeoman's daughter;
I have heard her tell Margett so, again and again; and now
she is made a great lady of, though she is no one's wife; and
she has all this grandeur about her, and she is caressed, and
flattered, and decked with velvet and silks and laces. I do
not like it—though I grant, when she was in the Island, she
was always prettily willing to serve Margett with tending the
garden, or the fowls, or anything that chanced; and now,
though she is cockered up like this, she is always gentle-
spoken and kindly of thought—"

"But why do you not like it?" I urged.

"It seems so absurd, and—I am not quite sure what an
actress is, but I think it is something wicked—"

"O no—not always; and she is a genius, they say."

"A genius? You must mistake. I have always heard
that a genius is something that they beat to death first with

sticks and stones, and set up on a great rock to worship afterwards.   Now they make her very happy whilst she is alive.
She cannot possibly be a genius."

"You are sure she is happy?"

"She would be crazed indeed if she were not," said Patch
with a little indignation. "A girl like that, who came starved
and half-dying, to be set up here like a queen, with lords and
gentlemen around her—of course she is happy, though I know
she grieves at times still for her lost people and Bronze."

"Ah, Bronze, dear Bronze!" I cried. "Where is he?"

"Bronze is dead."

Although I had felt so certain of the answer I should receive, that, coward-like, I had shrunk from asking it, the certainty struck me with a sharp and sudden pang.

"Dead!" I echoed stupidly. "Dead! Of old age?—of
illness?"

"Of neither.   The sea killed him."

I begged him to tell me all; and he told it, in a quaint,
poetic, simple fashion which had a sound in it that brought
to me the memory of old Trust.

"The girl Gladys came to us in Midsummer, and Bronze
came with her, and the dancer too," commenced the little sea-
bred dog. "The dancer did not tarry long; she was a saucy
feckless creature it was easy to see, with ribbons and roses
and all manner of follies about her; but she was soft of voice
and of foot, and she seemed quite shy, as one might say, with
Gladys, and to have taken quite a strange sort of love for her.
I call it strange, because I was told that they had never met
until a day or so before they were thus sent to us. The little
dancer was loth to leave Gladys, and she was bidden to stay
whilst she pleased; but the silence about and the sight of the
sea seemed to daunt her and fright her;—I cannot tell how.
'If I stayed long enow here,' I heard her mutter one day,
'it would kill me for the business. I should think, and think,
and think till every bit of heart for my work would go out of
me like; all the jigging, and the singing, and the punning,
and the—the rest of it, would seem such pitiful stuff, and so

foolish and vile; and where, I wonder, should me and granny
be then?' I remember her words, though I only half-guessed
what she meant. They let her do as she would, and she went
away after a week. It was sorrowful to see how she clung to
Gladys and sobbed—and Gladys so still and hopeless and
silent, like a frozen creature, as she had been, they said,
since the news of the death of her brother. 'I hope and pray
you'll never reproach me, dear?' Nellie cried over and over
again. 'I hope and pray you'll never reproach me!' I do
not think Gladys knew what she said: she seemed to hear and
notice nothing in those days. As for me, I could not tell the
meaning of the words. I suppose the dancing-girl must have
done her some wrong?"

I said nothing: to me such fear, such misgiving, seemed
intelligible enough. I knew that Nellie had sought for her a
succour that the world would have said was certain to be such
succour alone as the kite gives the wood-dove with talon and
beak. I doubted not that her mind had misgiven her for the
issue of her work many and many a time since the day that
she had rejected the old Roman scarabæi.

"Well, she went from us," resumed the little quaint,
bigoted narrator, "and Margett Llansaint was glad when she
was gone. All Margett's reverence for her master could not
make her see that it was fitting to have under her roof a girl
that wore mock roses in her hat, and mock laces on her bodice,
and mock gems on her fingers, and who showed herself in a
boy's dress nightly to the public, by her own confession.

"Gladys was different, you know, with that noble old-
world look about her; and that great grief that made her so
still and lifeless; and that grave simple fashion of her speech
which had a dignity in it too. And, besides, she was an innocent child, and had scarce been off the borders of her
father's farm-lands. So the dancer went her ways, but
Gladys and Bronze abided with us. It was Margett's lord's
will, as I say; and she strove her best to make them happy.
And despair is not natural to youth, you know: through the
long autumn and winter Gladys was ill, and very restless and

very sad, and seemed to know no pleasure save in watching the sea in its wrath; but when the spring came, and the white sails gleamed in the distance, and the almond trees put forth their bloom, and the little blue gentian blossomed in the clefts of the rocks, and the fisher children came out to play on the sands, the young life in her seemed to wake, and to take interest in the life around her. She was always beside the sea—morn, noon, and eve, and Bronze never left her side. The fisher-people all came to know her, and to care for her very much. The rudest amongst them grew to think it honour to take her out upon the waters, and would hang an old sail upon a spar to shield her from the sun, and deck their boat as gaily as they could with seaweeds and with spear-grass. Margett used to murmur to herself that it was a purposeless life for one who would have to find her own support in time to come; and once she plucked up heart of grace and dared to write so much—humbly—to Lord Beltran. And he wrote back only one line—'Let her please herself; and don't trouble me.' Was it not a heartless answer? I do not think he cared anything for her—in those days. He had placed her with us, and thought of her no more; as he would have thought no more of a spaniel placed with a keeper.

"Well, through all the summer it was the same. She spent well-nigh all her time drifting on the waters, or reading and thinking beside the sea. Our home was a little quiet chine, with no harbour or landing-place of any kind; where there was only a cluster of fishermen's cottages; and where no strange ships or strange people ever came. A yacht, indeed, would scud past now and then, but very seldom; for you know they go but little on the southern side. She was never disturbed or molested: and in the sea-air, and the southerly sun, and the salt-bitten winds she seemed to get beauty so suddenly; such a new vivid sea-born beauty, that gave such a glow to her hair, such depth to her eyes, such warmth to her lips; and I think she was happy—despite her sorrow and her loneliness—happy in her freedom, and in her youth, and in her dreams.

"And she did dream: I used to see that in her eyes when she would sit at night by the lattice of her little room where the moonlight would stream, bright as any lamp, upon the pages of her book; and through the open casement, across the brier-rose hedge, and through the boughs of the almonds, she would see the great silvered width of the sea, the sea that her brother had longed for in thirst and weariness, and had never in life beheld, they say.

"Well, all this time Bronze would never leave her. He was at her feet in the boats, at her side in the woods and on the shore, against her door by night, and continually within her shadow in the day.

"And Gladys clung to him beyond everything. 'You see he is all I have left, and he, too, knew *them*,' she would say to Margett. I suppose she meant her dead people. Bronze had never left her,—not an hour, I think, save twice in the rough weather time: once when he went to seek for some men lost on the downs above in a snow-drift; and once, on a wild night, when a cobble (smuggling a brandy keg or two, in truth) was wrecked on a rock hard by, and he swam to it, and brought safe to land the fisherman's two-year-old child, who had been asleep in its cot when father, and mother, and child, and nets and tackle, and kegs and all, had been tumbled out into the sea. For these two deeds the people about, of course, thought great things of Bronze, and always brought him pieces of their freshest fish and fattest bacon; and he generally gave it almost all away, letting all the small, famished, quarrelsome, unhappy dogs of the village come about him, and share it at pleasure.*

"Well, one summer day, in the forenoon, Gladys and Bronze were out on the shore, and I was with them. It was far in the afternoon, a splendid day, with a blue sea running calm yet high. The wind was fresh and the tide was down. We wandered somewhat far out upon the beach. The great rocks, that the water always hid when it was high, were so

* I have also seen a dog do this—sitting by in generous content whilst his lean brethren made feast on his goods.—Ed.

cool and smooth and brown; and the gray sand between them
had been all waved and marked in such pretty fashion by
the waves; and all about there were such clear, bright, shallow
pools, filled with the curling, sweet-smelling seaweeds, and
the many-coloured stars of the sea-anemones; and then beyond,
on what was always the land, the great wall of cliff, streaked
with many hues, and the woods above, and the little cottages
underneath, covered with fuschia and honeysuckle.

"We wandered far over the beach, so far that we almost
reached the lip of the last lazy wave as the sea went out on
its southward way; and we spent some time down there on
the low sands. Gladys had with her some books and a great
osier kreel that she used sometimes to cast over her shoulder
as the fishwomen cast theirs, and which she in her ramble
nearly filled with all kinds of sea-ribbons, and grasses, and
shells, and pebbles, and of the moist brown seaweed, for
which Margett had some household use. She used to look
very pretty there, with her garments tucked away to leave
her delicate limbs free for motion; and her head bare to the
sun; and the basket slung upon her back, filled with the
trailing algæ; and her cheeks warm and her hands wet with
the breath and the touch of the sea. She is a greater lady
now, of course, in her velvets and lace; but, to my taste, she
was lovelier then. I do not know if Lord Beltran ever thinks
so. I should suppose he would; he is a man of taste, they
say. He saw her so? Yes, once or twice, when he came
round to that part of the coast in a schooner he has for his
use. And, if I remember, he sketched her so—once.

"Well, this noontide was very warm, and when she had
filled the kreel she sat upon a rock to read. As she did so a
tiny skiff, with one tiny white sail, was putting off from land,
or at least from as near land as the shallow water would let it
approach. Catching sight of her, the sailor with it waded
back and came to her. He was a good simple fellow who
lived in one of the huts of the beach, and worked sometimes
with colliers, sometimes with fishing-smacks. He was full of
trouble now, and poured his sorrow out to her. It seemed

that he had been on shore seeking her. His wife, who was
on board a fishing-smack that lay off the land, some mile or
so westward, down the coast, was very ill—dying, he feared
—and had begged of him, if he could find Gladys, to entreat
of her to go and speak to her. He had been compelled to
come to the village for bread, and tackle, and other things he
needed; and the doctor he could nowhere find. This woman
was a delicate, pretty, good-living creature, and Gladys had
won her heart with many little tender services in the drear
winter-time gone by. It was a common thing with her to
visit the people on board their vessels, for she loved nothing
so well as to sail to and fro on the sea; and they had a super-
stitious belief in her because she was so different to themselves.

"She told him she would come at once, and laid the
wicker kreel, and the books, and a little rough waterproof
cloak, upon the brown boulder on which she had been just
about to make her seat, and on which Bronze and I were lying.
'Come!' she called to Bronze; but the sailor stopped her. 'I
durßn't take him, miss, not for our lives!' he said earnestly.
'He's the weight of a man; and the boat's so over-crowded
now with things as I've had to get in the Chine, that you're
to the full as much as ever I dare carry.'

"'I cannot leave him!' she answered, shrinking back;
and indeed she never had left him. He was always with her,
whether on sea or land, and they clung passionately to one
another.

"'I can go and come for you again, miss,' said the fisherman ruefully; 'but it will take a goodish bit of time—and
Jenny so bad, and nobody but the boy with her, and the doctor
not to the fore neither. Sure the dog'll wait for you here,
miss, safe enow. Not as I'd be pressing you.'

"But he did press her,—pressed her sorely.

"It was very 'reluctantly that she was induced to leave
Bronze there. Nothing save the knowledge of the value and
the misery of each fleeting minute to the sick woman would
ever have persuaded her. As it was, she threw her arms

about him and kissed him on the forehead; then pointed to the kreel of shells and seaweed on the red smooth piece of rock.

"'Take care of them, dear Bronze,' she murmured; 'and wait till I come back. Wait here.'

"She did not mean to command; she only meant to console him by the appointment of some service.

"Bronze looked in her face with eyes of woe and longing; but he made no moan nor sound, but only stretched himself beside the kreel on guard. I am always glad to think that as she went she turned, and kissed him once again.

"The boat flew fast over the water. When boats leave you, and drag your heart with them, they always go like that; and when they come, and your heart darts out to meet them, then they are so slow!

"The boat flew like a seagull, the sun bright upon her sail. Bronze, left upon the rock, lifted his head and gave one long low wail. It echoed woefully and terribly over the wide quiet waters. They gave back no answer,—not even the poor answer that lies in echo.

"It was very still there. Nothing was in sight except that single little sail shining against the light, and flying—flying —flying.

"Now and then you could hear a clock striking in the distant village, the faint crow of a cock, the far-off voices of children calling to one another.

"But where we were, there was quite silence, for the things of the sea are so noiseless. The little sea-mouse stole athwart a pool; the gray sea-crabs passed like a little army; the tiny sea creatures that dwelt in rosy shells thrust their delicate heads from their houses, to peep and wonder at the sun. But all was noiseless. How dared they make a sound, when that great sea, that was at once their life and death, was present with its never-ceasing 'Hush!'

"Bronze never moved, and his eyes never turned from the little boat that went and left him there—the little boat that fast became merely a flash and speck of white against the azure air, no bigger than the breadth of a sea-gull's wings.

"An hour drifted by. The church-clock on the cliffs had struck four times; a deep-toned, weary bell, that tolled for every quarter, and must often have been heard, at dead of night, by dying men, drowning unshriven and unhouselled.

"Suddenly the sand about us, so fawn-hued, smooth, and beautifully ribbed, grew moist, and glistened with a gleam of water, like eyes that fill with tears.

"Bronze never saw: he only watched the boat. A little later the water gushed above the sand, and gathering in a frail rippling edge of foam, rolled up and broke upon the rock.

"And still he never saw; for still he watched the boat.

"Awhile, and the water grew in volume, and filled the mouse's pool till it brimmed over, and bathed the dull grasses till they glowed like flowers; and drew the sea-crabs and the tiny dwellers of the shells back once more into its wondrous living light.

"And all around the fresh tide rose, silently thus about the rocks and stones; gliding and glancing in all the channels of the shore, until the sands were covered, and the grasses gathered in, and all the creeping, hueless things were lost within its space; and in the stead of them, and of the bronzed palm-leaves of weed, and of the great brown boulders gleaming in the sun, there was but one vast lagoon of shadowless bright water everywhere.

"And still he never saw; for still he watched the boat.

"I roused him, and he looked; only one fleeting look. His eyes went back to the gleam of the distant sail.

"By this time the tide, rolling swiftly in before a strong sou'-wester, had risen midway against the rock on which we had been left, and was breaking froth and foam upon the rock's worn side. For this rock alone withstood the passage of the sea: there was naught else but this to break the even width of water. All other things save this had been subdued and reapen.

"And the sea so long has reaped side by side with the reaper Death, that it reaps full sure and true, and will leave nothing ungarnered.

"'Will you die there?' I cried to him.

"'If so it be willed,' he made answer.

"'Are you mad? See the waters!'

"'I see them.'

"'See them! and know they are death?'

"'I know they are death.'

"'But you could swim to the shore?'

"'Yes.'

"'Then why do you tarry here?'

"'I must tarry till she comes.'

"'Though it is death?'

"'Though it is death.'

"'But that is madness!'

"'It is duty.'

"'To die, choked by the sea, is duty?'

"'To die, any how, at one's post.'

"'But she had forgotten.'

"'That may be. But she bade me wait.'

"'Then you will wait for your death!'

"'I must wait for whatever chances.'

"By this, the sea had risen within the height of the rock by the breadth of a man's two fingers. It was all deep water around; and the water glowed a strange emerald green, like the green in a lizard or snake. The shore, that had looked so near, now seemed so far, far off; and the woods were hidden in mist, and the cottages were all blurred with the brown of the cliff, and there came no sound of any sort from the land —no distant bell, no farm-bird's call, no echo of children's voices. There was only one sound at all; and that was the low, soft, ceaseless murmuring of the tide as it glided inward.

"I entreated him again.

"Again the same answer returned.

"The waters rose till they touched the crest of the rock; but still he never moved. Stretched out upon the stone,

guarding the things of her trust, and with his eyes fastened
on the sail which rose against the light, he waited thus—for
death.

"I urged no more, but struck off towards land. I was
light, and a strong swimmer. I had been tossed on those
waves from my birth. Buffeted, fatigued, blind with the salt
sea spray, drenched with the weight of the water, I struggled
across that calm dread width of glassy coldness, and breathless reached the land.

"By signs and cries I made them wot that something
needed them at sea. They began to get ready a little boat,
bringing it down from its wooden rest on high dry ground
beneath the cliff. Whilst they pushed and dragged through
the deep-furrowed sand I gazed seaward. The shore was
raised; I could see straight athwart the waters. They now
were level with the rock; and yet he had never moved.

"The little skiff had passed round the bend of a bluff;
and was out of his sight and ours.

"The boat was pushed into the surf; they threw me in.
They could see nothing, and trusted to my guidance.

"I had skill enough to make them discover whither it was
I wanted them to go. Then, looking in their eagerness
whither my eyes went, they saw him on the rock, and with a
sudden exercise of passionate vigour, bent to their oars and
sent the boat against the hard opposing force of the resisting
tide. For they perceived that, from some cause, he was
motionless there, and could not use his strength; and they
knew that it would be shame to their manhood if, within
sight of their land, the creature who had succoured their
brethren in the snow, and saved the two-year child from the
storm, should perish before their sight on a calm and un-
fretted sea and in a full noon sun.

"It was but a furlong to that rock; it was but the breadth
of the beach, that at low water stretched uncovered; and yet
how slowly the boat sped, with the ruthless tide sweeping it
back as fast as the oars bore it forward!

"So near we seemed to him that one would have thought

a stone flung from us through the air would have lit far
beyond him; and yet the space was enough, more than
enough, to bar us from him, filled as it was with the strong
adverse pressure of those low, swift, in-rushing waves.

"The waters leaped above the summit of the rock, and
for a moment covered him. A great shout went up from the
rowers beside me. They strained in every nerve to reach him;
and the roll of a fresh swell of water lifted the boat farther
than their uttermost effort could achieve, but lifted her backward, backward to the land.

"When the waters touched him he arose slowly, and stood
at bay like a stag upon a headland, when the hounds rage
behind, and in front yawns the fathomless lake.

"He stood so that he still guarded the things of his trust;
and his eyes were still turned seaward, watching for the
vanished sail.

"Once again the men, with a loud cry to him of courage
and help, strained at their oars, and drove themselves a
yard's breadth farther out. And once again the tide, with a
rush of surf and shingle, swept the boat back, and seemed to
bear her to the land as lightly as though she were a leaf with
which a wind was playing.

"'The waters covered the surface of the rock. It sank
from sight. The foam was white about his feet, and still he
stood there—upon guard. Everywhere there was the brilliancy of noontide sun; everywhere there was the beaming
calmness of the sea, that spread out, far and wide, in one
vast sheet of light; from the wooded line of the shore there
echoed the distant gaiety of a woman's laugh. A breeze,
softly stirring through the warm air, brought with it from the
land the scent of myrtle thickets and wild flowers. How
horrible they were — the light, the calm, the mirth, the
summer fragrance!

"For one moment he stood there erect; his dark form
sculptured, lion-like, against the warm yellow light of noon;
about his feet the foam.

"Then, all noiselessly, a great, curled, compact wave

surged over him, breaking upon him, sweeping him away.
The water spread out quickly, smooth and gleaming like the
rest. He rose, grasping in his teeth the kreel of weed and
shells.

"He had waited until the last. Driven from the post he
would not of himself forsake, the love of life awoke in him;
he struggled against death.

"Three times he sank, three times he rose. The sea was
now strong, and deep, and swift of pace, rushing madly in;
and he was cumbered with that weight of osier and of weed,
which yet he never yielded, because it had been her trust.
With each yard that the tide bore him forward, by so much
it bore us backward. There was but the length of a spar between us, and yet it was enough!

"He rose for the fourth time, his head above the surf, the
kreel uplifted still, the sun-rays full upon his brown weary
eyes, with all their silent agony and mute appeal. Then the
tide, fuller, wilder, deeper with each wave that rolled, and
washing as it went all things of the shore from their places,
flung against him, as it swept on, a great rough limb of drift-
wood. It struck him as he rose; struck him across the brow.
The wave rushed on; the tide came in; the black wood
floated to the shore; he never rose again.

"And scarcely that span of the length of a spar had parted
us from him when he sank!

"All the day through they searched, and searched with
all the skill of men sea-born and sea-bred. The fisher, whose
little child he had saved in the winter night, would not leave
him to the things of the deep. And at sunset they found
him, floating westward, in the calm water where the rays of
the sun made it golden and warm. He was quite dead; but
in his teeth there still was clenched the osier kreel, washed
empty of its freight.

*   *   *   *   *   *

"She grieved for him?"

"Yes. She was as one mad with grief awhile; crying out

that he was her only friend upon earth; and that it was
through her that death had come to him.

"But human grief passes so swiftly; see—you have heard
her laugh to-day! They buried him there; on the shore
underneath the cliff, where a great wild knot of myrtle grows,
and the honeysuckle blooms all over the sand. And when
Lord Beltran in that autumn came, and heard how he had
died in the fulfilling of a trust, he had a stone shapen and
carved; and set it against the cliff, amongst the leafage and
flowers, high up where the highest winter tide will not come.
And by his will the name of Bronze was cut on it in deep
letters that will not wear out, and on which the sun will strike
with every evening that it shall pass westward above the sea;
and beneath the name he bade three lines be chiselled likewise, and they are these:

'HE CHOSE DEATH RATHER THAN UNFAITHFULNESS.

HE KNEW NO BETTER.

HE WAS A DOG.'"

CHAPTER X.

"Milord, the Hawk."

THREE or four days passed in like manner, and I grew
attuned to the gracious harmonies of pleasure and of riches.
I wore my blue rosette, without too bitterly remembering the
coat of La Pipetta; and I basked in the fireside warmth,
without too poignantly recalling the icy moonlit nights in the
drear Parisian garret. I had the blood of aristocrats in me,
though I had been reared in a rush basket in a cottage; and
to my temper all ease and elegance seemed even as a second
nature. You shall keep the plebeian in a palace a score of
years, and he shall ever wear his purple, and bear his orb, as
though the one were a suit of rags and the other a ball of
lead. But you shall keep the patrician in a hovel a score of
years, and he shall ever wear his hempen shirt and bear his

reaper's sickle, as though the one were a princely robe and the other a knightly sword. *Bon sang ne peut mentir;* and against a throne it will cry out, "Ye who sit there are sots and fools!" and from a beggar's eyes it will say with a challenge, "My fathers once ruled in the land!" It cannot lie; and perhaps it is for that reason that the old blood is now hated, in an age which has exalted lying to a science—the one supreme social science of Success.

I was soon perfectly at home in this pretty *maisonnette;* but I was no nearer to penetration of its mysteries—if mysteries indeed there were. Gladys read her days away; her men friends came and went, the atmosphere was always full of flowers and birds, songs and pleasant voices, all the colours of art, and all the movements of thought. She lived in utter solitude here; but the world came to her on the tongues of those who knew it best; and all that was new, or rare, or welcome, seemed to find its way to her; and, if at night she went to the physical and mental fatigues of the stage, she went also to the brilliancy of victory and to the sustenance of homage.

I could not marvel that she was happy; happy with the vague, untroubled, slumbrous happiness of a dream. Too happy, surely, I thought, for shame to rest with her. I was perplexed; I was troubled; I could scarcely doubt that some wrong there was of necessity somewhere: but yet—when she came to me, and lifted me against her sweet rich lips, and murmured gentle words to me of that night when we had been first in wretchedness and solitude together, I could not disbelieve her innocence. I could not credit that the fair lone child, whom I had seen kneel down in prayer, had grown in this brief time callous and dishonoured.

Besides—the cream was so rich; the cushions were so soft; the cakes were so sweet; the hands that combed my curls were so gentle. I resigned myself to enjoy them, asking not if the source of my good fortune were tainted. It was wrong, I know; very wrong in the creeds of my race. I became almost as selfish as though I were human!

On the fifth night after my arrival I contrived to ensconce myself under the sealskins, and to revisit the Coronet unrepulsed.

I found it, as Fanfreluche had said, far more attractive than ere the rioters had wrought their wild work on it. Looking on the body of the house from the side, I saw that, in every detail, the artistic taste of its lordly lessee had provailed over all considerations of economy. It was indeed a model theatre. The hangings were of amber satin; the panels of the boxes contained charming little landscapes; the private boxes, of which there were many, were like tiny boudoirs, with their mirrors, their lounging chairs, and their lace curtains. The musicians played out of sight; the place of the former orchestra was filled by a moss-covered bank covered with evergreens and flowers. The officials were all good-looking girls, dressed in a pretty costume of blue slashed with silver. Out of the first corridor was a spacious smoking-room, with easy couches and a supply of the evening papers, where men could enjoy their cigars in the *entr'actes* without annoying any woman. All was light, bright, luxurious, fantastic, as befits a place that is the abode of amusement, and depends for success on the compensation which it offers to people for leaving their dinner-tables immediately after the ice.

It was as choice, as artistic, as seductive, as suggestive of every indolent enjoyment as a *bonbonnière* painted by Fragonard and fitted by Siraudin; and all that was fashionable and aristocratic in the town came to it. And yet I heard a man, whom I did not know, say on the staircase to another:

"Charming! perfectly charming! But it can't pay!"

And the other, in whom I recognised Dudley Moore, answered—

"It would pay if Beltran were Farquhar; if Gladys Gerant were Laura Pearl; if the music were from Canterbury Hall instead of the great composers; if the entertainment were witless buffoonery instead of delicate art; if everything were not what it is, in a word, which is the common recipe for the regeneration of all matters!"

"Why say that?" urged his companion. "It was all you describe under the old *régime*, and it was a dead loss also then!"

Dudley Moore took snuff.

"Ah! Our clever lessee has a knack of always falling in love with all his First Actresses. I don't know how any theatre *can* pay under those circumstances."

I had no business on the grand stairs; and I scurried away and took shelter in the dressing-room of Gladys.

It was tiny, as all such rooms in a theatre are; but it was tastefully fitted up with white and rose. No one ever came there, save her maid. She was alone, sitting still and thoughtful. She was dressed for Lady Teazle, and her face looked so youthful and so "flower-like" in its contrast with the powdered coiffure and the magnificent costume of brocade and of satin, with its train of cloth of gold, and the great cross of diamonds which glittered on her throat.

It seemed a strange career for one so young; a strange fate for a child reared in the grave pastoral simplicity of what must have been an almost puritan household. Yet that she was happy in it there could be no doubt; and that it had in no way tainted the proud purity of her nature seemed almost as little to be questioned.

I gazed at her, marvelling greatly, reasoning, as society doubtless reasoned, that a creature of her years, of her utter desolateness, of her absolute pennilessness, could never have come to be seated there, with the homage of all fashionable London hers, with those diamonds on her breast, with those golden robes trailing behind her, with that theatre for her arena, and its owner for her only friend, unless with all these vanities and all these successes she had not also accepted the usual price paid for them—dishonour!

And yet I could not look thus at her without shame for this thought. Despite her beauty, despite her position, despite her luxurious little villa, despite even that matchless rose, diamond cross, gleaming above the beating of her heart, it seemed impious to doubt that the dead boy's sister was one whit less innocent than when she had knelt down in the moonlight to pray for Harold—one whit less nobly proud than when she had repulsed the offered charities of the little dancer. The eyes were dreaming, indeed, looking far away, with the imaginative, poetic gaze of "one who beholds visions;" but there was not in them the look of one who gazes backward at a sin.

Though the diamonds seemed to me like the orbs of a snake—a snake that coils about a woman never to let her free again—yet I could not believe that she, though thus transformed, could be less fit to meet her father's sight than when she had stood beside him to read the Scriptures aloud at evensong, in the old homestead of her birth. Evil might be about her; but surely, I thought, evil had not as yet consumed her.

As she rose and opened her door there came in from the body of the theatre the ringing music of the orchestra, the buzz of the talking audience, the sounds of a rapidly filling house; the scent of some costly hothouse bouquets that had been sent her, and which her maid was bringing in;—I shivered and sickened. In this world—the world of Laura Pearl—was it possible for any woman to hold her honour, to retain her dignity?

At that moment she was called, and passed on to the stage. The piece played that night was the perennial *School for Scandal.*

In such pure comedy and elegant art she was supreme, they said; though her still greater triumphs were in parts of pathos and of power.

Lady Teazle is a rôle which any actress who is graceful and a gentlewoman can play with ease. There are but little light and shade in it; and there is not any kind of passion. But even here there was so much grace in her; all conventional readings were so utterly discarded; there were such charming alternations of playful piquance and of scornful dignity; whilst over the whole was cast the ineffable charm of a youth so seductive, that I no longer wondered at the celebrity with which the town had crowned her.

She was so entirely self-unconscious, too; so utterly negligent of the public that hung on her words: she played as a lovely woman might play for her own pleasure before her mirror, with none standing by; given with all this her personal beauty and her grace of motion, it was no wonder that even Dudley Moore confessed himself for once "satisfied."

"You play that perfectly, my dear," said the great critic, coming behind the scenes.

"Yet you say that they will never come to see anything that is even good," said Gladys, with a smile and a movement of her head backward to the crowded house.

"They will always come to see a pretty woman," returned the censor curtly. "I know too much of human nature ever to have denied *that*. What beautiful diamonds you have! They are new?"

"Lord Beltran lends them to me. They are his family jewels."

"That has luckily not been his habit before with his First Actresses," murmured Dudley Moore, as she passed on to the stage again. "If it had been, he would not have had them to lend now. If this child understand her *droits de largesse* the Beltran diamonds are lost to the house."

I thought that, with all his knowledge of human nature, the great critic did not very much understand Gladys Gerant.

When the comedy was over I found my way to that pretty chamber over which the marble god and dancing girl of Goethe presided. When I entered it was empty; but the chandelier was lighted, and on the table stood some ice, and wines, and fruits. Supper was rarely had here now, except on occasions when its lessee himself entertained after the first representation of a new piece, or on the opening night of the season. But she was accustomed to receive here, for an hour or so after her performance, all personal friends or persons of celebrity. The number of these was kept exclusively and carefully narrowed; and the *cordon* that was drawn around this place was quite as rigid in its way as that before the doors of a great duchess's drawing-room.

I had scarcely been there a moment ere Beltran and Denzil entered together. They had been dining with the Duke of Holyrood. Dudley Moore, Guilliadene, and one or two others followed; chatted of the gossip of the hour; lighted some rose-scented cigars; and drank some of the hissing iced waters.

In a little while she joined them, dressed in that simple black velvet, without jewel or ornament of any sort, except here and there a touch of old point lace, which always became her, I thought, almost better than any other fashion of attire.

The fire burned brightly, whilst its rosy glow beamed on the marble beauty of the god; the scent of the bouquets placed there in glass and china filled the air; the news of the hour passed laughingly from mouth to mouth; now and then Denzil struck out from the piano in the recess some deep full chords of German melody, or some half-gay, half-pathetic cadence of soft Irish song. It was all pleasant, amusing, blameless enough; but I suppose it would have been vain to tell the town that the society gathered round an actress in her supper-room was to the full as refined as, and not a whit more harmful than, the society gathered round a young peeress at her afternoon tea-table.

"'The exception proves the rule,' runs your proverb; but why, I wonder, is it that you always only believe in the rule, and are always utterly sceptical as to the existence of the exception?

"Why are people still amused by Sheridan, but always bored by Shakespeare?" propounded the mighty Editor, as Denzil brought to a close a buffo song of some Neapolitan composer, in which his voice had filled the room with melody.

"Why do people only tolerate Sheridan, and go into ecstasies over burlesques?" said Beltran.

"Because we want to laugh, and not to think," said
Denzil. "Now, to laugh at Sheridan, you must first think
with him."

"That is begging the question," said Dudley Moore. "I
don't want to know what the great mass of fools may do; I
want to know why people of intelligence and taste, who fully
appreciate the riches of Shakespeare when they read him,
are bored—undeniably bored—by him on the stage?"

He turned to Gladys, and she smiled.

"They will come to my Beatrice."

"No answer! They come because you look like a picture;
though they might prefer even your picture if set in Offenbach. What I ask is, why is Shakespeare a drug on the
English stage, ennui to audiences, and perdition to man-
agers?"

"If it be so, I think it is this: the Shakespearian plays
are all so utterly unlike our own life—it is so utterly impossible that men and women could ever have spoken such verse
as that—their words and deeds are so immeasurably removed
from all kindred with the language and the actions of this
present time—that when called from the world of the imagination, and presented visibly on the stage, they weary the
audience where they do not strike it with an irresistible sense
of incongruity and ridicule. It would be the same with any
of the great dramas of antiquity—with those of Euripides or
Sophocles, if we could play them. The more cultured the
mind, the more impatient does it grow of any attempt to
clothe in palpable shape any of the sublime ideals of a great
poet. Besides, surprise and expectation are charms essential
to the drama for all minds. How is it possible for people to
be either excited or surprised by plays that they have been
more or less familiar with ever since they learned to spell?"

"That is partially true," said Dudley Moore. "I am disposed to agree with you, that high culture makes the visible
personation of a poetic ideal both distasteful and vulgar.
High culture needs no aids to its imagination. But why,
then, do the French, the most cultivated people as a whole

of the world, still care so much for their Phèdre and its like?"

"'The French are naturally more declamatory than we are," said Beltran. "Attitude and sublime diction do not strike them with the same sense of unnaturalness that it strikes us. They are always *posing*, in school life, in home life, in public life. Besides, the workmen flock to see Racine, specially when Racine is to be had gratis; but the idle people have much the same preference for Hervé and Offenbach that we have."

"And it is ridiculous to quote the French," averred Denzil, "in any sort of dramatic contrast with us. Though they have not, to my thinking, one poetic drama in their language, except Victor Hugo's, they have excellences of every other kind —in the intellectual, the social, the satirical play, they are unapproachable."

"And then such power of adaptation in their actors!" pursued Beltran. "Such mutations, such ease, such effortless eloquence, such inimitable art! If we had such actors, we might perhaps tempt some English Hugo or Sardou to give his talents to the stage, instead of to the novel or the dinner-table. As it is, no genius or wit will write for our stage, on which he knows but too well that his gentlemen will be re-presented by counter-jumpers, his repartees be given with grins and 'gag,' and his good society be rendered by a *replica* of Margate or Cremorne."

"All this," said the Editor doggedly, "chiefly brings us back to Denzil's first proposition, that most educated people dislike to think, *ergo*, are fools. A curious fact, if true, and not in favour of education."

"I deny your deduction. It may be because we think overmuch—in our science, our profession, our jurisprudence, our intellectual composition, our political career, or whatever be the pursuit which we follow—that we are disinclined to think in a place of mere amusement, after our dinners."

"It would seem, then, that the decline of the drama re-solves itself into a mere question of eating."

"You are very perverse," said Denzil. "What I say is, that the mind is always so highly strained at its work in our day, that it refuses to make any additional effort in its mere relaxations. When you have been thinking all day, with little pause or peace, you do not want to think in the evening, when your mental strain is relaxed. You want light, gaiety, noise, pretty pictures—something that needs no thought whatever."

"And culture, though it have heightened one kind of imagination, has deadened another. And it has also sharpened the sense of ridicule," said Gladys. "In the old time, people wept for Imogen, and loved with Romeo, without any one of the aids to fancy of what we call 'scenic effect.' But now you would only laugh at the most poetic Juliet, if she played as she did of old, with a sign-post behind her that said, 'This is Verona.' And even with all the aids of admirable scenery, how seldom you seem to forget for one moment that you are sitting out a play! How seldom we can beguile you into the sweetest homage to us of all—delusion!"

"I don't think you need say so," said Beltran. "But I admit it is difficult. We are not imaginative—in that way. We are moved more nowadays indirectly—by suggestion, by illusion, by a line in a poem, a meaning in a picture, a gleam of insight in a writer, than we are by the broader and more direct appeals to our fancy of the drama. A generation which has found out that the moon is only a dried-up ball, and the Ultima Thule only a bit of water; that Wallace never lived, and Joan of Arc never died, may be pardoned for not very easily yielding itself to delusions."

"And therefore burlesques on delusions suit us best," said Denzil. "When we feel tickled at hearing Medea bawl that she'll whip her children, or Œdipus smash his tinted spectacles in a passion, we are amused, because, without knowing it, we feel a comical likeness, in such caricatures, with the strong tendency of our own time to dwarf all heroism, and make absurd all dignities."

"That sounds fearfully subtle, Derry," said Beltran; "but

I doubt if audiences like burlesques for any other reason than because they are nonsensical, showy, and full of jingling rhymes and catching music. And why shouldn't they like them? They can't be less intellectual than the old Farce was; and certainly they are much prettier."

"All this," cried Dudley Moore, "does not answer my question, Why does Sheridan keep his ground so much better than Shakespeare?"

"She answered you as to Shakespeare," replied Beltran. "As for Sheridan, he amuses us because his satires suit us so well still, and his characters are our own people disguised in wig and powder. Our society is artificial, passionless, insincere. So is his. He is a mirror in which we see our own faces; it is the costume only that differs."

"But we should not be driven to use a mirror sixty years old, if there were any quicksilver of wit extant wherewith to set up another," said Dudley Moore. "If the English stage be ever again to be worth anything—which I doubt lies not in its destinies—it must be rendered so, not by revivals of *King John* or of *Comus*, but by plays which shall faithfully show, and unscrupulously satirise, modern society. Our society is never represented on the stage. We have steam-engines, fire-engines, police-courts, gin-palaces, cabs and horses, pots and pans, all to the life, inimitably; but Society, *our* Society—that wonderful mass of indifference, intelligence, ennui, energy, licentiousness, decorum, corruption, and conventionality—is utterly unrepresented. On not one single stage do we ever see anything even dimly resembling the life of men and women of the world. Now, this must indicate one of two things: either that the power of satire and of representation is altogether dead, or that it finds in literature the vent that half a century ago it found upon the stage."

"The latter, no doubt," said Denzil.

"You think so, of course, as you write novels," assented the great censor. "But there is another reason too—Society, like most fashionable dames, is fond of self-delusion, and is very apt to break in shivers the mirror that reflects her *décolletée* too faithfully. Now, the novelist is a painter who draws his portrait on canvas which a stone or two of censure will not break; but the playwright's fragile glass falls to atoms unless braced in a gilded frame of popularity. Critical hostility is often the breath of life to the writer; but to the actor it is absolute damnation—"

"How many have you damned then!"

"Ah!" said Dudley Moore, taking snuff with an air of pleasant remembrance.

"What a deal of words they waste over it!" scoffed Fanfreluche to me. "I said all that they've been saying now a great deal better to you the other day in two minutes. The simple truth of the matter is that human beings love mere fun, mere prettiness, and a sprinkling of indecencies, all of which burlesques supply—only they hate a truth so; when it shows them just a little silly, and just a little childish, despite all their worshipful wisdom!"

I did not heed her much. I was lost in wonder that the child whom I had first seen with her dead bluebells, unpitied in the streets of Westminster, should have become this elegant actress, with her grace, her ease, her ready interchange of thought, her patrician calm of manner.

It was only when I saw the old childlike innocence in the eyes, the old childlike trustfulness in the beautiful arched mouth, that I could persuade myself she was in truth the same. And yet I remembered even then, in her helplessness, and her bewilderment, and her wistful, defenceless misery, there had been a certain noble pride, a certain grave repose, in this young daughter of an old Saxon race, whose forefathers had ruled as Earldermen ere ever a stone had been raised of Windsor or Warwick, of Longeat or Haddon. Race is stronger than circumstance. She had been reared in the severe simplicity of a yeoman's household, and amidst the harsh pains and privations of poverty; blown on by the winds of earth, sunned by the morning's rays, and drenched with the dews of the dawns, trusted to the freedom and the instincts of an open-air and hardy life; knowing not the world, nor the world knowing her; having no teachers save Shakespeare and Milton, save the sunrise and sunset, save the flocks and the herds. And yet Race had conquered Accident, and vindicated her title to it—in every limb and lineament; in every motion and gesture; in the accents of her voice, in the gaze of her eyes. The world may give costume, beauty, brilliancy, beguilement, many charms, many attractions; but Race alone can give—the hands, the glance, and the voice.

"Have you found out what she is to him, my dear?" grinned Fanfreluche that night.

"What do people say?" I asked cautiously.

"As if there were two opinions!—My dear—is it possible for a woman not twenty, without any sort of kith or kin; famous on the stage; living alone, in a charming villa with only men of rank for her companions, rich enough to drive in her own carriage and to give her own dinners—is it possible for her to have any verdict save one pronounced on her by Society?"

"Society's verdicts are often unjust?"

"Perhaps. But Society is a Vehm-Gericht from whose sentences there is no appeal. You may have all the innocence in life, yet if the dagger stick through you and the red hand point at you, why—your innocence is very little odds to anybody."

"But I am sure—"

"What's the good of buts, my dear? If people choose to occupy questionable positions, they shouldn't murmur because Society looks on them as questionable characters. The lamb that wore a wolf's skin couldn't with justice complain if its flock ran away aghast from it."

"But, with Society, it is the wolves who pretend to be horrified at what they know well to be a lamb, much purer than they themselves are!"

"Ah well! Then that only shows what a fool the lamb is not to become a wolf altogether—fangs as well as skin—and so get a brotherhood with the strong ones! Nothing is so

bad for a woman as to *be* innocent and to *look* guilty; she
gets the sympathies of neither side, and finds herself out in
the cold altogether."

"You believe Gladys only slandered, then?"

"My dear, 1 have seen moths in candles that were only
singed,—to begin with!"

"But he is so gentle to her, so generous to her!"

Fanfreluche grinned.

"Did ever you hear of the hawk who took into his protection a wood dove? There was not a question but that Milord
the hawk could, better than any one else, preserve her from
all the perils of the woods; all traps, and nets, and gins; all
ambuscaded sportsmen, all wandering night-owls, and above
all, from all the wiles and ways of hawks themselves, for who
should know these so well? And yet—when one fine day
Milord the hawk took the fancy of a nice dove for his own
eating, I am half afraid she did not find herself to be in such
perfect security after all!"

"Beltran has no such treachery in him!"

"My dear, he has been a hawk all his days, and it can't
be supposed that he can change his nature. Birds of prey
never do."

I soon came to know that Fanfreluche was right. Of the
relation of Gladys to her friend the town had but one opinion.

It judged from the surface, as it always does judge—
therefore fallaciously. Appearances are so and so, hence
facts must be so and so likewise, is Society's formula. This
sounds mathematical and accurate; but as facts, nine times
out of ten, belie appearances, the logic is very false. There
is something, indeed, comically stupid in your satisfied belief
in the surface of any parliamentary or public facts that may
be presented to you, varnished out of all likeness to the truth
by the suave periods of writer or speaker. But there is something tragically stupid about your dogged acceptation of any
social construction of a private life, damned out of all pos-
sibility of redemption by the flippant deductions of chatter-
box or of slanderer.

Now and then you poor humanities, who are always so dimly conscious that you are all lies to one another, get a glimpse of various truths from some cynical dead man's diary, or some statesman's secret papers. But you never are warned: you placidly continue greedily to gobble up, unexamined, the falsehoods of public men; and impudently to adjudicate on the unrevealed secrets of private lives.

Ah, if *we* could write your archives!—we who lie under your council-chambers, and sleep by your emperors' pillows, and watch your statesmen in the dead of the night, and see your mistresses in their solitude, and hear your absent friends when they speak of you, what a revelation there would be! I scarce can decide which you would find the falser, your mistress's kiss or your newspaper's news. I hardly know which would be the more at variance with their professions, the friend's opinion or the statesman's soliloquy. I do not think that any two members of society would keep on speaking terms; I doubt very greatly if any two lovers would remain in love; but there would be very few wars conjured up, I fancy, because leading articles would go out of fashion; and there could hardly remain any political differences, because you would see that all political creeds resolve themselves into the old moss-trooper's formula,—"Grab a' ye may, an' fire the rest!"

Could I have told the town that there was no life simpler than this of Gladys Gerant's; that there was no honour higher than that of this yeoman's daughter; that her friend had never touched even her hand with his lips; that although a beautiful and courted celebrity, she hardly knew more of the world's evil now than when she had been in her father's homestead; that of the darker lines of her career she had no knowledge, but lived in an idealic sphere of fair faiths and of golden fancies; could I have told them this—the mere truth, as I came to find it—none would have believed me.

And yet the truth it was. Life had opened before her like a dazzling wonder flower; and she had taken it without question, and rejoiced in it without fear.

As I came to know later, Beltran had glided imperceptibly
into his present relations with her. His pity had been first
aroused for the helpless, lonely, graceful child; there had
been much in her to charm the taste of a fastidious and
cynical man of the world; he had been interested, which was
not with him of common occurrence; and he had discovered
in her singular abilities, which it had pleased him to develop.
His first gifts to her he had induced her to accept by leading
her to believe them the fruits of her brother's talent; when it
was no longer possible to sustain this delusion, he had placed
her in a career where he could continue them to her as the
fruits of her own gifts. As it chanced, her success in that
career proved singularly great; yet not so great that it could,
of itself, have brought her in so brief a space all the pleasures
and all the luxuries which he contrived she should enjoy.

Owing to him she never traversed all the steep and weary
steps of that winding stairway of struggle and privation by
which most actresses are forced to toil. She never knew the
bitterness of probation, the fury of adverse cliques, the insults
of opposition, the slow agony of humiliating ordeals; all the
antagonism, annoyance, and insult inseparable to her career,
were warded off from her, and whatever he might encounter
of them, none of it touched her. From the first he had led
her to look to him for the guidance of her life; from the first
he had never allowed her to suppose that any of the gold she
received was his. The wage of the theatre was paid to her
in his treasurer's name; she never knew that he owned the
house; but she believed that his interest obtained her honours.
From her youth and her ignorance of all practical things he
had taken the management of her affairs and interests entirely
to himself. When he told her that she was rich by right of
genius, she believed him, and only felt that such riches had
charming uses and gracious ends.

Perhaps he had done unwisely in thus bringing her into
the midst of the world, with no more knowledge of the world
than a child gains from a tale of fairyland. Perhaps in the
very excess of his liberality to her he erred against her. It

was not a safe life for her; none knew that better than he.
It was a life, moreover, whereby her name was inevitably as-
sociated with his own in injury to her. But it had been hardly
possible for him to give her any other. From the onset he
had found this young creature resolute to receive no aid save
such as she could be brought to believe that she had really
earned. Finding in her both grace and genius, he judged it
the simplest and straightest service to her to give these free
scope. By her absolute desolation her fate was cast into his
hands entirely; he dealt with it after the fashion of a man's
liberal judgment and kindly indulgence; naturally he did not
regulate it by a matron's prejudices or with a philosopher's
severity.

He had ever seen the women about him surrounded with
elegance, pleasure, and pretty luxuriousness; he gave her
these because they appeared to him the privileges of her sex
and youth; and because a lavishness in giving was a charac-
teristic of his temper. But in all this he had been moved by
the generous impulse of a gentleman; never by those cold,
measured calculations of a libertine which society attributed
to him.

When he had endeavoured to induce women of his own
class to take interest in her, he had been baffled by their indifference or their incredulity, and could make no impression
either on their coldness or their scepticism. All things had
combined to throw her straight into his power. That he did
not abuse that power was, to my thinking, a gleam of purer
gold in the tangled web of this man's life than many more
virtuous men, of better repute than he, can show in theirs.
He was careless, contemptuous, indifferent, hardened in many
things; holding women lightly, and setting most moralities
at naught, after the manner of men of his kind. He had never
been a good man, as the world counts such. He had wasted
his possessions, spent his years in pleasures, and gained himself an evil name, often, perhaps, for evil he had not done;
but of old, when I had first seen the kindly smile gleam in
his tired gray eyes, I had known that he was more to be

trusted than very many better men, and that no living thing would ever place its faith in him in vain. And even so had she now found it.

With women of the world he was as unscrupulous as occasion might need; with other men's wives he had never been famed for discretion; his loves had had very little heart in them, and as little scruple. He had been quite capable of forsaking with easy negligence at the end of the season the same woman whom he had wooed with courtly beguilement at the commencement of it; some women indeed, they said, had found that gentle manner hard as steel, and that slight smile cutting as the north wind. But all this was but Greek meeting Greek; all these women were much as world-worn and as heartless as he, if they were more passionate and more tenacious. If here and there one of them had staked her life on his, the stake had seemed to have but little worth in it, because she who put it down was so inveterate a gamester, and had so often ventured "all upon a cast."

But many a man has honour who has not morality; many a man can be touched into generosity when he cannot be induced to care for duty; and he who smiles at all other religions may yet steadfastly obey the instinct which forbids him to abuse faith placed in him.

Such a man was he; and being moreover of a temper that, when once moved to do either, never gave measuredly or defended feebly, he had lavished all things possible on Gladys Gerant, and from the first time that her innocent eyes had met his own had dealt with her gently, reverently, purely; breathing no word to her that her dead boy-brother, living, could ever have needed to avenge.

Fanfreluche had said that birds of prey cannot change their natures; and, doubtless, you will say that it is entirely improbable that such a man could ever act thus by such a woman.

Well, I can only answer you as a little while ago I heard a novelist, as famous in the drawing-room as on cover-side and moor-side, answer his companion, when she demonstrated

to him that one of his stories—a love-story, which has thrilled
the hearts of many—was, charming as she and the world
found it, after all very improbable.

"Improbable?" he repeated. "Improbable? Yes, no
doubt it is—utterly improbable. Only, you see, it happens
to be all true, every word of it. But I don't know that that
makes much difference—to your theory."

CHAPTER XI.

"The Woman at the Lattice."

"'The morality of society is very beautiful. Look there,"
said Fanfreluche.

It was a mild noon in March, there were sables and sealskins in the Row, but the wearers thereof were already nume-
rous and aristocratic, and along the rails there already stood
some score of dainty equipages, all with fretting horses, and
some with coroneted panels.

The east still prevailed in the drift of the wind, but the
ennui had departed from the smoking-rooms of the clubs.
There might still be frost on the pavements, but there was
fashion in the footsteps that touched them. The spring had
scarce put forth her primroses, but Christie had put forth his
porcelains. The chestnuts had hardly their buds yet in em-
bryo, but the studios had already their paintings in maturity.
There were few leaves uncurled on the trees, but there were
several dinner-parties given in Belgravia. The mignonettes
had not begun to sprout in the window-boxes, but the love-
intrigues had commenced their up-springing.

London was at its pleasantest season, when dinners are few
enough to be charming; when little suppers succeed an hour
or two in the stalls; when the afternoon tea gathers its chit-
chat round a fire; when men and women have leisure to make
amusement a pastime and not a toil; when the great race-
meetings are still distant enough not to absorb every thought
and word; when the pictures of the year are only vaguely

known by tradition and prophecy breathed from private views; when scandal, and laughter, and flirtation, and gossip, all are unjaded; and when the soul of the cook, if it breathe a sigh for its game-loves departed, is yet filled with a soft glow of comfort before its visions of salmon and quails, its possessions of lamb and asparagus.

"Look where?" I asked her as we passed together down the Row, where my mistress, alighting from her brougham, was walking awhile, accompanied by Beltran and Guilliadene; all who passed her turning to look at that delicate face with the gleam of its golden hair, and the flush which the wind brought to its skin, set in the dark softness of sables, and velvets, and laces, as the bright hues of a porcelain painting may be set in an ebony frame.

"Everywhere," returned Fanfreluche comprehensively. "Look round, my dear, at them all. Look at that pretty woman in chinchilla and violet. That is Lady Hilda St. Maurice, who is not two-and-twenty, and who has had more 'affairs' already than there are rings in her dressing-case. Last year I lived with her a few weeks; one day at luncheon time, Colonel St. Maurice, her husband, you know, walked in to her with all her letters to Charles Flickers, the actor, in his hand. Dollie Flickers, his wife, who is horribly jealous of him on and off the boards, had got at them somehow, and had sent them on to St. Maurice. Hilda never winced once, though he made a scene out of it. 'Do be sensible, Frank,' she said when he'd stormed himself hoarse, she all the while sublimely indifferent. 'People who live in glass houses, you know— how would you look if we had a 'show-up'? And she ate a greengage as she spoke; and the Colonel was 'sensible;' and Lady Hilda went next day to the Drawing-room, as she will go next year.

"Look, now, at that haughty piece of dark still beauty in her carriage: that is the Countess of Grancedieu. With her blue blood, and her immense possessions, and her stainless name, she is the very type of the lofty and chaste aristocrat. Well, I have lived with her too; and if I spoke their tongue, and told of things that I have seen as I lay in my lady's private rooms when all the great house was still, they might maybe find that the days when Faustine called her paramour from the circus to the palace were franker and not deeply darker than ours.

. "Look, too, at that graceful creature so exquisitely painted, and dressed up to the eyes in the imperial sables; that is the . Duchess of Llandrysyl. She, the greatest of great ladies, has royalty in her veins; has revived the salon; and got her husband the vacant ribbon. People say that his grace is a gloomy, taciturn, listless, discourteous man, ill worthy of his matchless wife. An autumn or two since my people stayed at her magnificent domain in North Wales, and I with them. One evening before dinner his voice woke me in the great, dusky, splendid library; I listened; he was there, alone, with his wife. I heard enough to pity from my soul for evermore that great noble, who was more wretched than any cotter on his lands. And yet he held his peace, has always held it, so that the bright-haired lad that will reign after him, the only child of them all that has any look of his face or his race, may never know the truth of the mother who bore him.

"Look there, too, at that lovely, passionless-looking blonde, with all that guipure about her: that is Ida Warwick. Dudley Warwick is a baronet's son, very poor, very idle, very—good-natured! He has about 500*l.* a-year—and debts; Ida, a peer's daughter, has nothing—and debts. Yet they keep a charming little house in Belgravia; give very good dinners; have the first of fruits and the choicest of wines; two high-stepping bays and an opera-box; and their creditors never trouble them. How do they do it? Well, the Duke of Holyrood's bankers could tell, and handsome Holy's presence is a thing of course in the bijou house. But, then, Ida is quite 'in society;' her children are cherubs; her own people are fond of her; her husband lives with her. What more would you want to please all the Proprieties? O, it is a beautiful thing this morality of English Society! Look around, my dear, and only reflect that not one of these women whom I have named, and not one of their set or their order, but would deem her fair fame polluted, and her fair dignity insulted, if only asked to know—Gladys Gerant!"

She spoke the truth: the truth not only of those few,· but of many as corrupt as themselves, and of many more whose lives were really just, and whose honour was really honourable.

As Gladys passed under the leafless boughs the women of his world looked away from her, with that serene passionless look which *ignores*, and which is far colder as it is far courtlier than any scorn.· She herself, vaguely conscious of its·insult but unconscious of its meaning, gave back the look with a grave proud meditation in her eyes. She dimly felt that all the women of his order held themselves aloof from her; she thought it was because she publicly pursued an art for fame, and because she came of an old, humble, impoverished race, whose decay all, and whose ancientness none, had known.

Of the truth she had no nearer conception: all men who came near her dealt with her with an infinite respect; she did not dream that the mothers, and wives, and sisters of these men classed her with all that was basest and most venal. She knew that there were vile women; often she heard men talk of them; there were even those in her own theatre with whom he had requested her not even to exchange speech. But her knowledge of such was still vague. She thought scarcely at all of them save with a shuddering tender compassion. That she was classed amidst them never dawned, by its faintest suspicion, on her.

She was conscious of no sin; she was proud by nature; she was content in his protection and his friendship; she was of a temper to which the mingled isolation and publicity of her life added both strength and sweetness; she only knew the world as he chose to show it to her: that in the estimation of that world she was no better than Maude Delamere, no higher than Lillian Lee, no purer than Laura Pearl, was a fact that never brought its indignity within the scope of her sight or the sphere of her thoughts.

And she went now in the sunny noon of the still wintry morning, with her graceful head turned to him in happy careless speech, and a wild-rose flush brought to her cheeks by the wind; and her eyes glancing, clear as a deer's, dauntless as a child's, dreamy as a poet's, at the sneering, smiling faces of those women of whom he had forbidden her to have any knowledge; and at the cold, immutable countenances of those other women who had refused to have any knowledge of herself.

I think there was something in that look which baffled, perplexed, annoyed both classes of these her foes; for as I followed her I heard one of the former mutter with a laugh, noting the delicate warmth which the wind had fanned in her face, "Has to rouge a'ready, by daylight!—bet Fred Bruce a pound o' cigars that she did!" And I heard one of the latter murmur to a friend, noting the worth of the almost priceless black Chantilly which she had gathered about her, "How they do imitate all laces now; did you see that? You would almost think it was real!"

Now I believe that when a woman's own fair skin is called rouge, and her own old lace is called imitation, she must in some way or other have roused sharply the conscience or the envy of her sisters who sit in judgment.

Fanfreluche and I, as we ran, caught many such little phrases from the peripatetics of the Row. Almost all whom we passed had some word or another as they saw her.

"Is that the great actress?" said a country cousin with a stare. "How young she looks!"

"They know how to make themselves look young when they are seventy!" said her companion, who no doubt was a woman that knew the world.

"I wonder who she really was," said a man who had the look of the Rag about him.

"Don't you know?" said his friend arm-in-arm with him. "She was the natural daughter of the old Duke of Holyrood by an opera-singer. I can see a likeness in her to the young Duke myself."

"So can I, now you name it," responded his ally. "But I have heard so many stories that—"

"O, this is the perfect truth," interrupted the other. "I had it from a man who used to know old Holyrood very intimately."

"Is that she?" asked a handsome young girl very eagerly. "O, I never saw a real actress out of doors before! Somebody told me they were always so yellow by daylight. But she is as fair—"

"As you are," added the man with her, apparently her brother. "Actresses are the prettiest women we have. 'My face is my fortune, sir, she said,' is true of an actress, if not of the traditional milkmaid of the song."

"O, if I were but as lovely!" sighed the girl, who could only have been "just out," and unspoiled by lovers and ladies'-maids. "And what beautiful furs, and what exquisite lace! Ah, I am so glad you have got those stalls for to-night! And it is such a pretty name, too—Gladys Gerant. Is it really her name?"

"Heavens, no! I daresay her real name's Mary Stubb, or Martha Grubb, or something as euphonious," laughed the brother, moving her onward.

"Who is she really?" murmured an elegant woman, whom I knew to be Lady Cississiter, to her companion who had the look of a bow-window frequenter.

"God knows!" he responded. "Last thing they say is that her father's one of Beltran's gamekeepers; and that the keeper cut up rough about dishonour and all that, and got firing at him from a cover, Irish fashion, last time he was down at his own place. Keeper missed him by a hair's-breadth; and is put away somewhere in an asylum. Wish we could do as much by the Ribbonmen."

"Very romantic!" said Lady Cississiter with a little incredulous contempt. "What sables those are she has! Really, how preposterous!—"

Whether she meant the keeper's vengeance, or the sables' worth, I know not, for she also passed onward.

"My stars, what lace!" muttered Lillian Lee, putting up her eyeglass as she checked her horse by the rails. "By Jove, Jack, the virtuous dodge seems uncommon good to go in for—"

"I wouldn't try it if I were you," said John Beaudesert who rode with her. "You wouldn't look the part—quite."

"Beatrice Leintwardine has had an awful row with him. They'll never speak again," said a Guardsman, meaning the Countess of Leintwardine, Beltran's sister.

"About the property?" said another who was arm-in-arm with him. "I daresay she's fidgety. He's got rid of all he can; and her second boy's in the entail, you know."

"O, hang it, no! About the diamonds," answered the first speaker. "He's given the Beltran diamonds to that girl, and the Leintwardines are furious."

"The deuce! that's a new trick," murmured his friend. "Awfully pleasant. All St. John's-wood and Brompton will be flying at one's family jewels now; I'm sorry he's put it into their heads. All the racing-plate and shooting-shields will have to go next, I suppose."

"That's begun. Last season Mrs. Delamere asked poor old Brune to lend her his St. Leger cup for her sideboard at one of her big dinners—"

"O, Lord, yes, I remember. And when he sent for it next day she wrote him word back that she 'never returned gifts if people pleased to repent of them.' He raved; talked of law—"

"But he never went to law, and the vase is the Delamere's now."

"Did you get that box at the Coronet for to-morrow, Charlie?" asked a handsome matron of a handsome youth.

"Couldn't, aunt. Everything taken for a fortnight. Put our name down. But you can see her for nothing here—look."

"I never look at that class of persons," said the handsome woman severely.

"And yet you send me to take a box on purpose to look at her!"

"Don't be stupid, Charlie. That is on the stage. That is quite different."

"Who was she *really?*" asked a pretty dainty widow in pearl grays and swansdown: the fortieth time that I heard the same question asked in three turns of the Row.

"Well—really—I believe the story is this," returned tho man with her. "She was the wife of a poor devil of a painter, who married her when she was fifteen. Viscount Beltran met them at Dresden, where they were living in great wretched- ness; took a fancy to her; and entered into an agreement to bring her out on the stage here, and pay the husband five hundred a year to—absent himself. But they do say that the husband is waxing wroth because she makes so much money, and that we shall have the divorce on, and the whole story out before long."

"Dear me!" sighed the widow, who evidently thought simplicity her own great point. "But that seems a very wicked thing of Lord Beltran!"

"I never heard a good thing of him. It is hardly so bad as some others I could tell you," said the speaker, who, as I found afterwards, was a young clerk at the War-office, who knew Beltran about as much as he knew the Queen—by sight.

"Pray don't!" murmured the widow. "But how does it come, then, that she has the same name as that pretty green book you bought me? I thought somebody said she was the poor boy's sister?"

"Pooh! The boy's dead; he can't contradict them if they do. But it is all bosh. She is the wife of this painter in Dresden. McGilp, who is studying in Dresden, told me so. The name's a mere *nom de fantaisie*, picked out of the poems."

And they also passed on, amidst the chit-chat, the cigar- smoke, the perfumes, and the gay dresses, under the scarcely- budding boughs of Rotten Row,

"Mercy on me!" said Fanfreluche. "And to think all these people devoutly believe what they say! That is what is so comical. When Libel lies for a purpose it is comprehensible, if criminal; but when Gossip lies from mere wantonness it is such an awful fool; for pretending to have the eyes of an Argus it has all the blindness of a bat!"

"And yet you once said that the scandals of society, if false in the letter, are often true in the spirit," I said, for I loved to twit her with her own would-be smart sayings.

"I never said anything so foolish," snapped Fanfreluche. "What I did say was, that if you haven't the story you ought to have; society always supplies you with it, as a good corset-maker supplies a poor lath of a girl with a comely figure. If you occupy an equivocal position, you clearly ought to have an equivocal history. Supposing you are really innocent, and have not one, society weaves one for you, suitable in every respect, if not comfortable."

"A fire web for the Glauco it enfolds," I murmured. "Is it true that Lady Leintwardine has quarrelled about the diamonds? She used to be very attached to her brother."

"*Could* they speak truth here?" retorted Fanfreluche. "No—it was not about the diamonds. Beatrice Leintwardine is far too much of a gentlewoman to dispute about *them*. It was one day last month, in the railway-carriage. Beltran and she had been down with her boy, Beaulieu, to Eton, and coming back—we were alone—she took him to task about having old Margett Llansaint living with 'that girl,' as she called Gladys Gerant; and went so far as to lament that she herself could never take any notice of faithful old Margett now that he had placed her under the same roof with—with —she did not quite finish her sentence. Beltran was looking straight at her; and he has a way of doing that which often incommodes people. When she paused he answered her very quietly, 'My dear Beatrice,' said he, 'I suppose even brothers and sisters may know each other for over forty years and be strangers all the time. Since you fancy I could turn my dead mother's old servant into a pander to my vices, the less you see of me the better, I fancy. I'll order Beau's new boat, and look after him down there—good-day to you.' And as the train stopped just then at a station he got out, lit a cigar, and went into a smoking-carriage. He has never spoken to her since then, and to the best of my belief never will speak to her. And yet he is much attached to Lady Leintwardine."

"Did he ever ask her to know Gladys?"

"Yes, he did. He tried hard when the child first came out—and before, I think—to make the women of his own family feel some interest in her. But they were stubborn, and would not do so much as see her; and you know very well that he is not a man who will ask twice."

"And yet she is as innocent as their own little children that are at play in their homes," I cried indignantly; for by this time I had come to the sure knowledge that, howsoever it might look in the sight of the world, this life was stainless.

"What's that to do with it, my dear?" retorted Fanfreluche. "She is an actress."

"But still there are men who will believe in her?—men beside himself?"

"Ah, my dear," Fanfreluche replied with much energy; "but don't you know that whilst broad, intellectual scepticism is masculine, narrow, social scepticism is feminine? To get hearty, reverent, genuine belief in the innocence of a slandered woman, go to a man: where the world has once doubted, women, the world-worshippers, will for ever after doubt also. You can never bring women to see that the pecked-at fruit is always the richest and sweetest; they always take the benison of the wooing bird to be the malison of the hidden worm!"

Which metaphoric sentence seemed to please her, for she shook her golden bells, and went to gossip with the arrogant Astolat poodle.

A little later there passed us, going to her carriage, a very handsome woman, with gleaming hazel eyes, and a haughty languid mouth.

"That was Lady Otho," I cried to Fanfreluche when she rejoined me.

"Yes, my dear. There is nothing between them now. Two autumns ago he went to Africa and she went to Rome. He potted maneaters and she *monsignori*. Love died a natural death with absence; and when they met, with the next London season, they agreed by tacit consent to bury it decently in pretty cere-clothes of courtesy. Love used to die violent deaths, you know, in the old times of passion and poignards; but now-a-days its common disease is that gentle form of atrophy called *ennui*, and it yawns itself softly out of existence, polite and *bien posé* to the last, like the moribund beauty who asked for fresh ruffles and rouge ere she took the last sacrament, and drew the last breath."

"He never cared much for her?" said I.

"He never cared much for anybody. And that is why all of them care so much for him. Men of the world, to whom their loves are of about as much account as their cigarettes, get all the worship and all the devotion. 'How can you care so awfully for me, Effie? You know I care nothing about you,' I heard a man of that sort say once to a woman who had clung to him for years, with a vehement adoration which moved him with a little gratitude and a great deal of *ennui*. 'I know you don't, dear,' she answered him humbly; 'but I think that is just why I do care for you. You see men who love us much, always look such fools to us.' And she spoke with knowledge, for many much better and wiser than he had loved her."

"And yet you sometimes say men love more truly than women?"

"So they do. I have seen fifty instances of it. But it is true that their strongest loves are not always their most legitimate. 'The wife' may be poetised about and preached about; it is not always *she* of whom he thinks when he lies wide awake on a brown moonlit moor, or dull with fever in a hot sulphurous eastern city; but oftener of some fair sweet fate that might have been, or of some fond dead thing that loved him with tenderest unwisdom."

And I think she was right.

Not very long ago I was down away in the vale of Belvoir. I stayed with my friends at a great stately place, owned by as gallant a gentleman as ever swung himself into saddle. His wife was a beautiful woman, and he treated her with the courtliest tenderness: indeed, I often heard their union cited as one of almost unequalled felicity. "He never had a thought that he did not tell me," I heard his wife once say to a friend. "Not a single thought, I know, all these twelve years of our marriage." It was a happy belief—many, women have the like—but it was an unutterably foolish one; for the minds of the best and truest amongst you are, in many things, as sealed books to those whom you care for the most.

One bitter, black hunting-day, a day keen and cold, with frost, as men feared, in the air, and with the ground so hard that even the Duke's peerless "dandies," perfect hounds though they are, scarcely could keep the scent, there came terrible tidings to the Hall—he had met with a crashing fall. His horse had refused at timber, and had fallen upon him, kicking his head with the hind hoofs repeatedly. They had taken him to the nearest farmhouse, insensible; even dead already, they feared. His wife and the elder amongst the beautiful children fled like mad creatures across the brown fallows, and the drear blackened meadows. The farm, happily, was not far: I sped with them.

When they reached him he was not quite lifeless, but he knew none of them; his head had been beaten in by the plates of the kicking hoofs; and they waited for his death with every moment, in the little old dusky room, with its leaded lattices, and its odour of dried lavender, and its bough of holly above the hearth. For this had chanced upon Christmas Eve.

To his wife's agonies, to his children's moans, he was silent: he knew nothing; he lay with closed eyes and crushed brain—deaf, blind, mute. Suddenly the eyes opened, and stared at the red winter sun where it glowed dimly through the squares of the lattice-panes. "Dolores!" he cried aloud; "Dolores! Dolores!" It was the name of none there.

"My God! What woman is it he calls?" his wife asked in her torture. But none ever knew. Through half the night his faint pulse beat, his faint breath came and went; but consciousness never more returned, and for ever he muttered only that one name, that name which was not her own. And when they laid the dead body in its shroud, they found on the left arm above the elbow the word "Dolores" marked on the skin, as sailors stamp letters in their flesh. But whose it was, or what woe or passion it recorded, none ever knew—not even his wife, who had believed she shared his every thought. And to his grave his dead and secret love went with him.

This man was but a gay, frank, high-spirited gentleman, of no great knowledge, and of no great attainments, riding fearlessly, laughing joyously, living liberally; not a man, one would have said, to know any deep passions, to treasure any bitter memories—and yet he had loved one woman so well that he had never spoken of her, and never forgotten her; never—not even in his death-hour, when the poor, stunned, stifled brain had forgotten all other things of earth.

And so it seems to me that it is very often with you, and that you bear with you through your lifetime the brand of an unforgotten name, branded deep in, in days of passion, that none around you ever wot of, and that the wife who sleeps on your heart never knows.

It is dead—the old love—long dead. And yet, when your last hour shall come, and your senses shall be dizzy with death, the pale loves of the troth and the hearth will fade from you, and this love alone will abide.

At that moment both Fanfreluche and I were summoned; and while Beltran walked homeward, the little brougham, with its pair of small, spirited horses, swept Gladys away to the studio of Marmion Eagle.

Marmion Eagle was as handsome as ever, and had become much more famous; so famous, indeed, that he was almost fashionable, and that where people before had talked of his insanities, they now only murmured of his eccentricities. A man may flirt as wantonly as he will with colour when once the *Midas* has pronounced that his drawing is anatomically perfect, and that his meanings, even when obscure, are always profoundly poetic; and he may indulge as he will in stalking through the Park in an olive velvet Velanquez dress, with a mahl-stick in his hand, and a fez cap on his head, when once it is thoroughly well-known that he goes to the Premier's At-homes, and is admitted to the dinners of the Duchess of Llandrysyl.

His fair patrician, Gwendoline, had wedded her coronet; and he had locked up in a cabinet the miniature which he had once privily made of her, as he had met her first, when he was a wandering sketcher, under the oaks of her father's park. But she asked him to dinner with great regularity, employed her influence to have his pictures hung on the line; and, in fine, got him much talked about. Menus and notoriety are the favourite coins with which Love pays his debts in the nineteenth century.

We were soon at his studio in the heart of the "wilder west," where the brethren of the brush do congregate. When last I had known him, his atelier had been a big and barren room, with a few casts and a bronze or two, down somewhere in Chelsea, overlooking the Thames. Now it was placed in an atmosphere that is perfumed with successful talent, and in a suburb where the carriages throng by the hundreds on "Art Sunday" with every spring. And now the painting-room itself was cedar-panelled, velvet-hung, full of beautiful hues and grand outlines.

So swiftly will the word of the *Midas* and the cards of a Duchess persuade the public that genius is a thing, eccentric no doubt, but still not absolutely damnable—even, indeed, almost deserving of a stockbroker's patronage, and of a mill-owner's cheques.

13

Gladys now went to give him her last sitting for a portrait which he had painted of her for that year's exhibition.
He had drawn her as the Saxon daughter of Hengist, bearing in her hand the golden mazer, wherewith she bade her
lord Vortigern "Waes heal," and gave to the high tides and
holy-days of England the plegde and custom of the wassail-
cup.

The picture was beautiful; and a few great connoisseurs,
permitted to see it in progress, had pronounced that it would
be the picture of the year, when, with the king-cups and
hawthorns of May, the picture exhibition should unclose.

The figure was life-size, clad in white, with no colour at
all about it, save in the massive gold cup of wine which she
bore; in the purple border of the robe; and in the cool pure
blue of a northern sky at noon. The few great connoisseurs
talked very grandly, if not very luminously, of this wondrous
white; of its purity, of its crystal clearness exempt from
coldness, of its soft shadows that yet were white likewise,
and of its admirable management against the azure that
alone relieved it. But though they talked thus, the true
charm of the picture abode in the face which gazed out of
it: the grave, tender, proud, wistful face, with its meditative
eyes, and its exquisite hues, and its eloquent mouth, that had
all the smile of youth, and all the sorrow of genius.

The portrait was so perfected that I believe the artist only
demanded another sitting that he might have the pleasure of
noting the light glow on the fair waves of hair, and of seeing
the gracious form of the young actress move amongst the
dusky magnificence of his atelier.

There was scarcely anything more to be done; but he
stood for habit's sake touching this fold, and that detail,
whilst Gladys sat on a sort of daïs above, which was hung
with maroon-hued velvet, and filled with soft, pale, hothouse
roses—for Marmion Eagle had all that love of fragrance and
beauty, of grouping and grace, which is called, not with
much wisdom, the effeminacy of genius.

Pesently there entered Dudley Moore, who criticised the

picture with pungent acerbity, and complimented the original of it with all the suavity of which he could when he chose be master; a little while later there sauntered in Lord Guilliadene, who had been breakfasting with the Guards at Knightsbridge, and who was in his indolent way a dilettante of no mean knowledge or discernment; awhile after there came Beltran himself, bearing with him a small picture, and a very quaint piece of old Capo di Monte, on which he wished for Marmion Eagle's opinion.

Whilst the Capo di Monte passed from hand to hand, he set the picture before Gladys.

She looked long, and did not speak.

"You do not like it!" he exclaimed in some disappointed surprise.

"It is exquisite," she made answer. "But it pains me: it is unutterably sad."

"Nonsense! It is only a little study of pearls and grays; I bought it for its admirable management of half-tones."

"It is sad," she answered him, "intensely sad. Look—it is a woman alone; a woman without hope, a woman tired, not by work or years, but by the sickness of hope deferred. It is all twilight; rue, only, blossoms in the lattice, the plant they used to give to captives at the bar; in the bowl of water a purple butterfly lies drowned; in that landscape beyond there are evening shadows, but no evening stars. The whole picture has history."

Beltran laughed.

"You have the swiftest and dreamiest of fancies! The grays and the pearls would please *me* just as well if their subject were any old Ogham stone, or a *gris de Flandres* jug. —Ned, what do you say?"

The Earl sauntered up with his eyeglass.

"By Jove, where'd you pick up that? I offered any money for the thing twelve months ago, and couldn't buy it."

Dudley Moore just then, with the Capo di Monte for a theme, had commenced one of those charming disquisitions on Art with which he would occasionally favour people:

learned, Ironic, sometimes abstruse, always full of suggestion, to which painter and virtuoso were alike glad to
listen.

The opinions he gave forth in them were seldom, indeed,
similar to what flowed from his pen for the *Midas:* he was
one of those—they are many—who deem the Public a child
to whom it is not well to tell over-much truth. In the *Midas*
he would uphold that a recent National-Gallery purchase
was a quite undoubted Correggio, when in private he would
rend the Correggio to atoms as the most miscrable of im-
postors.

"Tom Glaze, who is my particular friend, bought it;
Lord Esprit, whom I always make it a point to disagree
with, attacked it; and the nation itself could not tell a
Raphael from a Frank Stone," he would say with a grim
chuckle to his intimates. "Besides, it is infinitely amusing
to hear Esprit raging like a wounded boar in the House of
Lords, and to see the public on its knees before that
wretched bit of canvas, begotten yesterday by some lad on
the Pincian hill, who couldn't pay his padrona's bill. I would
not disturb so admirable a farce for the world."

And so he would calmly continue to laud the Correggio in
print, and to chuckle in private, and would atone to the public
by flaying alive before it every hapless living artist he could
find.

"Modern painters do not owe you much, sir," said a
youngster to him once, writhing under the *Midas'* ruthless
flagellation of his first Academy picture.

"On the contrary," said the great censor, taking his snuff;
"they owe me much, or might have owed me much. If they
had only listened to me, they would have saved every shilling
that they have thrown away on canvas!"

Whilst they were busied in discussion with him, I stole up
to the little picture which Beltran had placed upon a low
easel. There, with the soft warmth of the hothouse roses
about it, I saw in its grayness, and sadness, and loneliness,
the sketch of the Woman at the Lattice.

To that easel, when the great critic had left, Marmion Eagle came, and paused long before it.

"You have bought this?" he asked.

"I found it in a bric-à-brac shop the other day in Paris," answered Beltran. "Do you know the artist? Is it of value?"

Marmion Eagle did not answer; he was lost in thought before the little painting.

"Twelve months ago he refused its weight in gold," he muttered after a while.

"Who did?"

"The painter of it."

"And why did he refuse gold then," asked Gladys, "and yet now lets it lie for sale in a public place?"

"Because he is no longer in love with the woman who sat for it, I imagine," said Beltran with his slight tired laugh. "The Madonna that we consider priceless at midsummer has a knack of turning, by Christmas, into a mere venal model, who may go for whatever her charms chance to fetch!"

"Because he is no longer living," said Marmion Eagle gravely. "To few men is it given to be able to secure fame for their work when their hand has no longer its cunning, and their brain no longer its skill."

"There is a story, then. Come, tell it us!"

"It is a very common story," answered the painter with a smile that had a little bitterness. "It was only that a man had some genius, and that a woman killed it."

Gladys, where she sat amidst the fragrance of the frail hothouse roses, turned her head towards them.

"The picture told us something; but do you tell us more. It was not *that* woman who killed him?"

"This woman? No; I do not know very much; what I do know, I will tell."

He sank into a chair near her, his hand playing with the delicate bloom of the roses, the faint afternoon light falling upon the little portrait that had been painted in the drowsy golden days of summer, at the Silver Stag, with the bees

booming amongst the lime-blossoms, and the seeding grasses
blowing in the wind.

"A year or more ago, Paris was mad about one young
painter. Paris had seen his pictures for ten years, and refused to believe; then suddenly it took a fit of belief, and
could not atone enough. It is the public way. Only, unhappily, the public is so often like a child, and leaves its
neglected bird so long to starve in an empty cage, that when
it comes to caress the bird, it finds but a ruffled heap of dead
plumage, which cannot feel its kisses. This young man was
kissed before he was dead; he had the good-fortune to con-
ceive a picture which drew the whole city to it. You will
remember it—it was called Faustine."

"Faustine!" echoed Beltran, to whom he had turned.
"Of course, a marvellous painting."

"Well, the artist of Faustine painted also yonder sketch
of the Woman at the Lattice. I wonder that you should have
overlooked that sketch when it was shown in the Salon. He
was offered any money for it, but he refused to sell it. 'Shall
a man sell his soul?' he used to say; but I believe no one
knew what he meant. I was in Paris a great deal last year,
and I saw but never spoke to him. He was the handsomest
man I ever beheld. Handsome is no word for him: he was
as beautiful as a god. When he walked in the Bois, people
turned after him as though he were a king or a woman; he was
like some Phydian statue incarnated. Unhappily, in an evil
hour Cléopâtre saw his beauty."

"I remember now," murmured Beltran.

"Who was Cléopâtre?" asked Gladys.

"Cléopâtre? Well, she was Cléopâtre. Paris knew little
more, neither need you. But it is told of her that when she
saw the scathing satire of the Faustine, she said, 'He has
dared to scourge us; very well, then, we will scourge him.'
I do not know whether this is true, or whether it was invented
afterwards as an *apropos*. If people do not say a suitable
thing, Paris always takes care that one is invented for them.

"It matters little what she said, or whether she was

moved by devilish vengeance or by devilish love. She set
herself to gain possession of him—of his heart, of his passion,
of his genius, of his life. She has a matchless beauty herself.
She succeeded. The leaves were just budding when she saw
him first, at sunset, by the lake in the Bois; by the time that
the trees were in full foliage, he had no god but his passion,
no heaven but her face.

"She made him paint her portrait in the first burning
days of the summer; and when all Paris flocked to the Cléopâtre, the Faustine was avenged. The satirist had fallen, and
kissed the feet of the courtesan. Well, just so long as the
portrait took to paint, just so long had be his fool's paradise.
When it was finished, and in it all Paris glorified her afresh,
then she turned and laughed him to scorn, and took in his
stead a gipsy-eyed prince, who came from the woods and the
plains where royalty still is half savage, and the European is
half Oriental.

"We know how men of the world take these things; but
this painter knew the world so little. He was young, ignorant,
maddened; and he loved a woman to whom love was a jest, a
scoff, a byword of theft. It is very terrible when a man really
loves a woman that is vile; it is terrible, but it happens.

"When he was jeered at, forbidden her presence, finally
thrust aside by her lacqueys, whilst she drove from her gates
with the gipsy-eyed prince by her side, and the jewels of the
prince on her bosom, then this man whom she had deserted
grew mad. Forgive him—he knew so little of the world, and
he loved a creature without mind or soul—a splendid animal,
made but to prey. I think the world does not hold a greater
curse for a man than that.

"He was mad; and he followed them on foot, turning once
only aside, and that once into a place where he had used to
paint, and where his colours, and draperies, and old armouries
were still kept. They drove with swift horses, and he turned
aside this once; yet hardly had they entered the Bois before
he entered it also. I saw this, because I myself drove scarcely
a yard behind them.

"It was at the close of a late summer day. I had gone there, and hundreds were there also, though the city was thinning. The sun was setting. Everything was reddened by the flush. The very waters seemed dyed crimson. Everywhere there was a hot hungry glare. I even heard the hoot of a mosquito—it did not seem to be Paris.

"Through the clouds of dust and the throngs of people he came, as swift as a hound runs; his head was bare, his hair was streaming back, his face, commonly so fair, was dark with a rush of blood; his eyes—I see them sometimes at night still. All his wonderful, godlike beauty seemed gone; he looked like some goaded wild beast—goaded to fury, and dying.

"He passed me like the lightning; there was a rush to stop him; but he tore through the crowd, breaking loose of all opposing hands, and darting like a meteor through the light. There was a flash—a shriek—a sudden oscillation of all the gay, laughing, pleasure-seeking mob. Through the dust I saw a straight steel dagger-blade glitter in the air; then the wind whirled, the dust rose again; I saw no more. But the voices that cried out around told me that in that moment of time he had stabbed both himself and his rival. With the prince the blow had missed of its aim, merely grazing the flesh as it passed; but he himself lay bathed in blood, in the dust, under the trampling hoofs of her horses.

"She supped that night in the Bois, in the café by the cascade; and she laughed, and she drank, and she talked of her diamonds, as she ate the sweetmeats a duke had provided. On the whole, no doubt, she was glad; the tragedy sent her name but more loudly down the stream of the world's babbling voices.

"For him—they took him to the horrors of the Bicêtre. He was not quite dead; when men loathe life they are hard to kill. Life lingered in him for five weeks—five weeks of raving fever, of intolerable torture. One burning, stormy night, a night with fire in the skies, and death in the air, his agony was ended. He died in unutterable torment, delirious to the last, gnashing his teeth like a mad dog at all who strove to draw near or aid him; and like a mad dog, dead, they buried him."

There was a long silence as his voice sank away. When one hearer raised her head, her eyes were heavy with tears.

"And *she?*" she murmured, glancing at the portrait of the woman at the lattice.

"Ah, I know nothing of her, not even who she was," he made answer. "I know no more than I have told. But this was the end of his genius; and already—Paris has forgotten that ever he lived; and your friend has bought that picture for a song in a bric-à-brac den yesterday."

CHAPTER XII.

Toy-Soldiers.

It is needless to say that I had quickly asked Fanfreluche of what had chanced to Nellie, the Wood-Elf; she had treated the inquiry with some scorn, as touching a little, half-obscure burlesque player, beneath the attention of *nous autres*.

"My dear," she made answer to my renewed inquiries, "girls like that little Courcey always remain just where they were. They are the rank-and-file of the theatrical army; they get little loot and still less promotion. They go on the stage, when they are in the freshness of their youth, because they have pretty little faces, trim limbs, and a fancy for jumping about in gay dresses, instead of sweeping, or baking, or washing, or trudging through life as a shopwoman, or as a mill-hand, or as a maid-of-all-work. They have very small talent, they have no education at all; they dislike work, and they like gaudy attire. The modern stage wants hundreds of such; and to it they go. They all are just so much tinder lying all ready for the devil's flint—we *say* the devil still, you know, because he is such a convenient synonym for all our vanities and wickednesses, though he went out long ago with the coming in of light wines, long beards, cigars, clubs, croquet, chignons, railways, five-twenties, and other conveniences. The life these girls lead is about as hard as most domestic servants', and they haven't their 'washing and board found;' but they like it because they can dress as they choose, and have a chance of bad champagnes and casino flirtations. They're not all immoral, poor children; some few are good enough girls, who keep their families out of their wages. But they are all of the same class; the class that naturally likes noisy fun, and tawdry glitter, and a sight of what they, God help them! call 'Life,' better than they do industry, and quietude, and the drear sameness of an English workwoman's existence. And now and then, out of their rank, a Lillian Lee or a Laura Pearl rises; and the poor little fools believe that the exception of one in ten thousand is the sure and invariable rule for all. The life is not, maybe, so odious when they are young and pretty; but it can contain no asylum for them as they grow in years and lose in beauty: and then—then one wonders vaguely what on earth can become of them, for they are seen no more, just as idly as one may wonder what becomes of all the lost pins."

"'The pins, they do say,'" I returned, "are always found in the bottoms of sewers in a hard, shapeless mass that they call, I think, 'slag.' I am afraid that these girls whom you talk of are found at the bottom of the social strata, hardened into evil, or, at the best, into wretchedness."

"Most likely," returned Fanfreluche, with asperity; she never liked any one to say a neat thing save herself. "The stage certainly has nothing to say to them. The stage may want armies of round-faced girls to skip about as mazurka-maidens, or as elves, or as shepherdesses, or as soldiers, but it never wants armies of middle-aged women. I suppose they do go to wretchedness of some sort—they must. But, then, so, I'm afraid, do whole multitudes of governesses, and housemaids, and shopwomen, and cottagers, who never did a naughty thing in all their days, and yet are left to starve on half-a-crown 'relief,' or drag out their decaying years in workhouses. There are so far too many women!—if two-

thirds of all the female children that are born were put in the
water-butt, where they put two-thirds of our puppies, the
world might be comfortable."

"If women had more spheres—" I commenced, but she
cut my words in two.

"Where did you learn that miserable cant? There are
more men than there is work for already; do you suppose
you would increase the harmony of the earth by setting
women to squabble with them for it as two of our mongrels
may quarrel over a bone?"

"But if they were educated?"

"Ah, my dear," said Fanfreluche with a grin, "we are
going to educate everybody, they say, so that everybody
shall be above doing anything. What a millennium that
will be!"

"But where is Nellie?" I persisted.

"She is just now, I believe, at the Palace Theatre, in the
Strand; a pretty theatre, as you may know, though not to be
called fashionable, and the chief home of burlesque and ballet,
now that *we* have gone in for Legitimate Art—whatever that
may mean: of course, every playwright thinks his own bant-
lings 'legitimate,' and other people's plays all bastards!"

"She is doing the same as ever, then?"

"Yes. They always stick to the same, till they are shelved
altogether. You know she is a spirited little dancer, and has
a certain small bright talent of her own, but she will never
be anything except Prince Goldenhair or King Charming in
a burlesque. She might have all the genius and poetry of a
Ristori, nobody would ever see in her anything except a
'jolly little girl' in a slashed tunic and white-satin tights,
singing doggrel to a catching air. If you begin with being
a job-horse, though you should win the Derby itself, nobody
would ever believe that you could have either pace or race in
you. Nellie has always done burlesque, and she will have to
do burlesque till the end of time. There are such scores of
such girls!—well, I suppose it is a good thing; if every-

body would only play Lady Macbeth, where would the theatres be?"

"But the stage is such a hard life anyhow! and without eminence in it—"

"Is it worse than making lace at a profit of a farthing an hour, or sewing fifteen hours for fourpence-halfpenny, or carding cotton in the mills at four-and-sixpence a week, or, for a few pence a ton, panning salt in the scorching steam, till their pallid faces are like a sodden sponge?—Well, yes, I think it may be even worse. *We* know that. But how should the girls know it when they are ignorant, and conscious of good looks, and wanting a bit of finery and a fling of dancing? and the floats and the green-room seem almost to them like paradise. The lives of women of the English poor are so abject, so colourless, so dreary, without any break of joy, or any pause of toil, or any gleam of hope, and full of such noise, and stench, and cursing riot, and bloodless apathy, all commingled, that one cannot wonder if they would sometimes exchange such lives even for hell itself!"

And I knew that she said truly; for indeed to live only to know the pains, the needs, the agonies, and the travails that lie in living, is a hard fate, though it be the fate of millions.

"And where they might be happy and innocent they will not," I answered, for my thoughts went back to the little cottage beneath the rosethorn, and to the honest smith's forge amidst the woods, where the woman, who had chosen vice and pillage, might have dwelt in honoured virtue and in homely peace.

Fanfreluche grinned.

"No, my dear—not often—and I suppose it's a very fortunate thing that they don't. If they would, we might perhaps get our salt panned, and our cotton carded, but we certainly shouldn't get our material for scenic effects of fine legs, and of gauzy tunics! I often think when I hear them talking, as it's the way to talk now, of bringing everybody to be so very virtuous, and so very refined, and so very intellectual, and so very divine, where on earth, if they were ever to succeed,

would the world go for the human *chiffons* out of whose bodies
and souls it manufactures all its amusements? So long as
amusement must be had I am sure they cannot afford to ask
their common men and women to be virtuous. The *residuum*
that they sigh over is what yields them gaieties, as the foul-
smelling ditch-mud yields the pretty painted myosotis. A
thousand nightingales died to make the Roman epicure's
pâté; tens of thousands of human beings perish in moral
death to give to one city—its pleasures."

And this was all that, for a time, I heard of Nellie.

She was playing at the pretty little Palace theatre, which
was of some repute at that moment for burlesques; and now
and then I heard two or three men say how awfully jolly
little Courcey was in that funny parody of the Bride of Lam-
mermoor, or how tremendously well got up she had been,
in crimson, and white, and gold, as the King of the Golden
River, in the pantomime that had been based upon that
story, at the Palace, at Christmas. She was leading the old
life, no doubt, learning doggrel, singing rubbish, dancing
hornpipes and jigs, delighting the gallery with appropriate
" gag," quarrelling in the green-room, supping noisily over
kidneys and "fizz," trudging home afoot in the grey break of
the dawn, or jolting wearily over the stones in an omnibus,
with its glandered dying horses; her appointed portion hard
work and coarse pleasure.

No other life was possible to her, once having enlisted
herself in this.

She was one of the "rank and file;" one of those innumer-
ables who, *tambour battant*, serve to make up a spectacle.
The conscription of Fate had drawn her to be one of the toy-
soldiers of King Joujou, who has a terrible knack of killing
his soldiers himself sometimes. So long as she could wear
her little gilded uniform jauntily and well King Joujou paid
her wage, and she held a place on his great parade-ground
of public amusement; if she were ever to faint or to fall it
would not matter—there were plenty as pretty and as alert as
she to catch her little pennant as it dropped, and fill her

place in that great army wherewith King Joujou plays the mimic war of Pleasure.

She was no genius, she was no beauty, she was only a little, blue-eyed, sturdy-limbed girl of the populace, with the *beauté du diable* in her cheeks, and her curls, and the freshness of youth in her voice that gave something of charm and of melody even to those vile slang inanities that she was appointed to sing. There were scores like her; what happened to her mattered to no one. She came to a workhouse at her birth: she would go to a workhouse for her grave. To the world this seemed excellently fitting; an arrangement proper, and quite harmonious.

And meanwhile—was it not much that a young creature, born of a pauper, and reared by the parish, should know the feel of silks and satins if only in her stage dresses, and should know the taste of champagnes if only made of gooseberries? On the whole, when you consider that a pauper child is an animal absolutely undesired by any one; very much lower than a pig, which can at least be sold so much per stone; and possessing nothing on the face of the earth except its hunger and its heartaches; it may be conceded that Nellie had done very well for herself when she had got leave to dance about in bright colours for some half-dozen years, and then could go leisurely to either death or perdition quite at her own choice and fancy. Several millions, you know, have to die in rags, and infancy—whether they may like it or not.

One day I got out "on the loose," as your slang phrases it; a reprehensible practice, no doubt, but one dear to dogs as to men, for better is a bare bone in the gutter, with the sweetness of free-will, than are fatted meats eaten within the curb and the gall of a chain.

My little wanderings were innocent enough in those streets and gardens of artistic South Kensington which stretched around the pretty villa where we dwelt. I was about to return of my own accord homeward, when I saw a girl walking

down one of the small and narrow lanes that do so curiously
intersect even your proudest lines of palaces.

There was something in the lithe step, the clusters of
auburn hair, and the supple yet sturdy figure that I knew; I
felt sure that they were Nellie's, and, quick as thought, I
darted after her. I could not reach her to attract her notice
before she turned in at the doorway of one of the small, poor
houses of the place, but I was near enough to follow
her in unseen, and mount the stairs up which she had disappeared.

There were three flights of these; and on the landing of
the third a door stood a trifle open: my instinct told me that
she had passed through it, and I squeezed myself through
its inch-wide opening, and entered the chamber.

It was a poor, meagre, little room; very dull, very mean;
looking upon leaden tiles and red chimneys, and gray gusts
of sulphurous smoke. There were the mansions of the nobles
and the traders, the villas of the fashionable actresses, the
artistic homes of the successful painters, all around in the
sweet, cool, living sunshine, with the greenness of budding
trees about them, and the colours of art and of luxury within
them. But this little room, with no look-out save on those
endless roofs and those drear columns of smoke, was almost
as cheerless and as wretched as though it had been in the
haunts of Whitechapel; whilst through its one narrow window
there only came upon the wind the scent of frying meats, the
stench of decaying vegetables, the screams of children,
and the throbbing of a steam-hammer at its never-ending
work.

There was a little linen-curtained bed standing in one
corner; and on it was stretched a girl, dying, it was easy to
see, of fever. She was very young, and though her face was
now so drawn and scarlet, it also was easy to see that but a
very little time before it must have been a pretty, brown,
baby face, with a little cherry-like mouth, and robin-like
eyes; such a face as would have been the pride of "mother"
and of "teacher" in some cottage home and village choir.

She also, doubtless, had been one of the toy-troopers of King Joujou. He sweeps into his conscription all whom he can find from far and wide, over all his kingdom; from the shepherd's hut on the moorlands, as from the crowded lanes and gullies of the city; from the little, humble, ivy-hidden village on the hills, as from the vast wards of the poor-house and the factory. And those he once has gained can never leave his service; until he breaks them in his gay caprice, or leaves them perishing by the wayside.

She was lying quite still and straight; with her brown eyes wide open, burning, and without sense in them: her cloud of dusky curls had been shorn short; her lips were parted with quick, painful, gasping breaths. She was muttering vague, broken words about father, and harvest, and going gleaning, and going blackberrying; her thoughts, no doubt, with some peasant life that she had led in childhood in the green level lands of the corn countries, or under the shelter of the oak woods of the west.

The other girl, auburn-haired and blue-eyed, who I saw was indeed the little "Wood-Elf," had dropped beside the couch, and was murmuring gentle words to her, and hushing her tenderly, and holding to her some fresh, cool, orange-scented drink.

The fever-stricken child drank eagerly; but she had no knowledge or consciousness in her regard, and when she had drained the draught she lay still and straight again, muttering huskily of the blackberries that were ripe in the lower wood, and that they would be late for school if they stayed to gather them.

On such a scene I did not dare to break; and yet I had not the heart to leave; so I crouched down in the shadow behind the door, and waited.

An aged woman came slowly in; a gaunt, shrivelled, cruel-eyed hag.

"It arn't no good fussing about her," the old woman muttered in a low voice. "The doctor say as how she can't live another day. And you're well-nigh wored out."

Nellie shook her head silently.

"This day do begin a new week," muttered the old creature hoarsely. "I thought as how she'd have gone off quiet
by now. Do you stand another week's rent—eh? She han't
got a shilling, you know."

Nellie, in silence still, opened a little purse, and counted
into the woman's wrinkled palm sixteen shillings. It was a
shabby, little, mean chamber; but rent, like all other things,
is so dear—to the poor.

"You won't ever sit up this night again?" pursued the old
dame, doubtless softened by the thrice blessed music of
silver pieces. "You've sat up nine nights already. You'll
kill yourself—and with all your work at the theayter, too,
as well."

"I sha'n't be harmed," said Nellie briefly, and turned herself away, and again sat down beside the bed. And there she
remained for more than two hours, whilst without, in the soft,
bright, cool spring afternoon the tender leaf-buds quivered in
the sunlight; and the carriages swept in hundreds through
the streets; and the fashionable crowds flocked to saunter
through the palm-houses, and to listen to music, and to laugh,
and to flirt, and to make their pleasant appointments, and to
draw their magnificent dresses slowly over the lawns, at the
first azalea show of the year.

It is the sharpness of its contrasts that lends all its poetry,
its vigour, its ambition, and its colour to your life; but sometimes—they are bitter.

Nellie sat motionless beside the bed, with the light from
the casement coming in upon her: in it I saw that she was
much altered.

The round cheeks, the smooth forehead, the ruddy mouth,
had all hardened, and got a curious, worn, coarse, pained
look. The soft skin and the bright colours of a woman cannot stand long the rouge, and the white paint, and the steam-
ing gas, and the late hours of the theatrical life of a bur-
lesque-dancer. They will "make-up" just as well as ever
by night; but by day—they make your heart ache, as does

a fresh rose lying soiled and stamped in the mud of the
streets.

And yet, despite this rack and wear of time, there was a
sweeter look in her eyes than of yore, a sadder, steadier, and
purer look, as of one who had suffered, and not vainly.

When the dying girl in the little white bed tossed and
moaned, Nellie touched her gently, moved her carefully, and
murmured to her a few soothing words, which, though they
could not reach the dulled and wandering brain, seemed yet
to bear with them some balm and hush. She was a little
wicked thing, of course; accursed of all good souls; gaining
her livelihood by ministering to the base senses of coarse
sight-seers; purchasing her daily bread by moral degradation, and in a sensual spectacle; and yet she came hither to
soothe the last dread hours of a creature poorer and lonelier
even than herself; and when her heart throbbed, and her
eyes smarted, and her limbs ached, after the work and the
noise of her theatrical labour, she had sat, night after night,
sleepless, worn-out, weary unutterably, only just for the mere
sake that a fever-stricken girl should feel a friend's hand
near when it sought one in its death-struggle.

Another hour went by: there was no change in the suffering she watched.

Sometimes the girl lay quite quiet, sunk in apathy, breathing hardly; at others she tossed, and moaned, and cried out in
pitiful ways of all the remembered things of some lost country
home—of pastured cattle; of running waters; of the hymn
that should be learned for Sunday; of the bilberries that were
ripening in the old birchwood on the moor; of the verses that
mother had given her to learn by rote in punishment for saying that she wished she were a lady.

In all the sorrowful, wistful, shattered words, it was so
plain to see the story that went with that little brown winsome
face; the story of the rebellious petulance, and fretful impatience, and vague discontent, which had brought the cotter's
prettiest sunniest child from moor and meadow, from burn and
byre, from the old safe ways, and the old healthful labour,

and the old summer gladness by hill and dale, and the old fireside nook by "mother's" side, to perish here of fever, and alone, amidst the noise, and smoke, and stench, and misery that are the birth-chime and the death-knell of the poor in cities.

"She had wished to be a lady,"—and she died here.

Poor little pretty sunburnt face, once bright as a brown brook, and ruddy as a berry of the yew!

Doubtless in that little cottage, wheresoever it stood, far away amidst grayhills, and soft mists, and sunny birchen woods, and calm green pastures, there was one name that was never spoken; one chair that was never drawn to the noonday meal; one voice, like a robin's, that the father missed from the girls' choir at the church; one kiss, given in smiles and tears, that the mother felt only in her dreams, when sleep came to her beneath the old thatched roof.

Yet another hour passed; the slow dull chimes of some distant clock swung six strokes through the air. Nellie started, rose, looked wistfully at the little bed, then stooped, and touched with her lips the child's flushed, knitted, aching brow. The girl moved wearily under the touch; her dark eyes still wide open, still without light or sense in them.

"Mother—mother," she murmured, "don't be angry. I did not mean to stay away from school. It was me, not Susie, did it. The wood was so pleasant this mornin', and the birds was singing so sweet, and the vi'lets was so many, I forgot—I quite forgot!"

And in answer there only came the dull fall of the steam hammer, the dull breath of the poisoned wind.

Nellie turned slowly away, and passed from the chamber, and down the steep flights of the stairs. Far below she met the old woman to whom she had given the money.

"Do look at her; pray do look at her!" she entreated. "I will come the moment the play is over."

The old woman muttered assent.

"But where's the good on't?" she asked; "'tis waste of time. The girl's a dead un, a dead un."

14*

Nellie went in silence out into the street. I followed her, and fawned on her.

She looked down, and started violently, as though she recognised me; with a quick glance at the name upon my collar, she raised me in her arms. Then, silently still, she went as rapidly as she could through the various ways that led to the gardens of Gladys' residence. Before the walls a groom was riding his own horse, and leading up and down a beautiful black mare, in which I recognised a favourite of Beltran's, by name Eblis.

As we drew near the gate it opened, and Beltran himself came out from it.

I felt her heart beat thickly against mine. She trembled, and would have fled; but he had seen and already approached her in the quiet road, under the shadow of the trees over-topping the wall. He thanked her for seeing to my safety.

"Not for the first time, either," he added. "It is the same dog you used to know. You are coming in here, are you not?"

Her voice shook as she answered him, "No."

"And why not?" he asked. "Gladys so continually regrets the way you shun her; you are always absent when she tries to see you, and you will never come here, or accept anything at our hands. Why do you do it, Nellie?"

"It's best, my lord," she said curtly.

"I am at a loss why you say so. She feels herself driven into a sort of ingratitude that is most abhorrent to her. Indeed, you give her great pain."

Nellie said nothing.

"Come in now," he urged. "She is alone; she will be rejoiced to see you."

"No, thank you; no, sir," she answered him. "Please let me go!"

"This is sheer obstinacy, Nellie. You rendered her too great a debt for her ever to forget, or wish to forget, it. You should not make her look, or feel, so negligent of it."

"She's neither, my lord. But—but—I'm not fit for the

likes of her. There's harm enough said of her without me adding to it."

His face flushed a little: it was he, now, who made no answer.

"Tell her—tell her," murmured Nellie, "that it's because I love her that I won't come anigh her; and tell her, sir, that I know her sweet, generous, tender nature a deal too well as ever to think she'd forget me—quite. Let me go—please let me go."

"Why, Nellie, what is the matter? You are crying."

"Am I, sir? It's only—I've just come from little Annie Dell as is a-dying—she's a dancer, like me; they calls her on the playbills Clarice Vaughan. It's fever; and she's only been a year on the boards; and she's a little soft thing like a kitten—it seems sad."

"Fever! Can I do nothing? There are many things she must want. Do let me help you—"

"She'll want naught no more, sir, when this night's over-passed," said Nellie very softly. "But you're very good—very. You've had a deal of goodness, my lord, again and again, to poor girls as was in want or woe; and all you've ever got back for it is a bad name."

Then she turned and rushed swiftly down the street, as though ashamed of her temerity, or fearful of his questions.

Beltran stood still and looked after her.

"A bad name! A bad name!" he muttered. "What does it matter for me? But for this glorious creature—when my lips have never even touched hers!"

Then he flung himself into saddle and rode away with Eblis.

CHAPTER XIII.

April Flowers.

"There was rather a good thing happened last night," said Fanfreluche to me a few evenings later in the supper-room of the Coronet, where Gladys had been playing in that favourite part of hers, the Beatrice, in which she had first challenged and won the suffrages of the London public.

Fanfreluche was accustomed to spend her nights out at pleasure; her present owner never heeded what she did nor where she went; she had established herself in his chambers unasked and undesired; and she had liberty to do just as she pleased—to go to perdition if she preferred.

Sometimes I think that this is one of the most exquisite enjoyments man or dog can have; no doubt we ought to be very grateful to those who will drag us to our good with collar and chain, but the process is apt to get excessively irksome to us; and I doubt very much if the poor suicides amongst you, who are hoisted out half-drowned from the mud of the Thames or the stench of the Seine, when they see all their trouble gone through for nothing, feel very grateful to the grappling-irons and the hot bricks that call them back nilly-willy to the woe and weariness of life.

"There was rather a good thing last night," she pursued. "We dined at Richmond; only men; a dinner that Claud Lucy gave to some members of the Cercle des Patineurs.

"The men were all right, except one, and he was an under-bred one—Abney Arcott. I don't think you know him. He's only been heard of the last year. He made a big fortune in agencies and things abroad; and by money, and luck, and flunkeyism, and a gorgeous place in the Forest, with a first-rate cook in it, he has got pushed amongst some of our *beaux messieurs dorés.* Only we don't take him amongst our own women; and always blackball him carefully all the way down St. James's-street, from the Bow-window to the Thatched-house; and only treat his Forest place like a very good inn,

where the host don't present you a bill. Lucan Phipps brought
him out; and Lucan generally trains pretty decently. Even
he can't polish this fellow, quite; but as Arcott always seems
to get awed when he's amongst his betters, he has never made
a real blunder before. Florance Fane used to give him awful
facers last season; and it's always seemed to put him into
tolerably fair form.

"I remember when they went first to dine at his place,—
Flo and seven other men of the Brigades,—old Flo, as they
went into the dining-room, stared hard through his eye-glass
at the dinner-table, and at the ninth place at the top, to
which Abney Arcott was moving.

"'I think you mistook us—quite,' said Flo, in his quietest
and most amiable tones; 'we said we'd dine *here;* we never
said we'd dine with *you!*'

"Well—last night Arcott was more loquacious than common. Somebody said he was *tête monté*, because the Duchess
of Astolat had actually sent him a card: somebody else said
it was because he was out without his trainer; Lucan being
over in Paris. Whichever it was, he let his tongue run far
more than usual. On his off side sat Lord Cississiter—you
may know the man; stout, florid, with a ruddy beard, and a
shady name on the turf; looks a bully, and is one when he
'feels a winner!' Beltran, whom he happens to hate, because our friend thrashed him at Eton some twenty-five years
ago, and has been down upon him on every possible occasion
ever since, sat on the other side of the table, some way nearer
to Lucy.

"Around Cississiter they got talking of theatres and such-
like; and of all themes in this world Arcott must needs harp
upon Gladys Gerant. He talked a great deal of her; and all
more or less in an offensive fashion.

"Beltran did not miss a syllable; but he went on with his
dinner and his own conversation as if he heard nothing.
Presently the millionaire grew coarser, and said one or two
things the meaning of which there can be no mistaking, and
which can only be said of women of the lightest name and

lowest life; and he ended with a sneer at her continual absence from places and pastimes that 'her sort' were only too
glad to be invited to enjoy.

"'Quite right, Mr. Arcott, quite right!' called out Cississiter in his loudest tones. 'It's the damnedest affectation.
She's as wild as any of 'em. But she's chosen to run dark in
that form, you know—they often do when they're young uns.
It's the commonest stable trick.'

"'Then, and only then, Beltran looked up, and without his
face changing a muscle, glanced across the table, and 'fixed'
both the men with eyes which can be very hard and cruel
when he chooses.

"'I'm glad *you*'ve come within range, Cississiter,' he said
very slowly and distinctly. 'One can't spoil powder on
vermin. I suppose you don't in the least know what you are
talking about. I do. The lady you speak of is quite as
good as your mother; and a very great deal better than your
wife.'

"Can't you fancy the dead silence that fell over the gay
and boisterous talk?

"It was straight hard hitting, a little more in the rough
and ready style, and less subtle than his reprisals usually are,
but he knew his foes, and it was the most effective he could
possibly have used with them. It fell with the force of a
sledge-hammer. Lady Cississiter is the wildest and worst of
her order.

"What happened after? Nothing ever happens after in
these days. There was a tumultuous, tempestuous scene for
a few moments; but Beltran calmly ignored the wrangle, and
only addressed himself to his host.

"'I'll bid you good-night, Lucy,' said he. 'I don't want
you to be bored with a row. Your friends know where to find
me—if they want.'

"But the sympathies of the table were with him; the common feeling was that he had been only *dans son droit*. Of
course they all believed that he had lied; but it was the sort

of lie which gentlemen like from a gentleman's mouth, and which becomes him well always.

"The upshot of it was that he did not leave the dinner, but Cississiter and Arcott did. That is Beltran's way of dealing with people who rouse him. But whether he cares for the woman he defended is quite another matter—he would take the part of an ugly old apple-seller if he were in the mood, and thought the odds strong against her."

As she concluded her narrative Beltran and Denzil sauntered in; they had just come into the house, it appeared, from a dinner with her Grace of Astolat.

They were speaking of this very occurrence of the previous night.

"It was hitting with the gloves off, Vere," said Denzil, as he cast himself into a chair. "It wasn't quite so polished as your usual style."

"I never put the gloves on with men like those," said Beltran, going up to the mantelpiece to light a cigar. "Pummel them as you may they don't feel, that's the worst of it."

"I should think they do feel—rather—with the story running wild this morning about the clubs and drawing-rooms."

"I'm afraid Bully Cississiter don't. Do you remember my thrashing him at Eton for stealing little Holyrood's champagnes?"

"He felt that—he was black and blue for a month. Have you heard anything from him?"

"Not a word."

"I don't suppose you will. It would be too ridiculous for him to meet you on the sands by Ostend about his wife—of all people in the world!"

Beltran laughed.

"O, I don't know. As long as your wife *is* your wife, I suppose she's *casus belli* enough for anything."

"All the men were with you; feeling ran very strong about it—"

"What's the good? Do you suppose any one of them thinks one whit better of the child?"

"I don't know that they do—"

"You know that they don't!"

"I fear that they don't, certainly. That is one of the peculiar successes of modern society—that there is no means whereby a man can declare the innocence and honour of a woman that shall not at once stigmatise her with darker slanders than ever touched her before."

"Yes. Now and then, though we know that, we are weak enough to let a cur get a rise out of us; but we are safe to repent it,—or ought to do for the woman's sake."

Then he began to talk of other matters, hearing a step that he knew without, and a moment later there entered the only person in all the town who had heard nothing of the scene at Claud Lucy's dinner.

Of course she had not heard of it; would never hear of it; you never do hear of any one of the million ways in which your world ruins, ridicules, marries, divorces, attaints, decides for you, prophesics of you, and even murders you—in your absence.

I asked Fanfreluche that night if Denzil had altogether forgotten his lost love; whereat she grinned.

"I don't know, my dear. Men do forget in seven days sometimes, and sometimes they don't in seven years. It just depends. They remind me of Clyde Paulett, when they were woodcock-shooting in the west of Ireland last year. They had very fine sport all the week, but Paulett was not in his usual spirits. No bags that he made seemed to give him much pleasure; and though, when they totted up the whole, he was found to have shot more than any other, he appeared to care little. They asked him what on earth was the matter with him—was it women or Jews, a plant on the turf, or a bad vein at *écarté?* 'Well,' he said slowly and sadly, 'to tell you the truth, I can't forget that one grand old cock that I blazed away at, like a duffer, and didn't bowl over. I *have* felt such a fool!' Now, you know, I think it's very much

with their loves as it is with their sport. However many head
of game may lie slain at their feet, they can't forget what
they '*blaze at and don't bowl over.*'"

A brief while later, in the balmy spring weather, we had
a little river-party—surely the pleasantest of all sunlit pastimes. Because Gladys was in a manner excluded from most
pleasures by her rejection of one world, and by the other
world's rejection of her, her friend did all in his power that
she should feel her loss as little as possible. Happily for her,
she was of a temper to which the meditative and intellectual
pleasures of thought and of art were far more suited than the
noisier and more frivolous diversions of society.

But yet there were in her the natural impulses of youth
towards gladness and gaiety, which, although bruised by the
sorrows of her brief life, had not been wholly broken. And
these he always sought to meet and to indulge, as far as it
was possible to do so without exposing her to that companion-
ship from which he had always warded her.

The boating-party usually consisted of two four-oars, of
which the crews were chosen from his own chief friends.
They used to take to the river some half-dozen miles out of
town; scull leisurely down to some pretty wooded resting-
place, to which servants had been sent earlier with choice
meats and light wines; lunch there; laugh and smoke; paddle
a little about amongst the tall reeds and the floating forget-
me-nots; and so row back to London in time for twilight and
for dinner. There were few pleasanter days, of simpler or
mere careless open-air amusement, than these river-days of
Beltran's; and it was held as an eagerly-coveted distinction to
be one of those invited by him to take a place in his boats.
It was well known that, though a man not commonly scrupulous in such matters, he was excessively scrupulous as to
whom he introduced to association with Gladys.

Men held their own opinions, doubtless, as to his relations
with her; but they saw that he chose to treat her with perfect
deference, and they had to follow his lead. Two or three of

them even, I think, credited the truth, and believed in her innocence almost as thoroughly as he did who knew it.

You, indeed, are very curious in this. In your clubs and your camps, in your mischievous moods and your philosophic moods, always indeed theoretically, you consider all women immoral (except just, of course, your own mothers); but practically, when your good-feeling is awakened, or your honest faith honestly appealed to, you will believe in a woman's honour with a heartiness and strength for which she will look in vain in her own sex. According to your jests, the world is one vast harem, of which all the doors are open to every man, and whose fair inmates are all alike impressionable to the charm of intrigue or to the chink of gold. But, in simple earnest and reality, I have heard the wildest and most debonair amongst you—once convinced of the honour and innocence looking from a woman's eyes—stand up in defence of these when libelled in her absence, with a zeal and a stanchness that did my heart good.

The boats this day went Henley way, and the pause was above Wargrave.

The river was a sheet of dusky sunlight; the meadows and banks were all golden with kingcups and daffodils; the hawthorn-buds were blooming on the great coiled swinging branches; the leafage was in all its sweetest and freshest green, and here and there a little water-bird was darting amongst the tall bulrushes and the green river-plants.

Under the skilled sinewy hands of men who, in their time, had won their honours on the Isis, the boats went as the rowers would—now skimming as fast as a swallow, now loitering like a slow-winged eider-duck—past the green, level, daisied fields, and the lofty walls of woodland, and the dark gateways of the locks, and the sunny reaches where the cattle stood, and the tufts of reeds and sedges that hid the soft blue of the forget-me-nots.

They landed, and lunched, and lingered over the fruit and the ice and the wine, under the blossoming hawthorns and the great boughs of the chestnuts; and then strolled hither

and thither, pulling down the plume-like hawthorn for a
standard for her boat, and gathering the primroses by thousands to fill her hands; carelessly enjoying such simple
country things, and wandering, these men of the world, as
though they were shepherds in a pastoral—save for the cigars
that were for ever in their mouths, and for the worldly gos-
sipry that they laughed over with one another.

With the freshness of the springtide, with the sunshine of
the waters, with the cool odours of herbage and foliage, with
the light easy laughter, with the gay friendly converse, how
charming they were, those river hours! And for one, at least,
amongst them, over the broad bright Thames, and over the
fields of flower-sown grasses, there shone the "light that
never yet was upon land or sea," save in the eyes of a woman,
when she lives in the first full sweet faith, the dreaming
idolatrous ideals, of a love half known, half answered, yet
still in all the deep untroubled peace of its birth-slumbers.

When the sun was slanting to the west, the boats were
sought for the return. Whilst they went for them, Gladys
remained where she had sat some time, couched in the curv-
ing roots of a great beech, whilst at her feet the water flowed
amongst the rushes, and the great green lily-leaves spread
out their splendour, though flowerless as yet.

She had been very still awhile, and Denzil also, who remained with her, had not spoken.

She was often very grave, when the stillness of the country
was around her. I fancy that her thoughts were with the
years when the boy Harold had been a child beside her, in
the old, cool, moss-grown paths of orchards, and in the tangled
ways of nut-tree coppices, binding the cowslips and the primroses and the daffodils with withes of ivy, and dreaming of
the imperishable things he should achieve when manhood
came.

After a while she raised her eyes from the water and
looked at Denzil. He had thrown himself on his side on the
grass; and his face, in the shade of the trees, was dark, stern,
sad exceedingly.

"Where are your thoughts?" she asked him.

Beltran's best-beloved friend seemed to her almost as a brother.

Her voice found its way to the closed recesses of his memory, and he answered her simply and truly, "Of a woman I loved."

Her eyes rested on him with their serious, meditative sweetness.

"Tell me of her," was all she said.

"I never speak of her."

"Never? She is dead, then?"

"Not that I know; she is dead to me. That is enough, you see."

"Who was she? What was she?"

"She was an actress, like you. You may hear them recall her now and then, when they speak, as they speak still sometimes, of Gertrude d'Eyncourt."

She raised herself on one arm; her eyes lighted and charged.

"Ah, I know! that beautiful woman whose portrait he has shown me—so heroic a face, so full of thought, of patience, of courage. But she was some one's wife, surely? She was married?"

"Ah, child! do not speak as if *you* had caught the world's cant. Yes, she was married to a beast, who only prized her proud beauty, and her bright graces, and her glorious gifts, as so many tools that were to bring gold to himself. There are men, you know, to whom their wife's honour is like their own—only a chattel to be sold, when they can! She loved me, and knew that I loved her. I had urged her to leave her husband for me with all the eloquence I knew; I don't deny that. I was justified. Although he hated me, because I treated him like the cur he was, he was ready enough to sacrifice her to any one of the richer *roués*, who would have purchased her of him just as one may purchase some beautiful wild hawk of a brutal keeper. But I ought not to speak to you of these things."

"Go on," she said quietly. Her great eyes were glowing where she sat in the shadow of the boughs, and her lips were parted.

"She loved me. It cannot hurt her to say it now. And, indeed, she could not have loved me much, or she never had done what she did; for one night in the height of that London season, seven seasons ago, she disappeared. Not a living soul knew whither she went. The town supposed I had taken her, but it was not so; I knew no more than the rest of them why nor where she was gone. I had left her that night in her own drawing-room, after the theatre was over. There had been other people present. I had been unable to see her alone, and I relied on seeing her, as usual, with the morrow. I recollect that she came out on to the balcony, and stood there looking after me as I went down the street. There was an awning over the balcony, for it was warm weather; the moonlight was strong and bright; she wore black, that drifted about her like a cloud, and she had a great gorgeous Brazilian lily that I had given her in her bosom. God! what fools men are to remember the veriest trifles that once belonged to women who never cared for them!"

"Did she not care? You said she loved you."

"Could she love me? Not as I count love. With the morning there came one of her letters to me; she often wrote to me and I to her, though we met twice every day; in it she told me that she had left the stage and the world for ever; that her husband had given her no choice betwixt flight and a lucrative dishonour; that she refused my love not less than she refused this abhorred passion that was pressed on her; and that she implored me not to seek to pursue, or to discover her. That was all. Am I not right to say she never loved me? Of course I did not obey her. I set all possible modes of inquiry at work. First, I went straight to their house and thrashed *him* till he was left half dead; then I began my search for her. It was utterly useless; it has been so ever since."

"She could not go to any evil?"

"Evil? No! Evil was not possible to her. She was the truest and the proudest woman that ever lived. Why she went I know no more than the dead; but I would stake my life on the purity, on the nobility, of her reasons, however exaggerated they may have been."

"And have you never found her?"

"Never. Once I heard of her accidentally; if the man who spoke were right, she was living then—in penury and wretchedness. I have tried every means, but all have failed. It doesn't matter, I suppose; they say that these things don't —greatly. Only, you see, I cannot forget her; and I cannot find heart in me to give to any other woman; and I talk to you, child, and look on you, not stirred one whit by your beauty; knowing you are fair indeed, but caring no more for that than an old worn dotard of ninety. Do you know that I would give my soul to love, and I cannot; just because this one lost woman will never release me?"

There were the fierce vibrations of an intense passion and sorrow under the half-quiet, half-reckless words; and his face was very dark where the shadows of the spring-born leaves drifted over it.

I cannot tell why, but I thought of the woman who had died in the bitterness of the winter time, in the poverty and the misery of Paris.

Through the silence there came at that moment the soft sound of moving oars and of rippling waters; amongst the twilight of the boughs a boat, with plumes of young green branches at its bow, glided gently to the little landing-place.

"Where are you, Derry?" asked Beltran's voice. "That duffer Ned has given over—says he can't pull back to town. Must get across and catch the express. He declares it's a sprain; I believe it's nothing but laziness and champagne. Take his oar, will you? They can have a waterman with your set."

"All right," responded Denzil, as he assisted Gladys into the boat amongst all the big bulrushes, and the broad water-docks, and the pretty, feathered, rosy-hued river reeds; and taking his coat off, seated himself on the bench that Guilliadene had vacated.

As he pulled us back to town in the stilly balmy evening, with his handsome head bare in the moonlight, and his grip giving true as ever the old marvellous Oxford stroke, he laughed as pleasantly and as often as any. It was Gladys whose eyes were dreamy, and whose face was troubled, as she sat under her fragrant banner of the hawthorn boughs, with a dark cloak drawn about her, and the field flowers that her friends had gathered for her dying in the coming of the night.

That night her acting lacked somewhat of its force, and had a languor and a lifelessness in it that were new to her.

As soon as her own share in the play was over she went to her home; Beltran was not in the theatre that night, and when he was absent she never received there.

She sat very silent, very thoughtful, before the fire that still burned in her pretty drawing-room, for the evenings were chilly, though the days were warm. Bright and full of rich hues though the chamber was, it seemed very still and solitary after the blaze and buzz of the crowded theatre.

Vaguely, perhaps, she felt how great this loneliness was in which she lived, at years when other women have all the light of home about them, all the tenderness of their mothers, all the gay companionships of their girlhood. It seldom weighed on her, because her life was brilliant and full of pleasures of its own kind; but to-night she seemed to feel how utterly alone in truth she was.

Her eyes were dim and full of languor as she looked at the delicate tender primroses of the woods and meadows, where they had been placed in an old costly vase of Venice glass.

"Whom did *he* ever love?" she murmured, with her lips against my forehead. "Did he love like that? So that he never again can forget?"

Denzil's words had stirred her heart from its rest; but it was for another, not for himself, that it awoke, troubled and still but half-conscious.

CHAPTER XIV.

"Victrix."

"Well, my dear!" said Fanfreluche, frantically rushing to me next day with breathless excitation and her most diabolical grin. "We have done pretty well, haven't we? Marchioness of Isla! Marchioness of Isla! When we began life, as *you* say, with bare feet, and home-spun skirts, and potatoes for dinner, in the Peak; and, as *I* know, with a shilling a week, and penny gaffs, and a glass of gin for a treat at Highbury Barn."

"What on earth can you mean?" I asked in some fear, thinking indeed that she had lost her senses.

"I mean what I say," she snapped angrily. "Marchioness of Isla! It is pretty well for a woman who began life by selling *you* in a market-place. Pooh, child, don't look so scared! Your friend of the Derbyshire wakes has won the great marriage-prize of the year. True; certainly it is true. The town is talking of nothing else. Avice Dare—Laura Pearl —Cléopâtre; what does it matter what one is called so long as one ends as Marchioness of Isla? What do I mean? O, you little fool! I mean this—Malcolm Kenneth, sixteenth Marquis of Isla, comes of age this winter; he has had a long minority; he has been educated by a foolish mother and a rigid Calvinist; he has seen no more of life than a young nun; he is a stubborn, simple-minded, frank, foolish boy; the first thing he does, on becoming his own master, is to go to Paris. Paris, in all the wonder of her exquisite spring season, for a lad who had only seen and known grim Scotch castles and sour Scotch matrons! The first night he went to the opera: there, in her box, blazing in the splendour of her beauty, and the living light of her 'sapphires, surrounded with princes and gentlemen, he saw—'Cléopâtre.' From that moment the world only held for the boy that one woman. She had the wit and the ambition to see that here was a greater prize than mere pillage. The boy was mad with his first delirium: she could do as she chose with him. She chose to marry him; she has done so. The marriage is valid; no efforts of his family will dissolve it; and the woman whom you once knew as the 'light o' love' of the lad at the mill in the Peak, is now a Peeress of England and Scotland, Marchioness of Isla, and Countess of Allanmore! That is to-day's news. Ah, my dear! I told you right that all the comedies of the playwrights, and all the romances of the fictionists, are not one tithe so amusing, nor one thousandth part so startling, as are the comedies and the romances that meet one at every turn in Life!"

Fanfreluche had in nothing exaggerated. To this amazing altitude had the betrayer of Reuben Dare arisen.

One sunny noon in that pleasant glad season when the leaves are as fresh as the toilettes, and the laughs are as light as the showers, I sprang down from the little carriage and roved to and fro, whilst the men passing by clustered round Gladys.

I roamed at leisure, viewing that scene, always familiar yet never hackneyed, because, on its wide stage the three imperious *impresarj*, Gold, and Ruin, and Death, never permit the same drama to rest nor the same players to tarry; but bring ever fresh names and fresh faces, if the old farces and tragedies still will react themselves under new titles.

The place was full: and all its crowd turned by one accord to gaze at a carriage which drove slowly down the road, as though to challenge that universal observation from that fashionable mob. It was an equipage fitter, with its outriders, its postillions, its superb liveries, its fracas, its display, for a ducal procession on the Heath or the Town Moor, than for a simple noon drive in Hyde-park.

Its occupants were a fair lad, with a stupid, feeble, ruddy face, and a woman of splendid beauty, enveloped in black

15*

guipures and black sables, for the last of which a chill in the air gave excuse.

"There go the biggest fool and the blackest witch in Christendom," muttered old Lord Shamrock. "Good God! If Ronald Isla had foreseen it, sir, he'd have strangled this lad—strangled him in his cradle!"

"Boy looks like an Ayrshire gilly," said Lord Guilliadene, to whom he had spoken. "Fearfully bad form: never saw worse."

"Malcolm Isla, his father, married a shepherd's daughter, off his own hills," growled Lord Brune. "Crosses always come out."

"But his grandfather, poor Ronald, was a gentleman all over," said Lord Shamrock, "though an awful fool to be sure. Do you know how he died?"

"No!" the earl responded with a yawn.

"He was shot in a duel," answered old Lord Shamrock. "Shot dead, outside Bruges. I was his second. 'It was all a mistake,' he gasped as I caught him. 'But I couldn't have explained unless I'd shown up a woman!' So he died, saying nothing. And that's the man whose grandson has made a wife and a peeress of—"

The language wherewith he designated her I dare not record for a polite age that blushes at Shakespeare and smiles at Schneider.

"I suppose she came over to make a dash here out of bravado," murmured Denzil, with a glance back towards Beltran. "The marriage only took place the other day. She will do just as she chooses with that wretched boy, no doubt."

"Isla House in Belgrave-square is being redecorated," said one of the loungers. "She is very stupid not to keep abroad: she will always be 'pilled' here."

"She will get the society she cares for," said Denzil. "All the men on the town will go and see her; and she will have a whole *cohue* of parasites—clergymen among them, if she like to become a 'patroness' of churches and hospitals, and I daresay, in time, even a bishop will dine with her."

"And I will bet you what you like," interrupted Guillia-dene, "that she will hold huge gatherings at Blair-Isla, and have festivities that will make all Scotland stare."

"If she don't give Isla's people a chance for a divorce," put in Lord Shamrock. "They will catch at a straw. I should not wonder if she were divorced by the autumn and married afresh by next Easter."

"Nor should I. She's awfully handsome," said Claud Lucy, "and awfully clever. She got De Ferras, and Bernaldés, and Prince Egon of Wallachia killed, and Lord knows how many she's ruined."

"Clever! She's the most stupid and most illiterate crea-ture that ever breathed," said Denzil contemptuously. "She never said a decently sensible thing in all her days."

"But she never did one not sensible," said Lord Brune quietly. "All her victims were solvent; she never forsook a man till she had plundered him as far as she could; she re-turned all small presents as 'insults;' she never got any one killed unless he were useless and troublesome; and she finally has married this lad. O, a clever woman, certainly; I do not believe she will be divorced. I believe she will now train for the Morality Stakes. They generally do when they have won a Gold Cup."

I overheard these remarks; my mistress did not.

"How beautiful a woman!" she murmured to Beltran, looking earnestly at the carriage as it passed. "She looks strangely at you. Who is she?"

"The Marchioness of Isla," he answered her with all gravity, but with a little, serene, contemptuous smile about his mouth.

"I have never seen her before, I think?"

"No. But you have heard of her—as 'Cléopâtre.'"

Fanfreluche had in nowise exaggerated: the woman whose first lovers had been found amidst the boisterous dalesmen and savage miners of the north, was now high in title, high in affluence, high in station. All the world knew her in-famy; but by the gracious fiction of your divine institution she had become blameless and without reproach—by marriage.

It seemed that she had drawn in this hapless boy beyond escape; and had wedded him with such scrupulous heed of all formalities that nothing which his frantic family could do could obtain any reversal of the hideous folly that had given all dignities and all nobilities to the wanton of the northern wakes.

He was but a lad; he was stubborn and simple; he had been reared in grim creeds and in childish ignorance; in the blinding blaze of his first liberty, in the sudden attainment of his mighty heritage, this woman had seized him as she might have seized some poor dazed bird long kept in darkness and confinement, and suddenly cast forth to stretch its untried wings in the full sunlight. He had been powerless to resist:—he had been held, and hooded, and fastened to that cruel and close-shut hand without a struggle.

You have seen such things before in this society of yours —seen them at least often enough for it to have become a known and dreaded thing that when the beardless boy of rank and wealth sits in the public places of pleasure beside the gorgeous thing of infamy whom you have made a household word, it will be possible—almost probable—that she will not pause at stripping him of riches, at forcing him to pawn all future heritages, at making him a gamester, a bankrupt, a beggar, an outlaw, but will go farther, and compel from him the old gallant name of his fathers, the old fearless repute of his race: the old gems that flashed in his ancestors' faulchions, the old home where his mother reigned in honour.

It is not moral to tell you this, you say? Ah, no!—life itself is not moral. But it is true—it is undeniably true—that whilst you repulse with a shudder the poor painted outcasts of the streets, you gaze with interest on the famous wanton throned in her jewels at the opera; and from this, your countenance and complaisance, whilst the painted outcast goes to the police-court and the prison, the jewelled wanton may steal the honour of your name unchastised, and wed your young heir to eternal shame, unarraigned.

Need you marvel then that, beholding this contrast of issue, women—low, ignorant, made full of greed by want, made sick for money and pastime by the inordinate envies and tawdry fashions of the poor of this age — say dimly to themselves, "Let us only be vile enough, we shall do well. All that are wanted are beauty and luck."

And verily they have cause to say it.

It has often seemed to me that you might do much to scare the female vultures from their prey upon the youthful curled darlings of your proud races, if you declared by law all marriages invalid wherever the vileness of the wife's previous life was a fact beyond dispute. It would be simple; it would be rightful: for shall the meed of the just pass to the unjust? shall the guerdon of honour abide with the thief? Shall Faustina claim a place beside Lucretia? Shall Phryne with the wine-dropping roses of shame on her temples, presume to mate herself with Arria Pæta, with the white lilies of courage and innocence bound on her beautiful brows?

But it is not done; and meantime the courtesan can laugh her cynical laughter, and say in her heart, "I will sin whilst it shall please me. When it ceases to please I can take the communion and—marriage!"

As for me, when I heard the world thus talk of her, I felt stupid and aghast. My thoughts were busied with that old dead time, when the woman who now drove there in her pomp and power, watched by all eyes, and spoken of by all lips, had stood in the cottage-door under the rose-thorn, and chaffered for glass beads and penny ribbons with the old pedlar of the Peak.

From the hour when she had stolen the coins of her brother's thrift and toil from under the moss by the apple-tree, this woman's life had been one long theft. Her hands had spared naught that her eyes saw and coveted, she had had no pity for youth; no mercy for ruin; no remorse at love;

no shame at trust; she had had but one law for her life—the
law of greed. If you would only bear in mind that this is
the law of all such women's lives, the world would be spared
much maudlin sentiment, and men much undeserved reproach.

That law Avice Dare, in all things the type and model of
her class, had obeyed, without one pause for its infringement
by any sort of gentler thought or better deed. She was cruel,
because all low untutored human creatures ever are more
cruel than any desert beast, or python of the swamps: she
was licentious, because women of her likeness, having but
splendid vitality and bodily beauty, without any conscience,
or intelligence, or soul within them, are always surrendered
to the dominion of the senses: but beyond all, more than all,
she was possessed with greed; the same greed which had
made her gloat over the mock stones and brazen jewelry of
the pedlar's pack, and steal, and pillage, and forsake all
duty, and betray the loyal heart which trusted her, that she
might flee to the ways of iniquity, and to the wages of shamefulness. Greed of the basest sort—greed for the things of the
senses; for raiment, and food, and wine; for horses, and
chariots, and treasure; for the laughter of fools, and the
license of venal kisses; for the envy of other women of the
gems on her breast, and the gold in her hands.

And having fallen upon an Age which has elected to deify
the courtesan, and wherein hard avarice, and keen passions
for pelf and self, do prosper more greatly than any genius
or attainment, or quality of the mind or character, this woman
was rewarded for her sin.

She had not intelligence, she had not knowledge, she had
no kind of pity nor any sort of comprehension; she was brain-
less as any savage that squats in his African hut; she was
only capable of such joys as the drowsy jewelled snake may
know in his Mexican swamps; she could eat, and drink, and
could glitter gemlike in the sun, and could uncoil from gorged
torpidity to kiss—or kill.

In a word, she was the courtesan of the nineteenth cen-

tury, who, to all the license and all the cruelty of the wantons that turned their thumbs downward for their brawny
paramours to die in Rome, has added all the vulgarities
of modern ribaldry and all the chicaneries of modern civilisation.

Hence, being thus suited to the Age which had begotten
her—being thus its creature and its likeness—she had thriven
in it as the snake thrives in hot and poisonous waters, which
for all purer and healthier things breed death.

Luck, of course, there had been in it; luck is the divinity
of the soulless. Many women, having all the will to do the
evil that she did, find themselves barred out for ever from
the chance. Many fishers in the sea-depths of vice angle all
through the day and bring to land nothing for their pains.
Many like her in their natures, and their passions, and their
aims, but lacking either her supreme physical beauty, or her
supreme good fortune, wander drenched and starving in the
slimy rains of city streets at midnight, cursing vice, as others
curse virtue, because its service is wretchedness, and its wage
famine. Luck, truly, there had been in this amazing fate,
which lifted the once sullen, ragged, unkempt peasant on to
this eminence where all the world observed her—clothed in
the purple, and environed with the "divinity that doth hedge"
the royalty of Gold.

But beyond all favours of chance, or circumstance, all aids
of accident or opportunity, the chief reason of her fortune was
that this woman was so entirely harmonious with her time,
so utterly its true daughter in rapacity, in licentiousness, in
egotism, in coarse hard lust of gold, and in dull dead indifference to anything save gain. She had been callous to
all misery she dealt, all need she left, all horror she entailed,
throughout her whole career—as callous when she had drawn
from the earth her brother's silver pieces that had been saved
by the hardness of his toil and the sweet patience of his self-
negation, as now when she trod under her foot a boy's guileless youth, and the lofty name of his race, and raised her
head in the world's sight, crowned. Crowned in greatness,

if crowned with a diadem from whose jewels the eagle-stone [*]
of Honour had dropped, with the same moment that had
raised it up to her shameless brow. Ah, well!—let but Kaiser
or Courtesan seize their crown and wear it, they shall find
courtiers and coveters enow; and for its gems—the eagle-stone
that knights held high as a stainless talisman, and that kings
wore in the old, fair, fearless years of old, is out of use and
out of fashion now.

CHAPTER XV.

Bonnet Blanc.

"What a wonderful woman that is!" said Fanfreluche to
me a day or two later, with a sigh of passionate envy. "What
do you think she has done? Not content with all the goods
of earth, she has even secured herself immortality—*she has
hired Philippe Rissôle!*"

And Fanfreluche for once held her breath in an absolute
awe of amaze.

"Immortality!" I ventured to echo in bewilderment.
"And who, then, pray, may be Philippe Rissôle, who can
confer it?"

"O heavens!" cried Fanfreluche, in a whirlwind of contempt, "what a thing it is to have lived in a puppet-box and
a garret! O you ignoramus, you barbarian, you most miserable of outsiders! *Who* is Philippe Rissôle? He is the artist
that made the Guards' Club sublime with his sauces; he is
the poet that made the French Embassy divine with his *hors
d'œuvres;* he is the *maestro* that made the Emperor of Russia
cry, 'I am greater than Cæsar,' as he ate a cutlet in curl-
papers; he is the genius of whom it has been said that the
Pope, embracing him after a *jour maigre* of thirty services,
mourned with tears that it was forbidden to send the Golden
Rose to heads crowned with the glorious *bonnet blanc* of the
kitchen. He is Philippe Rissôle, THE COOK! And she has

* The ancient *pierre d'aigle,* supposed to be found in eagles' nests. — ED.

hired him—she!—whom you once saw washing her own potatoes to eat with black bread for a noonday dinner. O, Lord!
Can' the 'masses' ask for a more absolute millennium of de-
mocracy than this topsy-turvy age in which an Avice Darc
can live to hire a Philippe Rissôle!"

I was silent: I was not alive to the imperial greatness of
a Rissôle, but I was struck dumb with a curious sense of marvellous strangeness as I thought of the woman whom I had
once seen greedily devouring the gilded gingerbread and the
painted peppermint-sticks of a wake fair-stall, now being
qualified to dazzle the sight of the world with banquets fitted
for princes!

"They call her a stupid woman," pursued Fanfreluche.
"Pshaw! she has the very wit and wisdom that suits her
Age. She is a splendid strategist; there is not a man in the
town, however lofty his rank, that will not accept invitations
to dinners designed by Rissôle. She knows that those who
are wise, seeking to rise, and desiring to win the *kudos* of
their compeers, will not ask themselves, have they genius?
have they beauty? have they wit? have they power? but
will ask themselves only—can they give a good dinner? If
they are sure that they can—not a good dinner in the mere
ordinary meaning of the word, but a dinner, original,
voluptuous, harmonious, dulcet, a 'thing of beauty and a
joy for ever'—then they may know that sooner or later the
world will be theirs. She sees this: she does not trust to
her beauty or her splendour, to her riches or her wicked-
ness, the world is full of such as these; but she obtains
Rissôle! The only living man in Europe who can make an
epic worthy of epicures! To secure the cook of the century
is to obtain the roc's egg. Who is the most successful
diplomatist? He who most successfully entertains. Is there
anything so humanising as a perfect dinner? Anything that
so tends to reconcile differences, and to smoothe aside prejudices? When a man eats exquisitely, he feels harmoni-
ously and he thinks placidly. What epicure would propel
a war that should ban the truffled turkeys of Paris from his

own frontier? What gourmet would urge a 'crusade for
ideas' when the campaign would deprive him of the *pâtés* of
Strasburg, of the *ortolans* of Lombardy, or of the *caviare* of
Russia? A statesman will cast a nation recklessly into feud
and famine when it is only the bread-rate of the poor that
will have to rise, only the porridge-pot of the pauper that will
have to be empty; but when he is a dinner-giver of consummate art, and understands the imperishable qualities of
the truffle, and the imperative necessities for the *foie gras*,
he will be no party to dissension that shall leave his *menus*
incomplete, and his cook disconsolate and unnerved. No one
understands so well as an epicure the mutual dependence of
the nations; for what dinner is worth anything to which all
the nations do not contribute? Strike any one nation off the
list of commerce, and you strike some one dainty off the bill
of fare. Were I a sovereign all my ambassadors should be
the best dinner-givers of their times.   Years ago I heard the
appointment of Lord Courtly to the Viennese Embassy sorely
questioned and sneered at; a man who I know well openly
attacked Lord Parmesan, then chief of F. O., upon the un-
justifiable choice. 'What single qualification does Courtly
possess for such a post?' he persisted. 'What single talent
does he evince for such an eminence? You cannot point out
one!' Parmesan laughed. 'Yes, I can; he possesses Rissôle.'
Parmesan was shrewd and all-seeing amongst men; he knew
that the pivot of all diplomacy turns within a stewpan. Avice
Dare knows as much.   Ere the season be over every man of
note will have dined with the Marchioness of Isla.   Philippe
Rissôle will give her eminence in the present, and in the
future immortality—for will not the dinners that he conceives
and executes for her table be shrined in the Golden Books of
gastronomic science for ever?

"The worst is," added Fanfreluche, ending with a sigh
her impassioned periods,—"the worst is, how can a woman
who once peeled her own potatoes be ever capable of ap-
preciating the genius of a Rissôle? She loves eating, indeed; but what has a vulgar love of eating in common with

the exquisite delicacies of gastronomical discrimination? The
palate requires education from birth upwards; your only true
epicure is ever of gentle breeding. But now—now—the
canaille have all the cooks; and Milord Rôture and Milady
Cocotte give dinners that would have brought tears of ecstasy
to the eyes of Brillat-Savarin, and all the while could not
themselves tell for their lives an ortolan from a sparrow, or a
canvas-back duck from a quack-quack of the gutter!"

I paid little heed to her; but her prophecies proved cor-
rect.

Isla House was opened with all the fresh magnificence of
Louis-Quinze decoration; the great cook created a series of
dinners which surpassed anything that he had ever conceived for prince or minister; and whilst the town talked of
her dauntless effrontery, of her *luxe effrayant*, of her infamy,
and of her ostentation, half its lords and gentlemen went to
criticise the wonders of her table; and their fair wives re-
gretted her shame and her sin because these debarred them
from honouring banquets prepared by Philippe Rissôle.

CHAPTER XVI.

Nellie's Prayer.

"I was at the Private View yesterday," said Fanfreluche,
with a grin. "How'd I get in? As I get everywhere, simple-
ton. I hide myself under a woman's dress,—for all the
world as if I were a sin! And I keep so quiet; not a soul
suspects me a bit more than the public suspects the money
that changes hands when the journals write a statesman into
office, or an archbishop into the primacy. I was at the
Private View. There is nothing there that comes near
Gladys' portrait. All that mob of ministers, fine ladies,
critics, dandies, and *litterati*, were unanimous about it. It
kills every other picture near; and yet there is so little colour
about it! 'That wonderful white!' they all say; but it is the
wonderful face above the white that charms them. Lady

Otho was there; and Beltran was entangled with her party.
He is always very courteous and friendly with her; he always
is with his old loves. She looked very long at the picture;
but she said nothing, except a few words of praise of the
artist; but awhile after, in the miniature-room, he stood beside her, some way apart from any others. Then she addressed him suddenly:

"'That girl is very beautiful!'

"'You have seen her on the stage, surely?' he answered
carelessly.

"She replied to him, with a touch of impatience: 'On the
stage,—of course! But they are so made up there—one never
knows—'

"He smiled.

"'She does not need to "make up." Have you any idea
how young she is?'

"I saw her long hazel eyes flash fire.

"'Is she not the girl you spoke to me of most romantic-
ally once—long ago? The sister of that dead boy, of that
poet?'

"He laughed.

"'*I* "romantic"! surely that can never have been! Yes
—she is the same.'

"'And is it true what the world says of you and her—
now?'

"She spoke hurriedly and almost fiercely; impulse must
have been strong on her, or she would never have deigned to
stoop to such a question.

"'Not in the least true,' he answered in his most
negligent fashion; 'though I don't know whom it can con-
cern.'

"'Not true!' she echoed; 'when you lavish all your wealth
on her, spend all your time with her, are seen everywhere
beside her!'

"'Not true,' he answered again more coldly. 'As for
wealth—I have none left, and if I had she would only take
the fair wage of her talent.'

"She laughed a little; that laugh that it never does one good to hear.

"'Indeed! Ah; pardon me if I cannot believe in your platonics.'

"'Perhaps it is natural you should not,' he murmured, as he drew her attention to a miniature. She turned to the art-subject with ease and indifference; but her cheek burned hotly under its delicate rouge: she spoke no more of Gladys. Do you think it was severe? Well—she should not have provoked him. Women will never understand the wisdom of the *non quieta movere*, and they never will let 'the dead past bury its dead,' and comprehend that to open closed graves is unsightly."

"But if she should still care for him?"

"My dear, as I told you, she cares enough to dislike to see him care for any other. Every woman loves enough for that. Even Avice Dare would know *so* much of the grand passion. 'Love!'—it is such a pretty synonym for all kinds of envies, and egotisms, and jealousies, and vicious desires. They are choice in their graceful synonyms, these dear human beings. They wrap a nauseous fact up in a gilded phraseology, until they take the pill like a bonbon. Pshaw! without that felicitous art do you think they would ever have managed to cheat themselves into forgetting their cousins the apes, and only acknowledging their cousins the angels?"

"There are men who hold to, and revere, straight simple truths," I said staunchly, for I thought better of men than she did.

"Are there, my dear?" she replied with a grin. "I never met them. I have heard a very great many men and women call the crows carrion birds, and the jackals carrion beasts, with an infinite deal of disgust and much fine horror at what they were pleased to term 'feasting on corpses;' but I never yet heard any one of them admit their own appetite for the rotten 'corpse' of a pheasant, or the putrid haunch of a deer, to be anything except the choice taste of an epicure!"

"But they do cook the corpses!" I remonstrated; whereupon she grinned with more meaning than ever.

"Exactly what I am saying, my dear. Their love of synonyms has made them forget that they are *carnivori*, because they talk so sweetly of the *cuisine*. A poor, blundering, honest, ignorant lion only kills and eats when the famine of his body forces him to obey that law of slaughter which is imposed on all created things, from the oyster to the man, by what we are told is the beautiful and beneficent economy of Creation. Of course, the lion is a brutal and bloodthirsty beast of prey, to be hunted down off the face of the earth as fast as may be. Whereas man—what does he do? He devours the livers of a dozen geese in one *pâté;* he has lobsters boiled alive, that the scarlet tint may look tempting to his palate; he has fish cut up or fried in all its living agonies, lest he should lose one *nuance* of its flavour; he has the calf and the lamb killed in their tender age, that he may eat dainty sweetbreads; he has quails and plovers slaughtered in the nesting-season, that he may taste a slice of their breasts; he crushes oysters in his teeth whilst life is in them; he has scores of birds and animals slain for one dinner, that he may have the numberless dishes which fashion exacts; and then— all the time talking softly of *rissôle* and *mayonnaise*, of con*sommé* and *entremet*, of *croquette* and *côtelette*—the dear *gourmet* discourses on his charming science, and thanks God that he is not as the parded beasts that prey!"

"Well," said I sulkily, for I am fond myself of a good *volau-vent*,—"well, you have said that eating is a law in the economics—or the waste—of creation. Is it not well to clothe a distasteful and barbaric necessity in a refining guise and under an elegant nomenclature?"

"Sophist!" said Fanfreluche, with much scorn, though she herself is as keen an epicure and as suave a sophist, for that matter, as I know,—"I never denied that it was well for men to cheat themselves, through the art of their cooks, into believing that they are not brutes and beasts of prey— it is well exceedingly—for their vanity. Life is sustained

only by the destruction of life. Cookery, the divine, can
turn this horrible fact into a poetic idealism; can twine the
butcher's knife with lilies, and hide the carcass under roses.
But I do assuredly think that, when they sit down every
night with their *menu* of twenty services, they should not call
the poor lion bad names for eating an antelope once a fortnight."

And, with the true consistency of preachers, Fanfreluche
helped herself to a Madeira stewed kidney which stood
amongst other delicacies on the deserted luncheon table.

We were in the inner portion of Beltran's chambers; I
occasionally strayed across the length of the park, and found
my way thither. I had grown wary of all thieves' beguile-
ments and stratagems; and I liked dearly to find myself once
more in those well-beloved spacious apartments, with their
deep, soft, blue colour, and their charming confusion of bric-
h-brac; their masculine litter and their artistic luxuries; their
familiar scent of cigar smoke, and their quaint bits of priceless vertù.

For picturesque charm, and for true comfort and luxuriousness, I do not think there is any mansion in the town
which can approach some of those perfectly arranged chambers that look out on the Green-park, or stud the various
streets of the quarter of St. James. They have all a woman's
elegance and all a man's negligence: the combination is perfection.

Whilst she ate her kidney, and I dozed on a couch, there
entered into the outer room his sister, the Countess of
Leintwardine; a woman of noble presence, wearing her forty
or more years with bloom and majesty. Beltran, who was at
that moment going out to his phaeton below, met her face to
face; he stood still and bent his head to her in silence.

She came quickly up to him; she was an impulsive woman
despite her dignity.

"Vere—don't let *us* be estranged," she said softly. "I
did not think what I said!—"

He gave her his hand instantly; he was not a man to refuse to meet such an advance.

. "I am afraid you did think," he said with a smile. "It was the thought I resented—"

"O no—O no," she said a little hurriedly. "I never think anything against you. Surely you know that?"

"Why do you not take my word, then?" he asked quietly.

"They are such very strange circumstances," she murmured; "so very equivocal!"

He raised his eyebrows a little, and moved an armchair towards her in silence.

"No, thanks. I am in a hurry homeward," she said, leaning her hand on the back of the chair. "I only came to see if you were here—one never has a chance to speak a serious word in society. As you were alone I could not help saying to you—let my injurious words be forgotten, and believe, O, always believe, Vere, that you have no truer friend than I am, no one who loves you more dearly than I do. And if I grieve over—over—some things in what seems to me a wasted career, it is only, only, my brother, because I remember too tenaciously and too fondly the hopes and the promises of your youth."

He listened, touched by the words, moved yet more by the tears that stood in the eyes of this haughty and worldly-wise woman of his race. He was silent a moment, then he answered her:

"You cannot be more dissatisfied with my life than I am; but—which of my contemporaries is more content with his own? Satiety lies like a curse on us all; and it is little odds whether it be born of ambition or of pleasure. Perhaps, if you knew all, you might not think mine so utterly wasted, though it is idle and barren of renown; but—that does not matter much; it is certainly selfish and useless enough not to be worth a defence. Yet—listen to me an instant. You know that I should not lie to you?"

"Nor to any one," she said, looking on him with a proud and sad tenderness.

He bent his head.

"Well—you say, too, that you bear me some love. Listen to me, then. More than a year ago, I told you that had my mother been living I should have taken Gladys Gerant to her. You heard—but you refused to assist me; you refused to lend her your countenance. What you refused to do, I could not ask of any woman less near to me. When I sought to interest any in her they met me with the question, 'What does your sister say?' To such a question I could give no answer; you had deprived me of one. What has been the consequence? That in lieu of being honoured by the world as her gifts and her purity demand, she is classed by the world with its most venal order, and nothing that I can do or declare can move one hair's-breadth of the weight of calumny off her. Now, on my faith as a gentleman, this woman you condemn is as innocent as your own daughters; of her beauty and her genius you have judged publicly; to the exquisite grace and nobility of her mind and heart no words of mine could ever render justice. You have spoken of my youth; in her presence alone do its better instincts revive, does its dead promise still seem capable of resurrection. Beatrice, it is not too late. Will you—even now—go to her; have faith in her; lend her the shield of your high name, prove to the world that my sister at least believes that I do not lie? It is not too late—you occupy the station from which it is possible to stem the tide of slander. Let her once be seen with you, and you will save her for ever from the vileness and the cowardice of calumnies which she is too innocent ever to imagine can assail her; and from which I—a man, and her reputed lover—am utterly powerless to defend her life. You believe me, you say—will you do this for my sake, and the sake of truth?"

He spoke for the sole time in his life with sad and passionate earnestness: it was not for himself that he pleaded; and his words followed one another eagerly, eloquently, unselfishly; with a prayer which one would have thought no woman ever could have heard in vain.

His sister listened, the tears in her haughty eyes; she bowed her head as he paused, and over her bent face passed tremulous shadows of yielding and of regret. She sighed, and stretched out her hands to him.

"Anything but that—anything! It is not possible—an actress—my daughters—think what the world would say of me!"

His teeth clenched on his lip; he was bitterly wounded.

"Need a woman of my race pause for *that!*" he muttered with passionate scorn. He had been unwise enough to hope; he had stooped his pride to plead. His disappointment was intense; his mortification supreme.

She laid her hands upon his arm.

"O Vere! I do believe—I do indeed. She is beautiful, exceedingly, and no doubt she is all else that you say, but the world holds her as your mistress; I cannot subject my children—"

"That is enough!" he said sternly. "If you came here for peace, not for feud, you had best say no more!"

"But you forgive me? You will not be angered again?"

He smiled; his coldest and most evil smile.

"Angered? Because you prove so true to your sex and your order! O no—O no!"

She would have answered him, but he went to the door, bade his servant call the Lady Leintwardine's carriage, and led her with grave and graceful courtesy down the stairway to the street below.

"Do you know what Gladys is to him now, my dear?" said Fanfreluche grimly.

"Scarcely!" I murmured, bewildered.

"Then I will tell you," she answered with caustic curtness. "She is the only woman whom he has loved in all the length of his life."

The voices of the dilettanti were echoed by the public crowd when the doors of the Academy were opened to these last. There was no picture so sought as that of the Cup-bearer of Vortigern. Its recognition as a portrait was its chief interest to the multitude; but even those who only came to it for this coarser reason were touched into silence and admiration before that spiritual, proud, poetic face, that had so little in its look of earthly care or earthly thought. Over the lightest and lowest that came thither it had a strange subduing power, which hushed the common parlance on their tongues, and sent them mute and wondering away.

"This picture has increased your celebrity tenfold, Gladys," said Beltran to her on the third day of its exhibition, when he strolled beside her through the green aisles of her pretty garden.

She smiled: the smile so pathetic in its meditation and its eloquence, that was on the mouth of the daughter of Hengist.

"I do not care for that! But—if it would make the people love me a little I should be glad."

"Why do you want that?" Beltran asked her gently.

"I do not know," she said with half a sigh. "But—when you see those thousands looking at you night after night, all strangers, all nameless to you, yet all caring so little for you that, if you died ere the play were ended, they would only feel themselves cheated of their spectacle, you cannot help wishing that you had a little of their friendship, a little of their love, and were not only to them just a mere toy to be watched, a mere mechanism to be dissected."

"With all your genius how little you are fit for the stage —for *our* stage! Great heavens!" he muttered, and he paced the lawn with his head bent as he spoke.

Then he came to her, and took her hands in his.

"Gladys, sometimes it seems to me like a crime to have brought your youth, your innocence, your divine nature into such a world as this of ours. O, my child, if ever you should reproach me!—"

She lifted her eyes to him in wonder; she seldom saw him thus moved. Then she stooped, and with an exquisite grace and obeisance in the action, touched his hand with her lips.

"Reproach! I! If you choose to kill me you would have

a right to my life—you, who have bestowed on me every thing on earth!"

"Hush, hush!" said Beltran almost harshly. "You owe me nothing! God grant only that you may never blame me."

She looked at him with a smile—that smile of ineffable exhaustless faith which ever makes the face it lightens half divine.

She loved him—it was so easy to see—with such perfect tenderness, such absolute adoration. She hardly knew it; he was "her friend;" he used none of the language of lovers; he had never, as he had said, touched her lips with his own; he subjugated whatever passion he might feel with a stern self-control unlike any other thing in his self-indulgent and too reckless life. But love for him had grown into the religion of her existence.

Although he had never let her know the extent of the services he had rendered her, veiling them under generous fictions of her art, and of its values, yet there was much that he could not conceal. Through him alone she had been raised as by magic from utter misery, want, obscurity, and desolation, to perfect ease, elegance, peace, and fame. In truth, her debt to him was measureless; and yet vaster than she even dreamed:—for she knew not of those depths of the world's dangers, or of the perils to her of his own passion, from which he continually defended her: defended her even against himself, because his simple creed, "the good faith of a gentleman" forbade him to injure what lay defenceless at his mercy.

Ah! revile that old faith as you will, it has lasted longer than any other cultus; and whilst altars have reeled, and idols been shattered, and priests changed their teachings, and peoples altered their gods, the old faith has lasted through all; and the simple instinct of the Greek eupatrid and of the Roman patrician still moves the heart of the English gentleman—the instinct of *Noblesse oblige.*

She loved him, as I say, with sweetest, highest, most innocent, and yet most passionate devotion. In her eyes, in her voice, in her unasked submission to him, in her countenance when he entered the place where she was, she betrayed it utterly, because utterly ignorant of the true meaning of this concentration of her whole life in his which to her seemed simplest gratitude.

He had been much loved by many women; men of his type ever are so; many a woman of the world had been stung by his listless contempt, or beguiled by his indolent wooing, into a passion that had become the one real, vital, undying thing in all her artificial existence. Many a young girl, like poor Nellie, had spent on him all the freshness and fervour of her heart in a worship won merely by some gentle, careless word, or some kindly glance from those eyes commonly so cold and weary, in which he had meant no more than a man means when he gives a caress to a playful horse. But although far and wide he had awakened more love than he ever needed or heeded, he had not ever been loved as he was now by this creature who owed all to him; this poet who had all the strength and the elevation of genius, this child who had all the innocence and trustfulness of infancy. To few men is it given to be thus loved, with a love in which the mind bears as great and pure a part as the heart, and the intelligence is centred no less than the passions.

It was a jewel of price which fell in his path, and often I wondered whether he would tread it down in the earth at the last beneath his foot, or whether he would raise it up as he went, and cherish it in safety in his breast.

Sometimes I thought that the mists of the sins and the antictics of the world were still so darkly about him that he saw not its value, and would crush it carelessly in mere negligence: and at others I thought that he knew its beauty so well that he deemed his own hand not unsullied enough ever to touch and to take it.

The world held him closely; he had been with it and of it so long; he was so deeply steeped in its tired, sceptical, gay, dissolute temper; he had so long learned to think with it that

nothing was desirable save the distraction of the immediate
moment, and the banishment of all emotional weakness.

But the world could not wholly absorb a man to whom, in
the years of his youth, a lofty ambition had murmured its
dreams, and an ideal love had shadowed its meaning. The
ambition had died, stifled by pleasure; the ideal had been
forgotten, supplanted by the senses. But sometimes I thought
that, when he gazed in the soul-lit eyes of Gladys, and heard
the eloquence of her poetic thoughts, both the dreams and the
faiths of his boyhood came back to him, and that he no
longer sought an intrigue, an idleness, a selfish indulgence,
a plaything for the passions, but at last also—loved. And
loved at length so well, that he denied desire and restrained
passion.

Meanwhile—whilst this struggle hid its violence in his
proud silent heart, and this self-negation was covered by his
proven armour of careless and caustic indifference—all his
familiar friends had, of course, decided for him that he was a
libertine, successful as usual, and that she was a toy for whom
he showed somewhat more gentleness than common.

Indeed I often wonder to hear the complaints that are
made as to the slightness and scarce sincerities of the friendship of this day.

I know not why you complain; there was surely never an
era when your friends took more active interest in the discussion and disposal of your affairs, or took more trouble to
insure that the very worst possible should be said of you.

What more can you want? I assure you that society
thinks much better of you the more evil it deems you. They
called him now fearfully immoral, and respected him: if they
had been told the truth and been brought to believe it, they
would have certainly thought him a fool or a madman, and
he would have sunk in their estimation accordingly.

When any of this that they said of himself drifted home
to him he smiled; he was a man of the world: but now and
then when he was alone he ceased for a moment to be a man

of the world, and then his teeth clenched and his eyes
darkened—because he thought of her.

"Good God! what a society we live in, in which a woman's
innocence is a thing incredible!" he said once in a rare moment of impulsive utterance to his friend Denzil.

"Nay," said Denzil with a smile that had all the bitterness of his dead love in it. "Let her lose her innocence, and
she will find champions enough!"

Is the saying dark to you who read? Ah, then! you do
not know society.

In the same week that the Academy opened I was lying
in the sun upon the lawn; the garden of the villa was blooming with jonquils and hyacinths; the hawthorn shrubberies
were in their first budding bloom; the birds in the conser-
vatory were singing, amidst azaleas and camellias, and their
music came through the open doors.

All was sweet and sunny; through one of the pretty mul-
lioned casements I saw the luxurious little library within;
Gladys sat there, reading at an oak lectern; the rich dark
velvet of her skirts had the colour of a Titian picture; and
her delicate head seemed painted in gold upon the shadow of
the deep-hued chamber. All was picture-like; all full of
fragrance; all eloquent of a peace around which gold had
drawn a charmed circle that pain could not break.

The roll of the carriages in the streets and roads beyond
the walls was only dully heard; only pleasantly suggestive of
the gay and endless life around.

As I half dreamed and half slumbered, in my calm re-
verie, in my sunlit resting place, there came to me Fanfreluche; pressing through the bronze scroll-work of the
entrance gate with the daring independence of her habitual
movements.

She approached more slowly than was her wont, and I
saw that her brilliant eyes were for once dim and troubled.

"I have ill tidings," she said simply. "Nellie is dead."

"Dead!" I could only echo the word dully and stupidly.

"Yes—you asked me of her some time ago. She is dead

of cold, and exertion, and fever; brought on by sitting up
many nights with a little ballet-girl of the Palace Theatre;
little Clarice Vaughan, who sickened and died first of a sort
of low fever, they say."

"Dead, dead, since when?" I muttered stupidly still;
death seemed to me a thing that it was impossible to utter in
the same breath with the name of that sturdy, rosy, blue-eyed
young creature, saucy as a boy, blythe as a bird, untiring as
a chamois, the little dauntless dare-devil, who feared neither
man nor woman!

"Since an hour ago—only," Fanfreluche answered me
gravely, without a touch of mockery or any caustic word.
"She was ill but a brief time, I think. We were about to
drive to Hurlingham to-day, when a little tattered boy came
up; the grooms pushed him away, but Beltran listened to him.
He said that Nell Brown was dying, and the old Granny had
sent him; would my lord let Nell see him afore she died? they
thought she wouldn't live an hour. Beltran, without a word,
turned his horses' heads to that poor place where she dwelt.
You saw it once? I was already in the phaeton; and descended
and followed him as he went through the house; the old woman weeping and wringing her hands, and crying sorely because she was all alone in the world at eighty year, and moaning out how 'Nellie, as was such a rare good child, if 'twarn't
for her wild humours, had been so wilful and so mad, and had
dug her own grave, say all as one would, a-tending little Annie
Dell, as had been down with fever, and dead and buried mor'n
two weeks agone.' Beltran answered her with a few words
of pity and consolation; and was ushered by her into the little
chamber where you once saw Gladys Gerant saved from
famine—and worse.

"Nellie was stretched upon her little truckle-bed; the sun
came in over the roofs, the canary moped in his cage, the
golden creeper hung withering for want of water; the little
room was full of gay and tawdry ribbons, and gauzes, and
tinsel, and all the glitter of stage costume. Her eyes were
closed; her face had lost all its colour and roundness; there

was a terrible blue pallor about the mouth. I thought that she was dead already; so did he.

"He went up to the bed, and stooped over her with a few gentle words. His voice seemed to electrify her; her eyes opened suddenly, with a blinded senseless look; her breath came fast and stifled.

"'Do you not know me, Nellie?' he asked her—so gently still. 'My poor girl—why not have told us of your illness earlier? If I had only heard—if I had only dreamt—'

"She gazed at him with more of comprehension, and a sudden flash came over the grayness of her face that gave it once more something of its fresh and rosy hues.

"'I sent—I sent,' she gasped. 'I don't know how I dared —but you was always so good, my lord.'

"'*Dare* is no word between you and me, Nellie,' he answered her. 'You had the courage to stay my hand once, in a passion that was making me a brute. I owe you much: only tell me how I can pay it.'

"Her dull strained eyes, that had lost all their old, smiling, azure light, looked up at him piteously. She gasped for breath—for speech—once or twice vainly.

"'If only you would have let me help you!' he said to her. 'But you would never take anything from me—not even such influence and interest as I may possess. It is not too late now, you are so young, so strong; I will get you all the aid, all the science, that the town holds—'

"She interrupted him with a plaintive motion of her bright curly head, that hung so languidly, like a wounded bird's.

"'I'm as good as dead,' she muttered slowly and feebly; 'else—I wouldn't have sent—never—never! But I want to say one word, sir—if you won't be angered—'

"'Say on, Nellie.'

"There was an infinite pity in his voice; he had seen death often enough to know that the hope which he had held out to her was utterly vain.

"Still, with her eyes gazing up at him, so woefully, so prayerfully, she spoke her feeble and broken words:

"'I wanted to say—I've heard, my lord, all manner of evil things of *her*—and you. I've heard that—that—she have come to shame, though it's a gilded one; and I know—I know —as it's a lie!'

"'It *is* a lie.'

"His face was very dark, his voice was very grave, as he answered her.

"'I said so!—I said so!' she murmured, her hoarse weak voice for the moment ringing with melody and strength once more. 'I said as she was innocent and pure as any little child—lie all they would. And I kep' away from her,—because the likes o' me seen near her couldn't but do her harm; me being so common, and so ignorant, and so low like upon the stage; and she so beautiful, and so learned, and so great a lady, one may say. But—but you know as they do say all them things of you and her?—you know what she be thought to be? You know as she'll never be cleared of what they talk—never, never, never!'

"'I know!'

"The wooden rail of the chair, on which his hands rested, was broken by the clench of them upon it as he spoke.

"'But it won't ever be *true?*' she cried, raising herself upon one arm, and conquering for that brief space the agonies and the weakness of death. 'You'll never make it *true?* It don't half matter if it isn't true. You see—you see, sir—it all came through me, her knowing of you first. I don't think I could lie quiet in my grave if she ever lived to curse me for it. And she *would* curse me—when she came to see as she was scorned! O, promise me, my lord, as she sha'n't ever have no cause—promise me, promise me, she'll live and die in honour!'

"He was silent awhile; then he gently bowed his head.

"'I do promise you—so far as in me lies to keep her so.'

"Her eyes closed; her chest heaved.

"'Thank God,' she murmured. 'I never doubted you—
I never doubted.'

"'If you did not, you had a rarer faith than any friend I
hold! But, Nellie, speak rather of yourself; tell me what I
can do for you. My poor child, you shall not die at such
years as yours!'

"A wan, faint, bitter smile played over her drawn, parched
lips.

"'What matter years?' she muttered. 'Maybe it's best.
I'd have had to go on for ever, act—act—act. And even now
—I was tired: very tired sometimes. Tell her I loved her
always—will you? Don't let her think as I'd ceased to
care—'

"'But tell me something you wish done—for yourself—
for yourself alone!'

"He spoke earnestly, urgently; he saw that, with every
second, sense and thought and sight were dying in her.

"'There's nothing,' she gasped feebly. 'Perhaps if you'd
be good enow to keep old Gran from want? She's nobody
but me; and I couldn't save—much.'

"He stooped over her tenderly.

"'She shall never need whilst she lives. Is there nothing
else—nothing?'

"Her curly head drooped more heavily still; her eyes
looked once more up at him through the dulness and mists of
death.

"'No—no. If so be you wouldn't mind—put your hand
once on my forehead; I think I'd die easier so.'

"He stooped lower, and in answer laid his lips softly on
her brow.

"A flush of dreamy warmth drove for one moment the
ghastly pallor from her face; she trembled from head to foot,
and her eyes shone with a deep ecstasy; then—even in that
same moment—she shivered, stretched her limbs out, and
died.

"He stood beside her, with his head bowed and his eyes
dim; he, whom the world deems callous to all pain and indif-

ferent to all tenderness, was touched to the heart by this
simple, pure, unspoken love that had been borne him, all unasked and unrecompensed, so long and so silently by this
little untutored, careless, audacious child of the populace,
who had shown her lithe form and her fair face to the public
gaze for the wage of his coin.

"The sun shone in over the roofs; the bird in its cage
began a low tremulous song; the murmur of all the crowded
streets came up upon the silence; and Nellie lay there dead;
—the light upon her curly hair, and on her mouth the smile
that had come there at his touch.

"Ah, my dear!" said Fanfreluche, as she ceased her story,
with a half-soft and half-sardonic sadness, "she was but a
little, ignorant, common player, who made but three pounds
a week, and who talked the slang of the streets, and who
thought shrimps and tea a meal for the gods, and who made
up her own dresses with her own hands, out of tinsel and
tarlatanes and trumperies, and who knew no better than to
follow the blind dumb instincts of good that, self-sown and
uncultured, lived in her—God knows how!—as the harebells,
with the dew on them, will live amidst the rank coarse grass
of graveyards. She was but a poor little player, who had
tried to be honest where all was corruption, who had tried to
walk straightly where all ways were crooked. So she died
to-day in a garret, my dear; and—have you heard that the
young Lord of Isla has bought his wife an estate in the south
that covers nearly one half of its county?"

                *   *   *   *   *   *   *

The night of Nellie's death there was a late card party in
his rooms. I had strayed there, and stayed with Fanfreluche.
There were none but men; they played long and gamed high;
it was the rule in his set. It was almost morning when they
broke up, and went on their ways. Denzil remained behind
them. He had strolled away to the great piano, and was
playing quaint, dreamy fragments of various melodies, whilst
he smoked.

"Go on," said his friend briefly, where he lay stretched on a couch by the hearth, and Denzil obeyed.

The gray smoke-clouds circled around them, as the dull vapour of satiety had drifted around all their pleasures and passions; the waves of sound rolled through the silence in soft, sad, weirdly eloquence; Beltran never stirred, he was lost in thought. Denzil arose and came to the hearth.

"What are you thinking of?" he asked.

"Your music."

"No doubt! But besides?"

"Besides," echoed Beltran slowly, as he raised himself and stood erect. "Well, besides—I was wondering whether Cæsar was true to his Order when he said that it was not enough for his wife to be pure, since she was not also above public suspicion; or whether he was but a cowardly cur, who cloaked social timidity in a grand period, and shrank before the mud pellets of social opinion. Which was it—eh?"

Denzil looked at him quickly: "You mean—?"

"I mean—that I must either be traitor to my race or traitor to a woman. I am undecided which to select. *Noblesse oblige.* It is an admirable creed, only a little unsatisfactory when it points two diametrically opposite ways. Get out with you;—it is late. Good-night!"

When his friend was gone he paced to and fro the length of the chambers.

"Am I a brute or a fool," he muttered, "when I know the purity of that perfect life?"

And he walked to and fro, to and fro, in that ceaseless, restless measure, till the sunrise glowed ruddily through the closed shutters.

As at length he passed to his bed he paused a moment before another portrait; a portrait of age, not of youth,—but of age in all its noblest benignity, its most venerable beauty. It was the portrait of his dead mother.

"The House might deem itself sullied; but you would not, were you living," he murmured. Then he went and threw himself on his bed, and slept as the sun rose. His rest was troubled, and on his face in his dreams there were the shadows of sleepless passions.

CHAPTER XVII.

"Glibe."

"Ir this play should succeed it will be a triumph of true art," said another critical writer to Dudley Moore, on the eve of a fresh play at the Coronet Theatre.

That great personage tapped his Louis-Quinze snuff-box with some impatience.

"Pardon me, but it is not possible to have Art at all on the stage. Art is a pure idealism. You can have it in a statue, a melody, a poem; but you cannot have it on the stage, which is at its highest but a graphic realism. The very finest acting is only fine in proportion as it is an exact reproduction of physical life. How, then, can it be art, which is only great in proportion as it escapes from the physical life into the spiritual?"

"But may not dramatic art escape thither also?" asked the critic, who was young and deferred to him.

"Impossible, sir. It is shackled with all the forms of earth, and—worse still—with all its shams and commonplaces. When we read *Othello*, we only behold the tempest of the passions and the wreck of a great soul; but when we see *Othello*, we are affronted by the colour of the Moor's skin, and we are brought face to face with the vulgarities of the bolster!"

"Then there is no use in a stage at all?"

"I am not prepared to conclude that. It is agreeable to a vast number of people: as a Frith or an O'Neil is agreeable to a vast number of people to whom an Ary Scheffer or a Delaroche would be unintelligible. It is better, perhaps, that this vast number should look at Friths and O'Neils than that they should never look on any painting at all. Now, the

stage paints rudely, often tawdrily; still it does paint. It is
better than nothing. I take it that the excellence, as the
end, of histrionic art is to portray, to the minds of the many,
poetic conceptions which, without such realistic rendering,
would remain unknown and impalpable to all save the few.
Histrionic art is at its greatest only when it is the follower
and the interpreter of literature; the actor translates the
poet's meanings into the common tongue that is understood
of the people. But how many on the miserable stage of this
country have ever had either humility to perceive, or capa-
bility to achieve, this?"

The other critic smiled.

"I imagine not one, in our day. Their view of their profession is similar to Mrs. Delamere's, when Max Moncrief
wrote that sparkling comedy for her. 'My dear,' she said
to him, 'why did you trouble yourself to put all that wit and
sense into it? We didn't want *that*. I shall wear all my diamonds, and I have ordered three splendid new dresses!'"

Dudley Moore laughed curtly.

"That is Delamere *aux bouts de ses ongles*. Our stage is
but an asylum for men who are tired of sitting on clerks'
stools, and women who are tired of using a seamstress's scissors. Yet such a stage as *this* we passively permit to be
lauded by our public writers, while we inanely chatter of the
decadence of taste. Good God! we might with as much justice make the House of Commons a cage for 500 parrots and
apes, and complain of the decadence of oratory and of state-
craft! And, indeed," he added with a grim chuckle, "the
parrots and apes would more nearly resemble the politicians
they would displace than do the players of our day resemble
the art which they affect to represent."

The eyes of the younger critic went to the figure of
Gladys.

"Surely she has genius?" he murmured; "you have yourself said so."

"Sir," said Dudley Moore very curtly, "I have said so
certainly; though what men say of a lovely woman is generally

to be taken with a pinch of salt! But because acting is not
art, it does not follow that an actor or an actress may not,
here and there, be an artist. The great player is like the
great orator—half a poet."

It was a few days previous to that pleasant water-party
that the mighty *magister* spoke thus, at a morning rehearsal
which he had deigned to attend—the rehearsal of a new and
picturesque play, which had been written for her by a scholarly and famous author, and cast in those old poetic and
heroic moulds which have been broken into potsherds under
the crow-bars of the felons, and the wheels of the street-cabs,
of the modern drama.

The play was indeed fraught with many perils. To commence with, it read so well in the closet, that it was almost
certain it must go ill on the boards; farther, it was cast in a
bygone time—the Saxon time of England—and was penetrated
with the high and simple spirit of that dead age.

It was slight of structure, inasmuch as the writer—wisely
doubtful of the powers of the herd of men and women who,
calling themselves artists, and receiving high wage in your
capital, would be hissed off the boards of any minor provin-
cial town of France or Italy—had centred all the strength,
pathos, and sustaining power of the piece on the one central
figure—a woman. Of course, this absorption of all interest
into one focus was not artistically symmetrical; but what is
a poet to do when he writes for a stage whereon the actors
declaim with the accent of Cockaigne, and move with the
grace of wooden *fantoccini?* His noblest diction will, he
knows, halt in false quantities through no fault of his own;
and the supreme art of the histrion—the art of gesture—will,
he knows likewise, be either unattempted or caricatured.

With these difficulties before him, he had cast almost the
whole burden of his dramatic creation on the one woman in
whose hands he felt that such a trust was safe.

He was sensible of the offences of his play; he was aware
that it was harmonious in treatment, subdued in colour, calm
in action, pandering nowise either to the prejudices or the

puerilities of the multitude; and yet it was hoped that all these offences might be pardoned to it through—not her genius, for genius alone is a *rococo* thing, who speaks in archaisms—but through the fashion of Gladys Gerant.

Besides, it was to be made a gorgeous spectacle; and it was trusted that in the splendid series of pictures, and the masses of men brought on in its groupings of camp and castle, monastery and witanagemot, the public would be for once induced to pardon intellect in the dialogues and nobility in the passions.

"Utterly unfitted for the present stage," said Dudley Moore, when the play was accepted after a noon reading of it at the theatre. "Utterly! But it is just possible that if you smother the sense of it under a weight of gorgeous decoration; that if you disgrace its classic treatment by a quantity of barbaric magnificence, such as the age it is cast in can afford; if you get some novel effect in moonlight or on water, and give two set scenes to each act, calling them *tableaux*, you may contrive, by dazzling the sight of the audience, to make them pardon their being asked to sit out a work of eloquence and of sense. Indeed, if you could introduce a *jongleur* or mumming scene midway, and get that new conjuror, who is performing miracles at the Egyptian Hall, to appear in it with his bouquets and serpents, the piece might not perhaps quite ruin you; it might even keep the boards for a month."

These sarcastic counsels had been followed seriously—all, indeed, except the adoption of the juggler—and the play was magnificently put upon the stage in a series of exquisite historic pictures, carefully compiled from Holinshed and Sharon Turner, Guillaume de Poitiers and the Roman De Rou.

"It will ruin you," they said to Beltran, who laughed in his negligent fashion.

"When one is to break one's neck, it don't much matter whether it's over a five-bar or a six, that I can see." And with the inborn recklessness that was covered under his quiet manner, he spared no cost accordingly.

So the play was to be put forth with the springtide of the year, and its various scenes—the encampment, the abbey, the vast untouched forests, the gathering of the monks for vespers, the noontide fight by the ford over the sumpter mules, the feasts of the Eorldermen in their Mead Halls—all were to afford spectacles that would to the uttermost serve to induce the public to pardon the startling heresies of meaning and of feeling in the words that were uttered. The scene-painter's skill had been strained to the farthest to purchase forgiveness of the poet's presence.

If you perfectly occupy the eyes of a London playgoer, he will not resent, because he will not note, that you offend his ear with the dead languages of eloquence and sense. Perhaps he may regret that such fine grouping and charming "sets" are not more worthily wedded to some punning doggerel; but he will not resent actively, though he will doubtless feel that he has scarcely had all he should have had for his money.

Moreover, this play was prepared and announced in those young April weeks, when first on men's lips came the rumours of the picture of the Cupbearer of Vortigern. Those who had seen it in the studio spoke widely of it in language that awoke interest and curiosity; and the portrait had scarce been revealed to the general public when the play of *Githa* was put forth, and it was known that she would appear in the old Saxon garb that was worn by the daughter of Hengist.

A trifle like this goes far to arouse and to rivet public attention; and served, amongst others, to make the town ready, and even willing, to excuse the mistake which had chosen an author in lieu of an adapter, a poem in the place of a police report.

The first representation was appointed for the day that followed on Nellie's death. Of that death he did not tell her, and it was too obscure for public rumour or record to take it to her ear. A little dancing girl—one out of hundreds—worth nothing when the lissom energy was once out of her limbs, what name could she leave? What moment of recollection could the busy world give her?

He knew that he must tell her sooner or later, but he shrank—with that kind of tender cowardice which so peculiarly belongs to men who are for themselves sternest, hardest, and least apt to fear—from wounding in any way this heart that had known so much of sorrow in its childhood, and had only so lately basked in joy. He withheld from her all things that could pain her, with an excess of care that had its perils for her; for, so perfect did this life seem in which she dwelt, that insensibly she grew to believe that its beauty must endure, shadowless, for ever; and insensibly, in her trust in him, she lost the strength and self-reliance that she had once possessed amidst adversity.

When her brief life had been but a little frail field-blossom, left desolate on the crumbled walls of a fallen house, to bear night and storm as best it should, and to be blown on by all rude winds of heaven, it had been steadfast and unblanched. But now that it was a hothouse flower, guarded from every chilling breath, and environed with perpetual sunlight; now—I sometimes feared that it would break and perish at the first rough touch—wither in the first lone hour of midnight.

"You are not afraid of your powers to-night?" he asked her in the afternoon of this day on which *Githa* was first to be given to the world.

She smiled in his eyes.

"When you tell me to be afraid I will be,—not until then."

The trustful words smote his conscience: if he dealt truly with her—truly as he had promised to the dead girl—would he not bid her be "afraid" now? Afraid, not of herself, but of him? I saw this thought told in his eyes.

"Do not depend so much upon me," he said gently and sadly. "You are a poet; you are an artist; you have genius; you must not rest your nobler existence on such a useless and prosaic life as mine. I am no poet, Gladys; I am only a tired, selfish, good-for-naught man of the world."

She smiled still; that beautiful serene smile of divinest faith.

"It's ever the noblest who most undervalue themselves," she said simply.

"O, child, I have no nobility!" he said, with a quick, impatient sigh. "If you knew me as I am you would hate me."

"*I!*"—it was only that one word she uttered, but in it there were all the glorious incredulity of a love which could never harbour credence of a stain on its idol, and—yet higher than this—the grandeur of a love which even if forced to condemn in judgment, would only still cleave the closer in tenderness. He looked at her and was silent; he had not the heart—what man would have it?—to shatter that exquisite, pure, untroubled faith in him. Perhaps also he thought—

"Almost thou makest me that which thou dost believe me."

That night was the first night of *Githa*. When the people came to its representation they were a little uneasy at the period in which the play was cast, and at the name of its author, which was of classic and scholarly repute. But the *grand art de plaire* had been long studied at this house; and a reassuring consolation had been prepared for them in a new drop-scene, which represented Dufresny in his Garden of Roses.

I do not suppose that many of them knew who Dufresny was: but the rose-garden was charmingly painted, and the handsome grandson of *la plus fraîche rose de mon parterre* was in his court suit and his lace ruffles: and these we know—to those who don't wear them—always seem suggestive of much elegance and amusement.

The play opened with a gorgeous festival scene, of the Saxon thanes with their purple peacock-broidered robes, their harpists, their skins of wolf and bear, their golden chalices, their rough and riotous revelry. This charmed the assembled house as a mere spectacle, and when, later, Gladys swept across the stage, with her slow, soft, haughty grace, and her white, purple-bordered robe, and her dark, lustrous, grave eyes gazing from under the golden fringe of her hair, they were in no mood to grudge her one iota of the triumph she might win.

And that triumph was great. Until now she had been but a gifted actress of extreme youth, for whom high patronage and favouring circumstance had done so much that it was almost a question if they had not done all. But with this night they knew that by her voice genius alone had spoken.

When the first two acts were over, friends and critics pressed eagerly around her. She bent her head with a dreamy smile; she was too truly an artist not to shrink from the lan-guage of flattery when it jarred on the consecration of her thoughts, the passion of her art.

Beltran scarcely spoke: but when her eyes met his she had the only tribute, the only answer, for which she cared.

Dudley Moore addressed her almost with emotion.

"You prove what none save fools—but many fools—doubt," he said to her. "You prove that the public can no more refuse to obey the influence of genius, than the tides can refuse to obey the laws of their flux and their reflux."

And he was right.

Breathed through her, shadowed forth by her, having in her all its vital yet spiritualised being, the vague dreams of the poet took life and became great. Interpreted by her voice, her eyes, her eloquence, her gestures, the shadowy fancy of the writer became a living creature, pure as the dew, generous as the sun, innocent as the blossom, grand as the tempest.

And the listless, ironical, surfeited, debased mental temper of the world of this your day was enthralled and subdued by an incarnation so unlike to itself, so far removed from its own narrowed passions and its own venal materialism; and yet which had reality within it, because it had the greatness, the truth, and the divine fire which can be evoked from your

human nature in its highest forms and in its noblest moments
—which, indeed, are rare, and found only in your impulses
of heroism, in your hours of self-sacrifice, but yet, though
thus rare, still are existent.

What is beyond all humanity ever fails to move it; it is
the reason why all the religions of your earth are things of
the lip, which scarcely influence the life: it is what remains
human, yet is human only in the highest sense, and by the
deepest woe, that can sway your hearts as the winds the
reeds.

It is scarce too much to say that such a creation was this
which the mind of the poet had conceived, and which the
living power of the actress placed visibly before the dimmer
eyes and the grosser intelligences of those who, without her,
would have missed its meaning.

There were cold cynics there whose eyes were dim with
tears; there were frivolous women there whose tongues were
hushed and whose fans were still; there was a fashionable
throng there that was forced to feel, that was compelled to
honour, that forgot to be inane, and did not dare to cavil or
to sneer.

Do you imagine that a corrupt age cannot revere, that an
artificial age cannot be stirred by truth, that an abject age
cannot rise to comprehension under the compelling force of
genius?—you are wrong to doubt. Was it not the vilest of
the pagan ages that gave credence, and foothold, and tenure,
to the faiths and the philosophies of Paul?

Even as men are to the kine of the fields, so is genius to
men: when its eyes are on them they dare not refuse to obey,
even if they obey in fear and in hatred. Stone it in the dark
they will, indeed—because men are oftentimes lower than the
beasts of stall and sty.

When the end had come, and the pent-up emotions of the
spectators had found their vent in tumults of applause, in
thunders of homage, the triumph that she had won was no
ephemeral glorification of a fair woman, but was the involun-

tary witness borne by a multitude to power that had vanquished it.

As she left the stage for the last time, the echoes of the
vociferations that still called for her, from an audience never
weary of beholding her, were yet resounding through the
house. Her face was very pale; her eyes were heavy; on all
her beauty there was a look of languor, of exhaustion, of
profound sadness: the forces whereby genius moves the
people ever recoil upon itself.

The story of the swan's song in death may be a fable,
doubtless; yet it is true in allegory of the suffering wherefrom is drawn the melodies that thrill the souls of men.

She turned with almost a shudder of distaste from the
congratulations around her.

"Let me go away; let me go home," she murmured to her
friend as he stood by her. "I could not bear the laughter—
the flattery—in the room to-night."

He led her almost in silence from the house.

It was a still, clear, moonlight night; above the narrow
street on which the side-door opened the stars were shining;
it seemed strangely cool and calm after the crashing plaudits
with which the theatre had reëchoed.

In that soft shadowy light her eyes met his. A quick
shudder ran through him.

"O God," he muttered half aloud, "that the world and I
were worthier of you!"

A sigh stirred her lips as she answered him:

"But for you what could the world have known of me?"

Her face was white as death; her eyes were languid
with fatigue; the suffering which is ever the tribute that
genius pays for its sovereignty was upon her; but as the
moonlight fell on her uncovered head, with the golden gleam
of its hair, her loveliness was greater than in her proudest
hours. He looked at her, then led her to her carriage; he
paused a moment irresolute, then for the first time entered it
also.

As he sank beside her, his hands touched hers; his lips

sought here; he drew her to his embrace in the first impulse
of passion that had ever escaped him.

Quivering and mute, she rested in his arms, and hid her
face upon his breast. The high courage, the poetic strength,
the eloquent powers wherewith a moment earlier she had
swayed the crowd, forsook her; and the woman whose divine
gifts had held a multitude in servitude shrank weeping to
him like a tired child.

The swift horses swept fast through the night, flying fleet
as the moments.

In the silence I could hear the loud hard beating of his
heart; in the dusky gleam of the lamp I could see that his
eyelids were wet with tears.

Brokenly, breathlessly, she sobbed as a child sobs on its
mother's bosom. The proud, passionate strength of a woman
breaks ever thus into weakness when the hour that needed
the strength has passed by. He let it have its way, waiting
patiently its exhaustion; but his arms pressed closer and
closer around her, and his kisses burned upon her trembling
lips.

When the carriage paused at length before her home, she
broke from him, and fled swiftly through the leafy shadowy
ways of her garden into the chambers of the house. He followed her rapidly into the little fragrant, velvet-hung room
that served her as a study.

The lights were burning low, the air was heavy with many
flowers, the casements were still open to the balmy spring
night.

She stood upon the hearth, her hands pressed upon her
breast; her face now deathly pale, now flushing scarlet; her
mouth quivering with swift breathless sighs, half terror and
half rapture; her eyes dilated with startled fear, like a roused
deer's, yet lustrous with an unutterable tenderness, an unutterable glory.

"Leave me—leave me!" she murmured brokenly. "I am
base in your sight—I am worthless—for ever!"

For to her pure lofty instinct, to her innocence reared in

simple stern creeds, which held honour a thing that a touch
could attaint, it seemed to her that he must have scorned her
utterly ere ever he had sought her thus with the wildness of
love: it seemed to her that because his kisses had burned
thus on her, she must be debased in his eyes and her own for
evermore. And yet with all this, beyond all this, there
reigned over her her belief in him as the law of her life, the
ruler of her fate, the saviour of her existence; and there
stirred in her, imperious and exulting, the sweet, blind,
tumultuous madness of the woman who loves and is loved.

He stood before her silent. His face was dark with riotous
passion held hard in curb, yet it was changed to a surpassing
softness and reverence.

He stood silent a while; how tempted, how assailed, his
own heart alone ever knew.

Then his hands touched her and drew her to him, and his
eyes gazed into hers.

"But—as my wife?"

Those brief broken words were all he said; it was his life,
his honour, his world, the fame of his race, the repute of his
name, that he gave her. Great gifts need slight phrase.

CHAPTER XVIII.

Slain.

WITHIN a day or two from that time he married her, by
those special laws which can be convened by gold.

In the humility of her intense love she had resisted him;
she had pleaded that she was not worthy; she had entreated
him to pause. But she could not withstand the force of his
persuasion and the yielding of her own heart. And she became his wife.

Denzil and old Margett were the only witnesses of the
marriage, and for a while no others knew it. His fortune was
so close to ruin, his affairs were so deeply entangled, that the
declaration of such a union at that moment was impossible.

So—bitterly against his will—he let her remain on his stage a while, and the town was left in ignorance of the relation that he bore to her.

Perhaps the tie had greater sweetness to them both because thus untold; the ecstasies of passion seemed yet more exquisite because seized from the midst of the world's brilliancies and levities. When their eyes met across the crowded theatre, their secret was dearer because unprofaned by publicity; when the laughter and gaiety of others were about them, their hearts thrilled at a chance word or a chance touch from each other, with purer rapture because their secret was unguessed.

Pshaw! Why need I dwell on what no words can paint?

They loved; they were undivided, In that brief phrase the uttermost passion of life's one perfect joy is told.

The hours fled apace. The spring grew into summer, and the summer grew languid with odorous heat. Three months drifted by; months filled, for her, with colour, with melody, with public homage, with brilliant scenes of pleasure, with sweet, dreamy days in the heart of blossoming woods, with hours of proud eloquence and lofty triumph, with the voluptuous trances of passion, and with the divine visions of love.

The last nights came, on which alone the public would ever behold her. With the height of summer the theatre closed: she loved the art which she followed; but his will was her law, and he had forbade her ever again to give the loveliness that was his to the eyes of a multitude. To go seaward a while; to wander in those southern and eastern lands of which her bright fancy had dreamed, and, whilst absent, to let the knowledge of his marriage be given to the world, was the future he promised her: there were now but six nights left betwixt that promise and its fulfilment.

On one of those nights there came to the royal place in the theatre a woman who took her seat there as though she were in truth a sovereign, her bosom and her hair blazing with the deepest lustre of sapphires, her fan flashing thousands of small diamonds in the light each time it stirred; her great, slumbrous, brown eyes watching the stage incessantly with a scornful laughter just stealing under their heavy amorous lids. To and from her box there passed continually half the "gilded youth" of the town; at the back of it, timidly hiding in the shadow like a chidden child, was a boy of ruddy cheek and simple air, who started now and again like a shy frightened hare: none noticed him; all passed him; he was her husband.

I shuddered as I saw: it was the same face that had glowed from the canvas of the Cléopâtre.

She spoke little: people would have said that she was devoted to the stage. She sat there almost motionless, gorgeous in the glare, nothing moving but those great dusky sleepy eyes, that glanced hither and thither over the house under their drooping lids.

Many present knew that her thoughts must be with the time when she, who sat there in her pomp and pride, had shown her half-nude beauty to the populace in the lowest pastime of the mime.

I alone knew that her thoughts might drift back to a still further season, when she who sat there, covered with jewels that were heirlooms, had envied the strolling players of the village-booth their spangles and their gewgaws.

Whenever Gladys was upon the stage this one gazer never withdrew her eyes from it, and they lost their laughter, and grew cold, intent, studious.

Wider contrast she could scarce behold to herself anywhere on earth. Perchance she felt it, for I saw her brow lower, and her red full lips tighten as though with a quicker drawn breath.

It might be that she felt—even as others did—that before this lofty, poetic, soul-lit loveliness her own voluptuous splendour was hard, sensual, earthly; for, look up from the diamond to the planet, what will you then see of heaven in the gem?

For me, I trembled as I saw that baneful presence there.

Looking on her as she watched thus, I thought of a glitter-ing, jewelled, ruby-orbed snake, reared motionless to watch the grace of a lithe-limbed, soft-eyed, and unconscious ante-lope—motionless, but ready to strike.

"Did you see that woman's eyes upon me?" Gladys mur-mured as they drove homeward. "She whom they say was 'Cléopâtre'?"

"Yes, I saw them," he answered simply.

There were things in his life that he loathed,—now that he loved.

That night in her sleep she moaned with a restless fear and awoke trembling.

"I dreamed of that woman!" she cried; "of that woman!"

"My love, my love," he murmured, "what can harm you, dreaming or waking, whilst I live?"

And she sighed softly, and fell asleep again on his heart, —content.

On the following night he did not come into the theatre as usual: she drove homeward immediately that the great play ended. She seemed anxious at his absence, the more so be-cause she had not seen him since the noon of the day; and she sat a while in her chamber, feeling sleepless and ill at ease.

The night was very hot; the casement stood wide open, looking out on to a mass of moonlit myrtle and syringa leaves; the heavy scents of dew-laden roses came up from the garden below; it was so still that all the starlit peace of some hill-sheltered country might have stretched around, rather than the countless roofs of a great city's fashionable outskirts.

She sat beside the window; the white folds of some loose *négligé* floating about her; her rich hair lying on her shoulders, gleaming to a dusky gold in the low lamp-light; her throat and chest half bare as the wind stirred her dress; her eyes looking out on to the dark, dewy, still night, with those dreams in them that only the happy dream. And her happiness was to her still a thing so breathless, so strange, so entrancing.

A church-clock somewhere without tolled midnight. As the last stroke sounded through the hot summer hush of the darkness, a man's step came up the stairs; the door opened, and he entered the chamber. She rose and went to him, with that beautiful flush and radiance which ever came on her face at his presence; and in his embrace there was a strange strength of passion rather like that of severance than of meeting.

"What has chanced?" she asked quickly, with the swift instinct of love, looking upward to his face, which had lost somewhat of its habitual colourlessness and calmness, and had warmth, and unrest, and almost eagerness upon it.

His eyes gleamed darker, and his lips quivered a little as he answered her:

"This, my love,—that I am rich once more!"

Her own eyes grew full of a tender surprise.

"Once more! But you have been so always, surely?"

He smiled.

"My child, I have been nearer to ruin than I cared to tell you, or than I care to remember now. For some years past I have had the worst sort of poverty, Gladys,—the poverty of a man who has rank to uphold, and self-indulgence to satisfy, and who has dissipated his heritage in pleasures which have palled on him, though he cannot yet bring himself to break with them. I have been as near ruin as a man may be whose good name has not been lost or jeoparded. But there is no need to think of it now. I am rich once more. I can command the world for you!"

She looked at him still in wonder: to her he had ever seemed even as a god in power and in possession.

"What is your joy, is mine. But for the world,—it is here for me," she answered him softly; and she pressed his hand to her breast, and bowed her head and rested her lips upon it.

He was silent; touched to passionate, dumb emotion. This

man, whom his world believed indifferent to all tenderness,
and callous to all devotion, felt a measureless gratitude to
this creature who loved him for himself alone.

"All other women I have known would have had but one
thought—how much my riches may be!" he muttered as he
drew her to the couch beside the open casement, and sank
down himself beside her.

"How lovely you are!" he murmured, as he moved back
the heavy masses of her hair and watched the soft night wind
stir amongst her dress, and drew her arms about him whilst
he told the history of his new-born wealth.

The tidings had come but that day to him. A distant
relative, old and childless, had left to him the whole accumu-
lations of a penurious and solitary life; utterly unlooked for,
undreamt of, because the dead man was of another branch of
his family; one which had ever been at variance with the
elder and loftier house. "Because he is the head of my race,
and because he never sought me, noticed me, even knew me,
therefore I bequeath, &c.," ran the strange testament; and
the bequest was one, in lands and in gold, to place him
amongst the richest and the most powerful of his Order.

To all men such sudden heritage is sweet; to him, at this
moment, it was precious, far beyond its actual and social
worth. He could not utter his thoughts to her, for he had
never let the phantom of the world's scorn come before her
glad and innocent eyes; he had never let the shadow of the
world's wrath fall across her sunlit, flower-sown path. But
none the less himself did he know that it would need all the
force of the fulcrum of wealth, all the massive weight of a
great dignity and a great position, to compel from the world
to her that world's honour without which both her life and
his own would be poisoned and incomplete.

For, to the man who is proud and of pure lineage, it is not
enough that he may know the innocence of his wife to be
without soil; it is as the very breath of his life, that it should
be unassailable by living lie or by dead rumour, and unapproachable as the stars on high. And, sooner or later, the

woman who learns that she has been suspected by the world will learn that, however deep her husband's love, or however imperishable his trust, there is one galled wound in his strength by which a passing touch can force his haughtiest pride to wince.

He knew this: she did not.

She could not comprehend the source of this vivid rejoicing which moved him at these tidings of his splendid inheritance; but she rejoiced with him, in all the sweet instinctive sympathies of love. And yet that humility, which is ever the companion of such love as hers, filled her with a vague sad sense of some unworthiness, of some unfitness, for such fortunes as his were.

"Perhaps it is not well that I should be your wife?" she said softly, whilst her face grew pale and her breath grew still, before that first shadow of a great unknown fear. "My people were poor and obscure; and I have followed a public art for gain; and when I cease to pursue it, as you desire, I shall have nothing of my own. I should not have been your wife! There are so many women, great, beautiful, noble, worthy of your name: will you never wish that one of them—? I can only love you, I have nothing else to give!"

He stayed her words with his kisses.

"O, child! Cannot you see that, with wealth and the world mine, such love is all, lacking, that I need? My God! how can I declare to you my pride in you? How shall I make you believe what greatness and what purity your genius, your loveliness, your nature, your mind, will bring to my race and my name? Stay but three days more, Gladys, and the world shall see in what estimate I hold these, in what honour I hold you."

She sighed, with a deep content.

"But will the world honour *you* for it?" she asked him, with that dim and wistful sense of some unfitness in herself that had but newly touched her, and was still so shadowy and so slight.

"It *shall*, my darling."

In another hour the memory returned to her that, ere he answered her, he hesitated for a moment; and that, as he answered her, his eyes darkened and his brows contracted, as with the resolve to encounter, to compel, to vanquish.

But in that moment she only heard the assurance given; she only felt the clasp of his arms and the touch of his lips.

She rested against him long in the deep, sweet, stillness of a joy, too sure and too perfect to be broken by words.

Once only she roused herself and spoke.

"Shall I know your friends—your sister—then?" she asked, with that happy light playing in her eyes, as she lifted them to his in the soft obscurity of the night.

"I hope so, love."

But I heard a short, impatient sigh from him as he spoke; and I knew that in his heart he was full sure that never would his sister's hand take hers in welcome and in friendship.

He was silent some time, his touch absently caressing the thick and gleaming waves of her hair. He had too true a manhood in him, and too haughty a temper, not to be ready to proclaim his honour of her to the world with all widest and highest publicity, and not to feel, with passionate sincerity, that pride in her—in her innocence, and her loveliness, and her genius—which he had avowed. But to every man it is bitter to know that the creature he delights to honour will be refused all honour by the world; to every man does it strike home, with a hateful pang, that the bearer of his name, the owner of his rank, the mother of his children, should be breathed on with the breath of libel and of imputed shame.

He knew the world too well not to fully appraise the cruel force of its incredulous contempt, its merciless censure; he had lived in it too long not to fully foresee the humiliations and insolences which it would be beyond all power of his to avert from the woman whom he loved. With time, indeed—and riches—he might be able to compel for her the lip homage of social respect, and to unclose for her the doors of the palaces of his order. But he knew that the work would be long—toilsome—and in the end but half accomplished.

For he knew that slander, having once seized on a fair name for its prey, does never altogether loose it; but, slumbering for a score of years, will yet, when it looks dead, have power still to lift its hydra head, and to spit poison. And so he sat there, thoughtful, weary, and half sad; yet with a thrill of old, dauntless, chivalric gladness in him, because to him it had now been given to show, at least in the world's sight, how high in honour he himself had held this life that trusted him with so supreme a faith.

Moreover, old aspirations stirred in him; old dreams arose.

Sitting there in the still summer night, with the light of the stars on the leafage without, and looking down into those deep, tender, soul-lit eyes, old fancies of his dead youth came to him. With gold, "the compeller of men," all things seemed possible to him. His wealth would be vast; his ambition might keep pace with it—a lofty and pure ambition, seeking the welfare and not the suffrage of men: seeking to rule and not to use them.

Of pleasure he had known every sense and satiety; of passion he had known every fury and folly; of the world he had known every bitter and every beguilement; a brief while ago his life had been tired, ruined, reckless, exhausted; but now—now in this soft midnight hour of summer—the fair and noble dreams of his boyhood returned to him, and it seemed to him that to give them fruition yet lay in his gifts and his destinies.

"You are thinking?" she said, looking up at him whilst her arms were about his neck. He smiled, and drooped his lips to hers.

"Yes. I am thinking of the future this day—and you— have given me."

And I believe that those dreams abode with him in his

slumber; for ever and again I saw a smile come on his face, as he slept, where the moonlight fell in upon it through the dewy foliage that half hid the casement.

Ah, God, that from some sleep men never awakened!

Early on the morrow he left her, compelled by some exigences of his new possessions to be absent in the north two days.

There were but three nights more of her public career. He would fain have shortened even these; but the interests of many were involved, and with the true soul of the artist in her, she parted from her world of art with pain and almost with unwillingness; and she clung to these few remaining hours in which alone the genius in her would ever utter itself to the multitude, and feel and use its powers.

He feared that it would be impossible for him to return before midnight of the second day at earliest. He left her with singular reluctance, with longing regret, even for so short an absence.

Towards the close of that day she sat alone in her little library; without there was all the glow of a summer evening at seven o'clock, but within the violet hues of the room seemed like twilight. She sat lost in thought; a smile and a flush now and then crossing her face at some memory; her book had fallen to the floor; her head was bent; in her bosom some little scarlet love-roses were fastened.

She did not hear the sound of steps without; she did not even hear the soft slow unclosing of the door, and the sweep of a woman's robes over the velvet of the floor. Lost in thought, the deep, sweet, visionary thought of a love that is half-earthly, half-divine, she did not even feel that she was no more alone.

The woman paused and looked at her, herself unseen. Her great, brown, slumbrous eyes glittered like jewels; her ruby mouth curled with a cruel scorn; her teeth set slightly, like an animal about to spring. I knew her—thus had I seen her, though then obscure of beauty as a diamond still

dull in its bed of quartz, look thirstily on the tawdry
treasury of the pedlar's pack; thus had I seen her in all the
haughty insolence of her shameful pomp when she had sat
in her amber-hung casement, and mocked the poor, lowly,
stainless life whose innocence and sublimity offended her.

She stood quite still, looking, looking, with the heavy
lids dropped over her eyes; she was attired for some festival
of the coming night; jewels glanced at every point upon
her; a gold-hued, tropical bird was fastened against her
breast, in its beak a flower of diamonds; with that scorn
upon her mouth, with that gleam beneath her lids, with
some gold-hued tissue, light as mist, about her, she seemed
to me to burn with an insufferable brilliancy through the
dusk as a tiger's eyeballs may flame through the darkness of
an eastern night.

Suddenly Gladys felt, rather than heard or saw; felt that
she was watched, and was no more in solitude; she started,
turned her head, and sprang to her feet, erect.

For the moment she was speechless in surprise; for the
moment this woman's face was strange to her, telling no tale,
bringing no history.

Avice Dare smiled where she stood. She had come un-
announced, unaccompanied; admitted doubtless through
some bribe of her gold, or some awe that her rank carried
with it.

"You know me?" she said carelessly, "I know you. We
are both on the world's stage."

Gladys gazed at her, still silent with amaze; remembrance
of the sole history that she had heard tangled with this
woman's name returning slowly through the confusion of her
shattered thoughts.

"I know you thus much," she answered, her clear pure
tones striking across the harsh voice of her questioner as the
note of a silver bell may strike across the dissonant clangour
of brazen cymbals. "Thus much,—that your presence only
is a dishonour. Why do you bring it hither?"

Avice Dare laughed aloud, with caustic insolent ease, and

for answer sank on to a couch by the hearth, and leaned her elbow on her knee, her chin upon her hand, in indolent action of familiarity.

"Dishonour? are you a fool? I am what all women would give their lives and their souls to be,—now. I came to look at you,—stand more to the light,—so! you are handsome enough!"

Gladys stood erect upon her own hearth, the last glow of the sunset falling upon her; her hand rested on the marble shelf, her eyes were dilated with a deepening amazement half touched with loathing and with fear.

She deemed this woman mad.

"Whatever be your errand,—say it and depart," she made answer. "Though you now were an empress, not less should I hold your life infamy."

Avice Dare laughed once more; with one hand she played with the diamond in the mouth of the bird, on the other she rested her chin, whilst her slumbrous, ruthless glances searched out every trait of face and of form, of limb and of feature, in the living loveliness that faced her.

"My errand is to look at you," she said curtly. "Well, you are beautiful, though not in my fashion. You are a genius, they say. What use is that? I had only good looks, and see where I am! Genius? Pshaw! what do *they* care for that? If you were an ill-favoured wench, though you had all the genius of heaven and hell, what would it serve you? You might die in a gutter."

The voice of Gladys, with its proud serene utterance, rang again across hers:

"Do you come here to tell me this? It was not worth while. I know nothing of you, save that you have been one who destroyed the lives and the souls of men; I desire to know no more. I only bid you go."

Avice Dare laughed aloud; her eyes glittered with a more sinister and savage meaning under the weight of their blue-veined languid lids.

"Destroy the lives and souls of men—know no more of

me than that! Pshaw! what is that more than to know me—
a woman? You speak fine and fair. I never did either. I
am a dullard at their hearts and their learning. But I am
no such fool but what I think,—sometimes. I think what
fools and what beasts they are: maddened by the red of our
lips and the white of our skins; ready to sell themselves to
any devil, if we will only be theirs when they craze for us;
flinging away all their gold, and their youth, and their good
repute, that we may spurn them, or kick them, or kill them
as our choice goes. I do think,—sometimes. I think what
fools and what beasts they are. There is your lover—he was
mine once."

The face of Gladys grew suddenly white as death; she
pressed one hand to her heart unconsciously, crushing the
roses.

"Will you go?" she said, calmly still, whilst her teeth
were tight shut. "Or will you force me to summon my servants?"

Avice Dare bent forward, the golden bird glowing brighter,
the diamond in his mouth shining with rosier light, the laugh
in her eyes growing broader and coarser.

"Call whom you like. It is no news to the town, if it be
news to you. It was only when I left him—left him because
he was well-nigh a beggar, and had dared to taunt me for
having no talent—it was only then that he gave his theatre
to you."

"His!"

She echoed the word unconsciously in the stupor of amaze
with which this woman's words had stifled her. Some vague
shape of some hideous truth, that loomed out from the gloom
of hidden years, was all she had vision left to see.

"His,—surely his,—what of that?" retorted the sullen,
scoffing, victorious voice, which in its moments of passion lost
all the finer and purer accent of tuition, and lapsed into the
rude and homely words of its birth-tongue. "*His* theatre!
You knew that well enow. It have always been his toy, to
set up his fancy of the hour in, and make the gabies of the

world run and stare to see a thing of wonder in his mistress. He's had it now a many year; and he've never had one as good in it as me, though he chose to dare and gibe me, and to say as I could only do the dancing. You were a girl he found in the streets, I've heard?—selling flowers and starving? And you'd a pretty face, and he took a liking to it; and he made a—lady—of you? It's his way; and it pays too. Naught draws like a handsome face to the stage. You are an artist, they say, and God knows what; I never did naught but dress and dance. But the town was as mad about me as you. So was he. I pillaged him pretty well; but they do say as how you have ruined him out-and-out. A playhouse is a pretty toy enough; but it beggars men quick—when we help too! You live very quiet, and proud, and innocent like, they say. Well, it seems to pay you high that way; but you chose to talk about 'infamy' a second ago. Now, I have been honest, at least; while you—"

Her laugh filled up the pause; more brutally than by jest or gibe.

Gladys stood erect; her hand clenched on the marble; her face blanched with a mute breathless disgust; her lips dumb in her own defence. An unutterable horror had seized her; in one instant all the truth, so long screened from her with such tender hands, was laid bare to her sight as the flash of the lightning lays bare the abyss.

For the moment she was speechless; her heart beat with a slow sickening effort that seemed to drain all strength from her limbs and all life from her veins; her eyes lost sight; her ears lost sound; a deadly faintness held her in its bonds.

Avice Dare watched her with a sleepy voluptuous cruel pleasure; even as in the old time gone I had seen her watch the lingering torture of a high-couraged, luminous-eyed falcon, caught in a trap in a green beechen bough, and struggling passionately for freedom, all through the hours of a burning thirsty summer-day, till death released it.

"Your eyes look strange; is this news to you?" she said coldly. "Ignorance is odd enough, surely. If it is not his gold that you live on, whose is it? Does gold grow, like your roses? You were a beggar, without bread, without home, without a hope in the world; yet when you were lifted up into riches and ease you never asked whence the wealth came that did it! Faugh! what liar durst tell any baby such a fable as that?"

The foul word roused her hearer like a dagger's thrust; the sickly faintness passed away; the blood rushed to her face in a bright passionate flood; her eyes flashed fire; her old form grew instinct once more with strength and gracious pride.

"Silence! Silence!" she cried, with calm contemptuous command. "What my life is, matters not to you. It cannot come for judgment to your vile imaginings. Go, and let me forget, if I can, that lips so foul as yours have ever dared to breathe to me the name I honour only second to my God's."

For one moment the low brutal nature of her antagonist was awed and cowed before the grandeur of that noble simplicity, the purity of that perfect faith; for one moment she, in whom womanhood was but a base and venal infamy, saw by one fleeting vision how great by the divinity of love can womanhood become.

With the next instant, the evil in her scoffed to scorn that one relenting impulse.

It has been written that there is not one man without some gleam of tenderness and pity; it is not written that there is not one woman.

Her dusky, sleepy eyes flashed with a sudden stupid wonder.

"Is it true?" she said curtly; "true, as some say of late, that you be his wife?"

Gladys answered nothing, but her face spoke. Where she stood, with her hands crossed upon her breast, and her eyes gazing against the sunset light, there was more eloquence than lies in words in that fearless dignity, in that conscious gladness and glory of a life which knew itself one with his for ever.

Avice Dare laughed aloud, gnawing with her ruby lip the diamond which the bird bore.

"So-ho! you have done worse by him than ever I did!" she cried, her hard exultant voice ringing through the soft sweet silence of the chamber; "I have done it by another, it's true. But *my* dupe is a witless lad, too great a fool to know what honour is. But yours!—Nay, hear me out. I have little to say, but I'll say that. I know him right well: he's a fool in his gifts, and a devil in his pride. Like enow you've drawn him on to give you even his name, out of pity. But maybe you've never thought how you've killed his pride in him for ever and aye. Do you know that the women of his rank would no more come nigh you than nigh me? Do you know that his world will say he has married his mistress, and that your sons will be taught, soon or late, to blush for their mother? Do you know that to live with you he must give up his order; and that, though you may carry its title, you will never pierce into its ranks? I tell you the truth; I've done the like myself. But I'm a 'vile woman,' you know; you —you're an angel of innocence! Well, you may be; you've a fair face, I see; and you hold yourself rarely and loyally. But look you here. When, through you, he is the scorn of friends and the jest of fools; when for you he gives up his old world, and his own race; when by you he has children who can be taunted by schoolmates with your name; when for you he lives beggared, restless, half obscure, shunning the eyes of the world because of the stain the world thinks that it sees on his scutcheon: *then* he will find little choice, I fancy, between my 'infamy' and your 'innocence.' You are his wife, no doubt; your eyes say so, though you stand dumb. Well, he will never tell it to you, because he is a gentleman born; but as sure as he lives, so sure will the day come when in his soul he will curse you for the selfish-ness that you cloaked in purity, for the cruelty that you

masked in love. I am a bad woman; yes, but I was never
so base to him as you! I only took his gold; I never stole his
name!"

Then, without another word, she passed across the chamber, the gleam of her golden tissues flashing on the gloom.

On the threshold she paused one moment, the brutal smile
gleaming on her full red lips.

"We go to see you act to-night; you will scarce be at
your greatest, I fancy!"

And the door closed on her slow hard mockery of joyless
laughter.

Gladys stood erect on her own hearth. A mute, breathless, numbing horror stole over her face, and blasted the
light from her eyes, and drained the life from her veins.
She gave no cry, no sign; she did not move; her eyes still
looked out steadfast at the light; and yet, ah, God! to see
that horror in her face was to behold death seize a living,
happy, sinless creature in the first fair radiance of its beauty,
in the first sweet summer of its years!

* * * * * *

Eight of the evening chimed softly through the silence.
It was the season when the world claimed her. She had
flung herself on her knees beside her couch, and still kneeled
there with her head bowed upon her arms, though more than
an hour had drifted by since the words of her destroyer had
echoed through the stillness of that peaceful place. At the
sound of the chimes she started, and rose to her feet; she was
white as marble; her breath came in slow agonised labour;
her eyes had a bewildered, tearless terror in them.

So brief a while before, a rapture so perfect had environed
her—a passion so shadowless had entranced her; and now—
the whole force of a hideous truth was round her like a web
of fire.

She knew that in the world's sight she was a thing dishonoured, and that the reflex of such dishonour was the sole
dower that she had brought her husband.

"To have harmed him—to have harmed him—O, my

God!" That was the sole cry that was wrung from her. Before her sight, like an abyss on which the lightning plays, there spread all the depths of infamy on which she, unwitting, had stood in joyous ignorance so long, and all the undreamt-of wealth of pity, tenderness, and countless gifts that she had owed to him.

All things were bared before her: she saw herself the creature of his alms, the beggar enriched by his mercy, the debtor kept in blindness because vision would have shown her all her debt. She knew now why all the women of his race had held aloof from her; she knew now why the assurance of the world's honour had hesitated on his lips, and his promise of it been, not confidence, but defiance. Even in her ignorance—even when she had deemed herself the creatrix of her fame, and the gainer of her gold—she had said ever in her soul, "What shall I render thee, O princely giver?" deeming that the world could never hold fit payment to him. But now —now—she beheld the past in all its nakedness; and now she knew likewise that her only recompense to him was to take to him, in marriage, the imputed shame wherewith the world had laden her! With all the sweeping cruelty of bitterest truth, the words of her enemy had scourged her, till they cut the living flesh of her bared heart.

Without a thought that was regret, without a dream that was fear, without a vision of dishonour that could ever taint her, of repentance that could ever assail her, she had lived her radiant life until this hour. And now—now—she knew that though she should live to the extremest years of age, she could never undo the evil wherewith she had paid him back his good.

Baser and more self-steeped natures would but have seen that, come what would, her own place as his wife was beyond challenge and beyond change. But to her the know-ledge that the wrong wrought to him could never be undone, though ever so passionately he should crave his freedom— though ever so wearily he should lament his loss—was an

agony greater than any woe or martyrdom she could herself
have borne.

"If only he were still free!" she cried aloud in her torture.
"If only I could be his servant—his mistress—his dog—so
that the world should honour him still!"

For to her, in the deep humility of her passionate gratitude, it seemed that there was naught in herself to recompense
him for his surrender to her of his honour and his troth: to
her, in the high, pure, stainless creeds of her old grave poetic
race, it seemed that to have lived upon his gold, though all
unwittingly, and to have been libelled by his world, though
all unrightfully, took from her for ever all fitness to the place
and to the name of his wife.

She was but a child, still; she was a poet, she had the
pride of lofty creeds, she had the self-abandonment of a love
that was absolute in its idolatry; she saw nothing, felt nothing, heeded nothing, save that she was shameful in the
sight of the world, and that she had paid a measureless debt
only by acceptance of as measureless a sacrifice!

One thought only folded her in its poisonous net, as the
fire folded Glauce. The thought that she had dishonoured
him—dishonoured him!—she, who would have given up her
young life to any torture or to any death, to spare to him one
moment's pang, to save to him one breath of scorn!

It may be, that if in this hour his voice had fallen on her
ear, his kiss had touched her lips, this paroxysm might have
passed, this horror might have unloosed her. But he was
absent: there were none near to counsel or to soothe: she
was alone with all this brutal truth that rose before her,
all this sense of irrevocable ruin brought on him by her love.

And in such an hour she could not reason: she could only
suffer:—suffer those tortures of hell which on earth only come
to the innocent.

    •   •   •   •   •   •

The eighth hour sounded.

She started to her feet. She knew that the public waited
her.

"O God! I cannot go!" she murmured, "I cannot!"

Her head fell on her breast; her white lips gasped for air; the crushed roses fell to the ground—dead.

But that moment passed. She had the courage of the soldier; the endurance of the martyr. Such women have. It was the fulfilling of his appointed place; it was the execution of his appointed duty.

On a side-table near there stood a flask of rich amber-tinted wine, that he had left there in the early day. By sheer instinct she poured it forth, and took deep draughts of it; it was rarely that she ever touched wine; its stimulant revived the warmth in her veins, quickened the dull uncertain beating of her heart, restored her for the hour to strength and consciousness.

"She shall not see me fail," she muttered in her teeth. "She shall see what force his love and honour give."

Then she rang, and bade them tell her people she was ready, and went, with a calm step and all her old grace of bearing, to the carriage that already waited at the accustomed hour. I followed her: she was not sensible of my presence.

The horses flew like the wind; it was already late; I looked up at her face in fear and trembling: it might have been cut in marble, it was so still, so fixed, so colourless. Her eyes still held that look of breathless pain, and her heart beat so loudly that I could hear the throb of its heavy and irregular pulse above the sound of the horses' hoofs, and all the manifold and confused noises of the busy streets.

The simple gold of the marriage ring was hidden under a weight of other jewelled circles on her slender hand; she drew the jewels from it, and looked at it with a strange passion, half glory and half horror.

It was the sign of her honour amidst women, it was true; but none the less did it seem to her the sign of his bondage, of his sacrifice, of his degradation in the sight of the world.

"They must not know: they must never know," she murmured; and she put back over it the gemmed rings that screened it from others' eyes.

What she would do in the future she knew not; she only vaguely felt that never, by the derision of the world for him, should the honour of the world be purchased for herself.

The carriage flew through the lighted town, in which the glare of the gas crossed the lingering light of the glad summer evening.

It paused before the familiar place where the world waited for her.

"If they see that I suffer, they will say evil of him," she muttered half aloud; and the meditative calm came back into her eyes; her colourless mouth wore a proud resolve; her head was lifted with a haughty grace: as she passed the people in the passage to go onward to her dressing chamber, I heard one stranger say to another:—"Is that fair-haired woman the actress? Heavens!—she might be an empress by her look!"

It was later than the appointed hour; the house called for her, growing impatient; there was not a moment to be lost. She robed herself hastily, and swept on to the stage with slow, graceful, negligent dignity, whilst the homage of the crowded theatre rang out again and again in their acclamations of welcome.

She looked once at the house; there, true to her word, her enemy was throned; seated laughing amidst her courtiers, as Faustina sat beneath the purple canopy of the Antonines to watch the gladiatorial show upon the blood-steeped sands below.

The amber tissues glowed around her, till she seemed bathed in light, and the golden bird in her bosom held his diamond in the light, as though in symbol of the sole wage for which the wise amidst womanhood sell love.

Her eyes met those of Gladys; they were full of the same merciless exultation, of the same sleepy, brutal, and voluptuous pleasure. As the noble courser answers to the barbed cruelty of the spur, so did the high courage of the creature that she tortured answer to that tigress' glance. The blood flushed to her face; strength rang in her voice; eloquence and inspiration returned to her.　She played with yet more consummate art, with yet more dauntless genius, than the world had ever beheld in her.　For she played to justify his love; she played to save his honour; she played, not for the world, but him.

I felt a strange fear as I watched her: I knew not why.

It seemed to me that the force of her self-command was too great, the fever of her strength too high, for the victory not to cost her some fatal price ere it should utterly be won.

And—at those times when she was no more in the public sight, but waited in the solitude of her chamber, my terror grew: for that deathlike whiteness of her face never changed, and I could see and hear the laboured beating of her heart, as though the youth and vital gladness of its pulse were crushed and suffocated beneath the weight of deadly knowledge.

Yet still she moved with a grace so exquisite, with a power so matchless, before the assembled multitude! She held them entranced as even she had never held them. When their cries rang to the roof, they were no empty or careless homage, but the tumultuous fury of a people moved to passionate and rapturous emotions. And where her enemy sat, with the golden bird nestled in her bosom, and the brutal triumph in her eyes, the eyes glanced with furtive doubt, and the wicked lips curled with an uneasy smile—her prey escaped her; her hate lost its sting.

The end drew near; the strain was well-nigh over.

As she went once more before the sight of the people I knew that the ordeal would soon be passed, the victory be soon accomplished, if—if—she had strength to endure to the last.

She went: and the echoes of the public acclamations greeting her again rolled in their muffled thunder on my ear where I waited in the loneliness of her little chamber.

Suddenly the door unclosed: Beltran himself entered. His return had been earlier than he had deemed possible.

He glanced round the empty place, and left it hurriedly: I heard his step die away down the long corridors which led to the public portion of the house.

I went forth from the chamber, and stole to that familiar corner where I so often had tarried to watch the play of the stage, and the crowds of the house. He, I saw, had passed amidst the audience, and was standing in his sister's box with his head bent to her. The theatre was hushed into intense stillness; some woman's sob, some man's deep-drawn breath, alone quivered on the silence; the listening multitude was held in that trance of sympathy in which genius can hold a world at will.

She was alone upon the stage: it was that supreme moment in the tragedy wherein the woman, whom she portrayed, learned that the love which she had deemed divine as heaven was but a thing of desolation and dishonour.

She stood erect, her hands crossed on her breast, the white folds falling about her limbs; the gleam of her hair like light above her brow; her eyes gazing out upon the upturned faces of the crowd beneath her feet with a mute blind anguish which chilled them as though they looked on death.

Her voice thrilled through the house with a strange, sweet, unutterable passion in it that brought tears to the eyes of those who heard—all meaning of the verse she spoke was lost to them, they only felt the meaning of that music of the voice, sad as the last sigh of a dying child, passionate as the last look of love in eyes that never more will meet on earth.

One alone in all that vast audience—one alone, her destroyer—knew what memories were in her thoughts, what truth was in her utterance, as the words of the poet left her lips:

> "I thought to give him honour,
> Liberty, fealty, peace—and all fair things
> That make men's lives divine. And, lo!
> The only dower that I take is shame.
> My arms entwining him will sap his strength,
> My kiss beget disgrace on him. My love —
> The only gift I ever had to give—will be
> Dishonour and corruption in men's sight.
> The harlot's jeer, the hired jester's gibe,
> And all the mockery and malison of tongues,
> Will now hoot at him, and drag down his name
> Through the foul mire of their public ways.

And I—I—I, his slave, his love, his wife,
Shall take him moral death and endless infamy.
Ah, God!—"

The breath paused on her lips; the words were broken and ceased; her gaze had fallen upon him where he stood amidst the women of his order in the centre of the lighted house, and in that one moment of sudden recognition the world about her died from her sight, and all she saw were those eyes, familiar and beloved, that smiled on her.

Her strength snapped like a bow overstrung. Her senses sickened and grew dull. With a faint cry she stretched her arms out to him, and reeled, and fell.

The curtain sank, and hid her from the public sight. Through the tumult of the panic-stricken multitude there ran the awe of one dread murmur—"death."

In one moment he was beside her; he scattered the people like sheep; he seized her in his arms; and bore her through the open doors of the supper-chamber where in other years the boy-statesman had fallen dead upon the hearth because a woman, vile of soul, had kissed him, and betrayed him.

Some fled in terror to seek succour; others huddled in terror on the threshold; about him his friends gathered, helpless, horrified, aghast, afraid.

He never spoke; but as he laid her down and threw himself beside her, he tore aside the lace and linen off her bosom, and sought to feel and listen for the beating of her heart.

Its pulse was still.

He flung himself upon her; he called her name with every caress of words that passion holds; he covered with his kisses her lips, her bosom, her limbs; he crushed her in his arms as though in his horror he could seize her and withhold her from the brutal ravishing of death.

The warmth of that burning embrace, the fire of those quivering lips, gave back for one fleeting moment a pang of movement to the numbed and strengthless heart: gave back a flush and glow of life to the languor and the coldness of the feeble blood.

Her eyes unclosed, and looked at him with that perfect love which never again on earth would come to him.

"The world need never know it—now," she murmured. "Kiss me once more—O God! O love! forgive!"

And with that prayer for pardon on her sinless lips, she feebly turned, and wound her arms about his neck, and drooped her head upon his breast, and sought his lips with hers.

In that last kiss, her last breath fled.

He, who so long had known no grief, and smiled at every pang, grew like a madman in his agony: he drove forth from the chamber every human creature, and barred the door upon them, and spent the watches of the night alone—alone, save for that beautiful dead thing that he had loved; alone, save for the gold of the heavy hair, for the calm of the closed eyes, for the caress of the lifeless lips, which stirred no more beneath his own, for the loveliness of the cold limbs and of the pulseless breast which thrilled and flushed no more beneath his touch.

All through that night I saw the deadliest sight that the world holds;—the despair of a strong man.

When, with the full light of day, his friends broke into the room, in terror at the silence that had lasted there from midnight unto noon, they found him stretched upon the hearth; his head upon her chest, his hands clenched in her loose hair, the full sun falling on her fair dead face and through the festal chamber of so many nights of mirth.

When they raised him they saw that her breast and hair were stained and wet and red—he had ruptured a blood-vessel, the dark stream had gushed from his throat and mouth, and he was senseless.

CHAPTER XIX.

Valete.

"I have not heart in me to dictate more."

There are many things that I thought to chronicle. I have many adventures left untold, many portraits left unsketched, many memories left unrecorded. But I have not the heart in me to tell more now; and, besides,—I am only to fill a certain number of pages.

Strange generation!—which has its literature measured like its yards of Coventry ribbon, or its pounds of Cambridge butter! I suppose, however, that it is a good thing that there is some such ruthless restriction, for, Heaven knows, without it poets or autobiographers might spin on at the wheel of their vanity for ever; for the thread of Amour Propre is a thread without an end, and tough as it is endless. In vain do the world's sharp scissors of scorn snap at it and cry, "Hold, enough!"—the thread is of stuff indestructible, and it only thinks that the scissors are jealous!

Since that awful night I have never quitted Beltran.

His life was long in jeopardy; but with time his strength prevailed. Those who care not for life commonly have life cling to them.

He never knew the truth of that early death. Men of science agreed in their judgment that her heart had been long feeble of action, and at length had suddenly given way; it is a disease not rare with those of vivid mind and delicate frame.

There was no one—nothing—which could reveal to him the secret of Avice Dare. For I could not bear witness against her.

Gladys' grave was made in the old green country of his birth, amidst the sepulchres of his ancient and stately race. This honour was all left for him to yield to her. By that grave the world learned that she had been his wife during that one, sweet, short summer-time.

One day I saw Dudley Moore stand by that simple tomb, almost hidden in the white blossom of roses, and his hard, cynical, keen eyes were dim with tears, the first that had ever dimmed them since they had seen the light.

From that night the theatre was closed. It can never more bring ruin to any, or echo with the laughter of a crowd. It has been razed to the ground, and on its site stands a poor-house.

Beltran does not heed that I am near. But I can watch him, follow him, guard him in his sleep—it is enough.

I ask no more. I am only a dog—I dare to love, I dare not even seek to be loved in answer.

Ah! when your poets have painted the fidelity of woman, they have found its likeness on earth, perhaps,—in their dog.

He leads the old life in the world. Why not? If all men in whose hearts lives a dull, abiding grief, whose throbs death and death only ever will still, deserted for desert or ocean your world of fame and of fashion, how strangely that world would look! How much eloquence would be dumb in your senatorial chambers; how many a smile would be missing from your ball-rooms and hunting-fields; how many a frank laugh would die off for ever from your ear; how many a well-known face would vanish from your clubs, from your park, from your dinner-tables, from your race-stands!

And how seldom would it be those that you had pitied who would go!—how often would the vacant place be that place where so many seasons through you had seen, and had envied, the gayest, the coldest, the most light-hearted, the most cynical amongst you!

Ah! let Society be thankful that men in their bitterness do not now fly as of old to monastery or to hermitage; for, did they do so, Society would send forth her gilded cards to the wilderness.

He lives the old life in the old world still. He could not dare to trust himself to solitude. Solitude!—sweet to the youth who first suffers; to the poet who finds in his thorn-crown his aureole; to the lover who is half-enamoured and half-proud of the pangs that devour him; sweet to those. But to the man of the world, to the man past his youth, to the man whose last hope is dead with his last joy and last passion—solitude would be but the gate of the madhouse.

He is in the world,—of the world; the great fortunes that have come to him bring the world about his feet. The man who is nobly born, and lately enriched, can have of the world what he will—except happiness.

"He is a man without a heart!" I heard a mother murmur, whose daughter he would not woo. "A man without a heart, and he has never loved. There was a beautiful young actress—his wife, we learned later, whom he had driven into public life to maintain himself in the days of his ruin—and she died on his own stage from his cruelty; and look! how utterly he has forgotten her now!"

Forgotten her! Heartless!

When they—they who are many as the woes and sins of the earth are many—whom he seeks out with unceasing patience, in their manifold sufferings, their innumerable needs, look up in his weary passionless eyes, and bless him for aid, for bread, for existence itself, given to them by a mercy which the world never dreams of—they know whether he is heartless.

When, in the stillness and darkness of dawn I watch him pace his chamber, sleepless and haunted by a ghost that will not leave him with the rising of the sun that day, or any day, in all the years to come—when I see him fling himself upon his bed as the morning light streams in, and see him writhe in his agony, whilst the great tearless sobs shake his frame in the torture of a memory that can never die while he has life—I know how he has forgotten.

Well—it boots little to dwell on this.

A "*vie manquée!*" says the world, when it speaks of. him, recalling the old fair promise of the talents of his youth.

Is there any threnody over a death half so unutterably
sad as that one jest over a life?

"*Manquée!*"—the world has no mercy on a hand that has
thrown the die and has lost; no tolerance for the player who,
holding fine cards, will not play them by the rules of the
game. "*Manquée!*" the world says, with a polite sneer, of
the lives in which it beholds no blazoned achievement, no
public success.

And yet, if it were keener of sight, it might see that those
lives, not seldom, may seem to have missed of their mark,
because their aim was high over the heads of the multitude;
or because the arrow was sped by too eager a hand in too
rash a youth, and the bow lies unstrung in that hand when
matured. It might see that those lives which look so lost, so
purposeless, so barren of attainment, so devoid of object or
fruition, have sometimes nobler deeds in them and purer sacrifice than lies in the home-range of its own narrowed vision.
"*Manquée!*"—do not cast that stone idly: how shall you tell,
as you look on the course of a life that seems to you a failure,
because you do not hear its "*Io triumphe*" on the lips of a
crowd, what sweet dead dreams, what noble vain desires,
what weariness of futile longing, what conscious waste of
vanished years—nay, what silent arts of pure nobility, what
secret treasures of unfathomed love—may lie within that
which seems in your sight even as a waste land untilled, as
a fire burnt out, as a harp without chords, as a bird without
song?

There are but three more things that I will tell you—
now.

In the spring-time of this year I was in Paris. It was a
beautiful brilliant night in the height of April. The chestnuts were full of bloom; the air was full of fragrance; there
were a million stars above and a million lamps below; lilacs
and hyacinths filled the balconies and casements; there was
the sound of music and of laughter everywhere.

I was curled on a satin cushion in one of the supper-chambers of a great gilded house, where all that is lavish, and brilliant, and dissolute in the city is wont to come. My friends had come thither after the opera; one of their guests was a great actress, with a wondrous dark beauty, and the luminous eyes of the East—a woman of many passions, of many follies, of many talents, of many caprices, yet of many virtues; a woman whom they called always Mariquith.

After a while, the supper ended, she moved a little away from the table and went out on to the balcony and sat there, leaning her arm on the gilded rail, and glancing at the crowds that stirred beneath the boughs below. One man followed her and sat there too, away from the laughter and glitter within, in the cool of the night, amongst the white and purple hyacinths that filled the place, and with the quiet stars above.

It was very still there; it was late in the night, and the street beneath was scarcely seen for the leaves of the limes and the hyacinth blossoms.

"You do not love me, Denzil," she said suddenly, when she leaned in the shadow, with her diamonds gleaming as they caught the rays of the moon.

He answered her simply, "No."

She looked at him with a curious, steadfast, dreaming look; whether she loved him or not I never knew. They played at love together.

"You are frank!" she said at last, with a smile; "and you are very singular!"

"No doubt. But you may as well know it—years ago I loved one woman so well that I never shall love another."

"Ah, how like a man! you can never love; and yet—you have a thousand passions!"

He flung his cigarette into the street.

"What has that to do with it? Nothing!"

She watched him curiously a while.

"Where is she?" she asked at length.

"God knows! If I knew, do you think I should be *here?*"

The dark magnificence of her face paled under all the scorn of the answer uttered. She was used to have the world at her feet, and the passions of men at her will.

She was quiet long; then she spoke:

"Listen, Denzil, you write stories that the world reads; I will tell you one that the world never knew."

He listened listlessly, leaning against the balcony, wearily watching the ebb and the flow of the street crowd beneath, under the linden boughs. From within there echoed the noisy laughter and the banal wit; out here the stars were shining.

She told him the story; it was one that I had known. He heard indifferently, striking alight another cigar, with his handsome dark head bent down in the moonlight.

When she had told it, she drew a little amulet-case from her bosom—an old worn leathern thing, though hung on to a necklace of onyx—the same case into which I had once seen placed the fragment of the paper that she had found in the death-chamber in the Quarter of the Poor.

"Here is the letter," she said, taking out of it a folded sheet torn. "I never showed it to any before. I do not know why I do to you. Only—see how women love."

He took it indifferently still; but as he saw the writing, he started and he grew deadly pale; he read it by the white clear moonlight, read it to the end. And as she watched him she trembled and was afraid; she, the famous and fearless and reckless woman, was afraid, with a terrible fear of this memory that she unwittingly had awakened.

She seized his arm in terror.

"O God! what have I done?"

He looked at her with a look that she will never till her dying day forget, though she live to the extremest years of age.

"Done, done? Nothing that I know, only—it was I who loved her!"

The laughter echoed from the supper-room, the sounds of music floated on the air; through the open window the lights

of the chamber glowed; beneath the leaves the crowds were
passing to and fro; from within the gay outcries of the women
of pleasure challenged his return; and he stood there in the
moonlight with the letter in his hands, only hearing a voice
for ever silent, only seeing a face for ever gone.

And thus the dying words of Gertrude D'Eyncourt came
to him at the last.

———

A little while later, more in the summer-time, leaving
Paris itself, we tarried a brief while in one of those charming
places in its precincts that lie hidden in those woods which
still seem to echo with the careless laughter, and breathe out
the amber perfume, and murmur with the mocking love, of
the dead Règne Galant.

I was left entirely to myself, and wandered as I chose
about the woods. One day I strolled far; and there seemed
to come to me a strange familiar feeling from the low level
meadows, the lines of poplar-trees, the fields of colza, and
the grassy orchards which met my sight. Gazing awhile, and
awhile drawing in that sweet scent of red rich earth, of cool
fresh air, of the breath of lowing cattle, and of the hearts of
unfolding spring-flowers, I knew it then. It was the country
of the Silver Stag.

Beside me there was a low wall overtopped with prickly
golden furze; beyond this stretched an orchard, its grass all
unshaven and daisy filled, its old tree-stems gray with the
fairylike leafage of lichens.

I crossed the orchard, knowing it well; here often I had
rolled the wind-fall apples to and fro in play, and here had I
often seen the homestead doves away drowsily in the moving
boughs.

It was evening now; the shadows were growing long; it
was all still; there was only the singing of the birds; for
whoso amongst you believes that birds do not sing after the
sunset-hour can surely have walked but little in the fields
and woods.

I passed on to the garden full of lilac and of chestnut bloom; treading the ground reverently as the soil of a place that had given me shelter.

We are ever mindful of succour bestowed, of hospitality received; where we have eaten bread there do we ever go with remembrance and thanksgiving; we have not learned your art of oblivion, your science of neglect; we cannot turn upon the hand that once tended us food; we cannot make a mockery of the kindliness that once befriended us; we cannot emulate you there—we are but dogs.

Outside the porch, at a table of rough-hewn wood, under the old-remembered sign of the Silver Stag that swung above amidst the foliage, there sat a little group of student lads— lads with flushed happy faces and noisy ringing voices, who were breaking white wheaten rolls and jostling their glasses together.

They were served by a stout strong woman, with a scarlet kerchief bound about her black brows. Within the chambers there were noise, laughter, strange faces, the glimmer of candles, the sound of chinking glasses.

In the doorway there stood a burly and bearded man, in a gray blouse, and with a pipe in his mouth. At his feet a yellow terrier was worrying, and worried by, an angry cat.

In the wide vine-hung casement of what had once been the painting-room of the Faustine, the lattices were pushed back, and there leaned a handsome dissolute girl with a velvet-tasselled cap on her head, and great ear-rings in her ears, and a square-cut scarlet bodice showing her bare chest. She was framed in the leaves and the coils of the vine; and was calling out, and laughing back, to the youths at the table in the garden.

At a glance I knew that there were no more present in this place the brave forbiddance of vice, the sweet clean ways of household service, the cheerful grace, the perfect purity, the honest kindliness to man and beast, the order and the quietude that had reigned beneath this roof when Madelon and her mother had been sheltered by it.

As I gazed out from one of the leafy grassy ways that
traversed the garden by so many paths, there came a youth
who had been smoking in a little arbour formed by lilacs that
arched above a rough-hewn bench. He was grave of face,
and clad in velvet; I recognised him as an artist who had
used to frequent this place until in the year of the Faustine
he had gone to Rome.

"You are landlord here—now?" he asked.

The man kicked the cat off the terrier, and assented.

"Where is Madelon Bris?"

The man kicked the terrier in its turn off the threshold
ere he answered: "Madelon Bris? She is in a religious
order."

"And the old mother?"

"Manon Bris? She is dead."

"It was on the death of the mother that Madelon became
a nun?"

"Eh? Yes: I think so. There was a day when Madelon
went to Paris; and was taken ill there; and the old mother
did not hear what had become of her for weeks, for months.
People were kind, but old Manon fretted herself into her
grave. When Madelon recovered of her fever and left the
hospital, she found her mother dead. It was a shock, I suppose. Anyway—she took the vows. She is a Sister of
Charity. Her hair was quite white when she came home;
she looked quite old; I suppose it was the fever."

He paused, and blew a cloud of smoke, and killed a night-
moth fluttering near.

"She is living still?" the artist asked.

"Ay—for what I know. When the cholera raged last year
she worked very hard, I heard, and, they do say, saved many:
as if by a saint's miracle."

"She was a saint herself," the painter murmured. "Have
you the living things she cared for?—the birds, the dog?"

"The birds are here; at least the fowls are; all but the
doves. I wrung their necks because they made such a noise.
They were very good in a pasty."

"And the dog—Russ?"

The man blew smoke into the air with a sullen shame upon his bloated face.

"He was here when I came. She was trying for leave for him to go to the convent. But he was always howling for her, and growling at us. So I got a fowling-piece, and shot him. He was very old, you know,—and savage. It was only safe to put him out of the way."

The artist turned from the porch without a word, and went down the path, and out by the little gate: I stole away, sick at heart, back through the woods and the meadows.

From the broad, vine-hung chamber where the Faustine had glowed into life, the laugh of the wanton, where she leaned from the casement, rang out on the stillness of evening; and the drunken, gay shouts of the students echoed over the leafy, silent, shadowy garden places, where, in his glad and gracious youth, the lips of Carlos had murmured of eternal love, and with the golden drowsy noons, and with the dewy summer nights, his dreams and hers had in belief beheld imperishable passion and immortal fame.

———

The other day I saw in your London a grand equipage sweep by me.

Within it, shrouded in ermine, was a woman whose broad, slumbering, brown eyes gazed with a hard, exultant scorn at the sun, as though to say, "Shine you on any more victorious thing than I?"

Beside her was a boy, with her look, though not with her beauty; who, holding in his hand a jewelled whip with a long white lash, curled the lash round the naked shoulders of a little tattered child of his own years, and laughed as his carriage rolled on, and the street-waif's shrill moan struck the air.

His mother laughed also; proud as the tigress when her whelp first tastes blood.

The boy was the heir to the Marquisate of Isla.

So great races decay, more foully than by poverty; and when the Mob curses the Noble for some act of greed, of tyranny, or of vileness, ten to one that it curses its own kith and kin, which, by base stratagem or illicit love, has foisted the cur's heart into the lion's hide.

Truly is Avice Dare amidst those of whom the Teacher of Galilee said, "Verily they *have* their reward."

Her young lord, dull, spiritless, cowed before her look as a slave before the scourge, drinks deep to find the death that his stubborn strength keeps at bay; and meanwhile grants all she wills to one whom he has learned to fear with the keenest emotion of which his feeble nature is capable. She has incalculable wealth, immeasurable luxury, possessions at which even her avarice halts satisfied; and all the power of a great race against her cannot shake her or her son from their stronghold.

Society holds aloof from her indeed; but with her riches she can summon crowds of courtiers, flatterers, and parasites. Moreover—she has become devout; has built a church, endowed a hospital, confessed a conversion. Cant, naked, is honoured throughout England. Cant, clothed in gold, is a king never in England resisted.

A bishop has not dined with her yet, but one will do doubtless ere long,—and then it will be possible enough that society will follow the apron, and consign to oblivion her antecedents.

From the hour that she sold me in the little street of the town in the Peak, she has been a woman with but one talent; but that one talent is worth all the powers, and graces of genius; it is the talent to use the age in which she lives.

Genius is oftentimes but a poor fool, who, clinging to a thing that belongs to no age, Truth, does oftentimes live on a pittance and die in a hospital: but whosoever has the gift to measure aright their generation is invincible—living, they shall enjoy all the vices undetected; and dead, on their tombstones they shall possess all the virtues.

It is thus well with her: meanwhile—

At the time when the warmth of the summer just touches on the ruddier, fresher weather of autumn, in the time when the flowers of summer are still blooming everywhere, but autumn is felt in the brimming fulness of waters and the cool fragrance of winds, I found myself this year in my home-country of the Peak; in the land where the altars of the Druid still stand on the moorland; where the murex-stone of the Roman still lies on the hill-side; where the pine and the fern fill the hollows and dells; where the woods are ever damp with the dews of earthborn waters; and where the old tongue of Shakespeare's England still is spoken in old-world houses and in brake-hidden huts.

Fate took me for a brief sojourn at a great mansion in that' district; and one day as I roamed amongst the lilac heather and the great plumed bracken, straying into a shady lonely dale, filled with stone-pines and fed by running brooks, with a shock of memory I felt that I was once more near my birth-place.

Once more I found my way through the old dim forest place, where timid leverets fled at my coming, and the pretty stockdoves were dabbling their rosy feet in the freshets, and the water was bubbling, and dripping, and murmuring everywhere, under ground and above ground, and the great horned cattle were lying asleep hidden amongst the huge stems of the burdock. It was all so still; so quiet; so strangely familiar; the very kine, as they lifted their sleepy heads from amidst the broad green leaves, looked old remembered friends.

With little trouble I found my way—for dogs never forget —to the little cottage, standing all alone, clothed in its rose-thorn; with the dusky woods shelving above it, and farther yet on high the slope of the wide moor flushed with the deli-cate crimsons and the deep lilacs of the heather that blent in that one soft melodious hue for which there is no name—a hue that glows in northern skies at sunset, as it glows on northern lands what time the heather blooms.

My heart was beating fast; memories thronged on me; old affection stirred: and yet—beyond all—there was a curious dull depression on me, a sense of irrevocable loss.

I felt that Ben was gone.

The sensitive nerves of our organisations feel the coming of woe as plants feel the coming of storms: when your hound moans on the hill-side be sure that the dangers of the hills are near; when your mastiff, howling, prays of you not to venture forth into the night, take warning that the snow will drive all wanderers to their grave; or that the swollen waters will sweep down the bridge and all who cross on it; or that above the wold the thunder-clouds are gathering; or that behind the hedge the ejected peasant hides with pike and musket; or that in some shape or another Death will walk abroad that night.

In the early years of your world your race, dwelling in forests and on plains, alone with the earth and the sky, was swift to read portents and warnings; and to this day the genius of the Savage, in the divination of signs and the smell of the tempest or of the foe afar off, ever laughs to shame and to scorn the baffled brain, and the muffled ear, and the purblind eye, of the civilised man. For, mustering in cities; ceasing to watch the things of the earth and the air; keen of pursuit for gold alone; environed in a web of artificial needs; burnishing the learning of the mind, but neglecting the instincts of the emotions; you have lost this faculty of the pre-vision of woe, as you have lost the nomad's power to trace the step that has yet left no prints upon a sun-baked path, and to scent that the air is pregnant with the storm though the heavens smile with sunniest light. You have lost it, but we retain it—greatly to our hurt.

With sickness of heart I drew near the little cottage. The rose-thorn was all red and white with its summer inter-change of rosy berries and white star-shaped blossoms. The brown brook ran underneath the grasses, glimmering golden in the sun. The old gray lichen, and the green wet mosses, clothed the stone wall, on whose topmost coping grew tufts of harebells glistening with dew.

The wide door stood open to the light, and amongst the great yew boughs above the roof the little birds were moving, and were murmuring, with tireless wing and ceaseless song.

Nothing was changed, and yet—I knew that one change was there.

On the threshold stood three figures: two were girls ruddy, well shapen, poorly clad, with sunburnt arm, and with bare feet. The third was the old, gray, bent, tough figure of the pedlar Dick o' tha Wynnats; before him, on the stone sill of the door, was his pack thrown open; and once more I heard his thin cracked wicked voice that was persuasive in the ears of maidens and of women as the subtlest and sweetest music, because it ever brought flattery to their vanities and temptation to their senses.

"Now, my dearies," he was crying to them in his wheedling, conxing tones, spreading out before their round wondering eyes his ribbons, and his laces, and his jewelry of brass. "Look'ee here! These arena goods to threap.* Ye'll busk ye'sells rarely wi' 'em, my wenches. And wi' wake time sae close tew 'ee, ye mun want a new bit of finery to dight ye up a bit. Eh? yer daddie'll niver say naught; for sure ye're kaded** as niver lasses was. Dew iver he gar*** ye dew whatna ye dinna like? I wouldna fang a farthin' o' yew gif I werena weel sure as yer old feyther be allus sae glad to pleasure ye. Ye're pratty as pratty can be—leastways when ye're prankt up wi' a bit o' dress; a' yew wimmen want dress; a'out it ye're ony like poor speckit hens that hanna a topknot, an' are ony good for nestin' and broodin' out o' sight. Look'ee, my dearies, I hae hitten on tha very things ta grace ye; jist these ribbons for yer bonny black hair, and this length o' lace for yer bonny white brists, an' these sparklin' stones to glower i' yer ears—"

* To argue about.
** Caressed, spolled: a pot-lamb in the Peak is called a "kade."
*** Compel.

But I turned away, sick at heart, and sure that my old lost master no more was there; and the rest of the pedlar's speech died away out of my hearing as I slunk back to return through the wood.

I left him there, in the sun on the threshold, holding up his glittering trash before the sight of the two country wenches; and coaxing them to buy and to wear, with all the old wheedling wicked wiles wherewith he had beguiled Avice Dare.

Of a surety the world that stretched outside the woods and the hills of the Peak had no better caterer for the food of its sins than wily Dick o' tha Wynnats, who bought the frail female souls with a glass bead and a penny ribbon that he might sell them again for his own profit of a silver piece and a quart of ale!

O Love! what offence hast thou done to mankind, that on thy mighty name should be charged the guilt and the vice that are daughters of Avarice, of Ignorance, and of Vanity?

I left them, not bearing well to see that once beloved little lowly home in the occupance of strangers, and found my road through the breadth of the pine-wood to that farther verge of it where the forge of Ambrose the blacksmith had stood.

On my way I passed the limestone quarry where Ben had been wont to labour, and where I had spent so many a summer-day.

I suppose they had ceased to work it; for already down its white jagged sides the grass and the bluebells were growing; already in its crevices the ferns were waving, and in its dells the sheep were grazing; the joyous deep-toned voice of Trust no more rang from hill to hill and called the straying lambs to fold; and where the blows of the pickaxe, and the laughter of the men, and the roll of the heavy wagon-wheels, once had roused the echoes of the woods and rocks, all now was silent.

I left it, quiet there, with only now and then the low pathetic bleating of a mother-sheep waking the stillness all

about; and wandered on through the maze of the pine stems,
and over the soft carpet of the mosses and mountain-grasses
sown with shining millions of fir-needles, and growing ruddy
now and then with the tiny fruit of the wild strawberry.

It was a long way, but I found it. The forge was standing
there, with the red light of its fire blinking through its square
ivy-hung window; and over its half-door the smith Ambrose
was leaning. It was high noon, and he was at rest awhile.
The little garden before his house was very trim and green
with its high walls of box, and its thickets of white and red
currant, and its one great walnut-tree that rose in a stately
pyramid of leaf.

On the wooden bench under that tree, on which the men
about were wont to rest whilst he within shod their horses,
there was a tattered dark-eyed gipsy sitting now. I knew
him again; they had used to call him "Daffe o' Sough Tor,"*
and he had been a favourite with Ben, as with the other people
of the moorside, for his docility, his vivacity, and his droll
waggish ways. He was accustomed to wander over the whole
north country far and wide; but the place where he loved
best to dwell was in a wattle hut made in a cavernous cliff of
the Sough Tor, a large mass of rock overhanging a deep
small sheet of shadowy reedy water in this wood.

Ambrose had just supplied him with a draught of milk,
and a half-loaf of rye bread, and was leaning over the doorway in converse with him. I had no dread of poor Daffe,
for he was, unlike most of his kind, very honest, and given
to harming no living thing; and I went near, and hid myself
under a burdock leaf, and hearkened to their speech.

For awhile it brought me no knowledge: it was speech of
oxen and of horses, of harvest and of fruit, of folk-lore and of
the northward wanderings of Daffe in the past year: but I
listened on—seeking news of him, feeling the sure presage
that there would be but one kind of tidings that ever would
reach me of my best beloved and earliest friend.

* The fool of the cliff by the pond.

20*

And it came at last,—the story which all things had seemed to tell me, from the soundless wood, and the grass-grown quarry, and the threshold on which the strangers stood.

"Ye hae niver took na wife, Ambrose?" said the wanderer Daffe.

"Na, na," answered Ambrose simply.

"Sure one 'ud ony frush ye," asserted Daffe thoughtfully. "Ye ha gotten a so tidy an weel reddup; an' gif she were a slattern,—most o' 'em mawthers is."

"Theer be tidy wenches for as wants 'em," said the smith; "but for mysell—sister Ruth, as wed wi' Isaac Cliffe o' Friggat Mill, and her wee uns, be fam'ly enow for me."

"Theer wur time as 'e thoct otherwise?"

"Theer be times as all o' us dew—e'en yerself, Daffe, tho' ye're so gi'en ta rovin' an reivin'—"

"Ay," assented Daffe, and he was silent a moment, when he sat under the walnut-tree, with a grave dreamy light in his wandering eyes.

"Ben Dare, he be dead?" he asked suddenly. "They telled me so by Darron's side."*

Ambrose bent his head, silently.

"When wur't?"

"Last simmar-time, i' th' aftermath."

"It were a ston' as killed him?"

"Ay," said Ambrose, softly shading his eyes with his hand from the sun that streamed through the aisles of pine.

"How wur't?"

"They was a blastin'. He'd allus thoct as he'd dee that way, ye know. They pit mair pooder i' quarry than common; and the ston' it split, and roared, and crackit, wi' a noise like tha crack o' doom. And one bit on 't, big as ox, were shot i' th' air, an' fell, unlookit for like, and dang him tew the groun', and crushit him,—a-lyin' richt athwart his brist."

"An' they couldna stir it?"

"'They couldna. I heerd tha other min screech richt tew here, an' I knew what it wur, tha shrill screech comin' jist i' top o' tha blastin' roar; an' I ran, an' ran—na gaze-hound fleeter. An' we couldna raise it—me an' Tam, an' Job, an' Gideon o' the Mere, an' Moses Legh o' Wissen Edge, a' strong min and i' our prime. We couldna stir it, till Moses o' Wissen Edge he thoct o' pittin' fir-poles underneath—poles as was sharp an' slim i' thur ends, an' stout an' hard further down. Whin tha poles was weel thrust under we heaved, an' heaved, an' heaved, and got it slanted o' one side, and drawed him out; an' thin it were too late, too late! A' tha brist was crushit in—frushed flesh and bone together. He jist muttered i' his throat, 'Tha little lass, tha little lass!' and then he turned him on his side, and hid his face upo' the sod. When we raised him he wur dead."

The voice of Ambrose sank very low; and where he leaned over his smithy door the tears fell slowly down his sun-bronzed cheeks.

"Alack a day!" sighed Daffe softly. "Sure a belter un niver drew breath i' the varsal world!"

"An' that's trew," Ambrose made answer, his voice hushed and very tender.

"He was varra changed like," murmured Daffe, his hand wandering amongst the golden blossoms of the stonecrop. "He niver were the same crittur arter the lass went awa'. He niver were the same—niver. Ta seemed tew mak an auld man o' him a' at once."

"It did," said Ambrose brokenly. "He couldna bear tew look na tew spik to nanc o' us. He were bent i' body, an' gray o' head, that awfu' night when he kem back fra' the waking. It were fearfu' tew see; an' we couldna dew naught. Th' ony thing as he'd take tew were Trust."

"Be dog alive?"

"Na. Trust he'd never quit o' Ben's grave. He wouldna take bit na drop. He wouldna be touchit; not whin he was clem would he be tempted awa'. And he died—jist tha fifth day arter his master."

"An' the wench? Hev' 'ee e'er heerd on her?"

"Niver—niver. Mappen she's dead and gone tew. She broke Ben's heart for sure; long ere tha ston' crushit life out o't."

"And wheer may he lie?"

Ambrose clenched his brawny hand, his eyes darkened, his swarthy face flushed duskily.

"Wheer? What think 'ee, Daffe? When we took o' him up for the burial, ta tha church ower theer beyant tha wood, the passon he stoppit us, a' tha gate of tha buryin' field. The passon he med long words, and sed as how a unb'liever sud niver rest i' blessed groun', sin he willna iver enter into the sight o' tha Lord. He sed as how Ben were black o' heart and wicked o' mind, an' niver set fute i' church-door, and niver ate o' tha sacrament bread, and niver not thocht o' God nor o' Devil; an' he wouldna say tha rites o'er him an' 'twere iver so, an' he wouldna let him lie i' tha holy earth, nor i' tha pale o' tha graveyard. Well, we couldna gae agin him—we poor min, an' he a squire and passon tew. Sae we took him back, five weary mile; and we brocht him here, and we dug his grave under them pines, and we pit a cross o' tha bark to mark the place, and we laid old Trust, when he died, by his side. I were mad with grief like, thin; it were awfu' ta ha' him forbad Christian burial."

"Dew it matter?" asked the gentle Daffe wistfully. He had never been within church-doors himself.

Ambrose gave a long troubled sigh.

"Aweel! at first it seemed awfu'—awfu'! And to think as Ben 'ud niver see the face o' his God was mair fearfu' still. But as time gees on and on—I can see his grave fra' here, tha cross we cut is tha glimmer o' white on that stem ayont, —it dew seem as 'tis fitter like fer him to lie i' tha fresh free woods, wi' tha birds a' chirmin' abuve him, an' a' tha forest things as he minded a flyin', an' nestin', an' runnin', an' re- joicin' arount him. 'Tis allus so still there, an' peacefu'. 'Tis blue and blue now, wi' tha hy'cinths; and there's one bonnie mavis as dew make her home wi' each spring abuve the grave-

stone. 'Bout not meetin' his God, I dunno—I darena saw nowt
anent it—but, for sure, it dew seem to me that we canna meet
Him no better, nor fairer, than wi' lips that ha ne'er lied to
man nor to woman, and wi' hands as niver hae harmed the
poor dumb beasts nor the prattlin' birds. It dew seem so. I
canna tell."

As the words died off his lips the sun fell yet more brightly
through the avenues of the straight, dark, odorous pines;
sweet silent winds swept up the dewy scents of mosses, and
of leaves, and of wild hyacinths: and on the stillness of that
lonely place there came one tremulous, tender sound. It was
the sound of the mavis singing.

"I canna tell; but for sure it is well with him?" said Ambrose; and he bared his head, and bowed it humbly, as
though in the voice of the mavis he heard the answer of
God:

"It is well."

Ah! I trust that it may be so for you; that the sweetness
of your arrogant dreams of an unshared eternity be not wholly
a delusion; that for you—although to us you do deny it—
there may be found pity, atonement, compensation, in some
great Hereafter.

L'ENVOI.

"My dear," says Fanfreluche with supreme scorn, and her nose in the air over the last of my proof sheets, "I don't think much of your Memoirs; and I can't say that there is any moral to be deduced from them, except one—"

"And that is?" I ask anxiously.

"That there is nothing on earth satisfactory except—A GOOD DINNER."

I think she is right; and my consciousness that in an earlier chapter I did my best humbly to add my small quota to that study of human happiness which lies in the great Art of Dining, alone sustains me under the rashness and the vanity which have led me to offer to the world of letters the adventures and the philosophies of your very obedient servant

Puck.

THE END.

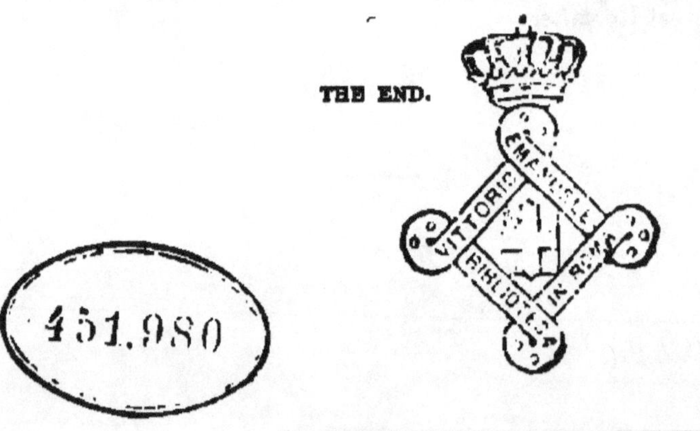

PRINTING OFFICE OF THE PUBLISHER.